"ARE YOU READY TO FULFILL YOUR VOW?"

"I have many vows to keep," I told the Elflord. "Right now, there is one that is more time-critical than returning your son's remains. Are you aware that the whole fabric of creation is disintegrating? That we seem to be running down to complete destruction.

"I have noted a few disturbances," the Elflord said.

"It's more than that. You'd better hear the whole story." And I gave it to him, the dragons in chicken eggs, the two full moons, our trips to the shrines of the Great Earth Mother, and the apparent outbreak of nuclear war in my world.

"There are now *three* moons in the sky," he said after I finished my recital. "Seven is the critical number."

"Then time is even shorter than I thought," I said. "I have to try to stop this spiral into chaos."

The Elflord shook his head, and said, "It is already too late to save this universe. . . ."

THE VARAYAN MEMOIR
3

THE
HERO KING

RICK SHELLEY

A ROC BOOK

ROC
Published by the Penguin Group
Penguin Books USA Inc., 375 Hudson Street,
New York, New York 10014, U.S.A.
Penguin Books Ltd, 27 Wrights Lane,
London W8 5TZ, England
Penguin Books Australia Ltd, Ringwood,
Victoria, Australia
Penguin Books Canada Ltd, 10 Alcorn Avenue,
Toronto, Ontario, Canada M4V 3B2
Penguin Books (N.Z.) Ltd, 182–190 Wairau Road,
Auckland 10, New Zealand

Penguin Books Ltd, Registered Offices:
Harmondsworth, Middlesex, England

First published by Roc,
an imprint of New American Library,
a division of Penguin Books USA Inc.

First Printing, May, 1992
10 9 8 7 6 5 4 3 2 1

 REGISTERED TRADEMARK—MARCA REGISTRADA

Printed in the United States of America

To the memory of
Alice Nehls,
Friend and mentor.
Without her help,
I never would have found
the cellar room with one door in
and so many ways out.

1

Arrowroot

If a regulation Hero is supposed to constantly get himself out of insane predicaments, I was doing at least *part* of the job correctly. I was getting myself *into* the predicaments like a pro. Forget all that about jumping from the frying pan into the fire, I was going from one popcorn popper into another.

Total panic doesn't lead to the most accurate memories. Too many impossible things had been happening at once. I had been out on an island in the Mist, the Sea of Fairy, stealing the left ball of the Great Earth Mother . . . to go with the *right* ball I had stolen a few weeks earlier in the Titan Mountains. More or less in order, I had faced an apparition of the Great Earth Mother herself threatening to destroy me, a beach full of rocks that picked themselves up and hurled themselves at my boat with the velocity of artillery shells, a sky filled with dragons that started to fall and change into other creatures after I swallowed the pecan-sized balls of the Great Earth Mother, and more rocks that turned themselves into soldiers from every period of history. Then Aaron, my new wizard, spit up a two-mile-long sea serpent to gobble up the soldiers.

Then came the earthquake.

My companions and I were faced with the choice of staying out on the beach and being eaten by the sea serpent along with all the bad guys, or retreating into the shrine of the Great Earth Mother—a building that was already in the process of collapsing under the shaking of the quake.

We went inside and Aaron Carpenter, my wizard,

managed to open a doorway back to Castle Arrowroot
and the whole batch of us—except Master Hopay, the
skipper of the boat *Beathe,* who had been struck and
killed by one of the flying rocks—got through the passage
before the shrine came tumbling down.

But the ground was still shaking.

It took me a moment to realize that Arrowroot was
also being shaken by an earthquake, if not as severely as
the island hundreds of miles away in the Mist. The tremor
ended quickly at Arrowroot, though, which was lucky.
Those of us who had just stepped through from the shrine
were shaky enough. Dropping to the floor to ride out this
tremor was all any of us was up to. And when the shaking
stopped, it took a moment longer for us to realize that it
was over. I know that it felt as if I were still shaking after
the building stopped.

"We've got to tell Baron Resler to get everyone away
from low ground," I said—louder than necessary, but I
was still thinking through the noise of the greater earthquake at the shrine. "There may be a tidal wave." Castle
Arrowroot and Arrowroot Town are right on the shore of
the Mist.

"How big a wave?" Lesh asked. He was the first to
get to his feet, the old soldier, recovering quickly from
all the insanity that had gone before, ready to meet the
next threat.

"Hard telling. It could be twenty, maybe even thirty
feet high or more, hitting with a lot of force." I just
didn't know what more to say about it.

"I'll find the baron," Lesh said. He staggered off toward the great hall while the rest of us got to our feet.

The head of Wellivazey, our dead elf, had fallen and
rolled to the side of the corridor when we came through
from the shrine. Harkane, formerly squire, now man-at-
arms, picked the head up. There were no complaints from
the elf, though. His ersatz life after life had finally ended
out on that island. To the end, he had contributed to the
general weirdness of everything. And his contribution to
weirdness didn't look like it was going to end even now.
All I had to do was look at Aaron to know that. Aaron

had a streak of pale white skin that ran from his left
temple to his jaw and a tuft of the elf's platinum-blond
hair above it, an eye-catching break in the black skin and
hair of my wizard.

Timon got up and went to look out toward the Mist,
presumably to see if the tidal wave was coming. He may
not have heard of such a thing before. I didn't bother
asking.

The eight soldiers who had crewed *Beathe* huddled together. I don't think any of them had been prepared for
anything near what had happened. They had seen their
captain, Master Hopay, squashed like a beetle, seen the
boat riddled by flying rocks and destroyed, all the rest.
They had been volunteers, soldiers with some experience
on boats, men willing to risk a voyage out of sight of
land. I doubted that any of them would ever be foolish
enough to volunteer for anything again.

"We're back at Castle Arrowroot," I told them. "The
stairs down that way will take you to the great hall." I
pointed, and all eight of them scrambled to their feet and
ran for the stairs. I didn't blame them. Anyway, it didn't
matter now. Their job was done.

"How are you doing, Aaron?" I asked. Aaron had
gone through a few more varieties of hell out there than
the rest of us. He shook his head but did meet my gaze.
The cloudiness was gone from his eyes.

"I'm wondering if maybe I made the biggest mistake
of my life when I got into this," he said, speaking very
slowly, spacing out the words. He wasn't the only one
asking himself that kind of question. I wondered the same
thing every time I got in deep trouble.

"Not that I had much choice," Aaron added after a
short pause. I nodded. The way he had kept popping into
Varay from Joliet, Illinois, back in the "real" world, he
could hardly help "signing on" in Varay. And after
growing from eight years old to an apparent mid-twenties
in a couple of weeks, he certainly wouldn't fit in anywhere back in the other world.

"If this is what winning feels like, I'm glad we didn't
lose," I said.

"We haven't won yet," Aaron said, and all I could do was stare at him. "All we've done is buy a little time to find the cure for the disease. That still lies somewhere else. It's some *thing* else."

"You're sure?" I wasn't pressing him just because he was new to the wizard business. I'd have pressed Uncle Parthet just as hard. My eyes were drawn to the white streak on the side of Aaron's face again. He didn't seem conscious of it—maybe he wasn't fully aware of it yet, even though he had seen the corresponding black streak on the elf's face—but I couldn't help but stare. The memory of how Aaron had pulled the elf's head on over his own started churning my stomach again.

"I'm sure," Aaron said. He reached up and traced the streak on his face. I know he hadn't been near a mirror, but maybe a wizard doesn't need one. "I don't know what the answer is yet. But all you've done is load the gun. You haven't pulled the trigger yet."

That seemed to be a peculiar analogy for him to draw, but I had to reach down and touch myself again, feel the extra set of family jewels. *How* they got there was more than a painful memory. I still hurt from it.

"Where do we find the answer?" I asked.

"I can't even be sure about that," Aaron said. We started walking toward the great hall. Timon and Harkane followed. Neither of them said anything. I doubt if they even thought of trying to contribute to the conversation. "If we still had Wellivazey to question, I might be able to find out."

"There's no chance at all of pulling him back enough for a few more questions?"

"No chance at all," Aaron said.

"Well, if not him, how about his father?" I asked.

"We send him a message?" Aaron asked.

"For a start at least." I took a deep breath. "I have to take his son home to him. Wellivazey fulfilled his part of the bargain. I can't back out. I gave my oath."

"I could argue that, but I won't bother. Even so, you don't have to take him home right away. I know you left yourself that out. And with general destruction hanging over everything, you *can't* do it now, not when the Elf-lord of Xayber wants you dead.''

"I know. But maybe he'll agree to a truce long enough to get the general problem solved. That affects him as much as anyone else.'' But I really wasn't confident of getting anything but agony from the elflord.

The great hall of Castle Arrowroot was in a state of complete upheaval. People were shouting and running around, trying to organize defenses against the possibility of a tidal wave, a tsunami. Part of the fishing fleet was out, as usual, and people worried about that but couldn't do anything about it. There were a number of small villages along the coast—most of them too far away to get a rider to in time.

"You have any real idea what we're looking for?'' Baron Resler asked when he saw me.

"Just in a general way, Baron,'' I told him. "An earthquake out at sea can send a giant wave against the shore. How big, I can't begin to guess, but it could easily be twenty or thirty feet, I think.''

"Strong enough to knock down castle walls?'' Resler asked.

"I don't think so, but no guarantee. I just don't know.''

He nodded and went off, yelling at people, trying to get work done. Parts of the town of Arrowroot might be in danger, but maybe not. The three hundred yards or so between the shore and the town might be space enough for any wave to break itself down. The castle was right *on* the shore, on a manmade island. But the courtyard was twenty feet above the mean water level, and the walls above that were very thick and secure. The waves would have to top sixty feet to come *over* the walls, and the water wasn't that deep close to shore. Any really huge waves would break farther out and roll in, so maybe the castle itself would be safe.

My companions and I wandered through the great hall. Each of us grabbed a flagon of beer. Lesh was already there, on his third or fourth round. Aaron got his beer and drank it straight down, and then filled it again.

"You sure you're old enough for beer?" I asked him. A couple of months before, he had only been eight years old.

Aaron looked at me over the top of his mug. "Right now, I feel even older than Parthet."

It was enough to bring a smile to our faces, something we both needed.

With a little beer in us, we were ready for food, so the five of us went back to the kitchen to scare up something to tide us over for a bit. With all the commotion going on, there were no servants handy to fetch food out to the great hall, not even for the Hero and heir of Varay. I didn't mind. Even after three and a half years all the fuss people made over me was embarrassing.

We found places to sit in the kitchen, helped ourselves to sandwich fixings, and ate. The cooks and their helpers moved around us. They were obviously nervous because of the earthquake and all the talk about a tidal wave, but meals still had to be prepared. There hadn't been any real damage in the kitchen—or in any of the other parts of Arrowroot we had seen. If any pots had fallen, they had already been picked up. Some of the kitchen staff relaxed a little when they saw the Hero sitting around eating and drinking as though there were nothing at all to worry about. They didn't know that I was too beat to get excited about anything.

"We should get back to Basil," I said after I had finished a two-pound ham sandwich and a couple of quarts of beer. There was no great enthusiasm in my voice, even though Basil was just a way station between Arrowroot and Cayenne, and Joy.

Harkane refilled my mug.

Aaron nodded. He was too busy eating to waste time talking. He was on his second sandwich. He had done all the magic. He had to be famished.

"In a few minutes," I mumbled, and then I started working on my third quart of brew.

"Was there a tidal wave after the *Coral Lady?*" Aaron asked quietly when his mouth was empty for a moment.

That caught my attention. It was the nuking of the

cruise ship *Coral Lady* in Tampa Bay that had started the latest string of disasters. Both of Aaron's parents had been on the ship.

"There was a tidal wave," I said, just as quietly. "A bad one."

"If one hits here, I want to see it," Aaron said.

"Okay." There wasn't much else I could say. I certainly wasn't going to carp about it being dangerous, not after the magics I had seen Aaron perform out in and around the Great Earth Mother's shrine. Now, I've always been very fond of my Uncle Parthet, but he just wasn't in the same class as Aaron when it came to wizardry, even if Aaron was the rookie and Parthet had been around for twelve hundred years or more. And it wasn't just a matter of Parthet's poor eyesight.

"I don't know how soon it might hit, so we'd better get our seats pretty soon," I said.

Aaron stood right up, and so did the rest of us. We went up to the battlements of the keep, even higher than the outer walls. I didn't anticipate any danger there, and my danger sense didn't kick up a fuss. Or maybe it was just overloaded like the rest of me after everything that had already happened.

The Mist. The Sea of Fairy. Mortals feared to travel out of sight of the shore. As far as anyone in the seven kingdoms was concerned, the Mist couldn't be crossed by mortals, though ships out of Fairy occasionally made the crossing. I had seen one of the Mist's dangers, a sea serpent two miles long. That was enough for me. A tsunami would be almost reassuring, make the Mist a trifle less mysterious.

We waited, but not idly. Lesh had carried a small keg of beer along and we all had brought our mugs. Lesh was the first member of my entourage when I arrived in Varay. He had earned his knighthood fighting at my side in Fairy and in the Battle of Thyme. Besides being a canny soldier with more than thirty years of experience, he had turned into an equally capable chamberlain since I had come into Castle Cayenne.

The wave, when it came, was less than I had imagined.

Two lines of heavy waves came in, several minutes apart. The second was larger. It actually splashed a little water over the curtain wall of Arrowroot—though not very much—and it washed halfway across the plaza that separates the castle from the town. Still, it wasn't very spectacular.

"Okay, let's get back to Basil," I said when it became clear that we had seen the main event. It probably sounded like a sigh. I was feeling more lethargic than ever. At the moment, it was all I could do to lift my beer mug to my mouth again. None of the others seemed very anxious to move either.

I looked at Aaron, then at Lesh, Harkane, and Timon—a slow scan. Nobody was jumping up to leave.

"We *do* need to get moving," I said. Aaron nodded slowly, but he didn't get up. Neither did I. I did look down into my mug to see how much beer I had left. About half a mug. I lifted it for a drink. That seemed to start a chain reaction. It's like yawning—one person starts and soon everybody's doing it.

That was when the sentry yelled.

"Rider coming!" He pointed to the west.

It wasn't much, but it was something. I stood to look.

"The wave must have caused trouble somewhere close," Aaron said. It hadn't been ten minutes since the second wave dribbled back into the sea. I nodded. It was the easy guess. It also pumped a little adrenaline back into my system. The lethargy receded.

"Let's go down to the gate," I said.

"It seems that the baron is curious as well," Aaron said as we started down the steps to the courtyard. He pointed. Resler was already hurrying to the gate.

The rider's horse was clomping across the wooden bridge when we reached Baron Resler.

"There's a strange iron ship, lord," the rider said, gasping for breath as if he had been doing the running instead of the horse. "It washed ashore, t'other side of Nerva." Nerva was the nearest village along the coast, about three miles away.

"Was it flying a flag?" I asked. I remembered the

reports in the other world of two ships being missing, a Greek freighter in the Aegean and a Russian frigate in the Indian Ocean.

"A red flag, with some design in the corner," the rider said, looking to me and then back to Resler. Well, not everyone in Varay knew who I was.

"It figures," I said, as much to myself as to anyone else. Then I cleared my throat and spoke a little louder. "It has to be the Russian ship, a *naval* ship—guns, rockets, who knows what all." It wasn't the fact that it was a *Russian* ship that bothered me. Any armed vessel would have been just as bad. The buffer zone would make any naval types edgy.

Resler looked to me. He didn't speak immediately, but a furrow appeared in his forehead as he thought over what I had said. I didn't jump into any fancy explanations. Perhaps Resler had never heard of Russia, but it seemed more likely that he had. The top people in the buffer zone had a fairly decent grasp of the main facts of the mortal realm. They had to.

"Trouble?" Resler asked finally.

I shrugged. "It could be." I looked up at the rider. He had made no move to dismount yet. "Was there any sign of the crew?"

"There were a couple of people on deck," he said. "I don't know if anything was said. The magistrate sent me riding at once." Every village and town in the kingdom had a magistrate if it didn't have someone higher in the feudal scale. He would be the local government, the representative of the king, and so forth.

"How many men should I send?" Resler asked me.

"Let's not go in *looking* for a fight," I said. "We'll go." I made a vague gesture with my head to indicate my companions. "This is your territory up here, so perhaps you'd want to come along. A few men, just an escort perhaps?" I did what I could to avoid stepping on the baron's privileged toes. It was a delicate point of etiquette, to be sure, since I clearly outranked Resler, but all the more essential because of that.

"Yes, Highness," Resler said, nodding formally. He

turned and yelled for horses to be saddled, then called for a half-dozen men to ride along.

"An iron ship?" he asked me softly while we waited for the work to be done.

"Steel," I replied. "Maybe a crew of two or three hundred men." I shrugged. "I'm just guessing on crew size. I don't know how many men a Russian frigate carries, or exactly what kind of weapons they would have. They will undoubtedly be very frightened men, Baron."

"Frightened men can be dangerous," he observed.

"At least there's little chance that their guns will work here," I added. Guns did work occasionally in the buffer zone, but not often enough to depend on them. But then, I had never been in the position of hoping that guns wouldn't work before.

2

Passages

We rode a mile and a half before I caught my first glimpse of the grounded ship. Part of the frigate's superstructure was visible over a low coastal hill. There was no sound of naval guns being fired. I took that as a good sign.

"How big *is* that thing?" one of Resler's soldiers asked.

"Not so big for a navy ship," I said. "It can't be more than a few hundred feet long." Of course, even a frigate would be much larger than any vessel ever seen in the buffer zone. It might be more than ten times the length of *Beathe*, for example, and *Beathe* had been a fairly large boat for the Mist.

The soldier didn't have anything else to say, not even something predictable like "It's as big as a dragon."

The village of Nerva wasn't very large, about thirty stone houses. None of the cottages had sustained any serious damage from the waves, though it seemed apparent that the entire village had been awash. The fishing fleet was another story. Two of Nerva's fishing boats had been washed ashore and damaged. There were already men looking them over to see if they could be repaired. For the families that depended on those boats, that was more important than the huge metal hulk that had also been grounded near the village.

And it had been *thoroughly* grounded. The frigate had apparently plowed directly ashore. More than half of the ship was up on the beach. It seemed to be listing only a few degrees to port. Two rope ladders hung from the deck, and uniformed men were already down on the beach, inspecting the hull of the ship, guarded by other uniformed men carrying submachine guns.

"Let me do the talking," I told Baron Resler softly. "While those guns might not be very effective, there is a chance that they could get off a shot or two." Resler nodded. After all, dealing with dangerous situations was my prerogative as Hero of Varay. "I don't want to see any weapons moving," I added, a bit louder, looking around so that everyone with us heard. "Let's not give them any additional reasons to be nervous."

I got a few grunts in acknowledgment. Resler's men were all too transparently awed by the size of the frigate. My own people weren't. Maybe Aaron was a little nervous at seeing his first ship since his parents were killed in the bombing of the *Coral Lady,* but he certainly wasn't awed by its size or its presence in Varay. And Lesh, Timon, and Harkane had seen enough television to be aware of big ships.

"They'll never get that boat back into the water," Resler commented. I glanced at Aaron.

He shrugged. "I don't know," he said softly. "If it becomes important, I'll try."

"In the meantime, can you cook up anything to make *certain* that their guns won't work?" I asked.

He hesitated for a second, then nodded once, decisively, and started a soft chant.

By that time, the seamen on and below the grounded frigate knew that we were heading for them. I saw several people up on the deck point our way, and the men who had climbed down to inspect the damage were all looking at us, their inspection put aside for the moment. I reined in my horse thirty yards back and dismounted. The people with me also stopped, but only Timon dismounted. He took the reins of my horse.

I took a few more steps toward the ship.

"My name is Gil Tyner," I said. "This is the village of Nerva in the kingdom of Varay." Meanwhile, I had a fervent appreciation for the translation magic of the buffer zone running through my head. I would be able to understand them, and they would be able to understand me. One of the sailors, obviously an officer from his uniform, took a few steps in my direction. One of the submachine-gun-toting men accompanied him, moving a step or two to the side.

"I am Lieutenant Dimitry Astakhov of the *Kalmikov*," the officer said. "What is this place?"

I repeated what I had said about that. "A full explanation of that is going to take some doing," I added. "Perhaps it should wait until I can speak with your captain. In the meantime, is there anything we can do to help? Do you have casualties that need caring for?"

"We have some minor injuries," the lieutenant conceded. "Our people are caring for them." He stared at me for a moment then. "You are attired strangely," he said then—a masterpiece of understatement.

I took a deep breath. "You must try to understand that you are no longer on the earth you are familiar with. I believe you were in the Indian Ocean?" I waited until he nodded. Then I pointed out to sea. "That is known as the Mist, sometimes as the Sea of Fairy. But, your captain?"

Lieutenant Astakhov seemed delighted to pass the buck to his boss. He led the way up one of the rope ladders, and I followed. The lieutenant hadn't even tried to make a fuss about my swords. The captain of the *Kalmikov* was Commander Eugene Sekretov, a man who looked much too young to be in command of a ship. He had trouble speaking—not any kind of *physical* disability, he was just so frustrated by his situation that coherent speech was quite an effort. Bull Halsey would have had just as much trouble.

"This is going to be difficult for you to believe," I said by way of preface, and then I jumped right into a ten-minute discourse on the buffer zone and its relation to the other realms, mortal and fairy. The captain's frustration grew sentence by sentence. His face flushed a deeper red. It was obvious that he neither believed me nor had a better explanation.

"I can guess that your engines haven't worked since your ship came to these waters, that none of your elec-

tronic communications gear works. You don't have radio
contact with anyone. Your radar and sonar don't function. I've never tried to use a compass here, but I would
guess that—at a minimum—it probably does not function
as you would expect. I can also guess that none of your
guns will fire—not your naval guns, not your pistols or
the submachine guns your sailors have down on the
beach. That is the nature of the place. If you haven't
already tried your weapons, please go ahead and do so
now.''

The captain held his hand out toward Lieutenant Astakhov, and the lieutenant handed him his pistol. "There
is a round in the chamber," Astakhov said. The captain
flipped off the safety and lifted the gun. I didn't suggest
that he aim it at me, but for an instant I thought he was
going to. But finally, he walked over to the side of the
bridge and fired it into the air.

At least he pulled the trigger. Several times. He went
through all the procedures, jacked new rounds into the
chamber, and so forth, and the pistol still refused to operate. Then I waited while he called men in and tried
several other weapons. Finally, he gave orders to load
and fire one of the deck guns—something along the order
of a four- or five-inch job by the look of it. It didn't work
either, not in four tries.

Then we did a lot more talking. The breakthrough
came when I assured the captain that we would be able
to get him and all of his people back to the other world.
I don't know if he believed me when I said that nothing
could be done for his ship, but there was undoubtedly a
lot of what I said that he wasn't ready to believe. And I
didn't broach the subject of just *where* in the other world
they would be going. I just assured him that the crew
would be able to get home. He could worry when the
time came about explaining how he and his crew happened to walk into the Russian consulate in Chicago when
they were supposed to be aboard their ship in the Indian
Ocean.

It was nearly sunset before Captain Sekretov and a third
of his crew accompanied me back to Castle Arrowroot.

The captain wasn't about to leave his ship unmanned. I told him that I would make arrangements for getting them all home. I assumed that he would be intent on destroying any documents and equipment that the Russian navy considered too sensitive for foreign eyes. I didn't care about that. I wouldn't have minded too much if he had ordered the whole ship blown to bits—if explosives worked in the buffer zone.

And then, *finally,* it was time for me to go home.

I was a little nervous about using the magic doorway from Arrowroot to Castle Basil after the way Aaron had tapped into the system to get us home from the island. The doorways are a family magic, controlled by sets of rings made by Parthet and only usable by the royal family of Varay, and people with whom the blood royal (pardon my blush) have had sex. A pair of doorways have to be matched between specific places, with the doors on each end lined by sea-silver, a seaweed that grows only in the Mist, along the Isthmus of Xayber. That was the way it had been for as long as the magic had been in existence. But Aaron, new wizard, not part of the family in either of the necessary senses, had confided to me that he could go between any of the sea-silver-lined doorways at will, not just the matched pairs, without the proper rings or the proper family tree. And then, out on that island in the Mist, he had opened a doorway that wasn't even part of the system to carry us back to Arrowroot. I was afraid that he might have shorted out the whole system, and magic *is* subject to interference and static, just like radio or television.

But we reached the capital without any difficulty. The passage worked the way it always did.

Castle Basil was more of a homecoming than Arrowroot.

We headed from the connection with Arrowroot toward the great hall of Basil. I knew that word of our return would spread quickly enough without any contribution from us. Baron Kardeen reached the hall as soon as we did. He strode across the room calling out his welcome before he got to us.

"You got what you went for?" he asked then.

I nodded. "We lost Master Hopay and the boat, though." I waited until he was right with us and spoke softly enough that I wouldn't broadcast that news throughout the room. "And the elf ran out of what extra time he had." I pointed. Harkane was still carrying the head under his arm. "Something will have to be done with that for the time being."

"We'll keep it safe," the baron said. The way he searched my eyes then, I knew the question that he didn't want to ask.

"I will keep my promise to him," I said. "We would never have made it without the elf. However, I have no deadline on the promise. I was careful about that. How is the king?"

Emotion rippled the muscles of Kardeen's face. He controlled it with a deep breath and an instant's hesitation. "He has been in a coma for more than a week now. Your mother or Parthet remains with him constantly."

Or you. I thought. I bet you take your turns as well.

"Who's with him now?" I asked.

"Your mother. Parthet, I believe, is in his workroom. He's one place or the other all of the time. I don't think he's left the castle since we came back from seeing you off."

Well, Parthet had been spending less and less time at his little cottage in the forest even before that. Even without a crisis, he had rarely gone farther from the castle than one of the pubs in the town of Basil, below the castle's rock, for more than a year.

"Harkane, you and Timon take the elf's head to Parthet," I said, and they hurried off. "Aaron, will you go up to see King Pregel with me?"

"Of course," he said.

"Have you seen much of the king?" I asked Aaron while we were on our way up.

"Parthet introduced me to him," Aaron said. "I've seen him only one other time."

Lesh followed us upstairs and took up a familiar position outside the door to the king's bedchamber while Aaron and I went in. Mother got up from a stool next to Pregel's bed and hurried to intercept us as far from him as she could. In *that* room, that meant about eighteen feet.

"You've bound him here too long," Mother whispered angrily.

"*If* I've bound him, it was only to give him a chance to heal himself again, the way he has so often before," I whispered back. I was still skeptical about Mother's belief that Pregel—her grandfather, my great-grandfather—remained alive only because I kept telling him that I couldn't take over his job yet. Anyway, the tension between Mother and me often means that I doubt *anything* she tells me about *anything*. Twenty-one years of pervasive deceit are hard to forget.

Mother and I stared at each other for a moment, then I suggested that she take a break. I would stay with the king for a bit.

"Will you never release him?" she demanded.

I bit back the impulse to snap an angry reply at her. I was too tired for patience, but I was also too tired for an argument. I was too tired for much of anything. It was more than just lassitude after weeks of short rations and mortal peril. I had never been so thoroughly drained in my life, not even when I was badly injured and holding on through sheer insanity during the struggle against the Etevar of Dorthin.

I continued to stare at her. Slowly, I collected enough energy to say, "If we can't find a way to stop this crazy spin into chaos, we'll all have our release, much too soon."

She brushed past me and left the room.

I leaned my head back to ease a throbbing pain at the base of my skull and closed my eyes for a moment. Disagreeing with Mother did that to me. Finally, I looked across the room at Pregel, so thin that he hardly dented the sheet pulled up to his shoulders.

"Aaron, will you see if there's anything you can do to

help him?'' Despite the unbelievable magics I had seen
Aaron pull off at the shrine of the Great Earth Mother, I
couldn't work up an ounce of confidence that he could
help the king. But I had to know.

"I'll try," Aaron whispered simply. There was no
bravado in his voice, but neither was there doubt.

We crossed the room together. I sat on the stool Mother
had vacated. Aaron stood at the foot of the bed and stared
at the king.

I could see the change in grandfather's condition, the
deterioration he had suffered in the weeks since I had last
seen him. He seemed to be—quite literally—wasting away
to nothing. The way people have to eat and eat just to
maintain themselves in the magical climate of the seven
kingdoms, wasting away actually made some sort of
sense. If you couldn't eat, you had to lose body reserves,
and people don't maintain great quantities of fat in the
buffer zone. Pregel was so thin that I thought he might
almost be translucent if I held him against a strong light.

At the end of the bed, Aaron started chanting very
softly. I felt the light tingle, like static electricity, that
comes from active magic (as opposed to the passive
magic that can't be escaped in the buffer zone).

"I'm back from another crazy quest, Grandfather," I
said, speaking softly but not actually whispering. I
reached over and took his hand. It was cold, impossibly
cold. I felt his wrist and could barely detect a pulse—
faint and irregular. His breathing was just as poor.

As briefly as I could, I reported on my quest for the
balls of the Great Earth Mother, and where they were
now, the way I had to swallow them, the way they now
rested between my legs. Talking about that seemed to
bring back the throbbing, the ache.

"We've got a chance now, Grandfather. Sure, everything seems to be going to hell in a hurry and we don't
know what we have to do to stop it, but I've got the
ammunition. As soon as we find out what has to be done,
I'm going to give it a try."

If there was time. If the runaway entropy didn't drop
the End of Everything on us first. It seemed strange that

only when everything was spiraling toward destruction did any sort of reasonable logic seem to hold in the buffer zone. It was as if magic was descending on its way to and through science.

"Do you remember the way I stormed out of your dining room that day?" I asked, knowing that the king wouldn't answer. "I didn't want any part of being Hero of Varay. I was madder than hell about the way I was secretly groomed for the job without being told, without being given a choice."

I shut up then. I didn't want to go down that path again. Not that I can ever avoid the memories. Every time Mother and I have a disagreement, it brings the pain and anger back again, full force.

Then I noticed the silence. Aaron had quit chanting. I turned and glanced up at him. He shook his head and gestured toward the door. We both walked over there.

"There's nothing I can do," Aaron whispered. "He isn't in pain, but his spirit is—well, I guess the word is restless."

"*Am* I holding him?" I asked.

"Mostly, but he *is* fighting on his own as well." Aaron shrugged. "He is aware of what's going on, I think, and I feel a tremendous sense of duty from him. He's fighting, but he couldn't make it for long without you. He seems to be getting impossibly stretched out, the way Wellivazey was near the end."

I closed my eyes for a moment when I realized that I could no longer argue the point. Maybe I couldn't see it on my own, but when Aaron pointed it out to me, I had to accept that he was telling me the truth.

"Wait here," I told Aaron when I opened my eyes again. I went back to the bed, sat on the stool, and took Pregel's hand again. For several minutes, I just sat there with him, knowing what I had to say, but still having trouble bringing myself to say it.

"I won't hold you any longer, Grandfather," I whispered. "I know you've done everything you could."

I'm not sure exactly what I expected to happen when I said that. I guess I thought that something would happen quickly, like in the movies—you know, a moment of consciousness, a dying message, and then a dramatic end. But nothing at all seemed to change. The king continued his oh-so-shallow breathing. His pulse remained the same. After perhaps another twenty minutes, I heard footsteps behind me. Mother had tired of waiting out in the hall. I'm sure she hadn't gone any farther away than that . . . not for more than a couple of minutes at least. I got up and let her sit again.

"It's just a matter of time now, I think," I told her, standing so my back was to the king. "I've got to get home for a little while. You'll send someone for me . . . if there's any change?" I didn't want to spell it out. Mother nodded and kept her face neutral, without expression.

Aaron and I left the room and headed downstairs with Lesh trailing behind.

"You'll have to brief Parthet and Kardeen on everything," I told Aaron. "Tell them about the Russians up at Arrowroot and ask Kardeen to start figuring out how we're going to take care of them all until I can get them back to the real world. I've got to get home to Joy."

"Don't worry. I'll take care of everything here," Aaron said.

Despite all the weirdness in general conditions and in his own personal, extraordinary experiences, Aaron had a sureness that was uncanny. As short a time as I had known him, and despite the circumstances, I already got the same feeling of reliability from Aaron that I got from Baron Kardeen or—within his expanding limits—Lesh. As dislocated as *I* had felt when I first stumbled into Varay, I at least had had a lot of training that helped me adapt and made it possible for me to respond to an immediate crisis. Aaron hadn't had that advantage, and his early days in the buffer zone had been infinitely more dislocating than mine. It wasn't just the way he suddenly appeared in Varay, or even his impossibly rapid growth. I remembered Aaron the way I first saw him in the great hall of Castle Basil, a scared little kid trying to sound brave with fake street talk. That was all gone, the street jargon, the pretense, the little kid. His speech had become homogenized—middle-class, middle-America—and I don't think it was the usual translation magic doing it.

That all hit me at once. I guess I stopped walking and stared at him.

"We all do what we have to do," Aaron said—as if he were reading my mind.

I shook my head. "How the hell have you managed to cope with all that's happened to you the last few months?" I asked.

Just for an instant, he slipped back—figuratively—into the little kid I first met. "It ain't easy, bro," he said. He grinned, and then we both laughed.

Parthet was in the great hall waiting for me, so nervous that he wasn't even paying proper attention to the mug of beer in his hand. But I aimed Aaron at him and held myself to a quick greeting and a single question.

"Have you found out yet what I have to do with the balls?"

He shook his head. "No, but we can conjure on them all we want now that you have them back." He held out his hand for them, and I laughed.

"It's not that easy," I said. "Aaron can tell you all about it. I've got to get home to Joy now. We'll talk tomorrow." I felt my smile wither. "Maybe a lot sooner," I said. Parthet looked from me to Aaron, then up—in the direction of the king's chambers.

I nodded, then collected my entourage and we went back to Cayenne.

Castle Cayenne had been my home for more than three years, but it still didn't have all the emotional connotations of *home*. It was part of my home, but with the magical doorways, *home* was an entire complex—Castle Cayenne, Castle Basil, my condo in Chicago, and the house in Louisville. My parents' house in Louisville remained part of the construct mostly on the strength of memory and childhood ties. I rarely went there except when I knew that Mother was in Varay. During the years between the defeat and death of the Etevar of Dorthin and the nuking of the *Coral Lady,* I had become accustomed to the double life I was leading, and even enjoyed it most of the time. I could understand the way my father had always seemed to enjoy life so fully while I was growing up . . . if not the way he and mother had concealed Varay and my heritage from me.

I enjoyed the life, and sometimes I got completely hysterical just thinking about it. I mean, in Chicago, I played the part of the rich young bachelor in search of the good life, good times, and the perfect party. But by simply stepping through a secret doorway, I suddenly became the Hero of Varay, Prince Gil of Varay, complete with costumes, fancy weapons, and a complete mythos. I was like Batman/Bruce Wayne with his Bat Cave, Superman/Clark Kent with his Fortress of Solitude. And sometimes I just got carried away with how ridiculous the entire concept was. At times I reached a point where I couldn't take *either* world completely seriously. I would hear people pooh-poohing magic, or fantasy literature, or whatnot, and I'd think how wrong they were, and how scared they would be if I hauled them off through a doorway into Varay and left them to find out for themselves. And in Varay, I'd catch sight of myself in a mirror—all duded up in my Hero garb with two long swords over my shoulders, maybe with bow, chain-mail shirt, and Cubs cap, and it would be all I could do to keep from collapsing on the floor in laughter. "Put that in your computer," I'd tell myself.

But death could be a sobering reality in either world. My first time in Varay, I had buried my father and watched a supposedly immortal elf warrior die fighting a dragon. I had seen men and trolls die—been the agent of death in many cases. I had killed and come close to dying myself. Killing does more to change you than the other does. It's something you can never forget, never get away from. It becomes a permanent part of you.

I think that's why I visited the crypt below Castle Basil so often. It gave me the sense of reality that I so desperately needed if I wanted to avoid slipping off into total insanity.

It's also why I occasionally went out and got stinking drunk in the real world, where it's not nearly as hard to do as it is in the buffer zone. Lesh and I would hit a bar, or a series of bars, and drink as fast as we did in Varay, where the magic of the seven kingdoms converted alcohol to sugar almost as fast as anyone could drink. Alcohol meant calories, just as food did, and the overall magic that maintained the buffer zone between Fairy and the mortal world would use any calories it could get.

Even wasting an old man away to a living ghost to get them.

Sometimes I think too much. I was ready for another heavy drunk, but I knew I couldn't spare the time.

Joy and I had one of those rousing greetings like those they used to show in the war movies: the ship docks in the States and the heroes go down to the pier and their wives or girlfriends are there to greet them—the big hugs, the whirling around, the kisses that are so passionate that you wonder that they don't lead to more frantic action right there in public.

> Home is the sailor, home from the sea.
> And the hunter home from the hill.

Our marriage was still new enough that Joy and I both had the same first impulse, to head for the bedroom and finish the reunion in the proper manner, but we had to put that on hold for a while. In Varay, eating comes before *anything* else, even sex. I was still famished, Joy had enough of an appetite of her own, and it was almost suppertime anyway. I think the first thing Lesh did when we stepped through to Cayenne was to head for the scullery to tell the cooks that we were all back so double everything for supper. Meals in Varay are protracted enough to get away with that. You start with what's already on hand while the extras are cooking.

I told Joy about Pregel. I also told her that we had gotten what we went north for, but that there was still more work to do once we found out what to do with the, ah, relics. I didn't give her any details of the quest . . . and I didn't tell her where the old family jewels were at the moment. I wanted to save *that* until we were alone and I found out whether or not they were going to interfere with my love life. I was starting to worry about that.

"I've been learning to ride," Joy told me as we headed for the supper table. "Jaffa has been teaching me." Jaffa was one of our new pages.

"Any interesting bruises?" I asked, leaning close to whisper in her ear. Everyone was gathering for the meal, and that wasn't the kind of question I wanted to share with all the help.

"You'll have to find that out for yourself," Joy said, hurrying on ahead of me to the table.

I kept dozing off during supper, and that's something I never do, certainly not in Varay. Lesh carried most of the table talk. He told about our adventures, some of them, but he was circumspect enough to omit the parts that didn't belong in the same room as food. I doubt that any of the Varayans would have been shocked at even the worst of it, but I still had a few civilized sensibilities and Joy wasn't completely acclimated yet, and Lesh recognized that. When he got to the bit about the room full of jewels in the shrine up in the Mist—walls completely studded with diamonds, rubies, and emeralds, with piles of precious stones almost waist-deep in the corners of the room—Lesh had everyone's attention. Some of the castle folk even forgot to keep shoveling the food into their faces for a moment.

What a letdown they'll have when they find out that we didn't bring any of those jewels back except the ones we had to have, I thought. They're going to want to see some of those treasures, and they *can't* see the two we have. Not with them lodged securely between my legs.

Surprise.

"How many did you bring back?" somebody asked Lesh.

Someone else said, "Can we see some of them?"

Lesh chuckled, and that opened my eyes. He looked my way and grinned, then he started digging into his pack. I hadn't even noticed that he had set the pack next to the table. Glittering bits of precious stones tumbled out on the table, the stuff that dreams are made of back in the other world. Even in Varay, rather blasé about riches most of the time, the shiny gems drew oohs and ahs.

"I didn't know you were so quick with your hands, Lesh," I said when he glanced my way again.

"I got some too," Harkane confessed, and then Timon blushed and nodded, so I knew that he had joined in on the grabbing.

I grinned and shook my head. "Why not," I said, and then I laughed. It seemed that I was the only one who had been too busy to grab a few extra goodies. Or maybe not, I thought then. Aaron was wearing the elf's head. He probably didn't think to grab anything extra either. Besides, he was still carrying that sea serpent around inside when we were in the room of jewels.

Enough of that train of thought.

"Have you liberators thought about what you're going to do with all those jewels?" I asked. There certainly wasn't much of a market for them in Varay.

Lesh got an embarrassed look on his face and shrugged. The others just shook their heads.

After supper, Joy and I headed up to the bedroom and I told her where the balls of the Great Earth Mother were. When I stripped to take a soak in the tub, Joy had to count for herself. That raised an erection, so I knew that there was still some life in me.

"I was worried abut that," I told her. I didn't mention that I was still very tender down there. Getting the extra family jewels in position had hurt like hell.

"Damn well better not mess up a good thing," Joy said. She climbed into the tub with me. It's big enough to hold three or four people without any crowding, though we've never tried it with more than the two of us. It was just sunset, so the water tank up on top of the castle still had plenty of hot water in it. The water was almost *too* hot.

We made love soaking wet, on the bedroom floor so we wouldn't get the bed sloppy. After the first bout, another bath, and a sensuous session with the bath towels, we did a rematch on the bed. By the time we finished that, I was almost asleep and trying to fight it off. I do have some sense of manners.

"I've got something to tell you," Joy said, snuggling closer against me.

I mumbled something that didn't take the effort of words.

"We're going to have a baby."

That woke me all the way. I sat straight up, dumping her head from my shoulder. Okay, I had seen a lot of magic, but . . . "You know *that* fast? We just got done."

And Joy started laughing hysterically. It was several minutes before she calmed down enough to inform me that my elevator wasn't going all the way to the penthouse. She had suspected that she was pregnant before I headed into the Mist. Now she was sure.

Finally, we got to sleep.

It was about one-thirty in the morning when Aaron came from Basil with the news I had been expecting.

3

The Crypt
and the Crown

"About ten minutes ago," Aaron said when Joy and I had pulled on robes and called him into the bedroom. "Quietly. He never regained consciousness. I came straight here."

Joy and I got dressed and ready to cross back to Castle Basil. I was in full regalia. I hadn't even needed Lesh's reminder to know that it would be expected. Joy and I led quite a procession. Aaron, Lesh, Harkane, and Timon went along, as did Jaffa and Rodi, our new pages.

The scene in the great hall of Castle Basil didn't look like the middle of the night. There were kegs of beer being tapped, and there was plenty of cold food sitting on the table. People would eat. People had to eat, no matter what. And there were a lot of people about, standing around, looking glum. Pregel had been King of Varay for more than a century. Except for Parthet, there wasn't anyone in the kingdom who could remember a time when he *wasn't* king.

When Joy and I entered the great hall, a lot of eyes turned our way and the soft conversations died away. We didn't linger. A guard told me that the king hadn't been brought down from his room yet, so Joy and I headed that way while the rest of our people stayed in the great hall.

Mother, Parthet, and Kardeen were in the bedroom with Pregel. The catafalque on which Grandfather would rest during the vigil had been brought in, but the king hadn't been moved onto it yet for the journey down to the chapel—the royal shrine to the Great Earth Mother.

I knew what the procedure would be, in a general way. Baron Kardeen had warned me what to expect one time before when Grandfather had seemed to be in particularly precarious condition. The rituals would be much the same as they had been for my father. I would be the chief mourner this time, since I was Grandfather's heir—whether I was ready for the job or not. The vigil would last until dawn. Then we would have a formal procession down to the crypt. Grandfather would be placed into his niche. That had been completed while I was out on the Mist. Before we left the burial chamber, there would be a brief ceremony investing me as King of Varay. It wouldn't be a fancy coronation, just a simple thing with the sword of state, the one Pregel had used when he named me Hero of Varay after Dad was sealed into the wall of the crypt.

Gil Tyner, King of Varay? I guess that didn't sound any more *or* less ridiculous than anything else about the buffer zone.

Baron Kardeen and I lifted Pregel from the bed and moved him to the catafalque. Grandfather couldn't have weighed eighty pounds, if that. Mother had dressed him in his fanciest clothes. He wore a jeweled chain around his neck. That would come off before he was interred. It was part of the regalia of office. The chain, the sword of state, and a scepter that looked a little like a stage magician's phony wand were the main trappings of the job. There was no crown, nothing like a crown.

We carried grandfather from the bedroom down to the main level, through the great hall into the shrine. We picked up people as we went, turning this into something of a preliminary procession. Everyone followed us into the shrine. Four soldiers from the castle guard carried the king and set the catafalque on a platform at the front of the chapel, under the eyes of the large painting of the Great Earth Mother.

The painting made me nervous, even though the figure didn't look anything at all like the apparition of the Great

Earth Mother that I had seen in her island shrine. In fact, just *being* in another one of her shrines made me edgy under the circumstances. It didn't matter that this was just one of the "ordinary" shrines that had been built by mortals and not one of the special, out-of-the-way colossuses that she had supposedly built—or given birth to—herself. I couldn't help but feel that she might appear—step out of that painting even—to have her revenge against me.

Parthet disappeared for nearly an hour without explanation, but when the rest of Varay's barons started to enter the shrine, I knew where he had gone—jumping from castle to castle to spread the news and to send the kingdom's nobles through the system of magic doorways to witness the funeral and the succession. Duke Dieth was the first to arrive, so I knew that Parthet had even made the jump over to Carsol, the capital of Dorthin. Dieth and each of the barons came in and knelt at the side of the catafalque for a moment, then came over and knelt before me. The embarrassment that caused me helped me get my mind off of the picture of the Great Earth Mother that was staring at me. Joy was as embarrassed as I was by the ritual. She gripped my arm tightly every time one of the peers came over to us.

Time scarcely seems to move at a vigil, a wake. I was determined not to move from my place next to the head of the catafalque. It took concentration, but I managed. Sitting there, half facing the rest of the mourners, I could see the play of emotion on their faces, see the way they were watching me when their grief gave them a moment's leave. And I saw real grief on most of the faces. It wasn't just that Pregel had been king since before any of them were born. It was grief at the passing of someone they really cared for.

And, perhaps, a little of the emotion was uncertainty at what life under Pregel's successor might be like. The encroaching chaos wasn't a state secret. Most people knew that strange things were happening, and the better-informed knew or suspected that the buffer zone was in deep trouble. The death of the king would have been evidence enough of that for most of the people in the room. The ones who knew more were more frightened. Even their faith in a "proper" Hero of Varay had to be challenged. I didn't hear anyone mentioning the promised "new Golden Age" that legend insisted would dawn on Varay when the same man was legitimately both Hero and King of Varay.

A deep fear seized me at some point late in the vigil, near dawn. It was as real and vital as anyone I had ever crossed swords with. It was almost a physical presence strangling my mind. Very soon, in an hour or less, I would be formally both King and Hero of Varay, the man who the legends said would bring that new Golden Age to the kingdom, to the entire buffer zone. But the fear came when I suddenly saw an alternative interpretation to the legend about the reunion of the two offices. One man, Vara, had been both King and Hero at the founding of Varay. Now, the first time the titles were reunited, Varay—and everything else—was likely to end.

Not a First Golden Age and a Second Golden Age, but a beginning and an end.

I sat frozen in terror until dawn. The fear grew. Once Baron Kardeen touched the sword of state (allegedly the Sword of Vara) to both of my rings to formally invest me with the kingdom, it might all end instantly . . . *all of creation.*

Dawn.

The procession.

Baron Kardeen led the way, carrying the Sword of Vara on a black silk pillow. The black wasn't for mourning. The sword was always paraded about on black silk. Four bearers—not the same men as before—carried the dead king. I followed immediately behind them, with Joy only a half-step behind me. Mother and Parthet were next, then Duke Dieth and the other peers of Varay, Aaron and my people, and finally the rest of the mourners.

It was a slow march, not quite in hesitation step, from the shrine down to the catacombs. We walked what might be the ultimate last mile.

Grandfather, was I wrong? Should I have bound you to us awhile longer?

If I had made a mistake, it might prove to be the last mistake anyone ever made. My mind raced, looking for alternatives, and I had to reject them all, even the most obvious. I couldn't simply refuse the rite of succession. Although the formality had not yet been observed, I had been king in fact from the minute of Grandfather's death, as Baron Kardeen had told me earlier, and as the obeisance of the barons had confirmed. If the reunion of titles was the catalyst for Doomsday, it was already working.

But we had not all died with Pregel.

So there was still time . . . but how much?

The headless body of the elf had been removed from the crypt—temporarily, no doubt—so that he would not be a distraction during this ceremony.

King Pregel's catafalque was positioned before his niche at the kings' end of the burial wall. That wall was getting crowded. Vara was in the center. At least, there was a capstone with his name and dates on it. Kings were to his left, Heroes to his right, with many more Heroes than kings. Heroes rarely lasted long. They were sought only when there was dire need for heroic efforts, and that kind of work had a high casualty rate.

Everyone got positioned in the room. Kardeen and I were right up next to the head of the catafalque. Parthet, Mother, and Joy were close. Dieth and the barons were behind them, and then all the rest of the mourners.

Baron Kardeen spoke of Pregel's life, his battles, his peaceful accomplishments, his wives and children, his love for the people of Varay, their love for him. Kardeen removed the jeweled chain from Pregel's neck then and hung it around mine.

Parthet intoned a genealogy that started with Vara and proceeded straight down the line of kings to Pregel . . . and then on to me.

Kardeen picked up the sword of state and stood in front of me. I extended my *trembling* hands palms down. Kardeen touched the top of my head and both of my shoulders with the blade while Parthet chanted some magic formula. Finally, Kardeen laid the sword across my hands so the blade touched both rings, the eagle and the signet, simultaneously. I scarcely felt the electric jolt and the influx of regal magic that the contact brought.

"The king is dead, long live the king."

Parthet whispered the formula, but everyone in the crypt, *everyone in the kingdom,* heard him speak.

I didn't cry until later, with just Joy to witness my tears.

I stayed in the crypt for a few minutes after the rest of the mourners left. I kept only Kardeen with me. My great-grandfather had been slid into his final resting place. A purple cloth had been draped across the opening, to await the fitting of a marble capstone later in the day.

Kardeen kept his eyes on mine while we waited for the last of the others to start up the stairs. Their echoes were a jumble of noise. Baron Kardeen remained silent, waiting.

"Just a question before we go on up for the rest of the formalities," I said when the echoes started to fade. Kardeen nodded politely.

"Supposing that there is anyone left to do the honors when the time comes, where will you put me?" I asked. "Both king and Hero. I don't suppose you'll cut me in half and divide me between the two ends."

"I trust you'll be around long after *my* days are done, Your Majesty," Kardeen said after a moment. "But your spot will be there." He pointed to the other long wall, to a spot in the center, precisely across from Vara.

It was my turn to nod. "I think I guessed that, way back when I first learned of the plan my parents had for me. But . . ." I paused, and then explained the fear that had come over me during the vigil. "Judging from the events of the last few months, that seems more likely than a second Golden Age."

Kardeen hesitated a long time before he answered. "Not all legends can be believed," he said. "We can only do what each day demands of us.'' He kept his voice steady, but I saw the shadow of fear that drifted past his eyes, and that was extraordinary in itself. The chamberlain always kept a tight veil over his emotions.

"I guess we should get upstairs before people start thinking that something else has happened,'' I said, and I started for the door. Before we left the room, I looked back along the tiers of marble headstones along the burial wall, and at the empty wall opposite it.

When we got up to the great hall, people were milling around the tables, everyone standing, waiting for me to arrive. Breakfast was being carried in from the kitchens. Joy came to me and we walked to the center of the head table together. For the first time that I could recall, the head table on the dais was completely filled. Duke Dieth, the man who had been my father's first squire and who had "held" Dorthin for me since that kingdom came to me after the death of the last Etevar, and all of the barons rated positions at the head table. We were more crowded than usual.

Eating took priority for its usual length of time. It was a quiet meal. Then there was one more bit of ceremony to go through before I could get away from all the people and find some time alone. That was in the throne room, after a side trip to Baron Kardeen's office to give everyone else time to get to the throne room and in place first—so *the king* could make a proper entrance.

"I hope this stage-managing isn't going to be a regular thing,'' I told Kardeen while we were waiting.

"However you want it,'' Kardeen said. "Your great-grandfather never stood much on ceremony, so . . .'' He shrugged and smiled thinly.

"And we have so many real problems to worry about,'' I reminded him.

He didn't have a smile this time. "Questions but no answers.''

"And maybe very little time to find the answers,'' I mumbled, the last of that around a yawn. "Sorry. When we get through this morning, I'm going to have to get some real rest. Then Aaron and I have to contact the Elflord of Xayber.''

''About his son?''

''Only in passing, this time. Mostly, we're hoping that the elflord might be able—and willing—to tell us what we have to do to keep all three realms from coming to an end.''

''I'll make arrangements to have the royal apartments prepared for you and the queen,'' Kardeen said, changing subjects. It was the first time I had heard Joy referred to as ''the queen.'' I held up my hand for a moment, to give myself a chance to roll it around in my head, before I said what I had to say.

''Don't do anything in Grandfather's apartments yet. Leave them just the way they are. I'll want to look them over first.'' I paused, then added, ''I may have some suggestions, or Joy might.''

''As you wish, Majesty.''

''And, *please,* can we dispense with as much of the formality as possible—at least when we're alone?'' I had enough trouble keeping my head on straight with all the Hero jazz.

Kardeen just nodded his acceptance. ''There is a traditional greeting to the barons on accession,'' he said after a pause to mark another change of subject. He had a copy of the greeting handy, of course. He gave me a small sheet of parchment. I read through it quickly— political-sounding stuff about doing my job and looking for the help of Vara and more of that kind of formula.

''It is also traditional to add a few words of your own at the end, words about what faces us and what your hopes are,'' Kardeen said. ''Perhaps it might be better to say little now?''

''Better, perhaps, but I don't think we can get away with it,'' I said. ''Everybody knows that things are in rotten shape. If I don't say anything at all, the rumors will get completely out of hand.''

Kardeen considered that for a moment. ''I expect you're right,'' he said, biting off the ''Majesty'' at the last instant. He glanced at the door of his office. "They should have had time to get there now."

Mother and Joy met us on the way to the throne room. Parthet and Aaron were standing outside the door. The two wizards went in first. Then Kardeen escorted Mother in and announced, "The King and Queen of Varay."

Joy and I went in.

The throne room was crowded with standing people, family, Aaron, Duke Dieth, and the barons up front, the rest wherever they had managed to squeeze in. The people hardly had room to bow when I made my entrance. I glanced at Joy and mouthed the word *help* at her, but she was just as caught up in the situation as I was—surprised, still in something of a state of shock. I had seen the startled look on her face at the way Kardeen announced us. I helped Joy step up onto the dais at the front of the room. There were no comfortable stairs. We got to the thrones. There was a second, slightly smaller, throne for Joy. I was sure that it had been Kardeen who thought of that touch. It was his efficient nature.

Somebody rapped on the floor with the end of a pike or something, and the bowing people straightened up as Joy and I took our seats—the only chairs in the room. The desk that had been in front of the throne when Pregel worked there was gone.

I had attended only one formal ceremony in the throne room before, back when Pregel announced that I was his heir designate, and there weren't nearly as many people present then. I didn't know what was expected of me that time, and I had only the roughest idea now. Without Baron Kardeen standing by, I would have had an even stronger feeling that I was about to make a complete fool of myself again.

Someday I'm going to drive a shrink off the deep end trying to sort through my brain, I thought.

The peers of Varay. I knew them all, to one degree or another. They knew me as Hero. From the expressions I saw on the faces in front of me though, some of them had doubts about me as king. Fair enough: I had doubts about me as king too.

Baron Kardeen knelt in front of the throne and recited an oath of homage. I returned words accepting his vow and confirming him in his title and so forth. Then he moved to the side and announced Duke Dieth and then each of the barons in order of seniority. We went through the same formula time and again. No matter what the intentions of those taking part, ceremonies tend to drag themselves out beyond all reason. That's just as true in Varay as it is at Hollywood awards ceremonies.

After the last of the vows, I read the set piece Kardeen had given me and went on into my "State of the Kingdom" speech, making it up as I went along. It's not something I would force on anyone. I told them what shape we were in. There was little new in that. The peers all had a fairly good idea. I didn't gloss over the dangers, but I didn't dwell on them either. I assured everyone that there was still real hope, that we had the tools to save the day as soon as we found out what to do with them, that we had some promising leads in that regard . . . and two wizards to help pursue this quest. Finally, I reminded everyone about the legends of a new Golden Age when someone like me came along who was rightfully both Hero and King.

I felt like a used-car salesman feeding them *that* line—since I didn't believe it myself—but from the worried looks I had been seeing, I had to give them something. I felt even worse when I saw that almost everyone in the room was buying every word I said.

At least nobody led a round of three cheers for good King Gil.

4

The Door to Nowhere

Eventually, that ordeal ended. But my work wasn't done. Resler was there after the ceremony, "begging" a few words. The Russian captain was being a most annoying guest. He had questions and demands. And so forth. The easy out for me would have been simply to tell Resler to do his best to keep our guests pacified for a couple of days, to tell him that Baron Kardeen was working on arrangements to care for the Russians until we could get them back to the other world. But taking the easy way out would hardly have looked proper on my coronation day. So I got Aaron and we made a quick trip back to Arrowroot with Resler. I talked to Captain Sekretov again. Among other things, I reminded him that none of his weapons functioned.

"We are still working on that," he said.

"I wouldn't dream of stopping you," I told him. "But another thing for you to consider. Have you looked at the stars since you've been in our waters?" The look on his face was instructive. "The constellations aren't even the same."

"You said that you could arrange for us to get home," Sekretov said, changing the subject quickly.

I nodded. "We'll do that in a day or two. Things are in quite a state here just now." I lowered my voice to add, "The king died last night."

Sekretov seemed torn between an insincere expression of sympathy and some old cant about the decadence of royalty. He finally chose to avoid both.

"We feel like prisoners here," he said after a moment.

"This is a different world, Captain," I reminded him.

"The men-at-arms are for your protection. There are dangers here." I hesitated before I said, "Like dragons several times the size of your frigate." I smiled and held up a hand to abort the instinctive protest that the captain was about to make. "I know. You don't believe me, and I don't blame you in the least. But, nevertheless, there *are* such creatures here, and others. As for getting you home, we'll get to that as quickly as possible. I'm afraid that it means taking you through to Chicago. We don't have any direct connections with Russia from here. But I can take you to the Russian consulate in Chicago and they can take over from there."

He nodded, if reluctantly. He might not have believed a word I had told him, but he had little choice but to go along with whatever was happening.

"Relax as much as you can. There's no shortage of food and drink. Look around. You're not restricted in any way, Captain. And if you, or any of your people, decide that you'd like to stay here, you're more than welcome. Varay can always use immigrants."

As soon as Aaron and I got back to Basil, Joy and I went on through to Castle Cayenne. For a few days, at least, that would still be our home. I went to bed and slept. The phrase "I slept the sleep of the dead" keeps taunting me. It did that day too, when I finally woke about sunset, smelling food on the air. I was still tired, but in Varay, hunger is almost always more insistent. I had to eat.

"Is any of this real?" Joy asked when she saw that I was awake. She was sitting on the window seat, arms clasped around her knees. She had been watching the sunset, waiting for me to wake.

I yawned and stretched, then sat up to look at her. "It's real, I'm afraid, all of it."

"I keep telling myself that I must be crazy, that none of this can be happening, but it doesn't help."

"Maybe we can get family rates when we go into therapy," I told her. I may even have managed to put a smile behind that. "But while it lasts, we've got to accept that we're King and Queen of Varay, and that we're all up the traditional creek without a paddle.''

"You don't think you're going to be able to stop— whatever it is that's happening." It didn't sound like a question.

"Yesterday . . ." That stopped me cold. Was it really only yesterday? I thought. It seemed impossible that so much could happen in just a little more than twenty-four hours. "Yesterday, Aaron said that I had the gun loaded but that I hadn't pulled the trigger yet. It's worse than that, though. I don't even know which way to point the gun." And then I recognized one of the things that had bothered me subconsciously about the gun analogy. Firearms only worked about thirty percent of the time in the buffer zone.

"And there's nowhere to hide, no place we can go to get away from it."

"Look, I know it all sounds crazy, that we're dealing with legends—myths—that got started so long ago that the big power in our world was the Egypt of the pharaohs, but everything so far has checked out," I said. "The odds are too heavy to hope that the threat isn't real."

I got up and started pacing. But before I could carry on with my ranting, there was a knock at the door and Lesh announced that supper was waiting.

"We're coming, just a minute," I called out. Then, more softly, so only Joy could hear me, I said, "But I've got to find a way to make sure our baby has a world to come into."

"A world?" Joy asked, getting up from the window seat.

I shrugged, hurried into clothes, ran my hands through my hair, and gestured toward the door.

"You're going down to eat looking like that?" Joy asked. "You're the king now—you can't run around looking like a bum."

T-shirt and blue jeans. I guess she was right, but I had just pulled on the first clothes that came to hand. I hurried to get myself presentable, and we went down to dinner.

Dinner was another ordeal, with everyone treating me different just because I was suddenly king. There was bowing and an overabundance of titles. I was glad when the meal was over. I was near the boiling point by then, but I knew that I couldn't take out my frustration on the people of my household.

"I've got to get away for a little bit," I told Joy when we went back upstairs. We went all of the way up to the parapets. Autumn had come to Varay. The evening was quite cool, but after the stuffy warmth of the great hall, that can be refreshing. At least there were no dragons hanging about overhead.

"Chicago?" Joy asked. "You've got those Russians to take back."

"Maybe, but not yet." I did have to get the Russians out of the way as soon as possible, and I didn't know anywhere but the other world where I could go to get away from the hoopla. But I also wasn't sure that I would be able go back to Chicago, or anywhere back in that world, ever. A memory: when I suggested that we take Pregel to that world to get him to a modern hospital, Mother said that it was impossible, that Pregel was so tied to the magic of the buffer zone that it would kill him to take him to the world I had been born in.

"Where else can we go?" Joy asked.

I took her in my arms. "I'm not talking about anything major yet, love," I said. "I just have to get off by myself for a couple of hours. Not *we*," I added as softly as I could. I kissed her. "I've got to find some way to come to grips with this."

Then I knew where I would go—whether it was the best place or not, the same place I always went to sort things out in my head in Varay, the crypt under Castle Basil. I had two people there to talk to now, maybe three. When the apparition of the Great Earth Mother confronted me in her shrine out on the Mist, she had initially mistaken me for Vara. "Vara, have you returned at last?"

she asked me. That was another bit of legend that I was going to have to have somebody check on. If there was time.

"I think we both need a few hours alone," I told Joy. "It's a big change for both of us."

"I've had too many hours alone lately," Joy said, turning away from me for a moment. She took a couple of steps away, then turned back to face me.

"We got married, or have you forgotten that? You've been off on these damned quests, one after the other. I'm just someone you come to see for a few hours between adventures." She walked off to the other side of the tower.

"It has been like that," I agreed, following about halfway. The word "damned" coming from her was a pretty clear danger signal. Joy rarely used anything stronger than "darn," and she didn't use *that* often. "I'm not thrilled about it either. There's nothing I'd like better than a chance for the two of us to go off somewhere all alone together. A proper honeymoon, if nothing else."

"But we can't, not yet?"

"Not yet." I shook my head. "If it's at all possible, we'll go lock ourselves away in the apartment in Chicago for a couple of days before the next round. Hey, I may not even have to go anywhere for this last part, if we ever find out what to do. It may be something as simple as performing some kind of ritual with the balls of the Great Earth Mother, some bit of conjuring that can be done right in Castle Basil."

Joy walked partway back to me. "Go on. Go get your brooding over with." She didn't sound angry, just sad. About the way I felt.

"A couple of hours," I said. "It shouldn't be longer than that. I just need time to sort through everything in my head."

"I know." She came the rest of the way to me. "You really cared for Pregel, didn't you?"

"Very much," I said. "And I really didn't want to get us tied down in his job this soon. I thought we'd have a few years of the simple life here first."

''Go on, get going. The sooner you leave, the sooner you'll be back. I think I'll stay up here for a while.''

I knew I had to leave, but I hesitated. I took Joy in my arms and we hugged with something that may have been very close to desperation.

And then I left quickly.

Somehow, I managed to get down to the doorway to Castle Basil and out of Cayenne without running into anyone. My leaving without some sort of entourage would have shocked all of the Varayans no end. At Basil, I couldn't escape notice for long, but only soldiers and servants saw me before I got to the stairs leading down to the crypt. That would give me the time alone I needed. Baron Kardeen would learn that I was in the castle. He *always* seemed to know who was around, within minutes of anyone's arrival or departure. It wasn't that he had magical means of discovering who came and went, it was just that he had the staff well trained, and decades of practice.

There are a *lot* of stairs to cover to get down to the crypt, more than a hundred of them, about eight stories worth. The steps are wide and shallow, running back and forth in straight flights past the cellars and on down into the heart of Basil Rock itself. According to local legend (and in a place like Varay, local legends have something to say about *everything*), Basil Rock is the hub of the universe, the center of all creation—all three realms of being: mortal, buffer, and fairy.

There are no banisters along the stairway, and you can look down between the flights of stairs, all the way to the bottom. But most people stay close to the wall side of the stairs, and few care to look down.

Going down is easy. Coming back up can be a pain.

The stairs and crypt are always well lit. Torches are kept in sconces along the walls at intervals. The duty guards maintain them, and in my years in the kingdom, I had never come across a burned-out torch along the route. They burn almost smokelessly, and there is just enough ventilation through the center of the stairwell and through air shafts bored through to the outside to keep the crypt from claiming new residents for itself with a buildup of carbon monoxide and carbon dioxide.

King Pregel's headstone was already mortared in place, with his name and dates freshly carved on it. Welliva-zey's body had been returned to the room also. Despite the months the elf had been dead, there had been no decomposition.

I stopped by my father's niche first, at the end of the Heroes' section of the burial wall, near the door, nearly eighty feet from Pregel's place.

"You've got someone down here to talk to now, some-one you knew, though you might have to shout at each other to be heard," I said. I had my hand resting on the marble capstone, the way I usually stood during those one-sided chats. I may have been heavily into the Hamlet routine, but I wouldn't say that I ever really heard Dad talking back to me in one of those sessions. My father, Carl Tyner, Hero of Varay before me . . . why would he talk to me about Varay's problems now? He had never said one word to me about the kingdom or his "job" while he was alive. I usually didn't feel the same sharp resentment against him that I still held against Mother, though. Sure, he was equally to blame, but my solilo-quies had eased my anger toward him. Dad never argued. Mother was still around, still alive, and every time I saw her, every time we talked, I thought of the *Big Lie* my parents had woven around me until my twenty-first birth-day.

"I'm still on the hot seat, worse now than before," I said. "I'm stuck with being king as well as Hero, and everything is falling apart—more than *you* ever had to contend with. And there's no sign of this legendary Golden Age, and wasn't that the rationale behind the ly-ing, the deceit?"

I stood there for a while, then moved on down the row of burial slots. The Heroes and kings of Varay. The He-roes were stacked three high, the kings only two high. And right in the middle, Vara was all alone. At one point, not long after I recovered from the wounds I suffered in and before the Battle of Thyme, I made an effort to memorize all the names and dates. I asked questions about who did what and when, and read some of the old books and scrolls that Parthet and Kardeen kept about the history of Varay and the rest of the buffer zone. But I gave that all up fairly quickly. The answers tended to be too depressing.

I made a long stop at Vara's niche. As I had many times before, I wondered if his remains were really in there, if he had really lived and wasn't just part of a legend cooked up to fill a gap . . . which led me—this time—to wonder if the set of family jewels I had swiped from the shrines of the Great Earth Mother *had* originally been his. That apparition of the Great Earth Mother in the shrine had promised to destroy me when she realized that I wasn't really Vara.

The balls, one ruby and one emerald, were they gemstones only or the somehow transformed testicles of Vara?

"If they are yours, at least they're back in the family again," I mumbled.

Two separate legends.

One told how the Great Earth Mother had wandered the void before the beginning of time, before Creation, until she found a mate that she considered suitable. Their coupling had resulting in the Great Earth Mother's giving birth to the entire universe. At some point after that, she had decided that she liked the offspring but not the sire, so she killed her mate and cut off his nuts as a keepsake. And they were apparently hanging with my own now, swallowed in desperation on the island out in the Mist when everything was falling down around me. They seemed to tingle while I stood by Vara's niche and touched his capstone.

The second legend told how Vara had been a renegade *in* and then a refugee *from* Fairy. His name was an obsolete version of the word "Fairy" in the language of that realm. Vara had come south through Xayber with a small band of loyal followers, fighting all the way. He had finally stopped all the forces of the Elfking at the southern end of the Isthmus of Xayber. With peace finally won, Vara had founded the Kingdom of Varay, or perhaps the entire buffer zone between Fairy and the mortal realm, to protect regular people from the magical depredations of the elves. His reign had been (in legend, at least) a Golden Age of peace and prosperity.

I had started to wonder if, somehow, the two separate legends might be parts of the same whole, if perhaps Vara was the stud who tumbled the Great Earth Mother, back before the beginning of time . . . or whenever. And there was only one person who *might* know the answer—Parthet.

I lose track of time when I'm down in the crypt. It may have been an hour, or only ten minutes, before I got to Great-Grandfather Pregel. I put my hand on his capstone. The edges of the newly carved letters and numbers were rougher than on the older stones. I stood there and couldn't think of anything to say to Pregel. Except, after a time, ''Goodbye.''

Before I left the crypt, I stopped and looked at the blank section of wall across the room from Vara. That was where they would put me someday, *if* there was anyone left to put me there when the time came.

''You're going to be lonely in there,'' I said. ''No next-door neighbors to rub elbows with.'' The thought twisted my gut—not the thought of being lonely on that side of the wall, just the idea of someday *being* there behind a marble headstone with my name, titles, and dates. I had been too close to earning a place in the wall over by Dad.

I left the crypt and forced a rapid pace up the stairs toward the living precincts of the castle. I went all the way up to the royal apartments above the great hall in the keep. To the king's bedroom.

There were no lights on in the bedroom. I left the door open until I found one of the oil lamps and lit it. Then I closed the door and looked around. As I had instructed, nothing had been touched yet. I wasn't looking forward to moving into a dead man's bedroom, or to sleeping in the bed where he had died, but I knew how tradition-bound Varay was. This was the king's

bedroom. This was where the king was *supposed* to
sleep.

The bedroom was vast—something like thirty by fifty
feet. Looking in from the hallway door down the long
dimension, there were windows on the wall to the right
and in the wall at the far end of the room. To the right
the view was down into the courtyard. The far end looked
down over the curtain wall, down the sheer northern face
of Basil Rock, several hundred feet to the River Tarn that
curled past the base. The royal bed was more than twice
the size of a "king-size" bed. It was centered along the
left wall. Three doors opened off of that wall into other
rooms of the royal suite, privy, bath and dressing room,
and study.

Before his health failed, Pregel had been an active
monarch. There had been a big desk up on the dais in
the throne room, and it was often cluttered. At some
point, between the time when Pregel publicly announced
that I was his heir and his death, that desk had been
moved up to the study, replacing a smaller desk that had
been there before. The study had been his working office,
most of the time I knew him. We had shared a few lei-
surely chats in that office. The only person who ever
dared disturb the king in his office was Baron Kardeen,
and the chamberlain knew when—and when not—to disturb Pregel.

It was an old-fashioned office. What else could it be
in Varay? The big desk was an antique that was probably
worth many thousands of dollars back in the other world.
There was a library, racks of deep pigeonholes to hold
scrolls, shelves to hold books. Ah, the books. Pregel had
medieval romances, modern sciences, an almost complete set of Louis L'Amour's westerns. He had Hitler and
Machiavelli, Gibran and Nietzsche. A twelfth-century
Bible copied in a Norman monastery was on a stand like
those that libraries use to hold their unabridged diction-
aries. There were also other religious books, copies dat-
ing from the Middle Ages or before, Koran, Talmud,
Zend Avesta, and others. It didn't matter what language

a book was written in, not in the buffer zone with its translation magic.

I opened the drawers in two wooden file cabinets, one at a time, wondering what exotic documents of state I might find. There were a few deeds and charters, a few letters, but five of the eight drawers were given over to magazines. I thumbed through the drawers. It looked as if Pregel had complete sets of *Penthouse* and *Playboy,* from their premiere issues up to about four years ago.

I chuckled when I shut the last drawer.

"It looks like I really didn't know you at all," I mumbled. I sat in the chair behind the big desk, reached out and stroked the smooth, worn desktop. The desk drawers were filled with working supplies, paper and pens, and the usual odds and ends that get chucked into drawers and forgotten.

There was a second exit from the study, leading directly out to the corridor, a way to bypass going through the bedroom all the time. Across the corridor was the king's private dining room, for those times when he wanted to avoid presiding over a meal in the great hall, or for private mealtime discussions. Back stairs led down to the kitchens, and to Baron Kardeen's office. Even after three and a half years I didn't know where all the secret passages were, though I had found a few of them.

I wasn't expecting the knock on the hall door. I jumped, then said, "Come in." I guessed that it would be Baron Kardeen. I was wrong. It was Aaron.

"I wasn't sure if I should disturb you or not," he said.

"Come on in and have a seat," I told him. "You're not interrupting anything but my brooding, and that needs interruption." He came over and sat in the chair at the side of the desk. So far, Aaron had shown none of the irritating "Your Majesty" routine, and that was a relief.

"You know, I'm going to need time to get used to that souvenir of our elf that you carry."

Aaron touched the streak of white skin on the left side of his face. "Ah, that. It is more than skin deep. At odd moments, I think I have a little of him inside my head too.''

"Enough to find out what I have to do with these spare balls?''

"No. That's the first thing I tried to find out. But Parthet is putting together some sort of special incantation. Something new, something not in any of the books and scrolls he taught me from. That's why I came looking for you. He says that he's going to need you present to run the spell.''

"And if that doesn't work, we're back to calling up the Elflord of Xayber and asking for his help,'' I said.

"It may not be necessary. Despite all the doom talk, there doesn't seem to be anything particularly rotten happening at the moment,'' Aaron said. "Maybe what you've done already *is* enough, despite what Wellivazey said.''

"I don't believe it,'' I said.

Aaron shrugged. "Parthet is trying hard to make himself believe it. He keeps talking about that Golden Age jazz.''

We sat and looked at each other for a bit.

"When is he going to be ready to try this new magic?'' I asked.

"A day or two, he says. He's working now, has been, just about straight through. He's even having his food brought to the workroom so he can keep going without interruptions.''

"That doesn't sound like he's had much luck convincing himself that the danger is past,'' I said. Aaron shrugged again. "A day or two?'' I asked. He nodded.

"I've got to make arrangements to get the Russians back to the real world. And Joy and I would like to get a little time to ourselves while we still can. The only way we're likely to get that time is to go back to Chicago or Louisville, and I'm not sure that I can anymore.'' I told Aaron what Mother had said about Pregel.

"I don't think you have to worry,'' Aaron said. "Before he started working on this new magic, and back when Parthet was teaching me about being a wizard, he did a lot of talking about Pregel. He talked about how they went to the St. Louis World's Fair together back in the beginning of the century, about being among the first people ever to eat ice cream in a cone. What your mother was talking about, that must just have been because your grandfather was already so sick.''

That sounded encouraging. ''I'd better double-check though,'' I said, getting up from the desk. ''Is Parthet so deep in his conjuring that I can't disturb him for a minute?''

''I don't think so. He's not in a trance or anything.''

Parthet confirmed what Aaron had said. After that, I could hardly wait to get back to Joy. It was almost midnight in Varay, which would make it about three in the morning in Chicago, but I was almost certain that Joy would want to go through right away, get away for as long as we could, as soon as we could, before anything could come up to keep us from leaving. I took just enough time before I left Basil to tell Kardeen where Joy and I would be and to tell him that we weren't to be disturbed unless it was absolutely a matter of life and death.

''As soon as I tell Joy the trip's on, I'll be back to go up to Arrowroot for the Russians,'' I told Kardeen. ''The sooner they're gone, the better. I'd hate to have any unpleasantness up at Arrowroot.'' Then I hurried back to Cayenne.

Joy was still up on the battlements, staring at the night sky.

''You ready for that honeymoon?'' I asked.

''Aren't any of the stars here the same as they are back home?'' she asked. I looked up at the sky.

''I'm not sure. I think they must be, but we're seeing them from a different perspective. I know what you mean, though,'' I added before she could say anything. ''The patterns are different. There's no Orion, no Dippers, nothing to recognize. It bothered me at first too, especially not being able to see Orion. But you get used to the new patterns.'' As long as you avoided dwelling on the paradox of the same moon being in the sky with different constellations.

"I wonder," Joy said, and then she switched topics. "You mean we *can* go back to our world?"

"Anytime we want. The trouble with Grandfather was that he was already so sick. He just couldn't take the strain of being away from the source of the magic that was keeping him going. He was even in our world when I was born. He came to see me while I was still in the hospital."

"Can we go right now?"

I smiled. I knew her well enough to predict that response. "I hurried back as soon as I found out. We can go anytime you want. It'll be about three in the morning there, though."

"As long as there's hot water in the shower."

"There should be." And then I decided that the Russians could wait for a few hours, until morning. There was no sense waking them up now. Joy and I deserved a little treat.

"But will it be safe? Will the police be waiting, about Aaron?" Joy asked.

I laughed. "So I'll claim diplomatic immunity. I'm the head of state of a sovereign kingdom."

The joke came at a good time. We both laughed, and we *needed* a laugh.

"Okay, your high-and-mightiness, let's go take a hot shower."

We went down to the bedroom, grabbed clothes to change into after our shower, and went to the doorway leading to the bedroom in the Chicago condo. I handed Joy the clothes I was carrying so I would have both hands free to open the passage. I put my rings on the silver lining . . .

And nothing happened.

"You miss the silver?" Joy asked.

I shook my head and looked. The rings were on the sea-silver.

Something's wrong, I thought, but I didn't say it yet.

"I'll try the door to my office in the Loop," I said. I

kept office space just to have an extra bolt hole in Chicago—and to let me get downtown and back a lot faster. My office was only a couple of blocks from the big Kroch and Brentano bookstore on Wabash, even closer to Marshall Field's. Convenient for shopping.

That door didn't work either.

Neither did the one to my bedroom in Louisville.

''I think we've got big trouble,'' I told Joy.

5

The Day

Joy dropped the bundle of clothes. She guessed what had happened as quickly as I did. Neither of us screamed. We were beyond that. I went back and tried all of my doorways to the other world again. There was nothing, no tingling, no opening. I didn't get a kick in the gut from my danger sense, because I couldn't get through to where the danger was.

"World War Three," Joy said. She seemed to choke on the words. Who could blame her?

I nodded and cleared my throat a couple of times. "Maybe not," I said, even though I didn't believe what I was saying. "It may just be a malfunction in the magic. Aaron might have shorted out the system when he created the passage back from that shrine."

"That was days ago. Why would it wait till now to blow? Try one of the doors to Basil."

"Not days ago," I said. "Less than two days."

Was it really only that? I asked myself. It hardly seemed possible that so much had happened in a day and a half.

Try one of the doors to Basil. I would have thought of that fairly soon even without Joy's prompt. As soon as I got hold of the shock of not being able to get through to Chicago or Louisville, my first impulse would have been to run to Castle Basil to spread the alarm and start everybody working on ways to deal with the crisis. It *would* be a crisis and it *would* spill over into Varay and the rest of the buffer zone one way or another. Even without all the other weirdness going on, something that major would be reflected in the seven kingdoms. That's how closely the realms are tied together.

The door to my (now former) bedroom in Castle Basil worked.

I looked through the doorway for a moment, then broke the contact. "Okay, it's not all the doors," I said. "I'll get Lesh. This isn't a time to be going anywhere without an escort."

I opened our bedroom door and yelled for Lesh. He may be a heavy sleeper at times, but he woke fast enough that time.

"We're going to Castle Basil," I told him. "There's some kind of trouble with the doors leading back to my world."

"Aye, sire. I'll grab my things." Lesh turned and raced back to the level where he and the rest of my people slept. Lesh was soon coming back, with his weapons—and with Harkane, Timon, and the new pages, Jaffa and Rodi.

"We're ready, sire," Lesh said. It had taken me ages to break him of calling me "lord" every time he opened his mouth. I wasn't sure that I would ever be able to break him of the sires and Majesties now that I was king.

"Not all of us," I said. "Harkane, you'll stay here as my steward for the time being." Giving the job a title would make it easier to accept. That lesson had taken some learning for me. "I don't know how long we're going to be gone, but you're in charge here until we get back."

"Yes, Your Majesty." Harkane was even worse about it than Lesh. Supper had been so full of titles that I'd almost choked on them.

"When we get to Basil, I'll need Baron Kardeen, Parthet, Aaron, and my mother. I'll be in the king's . . . in the private dining room upstairs, waiting. You know where I mean?"

"Aye, sire," Lesh said. "Timon and I'll round 'em up quick."

"Quickly, yes, but gently, Lesh."

"Aye, sire. Ah, your weapons?"

I sighed. "Yes, my weapons." I was still Hero of Varay, and the Hero must always be armed in public. Well, with the collapse apparently on again, it was a good idea anyway.

Even with the delays, we stepped through to Castle Basil less than twenty minutes after I discovered that the doorways back to the other world didn't work. It was barely an hour since I had left Aaron and Parthet in the workroom they now shared.

The guard who spotted us just after we arrived at Basil snapped to attention and Lesh commandeered him to go after Baron Kardeen. Joy and I went straight up to the private dining room across from the king's bedroom. I sent Jaffa and Rodi to stir somebody in the kitchen—one of the cooks was always on call—to make coffee and something to snack on and get them hauled upstairs. The boys knew their way around Castle Basil. I wouldn't have been surprised if they knew back passageways that I hadn't found yet.

"Where do you want me?" Joy asked when we got to the dining room and got some light in the room. Timon lit a torch from one out in the hall and stuck it in a wall bracket. Then he lit the other wall torches in the room from that one.

"Right at my side, where you belong," I told Joy. I shifted one of the chairs around next to the royal "throne." Physical labor. It made me feel good to do things that my people would scarcely permit if any of them were close enough to get in the way. I barely beat Timon to it, though.

Baron Kardeen arrived almost as I got the chair in position.

"How bad is it, Majesty?" Kardeen asked.

"The doorways back to my world don't work. At least, none of them from Cayenne do. I haven't tried the ones here in Basil yet. My guess is that nuclear war has broken out back there. If the doorways are all shot, I'm not even sure how we could find out." The idea of being stranded permanently in the buffer zone was almost as frightening as the idea of nuclear war back home—the war that ev-

eryone said could no longer happen because of the de-
cline of Communism.

"There are ways," Kardeen said. "Parthet will
know."

Almost on cue, Parthet and Aaron came in. Mother
was just a minute behind them. I told the others what
little I knew and what I suspected. Nuclear war wasn't
gibberish to either Parthet or Kardeen. They knew enough
about my world to follow the talk without any trouble at
all. And Aaron . . . well, he had more reason than most
to know what nuclear weapons could do.

"It seems that the *first* thing to do is to check *all* of
the doorways leading to the lesser world," Parthet said.
It was the first time I had heard him call my world "the
lesser."

"The doors in the cellar in Louisville might have survived even holocaust," Mother said. "Unless the magic
can be disrupted by EMP, like electronics."

"Electromagnetic pulse?" Parthet said, rubbing his
chin. "It's a distinct possibility. Carl once offered a guess
that our magic might be a function of an electromagnetic
force, something at the extreme short end of the spec-
trum. I suppose that might do it. Of course, even if there
is disruption, it might be temporary. Who really knows
enough about things like EMP? It's all theory, like nuclear winter."

That's right, we sat around in the middle of the night,
in a medieval castle, discussing the ramifications of nuclear war—an ancient wizard, a new young wizard, and
all the rest of us. And down in the crypt, we had the
headless body of a dead elf warrior. We were in a kingdom that couldn't exist by any rule of logic. Magic forces
assailed us from every side and dragons the size of ocean
liners sometimes flew overhead and dropped two-ton
loads of crap. Our pages and two kitchen workers hauled
in wooden platters of food, a pewter pot of terrible coffee, a small keg of beer, and the "tools" to handle it
all.

Joy and I were both trained in computer science and
there wasn't a computer in the kingdom. At the moment,

the insanity of the entire scene seemed to have a macabre undertone of danger. There was no laughter, not even a smile, not with the likelihood that World War Three had indeed broken out back home.

"Which of the doorways is nearest?" I asked.

"Down the back stairs here, and off to the left," Kardeen said without hesitation.

I stood. Everyone else stood. That's one of the annoyances of being king. "Parthet, Aaron, can you come up with something to shield us from radiation if the passage does work?" Aaron and Parthet looked at each other. Aaron was the first to nod.

"I'll let the lad take care of it," Parthet said softly. "His magic is already much stronger than mine ever was."

We all went down the stairs. "The rest of you stay back here," I said, thirty feet short of the door. "No call to take more risks than we have to." Aaron and I went on together. We looked at the silver tracing around it.

"Let me know when you've got the shield up," I said. "And if I do get the doorway open, I may jump back in one hell of a hurry. My danger sense gets quite insistent at times."

"I can dig it," Aaron said. Then he shifted to a magical chant.

The spell he wove was visible, a shimmering in the air across the doorway. There was a slightly greenish cast to anything beyond the shield—not the most attractive shade of green.

"Go ahead," Aaron said quietly. I could hear the tension in his words. I looked at him and he nodded.

I reached for the silver on both sides of the doorway. The motion didn't merely appear slow, it *was* slow. I was scared. I could draw on memories of enough books and movies about nuclear holocaust to be about ready to brown out at the thought that I might be opening a doorway into the middle of one. Even in a limited exchange, Louisville would certainly be a target. Fort Knox was out there south of the city, and there were other strategic targets in the area as well.

When I touched the silver, within the green haze of Aaron's shield, there was a scream inside my head as my danger sense overloaded—even before the cellar room in Louisville came into view.

The room was still there. It was a mess, but it was still there. One leg had snapped on the big table in the middle of the room and spilled everything to the floor. The floor was littered with papers, books, weapons, and pieces of armor, not all of it from the table. The antique rolltop desk seemed to be intact. I guess it would take a direct hit to destroy *that*. The rest of the room? Well, one door had blown in, the one that led out to the rest of the basement. But there was no evidence of fire.

The bile-green shimmering of the shield Aaron had raised started to show orange flecks that quickly multiplied and started to overshadow the green. Aesthetically, it was an improvement, but Aaron didn't have to tell me to break the connection before the shimmering went completely orange.

"Radiation of some kind," Aaron said after I stepped back and the cellar room disappeared. "I had no way to guess how much there might be. There are some weak spots in the education this place gave me."

"A cellar under a stone house," I said. "I would have guessed that that room would have made a decent fallout shelter."

"It's still intact, except for the door," Aaron pointed out. "That's wood, isn't it?" I nodded. "I can't say what the level of radiation is. I don't have a scale to compare it to."

"Back upstairs," I said.

When we were all seated around the table again, we were all silent for a considerable time. Parthet was the one who finally broke the silence.

"We'll be picking up the backlash here before long."

The obvious questions would have had something to do with the kind of backlash we might expect and how long it would take to start. I had something different come to mind, though.

"Uncle Parthet, how well do you remember Vara?"

He started to answer automatically before he fully comprehended the question. When the question did register, it seemed to jolt him like an electric shock. He stared at me for a moment, then he seemed to slowly focus beyond me. His face went blank, his skin pale. I didn't pay much attention to the others at the table, just enough to register the shock or surprise they felt at my apparent non sequitur and its sequel. I suspect that Aaron was affected least. And Kardeen recovered quickly, before Parthet spoke.

"As well, I imagine, as you remember *your* father," he said—eventually, and *very* slowly. His voice sounded as if it were coming from far off, in time if not in space.

I had been expecting something of that nature, but the others were obviously taken by surprise . . . by something even beyond surprise. Mother's mouth dropped open. Kardeen's lips pressed together more tightly. Joy's hand gripped my arm as tightly as a fully inflated blood-pressure cuff. Aaron showed no reaction at all.

"Just how old are you?" I asked Parthet. "Straight out this time." I had asked him often enough before, and he had never given the same answer twice. But I had never asked as *king* before, and never in such constricting circumstances.

"Straight out? I *can't* say precisely," Parthet said. There was something wistful, and terribly sad, in his voice. "Time isn't a constant. You found that out on your journey up the Isthmus of Xayber." I nodded. "And time hasn't always run at the same rate here as in the world where you were born. There used to be a"—he hesitated for a moment—"a considerable differential. Time ran slower here before the lesser world discovered clockmaking."

I may have raised an eyebrow at that. If I did, Parthet didn't seem to notice. I had started his mind down an ancient trail. The answers we needed might be buried back there, and if no one disturbed him at the wrong moment, the answers might surface. I hoped.

"I was his second son, of course," Parthet said after a long pause. "My brother Paterno inherited the kingdom. I came into this calling. Perhaps the kingdom would have been better served if Paterno and I had reversed our roles. His gift for wizardry may have been greater than mine. Wizards are—to a great extent—born, not made, and they are *not* born equal.'' He glanced at Aaron, and then he shrugged. ''I used up all of my envy before the fall of Camelot.''

Statements like that didn't surprise me any longer. Parthet had hammered one lesson home over and over since I first came to Varay. *We create our own history, changing the past generation by generation, sometimes moment by moment*—not just the interpretations, but the facts themselves. It's something we all contribute to, some people more than others, according to Parthet. Call it an alternate-worlds theory turned backward. Parthet claimed Merlin as a mentor and friend. He talked about Robin Hood, King Arthur, and Prester John as freely as I might talk about people I knew in high school.

''Things were different here in the days when Vara was still King of Varay. The distinctions among the three realms were . . . different from what they are now. Fairy was more advanced than the buffer zone, and we were more advanced than the lesser world. The pyramids had yet to be imagined. It was possible to move back and forth quite freely from one realm to another—not that many people had much cause to travel far. There was the occasional lordling who wanted primitives to impress. I guess that at one time or another, there were plenty of those—men and women of Fairy who liked the idea of being worshiped as gods and goddesses in one area of Earth or another.''

He fell silent again. I waited a bit and then asked the next important question. ''How did Vara die?''

''We never knew exactly. It happened in Battle Forest. He didn't come back from a hunt. The few soldiers he had taken with him were found first. Vara was found nearly three miles away. A patrol from Coriander found him.''

''What kind of condition was the body in?'' I asked.

''Mutilated. He . . .'' Parthet stopped and looked up

suddenly, and his thoughts were clearly reflected on his face. He realized what I was talking about, and put together the legends that had grown during the millennia of his forgetfulness. "He had been . . ." Parthet shook his head and needed a moment to get his thoughts organized again.

"He never talked about anything before Varay. He never told us about our family's past. Back then, it wasn't even something we would have thought to ask. We had Varay. It was our heritage. It was enough."

"So you're half brother to all of creation?" I asked, speaking very softly so I wouldn't disrupt the mood.

Parthet's gaze seemed to stretch out toward infinity. "I have to get back to my workroom," he said. "There may be some . . ." He got up and left, almost as if he were floating out of the room.

After Parthet left, the rest of us did one of those numbers where everybody just looks around at everybody else.

"What was that all about?" Mother asked finally. "I've never seen Parthet act like that—so strange."

"I had to shock him back to our roots," I said. "It may be the only way to find an answer."

"You've given up on the elflord?" Aaron asked.

"Not necessarily, but I like the idea of having alternatives, and if Parthet can really keep his thoughts together on this, he may be a better source than Xayber could be at his most willing."

"I never suspected," Kardeen said slowly, and the shock of that realization, rather than the revelation that caused it, seemed to get to the chamberlain. He looked toward the door. "I knew he was old, but I didn't know he was *that* old."

"I don't think Parthet remembered it himself," I said. "You've heard him talk about how history changes. He had been affected by those changes like everything else. I shocked him back to an earlier release, back to the roots. I hope. Aaron, give him a little time alone, then keep a close watch on him. Anything could happen now."

Aaron nodded.

I closed my eyes for a moment. I wasn't working from any set plan. I was just jumping from one thought to another, trying to catch up.

"I'm still going to have to talk to the elflord," I said.

"When?" Aaron asked.

"It had better be soon," I said without much hesitation. "We don't know how much time we have, so we need to pursue all our options at the same time."

"In the morning?" Aaron suggested.

I thought about it for a moment. "Maybe we shouldn't even wait that long. Mother, will you stay with Parthet until Aaron and I get done?"

She nodded abruptly, started to say something, then changed her mind.

"It had to be, Mother," I said, assuming that she was about to question what I had done to Parthet. "Right now, there's too much at stake to worry about what might happen to *any* of us as individuals."

Mother got up and left.

"Joy, you'd better go with Baron Kardeen. Or try to get some sleep. We still have my old bedroom here. I'll come get you after I talk to the elflord."

"You don't think I could actually sleep, do you? Gil, we *have* to find out what happened. My family is back there."

I turned toward her, took her hands in mine. "I know, dear. I'll do everything I can."

There were tears on her cheeks that I hadn't noticed before. *Her family.* Caught up in everything else, I hadn't even thought about them. I couldn't. I had a lot more to worry about, as heartless as that might have sounded to Joy. I didn't say that, though, and Joy didn't press. Not then.

Kardeen escorted her out.

"Do you need to do anything special before we try to contact the elflord?" I asked Aaron when we were alone in the room. Timon, Lesh, and the pages were out in the hall, close but not in the way.

"I don't think so. I just need a few minutes to make

some preparations. Are you sure it's wise to call in the middle of the night?''

"I'm not sure it's wise to call him anytime, but night or day won't make any difference to the elflord. It may not even *be* night where he's at."

"Xayber is straight north of here, isn't it?"

"Near enough, but day and night don't necessarily co-incide between here and Fairy. A week inside Fairy can be ten days out here, or two weeks, or even longer."

"That's what Parthet was talking about?"

"Part of it."

I got up and paced, over by the windows, while Aaron worked up his preliminary magics. While I couldn't fol-low any of the mumbo-jumbo he chanted, I had a rough idea of what he was doing. He knew that the Elflord could be dangerous, even long-distance, so he was build-ing what defenses he could around us before he made any connection to Xayber. I had been through a couple of psychic confrontations with the elflord, and I was all in favor of getting any extra protection I could before chatting with him this time.

Calling the Elflord of Xayber was a little more com-plicated than picking up the telephone and dialing a num-ber. I knew that Parthet had communicated with the Elfking something like this, back when I was trying to distract Xayber long enough to let us deal with the Etevar of Dorthin, but I hadn't been around to observe the pro-cess. I was off on the isthmus looking for sea-silver to line new magic doors and getting myself in more than enough trouble on my own. And the Elflord of Xayber had found my ''number'' while I was raising a little hell among his subjects. When it worked, this magic long-distance communication was a lot more comprehensive than the telephone. It really brought you close enough to ''reach out and touch someone''—in my limited experi-ence, usually to the dismay of one or the other of the parties.

"You do know that there are certain hazards to this, don't you?'' I asked when Aaron paused in his prepara-tions.

"I know about the time Parthet got caught with his spells down, and how you rescued him," Aaron said. "I know that the elflord controls a more powerful magic than I do, than you and me combined." He looked at me. "Even with the ruby and emerald contributing."

"Are they?"

"I can feel the magic," Aaron said. "If all this jive is right, they helped create the whole ballpark. Makes Adam and Eve sound like kid stuff." He circled the table, mumbling another chant. When he finished that one, he stopped at my end of the table.

"You're a regular riot of magic now, you know? I can feel the static complicating what I'm trying to do."

"Parthet told me that everything here has its own kind of magic about it," I said.

"No different anywhere," Aaron said. "But *you're* something else."

I nodded and tried to divert my mind from worrying by listing all of my contributions to the static—the magic of the Hero of Varay, the magic of the king, the magic of each of the elf swords (hung across my back in an "X marks the spot" arrangement, so I couldn't even sit back comfortably), and the magic of the balls of the Great Earth Mother. Each packed a potent *sui generis* magic. Maybe I had picked up a little extra zap from the elf and the dragons I had killed along the way—something like the primitive belief that you could get some of the lion's power by eating the heart of a lion you had killed. Only in the buffer zone, that sort of thing seemed to be fact rather than superstition.

"The static won't get in the way of your precautions, will it?" I asked.

"Give the elflord something extra to think about. Almost ready now. You know what you're going to say to the man—or whatever he is?"

"I didn't write a speech, but I've got some idea what I need to say." Only mildly sarcastic. "There going to be any trouble holding this long enough to say it all?"

"From what I've heard, the only worry is can we hang up when we want to."

"I'm ready whenever you are," I said. I sat back down in my place at the head of the table.

Aaron sat in the chair to my right, along the side of the table, and started chanting again, a different line, louder than before, more insistent. Judging by what I could feel and see, it was a stronger, or at least a more active, magic than his preparatory spells. My skin tingled, itched. The hair on my arms stood on end. The lights seemed to fade and flare alternately. The entire room seemed to pulse.

And suddenly, the Elflord of Xayber was seated at the far end of the table, staring at me, drumming his fingers—audibly—against the tabletop.

"I've been waiting to hear from you," he said. The voice was intimately familiar, recalled in every nuance from our earlier "meetings." There was a hint of condescension in his voice now, as there had been before, and a hint that he hadn't really expected me to make contact. I sat quietly and stared at him for a moment. I couldn't distinguish this magic from reality. To all intents and purposes, the elflord was actually there in the room with me . . . and he had brought along his own chair. Ma Bell should work so good.

"Are you ready to fulfill your vow?" Xayber asked. He looked much as I remembered him from our psychic duel years before—tall, even sitting he seemed to dwarf me; thin, with coal-black hair and a face that was so pale that it was *really* white, bone white.

"I have many vows to keep," I told him. "Right now, there is one that is more time-critical than returning your son's remains. Are you aware that the whole fabric of creation is disintegrating? That we seem to be running down to complete destruction?"

The elflord glanced toward Aaron at the side of the table, then said, "I have noted a few disturbances."

"It's more than that. You'd better hear the whole story." And I gave it to him, as complete as I could, the dragons in chicken eggs, the *Coral Lady* and Aaron, the two full moons. I covered his son's interpretation, the basics of our trips to the shrines of the Great Earth

Mother, and the apparent outbreak of nuclear war in my world. Xayber asked a few questions, but even the elflord seemed to have a passing acquaintance with the vocabulary of the nuclear age—either that or the translation magic put it in terms he *could* relate to.

"There are now *three* moons in the sky," he said after I finished my recital. "Seven is the critical number."

"Then time is even shorter than I thought," I said. "And before I can bring your son home to you, I have to try to stop this spiral into chaos. If we go down to general destruction, it wipes us all out."

The elflord looked toward the ceiling. His image seemed to flicker out for just an instant before he looked at me again. He shook his head.

"It is already too late to save this universe," he said.

6

Death Dawn

"No!"

The negative was ripped out of my throat without thought, but thought didn't alter my rejection of Xayber's verdict. The elflord stared at me. I saw pity on his face, and that added anger to the other emotions I was feeling.

"There are some things that wishing cannot change," he said.

I paused, took a deep breath, and set my jaw. "Perhaps, but you must be wrong about this."

"Doubtful," he said.

"There must be something we can do. I have the balls of the Great Earth Mother!" After all the hell I had gone through to retrieve them and the utter agony of . . . assimilating them, I couldn't bear to contemplate the possibility that it might have been in vain.

"This world, this universe, must pass," Xayber said. He seemed to flicker out and in again. Then he shrugged. "Perhaps it is best. The old must pass before the new may come." Fatalism. "Will you bring my son home before the end?"

"I won't give up."

Too much was flooding through my mind. I tried to focus on the elflord, but the thought of total eradication, the End of Everything, was overloading my circuits. I thought only of what *I* would lose in the total disaster. How can anyone really comprehend the greater disaster? I thought of the unborn child who would never be born. I thought of losing Joy, of losing Varay after the world I grew up in had already suffered nuclear catastrophe. There was no way that my mind *could* accept Xayber's sentence of futility. Hey, I thought. This is a fantasy world. Never-Never Land. It *can't* end like this. I got so wrapped up in all the internal byplay that I didn't hear what Xayber said next.

"What was that?" I asked when I realized that I had missed something.

"I said that the old world *must* pass, but that if you are a true heir of Vara, you may—*may*—be able to see that some portion of this world is recreated in the next. You carry the seed."

"I don't understand what you're talking about."

"The seed. The *seed*. Are you dense? You must do what Vara did. The seed and the egg."

The seed? I stared at him for a moment. Perhaps the old euphemism was what threw me. "You mean I have to find the Great Earth Mother and knock her up?"

"If you are truly the heir of Vara, you have the seed of the new world in you," he said, nodding.

"The Great Earth Mother is already looking to kill me for taking the family jewels in the first place. And I don't think my magic is strong enough to let me take her against her will." Not to mention my own revulsion at the idea of forcing *anyone*.

"If you want to have any hope of preserving anything of this world, if you want to ensure that there *is* a next one, you must create it with her. There is no other way."

Long pause.

"There don't seem to be a lot of alternatives," I said, shaking my head at the images running through my mind. "Granting that it means that I have to try, where do I find her and how do I make my approach?"

Another long pause.

"Difficult questions," the elflord said. "It will take time to find the answers."

I hope you're not going to pull a Deep Thought on me, I thought.

"How much time?" I asked. "That commodity seems to be in particularly short supply."

"There will be a price," Xayber said. "The return of my son."

"If there is time, and *if* I have your guarantee that you won't do anything to hinder my attempt to find the Great Earth Mother.''

"Agreed. Anything I might do would be less than you will experience in your frustration to save what can't be saved.'' He paused and cleared his throat. "I won't do anything to hinder you. You have my word on that. You could even return my son now. Bring him to this room and I can take him home with me.''

I kept my voice level and my face straight. "I think that might be premature,'' I said. "When you have the answers I need.''

"As you will.''

"For what it may be worth, we could never have come this far without the help of your son, even after he was dead.''

"I know.''

I thought you might.

There was a loud noise from the corridor, something—or someone—falling against the door. I turned, distracted, and started to reach for a sword instinctively. The elflord also looked toward the door. Aaron was facing it. The door swung open and Annick hopped over Lesh. He grabbed for her ankles but missed.

"I *knew* there was an elf near,'' Annick said, not quite in a shout. A long dagger flashed through the air—through the head of the image of the elflord—and clattered off the wall behind him.

"You, the hellhound.'' Xayber hadn't even blinked at the dagger she threw at him, a calmness I could never have maintained, even if I knew that it was just an image of me being threatened.

"Me. Tell my father that I'll get to him yet. I'll take off his head the way he''—she pointed at me—"took the head off of that other crud.''

Lesh levered himself to his feet and lurched toward Annick. She started to jump sideways, but Aaron pointed a finger at her. She went rigid and fell. Lesh broke the fall but couldn't stop her from going down.

The elflord looked at me. "I will contact you when I have the answers you seek."

"How long?" I asked.

He shrugged. "It will take time. The Great Earth Mother is always elusive."

"Hours? Days?" I wanted *some* idea.

"Days, at least, more likely weeks." The elflord glanced at Aaron again, then back to me. "I will find you then."

And then he was gone.

Tableau vivant. *I'm sitting on the almost-throne at the head of the table. Aaron is to my right, standing about a third of the way down the table. Lesh is on one knee, his left arm still supporting Annick's head, just off the floor. She is sprawled, still held by Aaron's restraining magic.*

I don't suppose that the scene held motionless more than a couple of seconds, but it seemed much longer. That kind of frozen moment always seems impossible, a device, unless it's actually happening to you. I had one of those moments when I heard about the *Challenger* disaster. Dad said he experienced the same thing when he heard that President Kennedy had been killed, a frozen moment with everything about it impressed indelibly in the mind.

A blink. A deep breath. The moment ends.

I glanced at Aaron, then turned my attention to Annick. She picked herself up off the floor.

"I didn't drop you hard on purpose," Aaron said. He got up and went around the far end of the table, moving slowly. "It's just that you didn't give me the time to do it gently."

Annick flashed a fierce look at Aaron. Behind her, Lesh stood up, ready to grab her again.

"It's okay, Lesh," I said. "There's no one for her to attack now."

That turned Annick's attention from Aaron to me.

"What the hell did you think you were going to accomplish?" I asked. "The whole universe is falling apart and you've got to stage your damn theatrics."

"I came back when I heard that the king had died," Annick said. "I find a new king and a new wizard, dealing with the enemy."

"There are no enemies right now, Annick," I said. "We're all facing the same disaster."

"*I* still have enemies!"

She had held that level of hate when I first met her. It seemed to sustain her. She had never been able to let go of her hatred for the elf warrior who had raped her mother. Her father. And her hatred for everything in and of Fairy. That was why I had never doubted any of the fantastic tales that were told about her exploits in Fairy. I knew she was capable of the most extreme of them.

"I appreciate your help with the forest trolls," I told her, trying to forget a chance vision of the Queen of Hearts screaming, *"Off with her head!"* As far as I knew, Varay had never used capital punishment. Serious crime was extremely rare among Varayans, and the Kings of Varay had always had a more potent sentence to impose, exile. People who couldn't get along in Varay could be dumped in Fairy or in my world to fend for themselves. But exile to my world looked like capital punishment at the moment, and shipping Annick into Fairy would have been no punishment at all. It would just have given her a chance to go on with her killing . . . until somebody, or something, killed her.

"But right now, you're a distraction I can't afford," I told her. But I needed a moment to figure out what to do with her.

"Aaron, have you been to Castle Curry yet?" I asked.

"Only briefly."

"You met Baron Veter and his guardian, Sir Compil?"

"We met." He seemed unusually terse. Aaron was watching Annick as closely as Lesh was. He was learning fast. In her killing moods, Annick needed close watching.

"I would like you to take Annick to Castle Curry and put her in the care of Sir Compil. She is to be held there through the crisis, not harshly, but with as much security as they can manage. Restrained from leaving. Have Baron

Kardeen prepare a letter to that effect.'' Aaron nodded.''Take Lesh with you to help keep an eye on Annick until you get her turned over to Compil, then both of you get right back.''

If it had been up to Lesh, I'm sure he would have hogtied Annick to make sure she didn't give him any trouble. He might even shackle her with handcuffs and leg irons, if any were available. Maybe it would have been a good idea at that. They left. Annick glared at me over her shoulder as Lesh nudged her toward the door. I doubted that Castle Curry would hold Annick for long, but it was the most distant point in Varay from both Basil and Xayber that had a magic doorway. Once Annick managed to escape from Curry, it would take her a week to ride to Basil, nine days or more to reach Arrowroot, even if she managed to steal a good horse. That bought me some time without her. And every day that Compil managed to hold her in custody would add to the margin.

Sitting alone after the others left, I had to start thinking about what the elflord had said. *This world must pass.* I might be able to save a little of it—somehow add it to the next world. That was more than a little vague, but it did give me some hope to hang on to. I was ready to grab for any thread I could. Vara had managed to stick around and enjoy his new world for a time before the Great Earth Mother carved him up. If I could save enough from this world to let my mind survive in the next . . . if I could save Joy, maybe a chunk of the buffer zone as well . . .

If not? I wondered what the end would be like. Would there be a show, fireworks and earthquakes, the wild special effects of a Hollywood disaster film? Or would we just fade to black? With a whimper or with a bang.

Joy. No Joy.

I thought about movies I had seen where the hero is told that he's dying and there's no hope for a cure. John Wayne's last picture, *The Shootist,* was the first I thought of, where Jimmy Stewart tells the Duke that he has a cancer, and then the follow-up, with Wayne's character trying to come to terms with the end and managing to go out with style.

But it wasn't enough. It wasn't just my death in the offing, but the End of Everything—all of creation perhaps, the far end of time, when the entire universe fizzled out. According to the cosmologists back home, that wasn't supposed to happen for billions and billions of years, the heat death of the universe, entropy run down to its final chaos. And we hadn't even landed men on Mars or met our first extraterrestrials yet. No E.T. No Alf. No Mork. No Starship *Enterprise*.

No "Mr. and Mrs. Gil Tyner announce the birth of their first child."

No "Someday, son, this will all be yours."

Shit.

Somewhere along the line, I noticed that tears were running down my face, quite freely. My nose had started to run as well. I sniffed and snorted and wiped at the tears. I was still doing that when Baron Kardeen entered.

"It's as bad as that?" he asked.

I nodded, then gave him the short version. He took a moment to run it through his mind—the closest thing to a computer I had found in the buffer zone.

"Some little hope, perhaps. Not much," he said. "What will you do?"

"Whatever I can. As long as there's any hope at all, I have to go for it."

There was a silence then. Kardeen seemed almost embarrassed, and I didn't think it was because of the way he had seen me. He had been around the royal family too long for that.

"What is it?" I asked as gently as I could.

He didn't flinch. "Two things, actually. The first I hesitate to mention just now."

"Go ahead. It can't be worse than what I've already heard."

"The, ah, Russian sailors. It will be impossible to get them home just now."

I nodded. The Russians. Of course, I assumed that the Soviet Union was behind the nuclear war that had apparently engulfed my home world. I didn't think that there was any other nation capable of mounting an attack that could wipe out cities in the middle of the United States. And I also assumed that the Russians must have started the fray, though I admit that it was a knee-jerk reaction and not any exercise of logic that led me to *that* assumption.

"I think I had better steer clear of the Russians for a bit," I said, uncertain how I might react if I had to face Commander Sekretov just then. "And it might be better if no one mentioned the fact—the supposition—of a war back in the other world. At least for the moment. What else is there?"

"Ah, the queen is quite distraught," Kardeen said. "About her parents and her brother's family."

"Yes, they must have been caught by the war in my world." The other world, the one I was born and grew up in, was still the one I thought of as mine, not Varay and the buffer zone. "If they went right away, in the first minutes, they may have been among the lucky ones." If Chicago and Louisville had gone, St. Louis would hardly have escaped attention. McDonnell Douglas, the confluence of the Missouri and Mississippi Rivers with important bridges, locks and dams.

"The queen . . ." Kardeen started again.

"Where is she?"

"In your old room here."

"I'll go to her now. When Aaron and Lesh return, we'll have to talk with Parthet. You'll let me know?"

"Of course, sire."

I stood up. I had to go comfort Joy. And I wasn't sure that I had any comfort to give.

The room that had been mine as Hero of Varay was on a sort of mezzanine, a corridor about halfway up the side of the great hall, reached through stairways at either end. I wasn't precisely sure of its position in relation to the king's apartments above, but I thought that the Hero's room had to be almost directly below the king's private study. But, as far as I knew, there was no shortcut. I had to go downstairs, around the great hall, and up a shorter flight of stairs on the other side.

Jaffa and Rodi were standing outside the door.

"She's very upset," Jaffa said. His eyes were stretched wide. Rodi didn't look nearly so fearful. "She sent us out."

"It's okay," I said. As if anything was okay. I told Timon to stay out with the pages, then I took a deep breath before I went inside.

Joy was lying across the bed sobbing. She didn't hear me come in. I crossed to the bed and sat next to her.

"Are they all dead?" she asked.

"I don't know," I said, putting my hand on her back. I started to rub between her shoulder blades. That normally relaxed her, but not this time.

"I don't know either, and that's what's tearing me up," Joy said. She rolled over and looked up at me. Her eyes were red-streaked. Her face was wet from all the crying. "Are they dead, dying, or somewhere safe? They *might* be safe. I gave them all your warnings about being ready to leave the city. After my parents came here and saw this place, they might have believed. Maybe there was enough warning to evacuate."

"I don't see any way we can find out, dear," I said. "Not yet. Maybe not for a long time."

"We could go there, drive to St. Louis from Louisville."

"No, we can't. If the basement is so messed up, the cars probably didn't survive in the garage, and"—I made a helpless gesture with both hands—"even if the cars did survive, we wouldn't be able to get gas anywhere, and there's not much chance that any of the bridges survived across the Ohio or Mississippi. Not to mention the radioactivity. Louisville's hot. We might not be able to get clear of it fast enough to avoid a fatal dose."

"There has to be a way."

The echo of what I had told the elflord knotted my gut.

"I'll ask Aaron if he can conjure up a spell to get news about your parents and your brother Danny's family," I said. "I don't know if he can. Contacting the elflord was different. Xayber has his own powerful magic."

"I have to know, Gil. I'll go crazy if I don't."

I picked Joy up and held her against me. She seemed very fragile just then, close to the breaking point. I could see the hysteria lurking behind her eyes, looking for a chance to break loose. That meant that I couldn't even begin to tell her what the elflord had said was waiting for everybody—or what I would have to do in order to save anything at all.

"Aaron can make a spell to protect us from the radiation," Joy said. "We can ride horses if we have to. I've been taking lessons, remember? And if the bridges are out, horses can swim."

"Aaron's spell against radiation barely lasted the few seconds I had that doorway open, remember?"

"I have to find out, Gil, one way or another."

And she had a set of the rings.

"I'll talk to Aaron. Don't you go doing anything foolish. Even if there is a way to go back and get to St. Louis, *you* can't go. You're pregnant, remember. You can't take *any* risk of radiation, spell or not. You can't risk the baby." It hurt talking about the baby, but you have to go on as if there was a certain future. It's either that or curl up in a corner and suck your thumb until the end comes.

"Promise you won't do anything foolish like trying to go through one of the doors to Louisville?" I said.

"I have to know, Gil."

"Not that way, Joy. Not that way."

She turned away from me for a moment, and I wondered if I was going to have to tie *her* up to keep her from doing something stupid.

"You'll find out for me?" she asked.

"If there's any way possible," I promised.

"If you don't, I will try myself," Joy said. "I have to *know.*"

Baron Kardeen knocked and came in when I called. Aaron and Lesh were back. Annick was "safely" in the hands of Sir Compil at Castle Curry. The others were in Parthet's workroom. Aaron was briefing Parthet on what the elflord had said.

"Come on, Joy," I said. When I stood up, I was still holding her. I let her down and put my arm around her.

"We've got a lot of business to deal with, and not just seeing how we can find out about your family, I'm afraid."

I hesitated. She had to know how desperate the situation was, but I was still afraid that she wouldn't be able to handle it—and not just what I was going to have to try to do to rescue some part of our universe.

"There's worse trouble than World War Three back home," I said. "There's only the slimmest chance that I'll be able to do anything to help, but nobody else has even *that* much chance."

She didn't respond. As much trouble as I was having relating to the greater crisis, I couldn't expect her to get beyond her worry over her family, not without a little time . . . and maybe some news.

Parthet seemed almost cheerful.

"What are you so tickled about?" I asked. I'm sure it didn't sound very good-natured.

"The news was much better than I expected," Parthet said. "Much, much better."

"You think the End of Everything is better?" I asked.

"No, no, the beginning, the *beginning*. Haven't I told you?"

"Told me what?"

"We all recreate our past, and some people do it more effectively than others." He jabbed a finger in the direction of my groin. He wasn't close enough for me to need to flinch, though. "If you can find the Great Earth Mother and, ah, get close enough, you have the balls to do the job right."

"What's he talking about?" Joy asked.

Thanks a lot, Uncle, I thought. I took a deep breath. "It means that I have a chance to save something of this universe by doing what Vara did back at the beginning of time."

"Does that mean what I think it means?" Joy asked.

"It means that I have to try to track down a mythological being who may or may not be the goddess who gave birth to our universe, and I have to use the family jewels we swiped from her shrines to get her to do it all over again. It's the only hope any of us has to survive, to keep anything alive anywhere.'' I had to stop to suck in air. ''There *are* a few obstacles. First off, nobody has any idea where to find the Great Earth Mother, if she really does exist.''

''She does exist. Count on it,'' Parthet said, interrupting.

''Next, she's already sworn to kill me, or her ghost did, just for taking the jewels. Those are a couple of rather hefty obstacles.''

''When?'' Joy asked, not at all what I thought her next word would be.

''I don't know. The elflord said that it would be days, more likely weeks, before he could trace the Great Earth Mother, and I can't do anything until I know where to find her—or even if she can be found.''

''And remember,'' Parthet said, ''that it will almost certainly take more of our time than it does his. A week in Fairy can be ten days or more here.''

''Then you have time for the other first,'' Joy said.

One track.

''Aaron, do you think that either you or Parthet could come up with a spell that would protect a horse and rider from radioactivity long enough to ride from Louisville to St. Louis and back? Joy is desperate to find out what happened to her family.''

''Very desperate,'' Joy said, intensely enough that everyone stared at her.

''I can put together a spell for that,'' Aaron decided after a moment, ''but not by remote control. I'll have to go along to keep it up. I would have to go anyway, if you intend to go,'' he said, meeting my eyes. ''When the elflord calls, I can bring us back here from wherever we are in the other world.''

''Will you be able to stay there long enough to do any good?'' I asked. ''Won't you just pop back here like you did before?''

''I think not. I've found my place here. And I am a wizard now, not a lost little kid like I was then.''

"I'll get the horses and gear, sire," Lesh said. "That'll be three of us riding?"

"Four," Timon said from near the door. "I'm not a page to be left behind when things get dangerous anymore."

I looked at him and nodded. "Four it is," I said.

7

The Four Horsemen

Running off to the other world just then certainly wasn't the most logical decision I could have made. I had a bigger load on my shoulders than going off on another crazy quest, this one to find out what had happened to my in-laws. And this looked at least as wild as the other quests I had gone on. Even if I could get from Louisville to St. Louis, it might prove almost impossible to find out anything about Joy's family. But it did serve a purpose. Just sitting around Basil, waiting for the elflord to call—possibly for weeks, while the sky picked up extra moons and brought us closer to doomsday—would really have driven me crazy, or crazier than I already was. Worrying that Joy might slip off and try to find her way from Kentucky to Missouri alone would have been even harder to bear.

It was just something that I had to do. I did question Aaron at length to make sure that the elflord would be able to contact us even in the other world and that Aaron would be able to pop us straight back to Basil when that call came.

Aaron was positive. Parthet didn't demur.

With Lesh and Kardeen hard at work making the preparations, there was really nothing I had to do but talk with Joy. I got her to tell me about the neighborhoods where her parents and her brother lived. I had been to her parents' place, but never to Danny's. I asked about places they might have headed for if they had left the city. There were two places that Joy thought were possible, a state park southwest of the metropolitan area and another spot out along the Missouri River.

Once Joy was sure that I was going to do something to find her family, she was calm. We sat in the private dining room, ate, and waited. Grabbing a couple of hours of sleep might have been smarter, especially for me, but there are times when you have to forgo things like that.

Parthet came wandering in about dawn.

"There really is a chance to save quite a lot," he said, more subdued than he had been before. "While you're gone, I'll try to get some of my memories written down. It's important that I do that as soon as possible."

"When we get through this, you can tell me all the stories over Old Baldy's beer. That'll be even better."

He shrugged. "Who can tell what time there will be, especially at times like this."

"You been skipping meals?" I asked, puzzled at his sudden melancholy.

He smiled and shook his head. "I've not come to that yet. It's just that you brought back so much that I had forgotten for so long." He stopped and shook his head more vigorously. "I'll tell you when you return and we know where to find the Great Earth Mother."

"We'll have to pop back to Cayenne for a moment before I head out," I said, more for Joy's benefit than Parthet's. "Going back to the real world, my guns will work at least." There would likely be call for all the weapons I could carry. "And I've got to tell Harkane that he's in charge awhile longer."

"He's going to want to go with you," Joy said.

"This time, he has other duties, like running Cayenne and keeping an eye out for you. Or do you want to move into the royal apartment here before I get back?"

"I'll stay at Cayenne. I was just starting to get used to living there."

And even before that, I had to give Baron Kardeen a few more instructions about our Russian visitors. That was difficult, but I went out of my way to keep emotion out of it. "Have someone explain that there is a glitch in our communications with the real world. They are our guests in the meantime, and that's the way I want it played. Watched but not too closely. Nothing hostile." I just hoped that *I* would be able to play it that way after I came back from seeing the destruction.

Sunrise arrived. It would be midmorning back in Kentucky. The detour to Cayenne took only ten minutes. We got everything set to go.

There were some minor inconveniences we knew we would have to work around right at the start. We were taking horses. Horses don't take to stairs easily, but none of the doorways leading from Castle Basil to the basement in Louisville were at ground level. And getting the horses up the stairs from the basement in Louisville was going to be another problem. At least there were stone stairs leading up to the outside basement door. I wasn't sure that there would be enough clearance for our chargers to get through easily, but options were rather scarce.

Four riders, two spare horses loaded with provisions. We wouldn't have to eat as heavily in the other world as we would in the buffer zone or Fairy, but we couldn't count on finding much along the way. Game would have been sparse even without World War Three through most of the area we had to cross.

Joy and I said our goodbyes in private, but she came to the doorway to watch us leave—after Aaron assured me that he would be able to keep any radiation from leaking through the doorway while we left. Parthet was there to add a spell or two of his own if necessary.

"We'll stay with this as long as we can," I said—a sort of general announcement. "When the elflord calls, we'll pop straight back here." I looked at Joy. "We may be running against a tight deadline"—a real *dead*line— "by then, so that will have to take priority." I shrugged, gave Joy another kiss, and told Aaron to start spreading his shields.

There was another green shimmering over the door, a deeper green than before. The four of us who were going through, and our six horses, were covered with a similar twinkling, something closer to aqua, that settled on us and in us. We had to be protected inside and out, covered from everything, including the food, water, and air we would consume. The shield seemed to tighten my skin, like a strong astringent. I had a moment of doubt. If the shields didn't work, we might be in deep trouble very fast.

"We're ready," Aaron said.

When I opened the doorway to Louisville, I couldn't help thinking that this ridiculous quest was a properly adolescent way for a certified *Hero* to go out in a blaze of glory. And the song started to echo in my mind.

I stood with my hand, my ring, on the sea-silver while Aaron, Lesh, and Timon went through with all of the horses. I stepped through to the basement in Louisville after them, then looked back through the green-turning-orange shield over the doorway . . . for what I hoped wouldn't be my last sight of Joy and Varay. And then I turned loose.

The basement was in pretty bad shape. The others had led the horses straight out into the main cellar room. Dad's private little retreat wasn't large enough to hold more than two horses at a time. Their stalls back in the Castle Basil mews were each as big as the "secret" room.

There were no real windows in the basement. When Dad built the place, it wasn't that many years past the time when the federal government was actively encouraging people to build home fallout shelters. There were no windows, but there were a couple of light wells walled off with glass blocks, several feet underground, that let in just enough illumination to keep the cellar from being pitch-black.

There was more light in it now. The kitchen door was gone, off its hinges, broken in pieces and blown down into the cellar. The door leading straight to the backyard was metal, though, and it was still intact.

"We'd better go up and have a look around before we start maneuvering the horses upstairs," I said.

Lesh and I couldn't raise the outside door together—one of those angled bulkhead doors—so we went up through the kitchen to see what the problem was.

The house was still standing, though a lot of the interior was scorched. Everything that wasn't bolted down had been hurled toward the northeast corners. All of the windows and doors were gone, either splintered or completely lost. But from the odds and ends that were still sitting around, I guessed that no looters had been through.

Looters would have been an encouraging sign, evidence that there were still *some* people around.

"I'm going up to the second floor for a minute," I told Lesh. I felt silly when I realized that I was whispering. "I want to see how much more damage there is. And that'll give me a better vantage to see what the rest of the neighborhood looks like." Lesh nodded and followed me to the stairs.

The steps were shaky, as if there wasn't much holding them up but habit. I went from room to room upstairs. Big sections of interior walls had been destroyed. There wasn't a trace of sea-silver left around any doorway. There wasn't much of anything recognizable up on the second floor. The place had been gutted.

"I don't think we should be here," Lesh said.

My danger sense agreed. Aaron's radiation cocoon had kept that from going berserk when I opened the passage and stepped through, but it recognized that a spell against radiation wouldn't keep us from falling through a floor. Lesh and I went back down to the first floor and then outside.

All of the greenery, the carefully cultivated pseudo-wilderness that Dad had arranged around the house, was gone. The whole neighborhood was a wasteland, charred and empty except for ruined foundations and our house. None of the other houses in the development were standing. Of course, the others had all been simple frame houses. Ours had been the only one built like a fortress, with thick blocks of limestone instead of wood or aluminum siding.

"I'd never have believed this," Lesh said. He walked away from the house, turning slowly, looking around once, and then again. He knew the neighborhood from previous visits, most recently from the time he waited for me to get out of the hospital after Wellivazey's attempt to kill me.

"And this has to be some distance from the nearest explosion," I said. We were more than thirty miles from Fort Knox, closer to forty miles. The Naval Ordnance plant and Ford were closer, over by the airport, but still some seventeen or eighteen miles in a straight line. "We'll see worse before we see better."

Some of the ruins in the neighborhood were still smoking. I wondered how long it had been since the rockets hit. All I could do was guess, but I doubted that it had been more than a day or two, maybe not very long before I discovered that the doorways to Chicago didn't work.

If Joy and I had been a little quicker to take off, we might have been in the middle of it, I thought, which caused blood to drain from my head.

"Let's get around back and see what's blocking the cellar door," I said.

Part of the chimney, tumbled, crumbled, was piled over the bulkhead door. The stones were shattered, so it was just a matter of lifting and shoving about a ton of rubble to the side, about twenty minutes' work after Aaron and Timon came around to help.

The garage wasn't as badly damaged as the house. Some of the rafters had fallen, but the roof had held and even the aluminum doors were intact, though dented. Of course, if the explosions had all been to the west and southwest, the house would have sheltered the garage from the worst of the force. The Citroën and the van were both inside, but damaged. The rear end of the van had been slammed sideways into the Citroën. I didn't think that either of them was drivable. But the engines worked on both cars. I turned on the van's radio and searched through the bands for some kind of working signal.

It's a good thing I was patient. I needed twenty minutes to catch anything, and then it was just a brief announcement giving the time and a frequency to turn to for news on the hour—fifteen minutes off.

"Timon, you'd better keep watch over the horses. We're going to wait for the news," I said. The horses

were up out of the cellar and tied along the north side of
the house, in what little shade there was early in the afternoon. I sat half out of the van with the door open. I
couldn't have sat all the way inside without taking off my
elf swords. Lesh and Aaron stood close. There was a lot
of static on the radio. I switched over to the frequency
mentioned in the announcement, then turned off the radio to save the car's battery. But I didn't have a working
watch with me, so I turned the radio back on almost
immediately. I was afraid to miss even a single word of
the broadcast when it came.

"*It is now two p.m. central daylight time,*" an anon-
ymous voice said. "*Here is the news we have. Yesterday,
the United States and the Soviet Union exchanged a considerable number of nuclear warheads.*

"*There are no numbers yet, but damage in this country
is extensive and there is no way to even begin to estimate
casualties. There is no contact of any sort from any of
the nation's thirty largest metropolitan areas.*

"*All members of the Reserves and National Guard are
immediately activated and directed to take charge of local rescue efforts and emergency requirements. It may be
days before any real help can be organized.*

"*There are major rural areas of the country that have
not been touched by the bombs and missiles. Power and
other utility services appear to be spotty everywhere,
though.*

"*To the best of our knowledge here, the fighting has
stopped, but international news is almost impossible to
come by. We will be on the air every two hours, dawn to
dusk. I'm sorry, we don't have much solid information
yet. There is no telephone service, little power, and only
scanty radio contact with other parts of the country. We
can't even guess how long it will be before we have any
of those services.*

"*We will return to the air at four o'clock.*"

"That's it?" Lesh asked when the voice stopped and
the static took over the frequency again.

"That's it," I said. "The war was just yesterday."

"St. Louis is one of the thirty biggest cities, isn't it?" Aaron asked.

"Easily. Well, no use sitting around. We'd better start riding. We've got a long way to go."

"They said some of the rural areas are okay," Aaron said.

"Those may be the areas we have to be most careful of."

I didn't have a map, but I had a decent idea of the route we had to take. I figured that the natural hazards that would pose the most trouble were the rivers. No matter how we went, to get from Louisville to St. Louis we would have to cross at least two major rivers, and I wanted to hold it to just two. That meant that we had to head southwest along the Ohio River, and find a place to cross it between the Wabash coming down along the Illinois-Indiana line from the north, and the Cumberland River coming up from the south. Then we had to head across southern Illinois to find a place to cross the Mississippi.

We would look for intact bridges, but I wasn't ready to hold my breath. Even bridges that hadn't been too close to a mushroom would have to stand up against debris and raging water being hurled downstream from other areas. Many of the backcountry bridges, and even some of the main-road ones, had all they could do to support their own weight in the best of times.

We started riding.

Aaron surprised me. Although he looked awkward in the saddle, he didn't have any trouble staying aboard.

"I managed a few lessons in Varay," he told me.

Obviously, he had absorbed enough.

"You'll have time to get a lot better before this trek is over," I told him.

Aaron nodded. Then he said, "You agreed to try this even though you think it's impossible."

"It makes looking for a needle in a haystack as easy as finding the ground when somebody kicks your legs out from under you," I said. "Even if any of them are alive, there's almost no hope of finding them."

"If that's the way you feel, why did you agree? Just to keep your wife from trying?"

"Mostly. But even if I had been willing to take away her rings and keep her under guard to make sure she couldn't try to find her family for herself, I think I would have welcomed the excuse. Sitting around Basil for who knows how many weeks waiting for the elflord to find something, playing king and trying to act as if there was any point to it, that would have driven me completely out of my skull. I operate close enough to the edge without that."

"If it helps ease your mind, the search may not be as hopeless as you think," Aaron said. I turned to look at him. "*If* her parents and her brother are alive, I may be able to home in on them. The brother's wife and kids, that's something else, but if we get within—I'm not sure— maybe a hundred miles of the others, I think I'll be able to guide us the rest of the way."

"You *think?*"

"It's a stretch for me, as they say, but yes, I *think* I'll be able to. I'm not positive." He shrugged. "A hundred miles may be a bit far. The distance is all guesswork. But, whatever, the signal should grow stronger as we get closer to them."

I thought about my first ride to Castle Thyme, back when I was trying to rescue *my* parents, before I knew that Dad was already dead. Parthet had homed in on Mother finally, but at that point we were only about five miles from her. Of course, Parthet had said that he was vaguely aware of her for quite a while before that. Maybe it *was* possible.

"If they're alive," I said. "That's still a long shot."

When we left the house, we rode due south. I wanted to avoid as much of the Louisville metropolitan area as possible. Grass would be easier on the horses than pavement, and I wasn't sure how close to a ground zero I wanted to get, even with Aaron's magic shields. Going south, all the way around Fort Knox, would add miles to an already long trip, but we might have a month to spend if we needed it. Or not.

There was destruction all around. For the first hour or so, I was strangely drawn by the havoc the war had unleashed. The ruins, the broken and smoldering trees, all might have been from the mind of an artist with a particularly vivid—and gruesome—vision of the Apocalypse. There were hills that looked as though they were modeling clay that someone had smashed a fist into. We saw bodies stripped of flesh, little more than bones with just a few shreds of muscle and meat attached.

But after that first hour or so, my mind went numb. I simply couldn't absorb any more. Blank. There were the four of us and our six horses, the only living creatures around—no people, no dogs or cats, not even any birds. The vultures hadn't even gathered to pick the bones yet. Maybe there were no vultures left to perform the office.

It must have been six o'clock before we saw anyone at all. By that time, we were well south of the city, about due east from the northern portion of Fort Knox, almost to Highgrove on US 31W. Three men were standing in front of a little country grocery and gas station. If the building hadn't been badly burned and ready to fall, I would have thought that they were looters, but they couldn't have gotten much from that wreckage. They were armed. I wasn't looking for trouble, so we gave them a wide berth. Since we were mounted and they were on foot, that was no trouble.

"We might be safer staying close to the hot spots," Aaron said. "Less chance of having to fight off people."

I nudged my horse, Electrum, a little to the right, southwest instead of south, and the others followed my lead.

"You ever get down this way with your folks, Aaron?" I asked.

"Naw. We used to go to Florida or California every year for vacation. I think I had a whole closetful of Mickey Mouse stuff at home. Don't think I ever touched most of it once we got back from whichever Disney place we'd been to last. But my dad couldn't get enough of it. He used to say that Mickey was a soul brother."

It didn't get much of a laugh.

We rode until sunset and used the shortened twilight to make camp and eat supper. The sun was a muddy red as it got close to the horizon, and the red seemed to bleed all the way across the western sky.

At a guess, we might have been eight miles from the Federal Gold Depository, fairly close to the edge of the Fort Knox reservation, but there was no way I could be positive of our exact location. We had crossed Interstate 65 well north of where I killed the dragon, and had angled more to the west. I was navigating by dead reckoning, but if I had our location approximately correct, all we had to do then was ride due west until we ran into the Ohio River, somewhere near Shawneetown, Illinois, a few miles downstream from the Wabash. The only population center we would approach in that stretch was Owensboro, with maybe sixty thousand people . . . before the war.

Aaron put an extra shield around us when we camped, not against radiation, but to make us harder to see if anyone came near, something like the veil Parthet had put over us in eastern Varay to hide us from a dragon. We kindled a fire and prepared supper without magic, though. I still had a large supply of packaged almost-instant camping meals. We would use those as long as possible. Despite the flair Aaron showed for every magic he attempted, I wasn't eager to find out what a meal conjured up out of nothing but magic might taste like.

We had to treat this as an excursion into enemy territory, just as was my trek north along the Isthmus of Xayber years before. Maybe the dangers weren't the same, but they could be just as great. People running from the horror of nuclear war couldn't be expected to observe all the niceties of civilization. To put it mildly. And a lot of civilization hadn't been very civil even before. Hungry people might covet our horses, or whatever supplies they might be able to take off our dead bodies.

"How much of this will we have?" Lesh asked before I turned in for the night. He was as shaken by the devastation as I was, and he had fewer ties to this world.

"I don't know. Maybe today was the worst we'll see, at least until we get close to St. Louis. It's probably just as bad there. In between, who knows? Remember, the radio said that some rural places were okay." Relatively okay maybe, but I doubted that anyplace was anything near normal.

"How long do you figure this ride will take?" Aaron asked.

"It must be nearly three hundred miles to St. Louis," I said. "Something like that, anyway. All things considered, we may be lucky to manage twenty-five miles a day." I thought that was a properly pessimistic estimate. There was no telling what we would face—in addition to a couple of major rivers.

I woke a little before dawn, not with my danger sense clanging, but just because I was sleeping lightly. I had spent a disturbed night, part of it apparently in conversation with the recurring dream of the Congregation of Heroes. I still hoped that it was *just* a dream.

I sat up and stretched, feeling troubled, less rested than I should have been. Dreaming about my father, Vara, and all of the other dead men who had been Hero of Varay in turn always did that to me. Timon was on guard. He spotted the movement as I sat up and came toward me. The sky was thickly clouded, but there was still a faint trace of illumination in the night, mostly a touch of red reflected from the base of the cloud cover. I wasn't sure if the red was a reflection of distant fires or a more direct remnant of the nuclear exchange.

"An eerie night, sire," Timon whispered. He had waited a moment to speak, probably wondering if I had awakened because I sensed imminent danger. When I didn't leap to arms or call the others, he assumed that I hadn't.

"Eerie," I agreed. "Have you heard any noises?" We had camped fifty yards off a road, back in an area where there were rock outcroppings to hide us from prying eyes—in case Aaron's magical blanket wasn't enough. There was a little grass in the lee of the rocks, grass that hadn't burned when the nuclear explosions seared everything in their path.

"Naught but the wind," Timon said. "Not even a cricket."

A long night, I thought. Too long. I stared at the clouds. They must be awful thick, I decided. To the east, there was still no recognizable hint of dawn. I didn't think nuclear winter was supposed to start with a total blockage of sunlight, just with enough debris held in the air to keep out a significant portion of the light in the frequencies that plants need to grow.

"The days may be dim for a while, Timon," I whispered. "As if the Titan Mountains had been pulverized into the finest dust and scattered to the winds." Sunset the night before had been short but fiery. I expected sunrise to be about the same.

If it came.

Lesh yawned and stretched as if he were waking in his own bed. Then he sat up quickly as he remembered where he was. Aaron propped himself up on an elbow as if he had been awake for some time.

"A fire?" Lesh asked softly.

"We might as well," I said. "I think we're still too close to ground zero for anyone to be prowling around." I wondered how many warheads had been targeted against the area. It had to be at least two, maybe three. There was an Army quartermaster depot across the Ohio River in New Albany, as well as all the targets on the Kentucky side. No single bomb could be certain to take out both Fort Knox and the depot, forty-odd miles away.

Lesh had stockpiled enough bits of usable wood the night before, stuff that was charred but hadn't completely burned. There were tons of it around. Aaron lit the fire and Lesh and Timon went about preparing breakfast.

"I had nightmares," Lesh said when he had a chance to talk to me a little apart from the others. "I've never had nightmares in all my life."

"You've never had such good reason," I told him. "Nuclear war—that's more concentrated evil than all the elflords in Fairy rolled into one. If an H-bomb went off over our heads now, maybe even five or six miles straight up, not all the magic in creation could save us." Lesh looked up at the sky. There was finally a little light coming from the east.

"Evil dreams," Lesh muttered, and then he went off to check the horses.

"Evil dreams," I echoed softly. And waking up didn't get rid of them.

8

Legions

Rain came not long after dawn, a dirty rain that had to
be loaded with radioactive dust—the dust of civilization
and hundreds of thousands, even millions, of dead people. It poured for two hours or more while we rode west,
but there were no fresh smells of nature following this
rain. The odors were all of death and rot. Over and over,
I found myself worrying that Aaron's magic might not
be enough to protect us from the radiation. He had re-
newed the spells before we broke camp.

"I don't think it's really necessary yet, but there's no
use taking chances we don't have to," he said.

I agreed wholeheartedly with that.

We started to come across badly burned bodies, some
with mutilating injuries. These weren't stripped bones.
These were the bodies of people who had lived long
enough to start fleeing west, away from Fort Knox. And
we started to see abandoned cars along the road. The two
I bothered to check were both out of gas. The riders had
driven as far as they could, then continued on foot.

"We'll start coming on live folks soon," Lesh pre-
dicted, and he was right. Within an hour we saw people
walking along the road. Even in disaster, they thought
that there was some advantage to staying on the roads,
as if help would come driving up.

Maybe it would, for some of them. Kentucky has a lot
of wild country. There might be hollows that had escaped
the direct effects of the bombs, even fairly close, places
where people might attempt to rescue outsiders . . . until
they started to worry more about their own supplies and

long-term survival. I thought that hospitality would run out quickly, even among most of the church groups.

"Let's move a little farther away from the road," I said. "Some of those people may have guns and the will to use them. Our horses may look like steak on the hoof."

We turned off into a valley that headed a little north of west and took us out of sight of the road. There was a trail along the bottom of the valley, but from the ruts that the rain hadn't completely washed away, it looked like only jeeps had used it in ages.

I tried to blank out any feeling, without notable success. How could anyone view such destruction without feeling it rip at their guts? I could call it a waking nightmare and write it off like that if I could, but the reality was so much worse than any nightmare, so insistent, so *total,* that I wanted to scream. I wanted to close my eyes and curl up in a ball and just wait for it all to go away. I wanted to run, as far and as fast as I could, anything to get away from it.

But there was no escape.

We reached an area where the trees were still standing. Autumn had come to western Kentucky even before the war, so only the evergreens still showed green. The leaves of the deciduous trees had already turned color. Most had fallen and matted the ground. I saw a few squirrels, but there were still no birds in evidence.

"It's all so dead," Timon mumbled. He was riding close behind me, leading the packhorses.

"Deader than anything you ever imagined," I said.

"There's water not far ahead," Aaron said. He was leading the way at the moment. He pointed off to his left. "I just caught a glimpse of a creek or something."

"Let's check it out. The horses could use a rest and a little time to graze," I said. "We can use a break too." We had been riding for most of the morning by then, with only a couple of very short stops.

The business of stopping, dismounting, and loosening the cinches on our horses used up a couple of minutes. Lesh and Timon linked the animals on a picket line, and

Timon was there to keep them away from the creek until they cooled off.

The creek wasn't much, just a couple of feet wide and not even that deep, but it was running water, and almost clear. I stood on the bank and stretched. My chain mail, the swords hanging across my back, even the old jeans I was wearing seemed to chafe and drag at me. Aaron came up beside me. He was wearing a shirt and trousers made in Varay out of something like sailcloth. The only weapon he wore was a small dagger on his belt. He had no wand, no pouches of paraphernalia. All Aaron needed for his wizardry was his head—eyes, mouth, and mind—and whatever special magic that initiation into the craft conferred. He didn't need props.

I turned to Aaron and had started to say something when I heard a noise, off along the creek. It sounded like a baby crying, then being silenced quickly. I listened closely and then I heard a very soft shushing sound and knew I was right.

"Is somebody there?" I called. "It's all right. We won't hurt you." And I hoped they wouldn't panic and hurt us. My danger sense got a little more active, but it didn't sound a full-blown warning.

"Do you need help?" I asked, taking a couple of steps in the direction the sounds had come from.

Aaron stepped across the stream and moved parallel to me, just a step or two at a time. With everything wet from the morning rain, we didn't make any noise. No twigs snapped or anything like that. I tried to use my danger sense to home in on the noises, but the threat wasn't great enough for me to read it that precisely.

Aaron had less trouble. He pointed, farther downstream, at my side of the creek. There was a thick area of vines that had grown around the remains of a tree that had fallen long ago and started to rot.

"It's all right," I said, not quite as loud as before. "We're not going to hurt anyone or take anything from you. If you're hungry, we have food to share."

I heard a soft whimper that was almost immediately cut off, then the rustle of vines. Aaron spotted them just a second before I did, deep in the tangled thicket. A family. The man stood up first. The woman was holding a baby, not newborn, but not more than a few months old. And there was a boy who couldn't be old enough for school. They were all wet, bedraggled, and quite obviously scared.

"I know we look strange, but really, we won't hurt you," I said.

Off to the side, perhaps even closer to the family than either Aaron or me, I heard Lesh's voice. "Sire?"

The man and woman looked off that way. Sire, I thought. That's just what we needed. As if seeing the long swords on my back wasn't enough to convince frightened people that they had fallen into the clutches of lunatics.

The man and woman looked at each other then. He shrugged.

"We have nothing left to lose but our lives," the man said. "Hard enough holding on to them now."

"Do you have a clear path out of there?" Aaron asked. His voice sounded strangely gentle, reassuring, even to me. I decided that he was weaving some sort of spell with his words.

"We crawled in, as far as we could," the man said. "Last night, hiding."

"That's why you're all scratched up then," Aaron said. "Here, I can make it easier for you to get out." He hummed, then chanted and started to sway, using a magic I had once seen Uncle Parthet use. Maybe it was the one piece of magic that had really convinced me that the buffer zone ran by different rules from this world's. The vines started to untangle themselves, opening a way along the creek from the family toward us.

"Hurry through," Aaron said when the path was complete. "It takes some effort to hold this for any time."

Maybe substituting something supernatural for them to worry about was a step in the right direction. I'm not sure. But they came through, looking more frightened the closer they got.

"My name's Gil Tyner," I said when they were free of

the brambles. "My friend here is Aaron Carpenter. He's, ah, something of a wizard. There are two others waiting with our horses, Lesh and Timon. You'll meet them in a minute. And no matter how different, how strange, we look, you won't come to any harm at our hands."

"We're the good guys," Aaron said, still in that abnormally reassuring voice.

"I'm Charley Ingels," the man said. "My wife Mary. Little Charley and Marie." The children. "We were on our way to visit Mary's brother at Fort Knox when it happened."

"There's nothing left of Fort Knox," I said, trying to look sympathetic.

"We know," Charley said. "We went on as long as we could, then we had to turn back. We ran out of gas. I didn't want to stay with the car. We had . . . we saw some pretty ugly things happen to people."

"You were trying to get home?" I asked.

Charley nodded. "We live in Missouri, in Rolla. I teach engineering at the university there."

"Rolla? How far's that from St. Louis?"

"About a hundred miles," his wife said. "Southwest, out toward Fort Leonard Wood." Which might be in the same shape as Fort Knox.

"I don't know if you could get that far, even if you still had your car," I said. "Not much chance of finding a bridge over the Mississippi. Hey, I don't know if they've got refugee camps set up yet, but I think that's about the best anyone can hope for right now."

"But where?" Charley asked. "I don't even know where to start." He didn't look like any of the professors I had in college, but then I had never seen any of them in circumstances like these.

"How late yesterday did you hear any news?" I asked.

"Noon. And we ran out of gas not a half hour later."

I shook my head. "The only news I heard was at two, and there wasn't much then, nothing about a relocation center. I guess nobody's that organized yet."

"You must be hungry, and we're just standing around

gabbing,'' Aaron said. ''We have plenty of food.'' He gestured back toward where we had left the horses.

Lesh must have caught the hint when I said that he and Timon were both back with the horses. And more than that, he had a fire going to cook some of our packaged meals and had a kettle of water on too. In a few minutes, we could offer instant coffee.

''We have powdered milk for the children,'' Aaron said. Timon hurried to one of the packs, right on cue. ''It's not the best stuff, maybe.'' Aaron crinkled his nose. ''But maybe this will help it go down.'' He knelt by Little Charley and offered him a Milky Way. Little Charley looked up to his parents for permission before he took it.

''We might as well all sit down and rest,'' I said. ''Lunch will be a few minutes.''

''Just who the hell are you anyway?'' Charley asked. His shock was giving way to something else.

I smiled and shook my head. ''You couldn't possibly believe that story,'' I said.

''I see guns, swords, bows. You're riding horses that make the Budweiser Clydesdales look puny. What the hell is this?''

I gave him the one-word explanation. ''Magic.'' I expected some kind of indignant outburst at that. Charley opened his mouth, but shut it again without saying whatever he had planned to say. He waited a moment to speak.

''You mean that, don't you?''

I laughed. ''Delicate phrasing, Professor.''

''You saw the vines,'' Aaron said, and Charley nodded. ''By the calendar, I'm not quite nine years old yet. Four months ago, I stood about this high.'' He held a hand out just above waist level. ''I was small for my age. My parents were both on the *Coral Lady* when it was blown up. I heard the news and disappeared from my grandmother's home in Joliet, Illinois. Where I turned up was in this fairy-tale kingdom called Varay. I grew up in just a couple of weeks. Gil Tyner here was Hero of Varay. I mean, the man fights dragons and elf warriors. Did you hear about that dragon that was killed here in Kentucky? That was him too.''

"I saw that on TV," Mary said. Her husband nodded.

"And I remember hearing something on the news about a little kid disappearing somewhere, just after the *Coral Lady*," Charley said.

Timon fixed up two mugs of instant coffee and gave them to the Ingelses. "He *was* Hero of Varay," Timon said, jerking a thumb toward me after he got the mugs out of his hands. "Now he's King of Varay too."

"King?" Charley asked.

"King," I agreed. "Aaron is my wizard. Timon is my squire. And Lesh, Sir Lesh, is my right-hand man when it comes to battles and fighting dragons."

Charley looked at his wife. "I think I've gone crazy, dear," he said.

"If you have, then so have I," she said. "I'm hearing things too."

"Did you really kill a dragon?" little Charley asked. He had finished his candy bar, though he looked as if he was wearing as much of it on his face and hands as he had eaten.

"I've had to kill a couple of dragons," I told him.

"You kill any wicked witches?"

"No, no witches. We don't have any witches, just a few wizards, and the ones I know are pretty good guys."

"This is crazy," his father said again.

"I know how you feel, believe me," I assured him. "I was six weeks short of a B.S. in computer science at Northwestern when I stumbled into this other world a few years back."

"My daddy builds bridges," little Charley said.

"There'll be a lot of work for him then when all this gets straightened out," I said. I squatted down by the boy so I didn't tower over him.

His mother started to feed the baby. It was a delicate operation. The baby didn't care for the powdered milk mixture, and mama had to coax and coax.

"Food's ready," Lesh announced. And, at the moment, food was more important than talk, for everyone. While the Ingelses ate, I took Aaron off to the side, past the horses.

"How much radiation you think they got?" I asked softly.

"No idea. Radiation is still a little foreign to me. We didn't cover that in the third grade. But you know, if we leave them here, they're not going to make it. Not with two little kids."

We looked at each other for a moment. "Can you get them through to Varay?" I asked.

Aaron grinned. "Varay needs somebody who knows how to build bridges. That one across the Tarn scares the pants off me every time I cross it."

"Yeah, me too. You got a pen and paper?"

"I'll get it," Aaron said.

"And I'll make the offer. It has to be their choice."

"You think there's any chance at all they'll refuse?"

No, I didn't.

I went back to the others, sat down, and started on my own food, but I didn't give it the attention it deserved at first.

"I know you think that either you're crazy or we are," I told the Ingelses while Aaron was getting the writing supplies. "But I can offer you a refuge from all this. The four of us have to go on toward St. Louis. We're trying to find my wife's family. But we can get you to a place of safety before we go on. And maybe we can do something to counteract whatever radiation you've been exposed to."

"More magic?" Charley asked.

I nodded. "We can get you through to Varay. I'll give you a note to give to Baron Kardeen, the chamberlain. There's a doctor handy, another wizard, and plenty of everything. It's a good place, but a bit primitive."

Charley looked at his wife, spoke to her. "Whether we're crazy or not, we've got to play the cards the way they're dealt." She nodded.

Aaron brought me a small notebook and a pen.

"This is going to take a few minutes, so you might as well finish eating," Aaron said. "Lesh and I have to build a doorway first."

I just nodded, but the Ingelses exchanged another of those

who's-crazy-here? looks. They went right back to their eating, though. Little Charley had already finished. He shook his head when Lesh asked him if he wanted more.

I started my note to Kardeen, telling him how we had come across the Ingels family and asking him to see that they had what they needed until we got back. I heard pounding behind me. When I looked, Aaron was holding a sapling across two other trees, about seven feet off the ground. Lesh was pounding nails, and I have no idea where *they* came from unless Aaron conjured them up, to hold the cut tree in place against the two that were still in the ground.

"Why is he building a doorway?" Mary Ingels asked.

"We have a magic that lets some of us open a passage between a door in one place and a door in a different place. That's how we get between Varay and this world, and we do some of our traveling in Varay the same way. He needs a doorway, a *frame*, for the magic."

I finished the note to Kardeen with a warning that there might be others coming through the same way. I knew I couldn't ship off everyone we might come across, but I wouldn't rule out sending some. Varay always needed people.

I folded the paper and started to hand it to Charley, but Lesh was there at my side with a burning candle, to drip wax on the letter so I could put my seal on it. The signet ring. I wasn't used to that. Every time I saw somebody standing at my side ready to drip wax on paper, it gave me a start.

"Show this to whoever you see first at Castle Basil," I said while I pressed the ring into the wax. "Tell them to take you to Baron Kardeen. The letter will pretty much stop any questions before you get to him, and he'll take care of everything afterward."

"Baron Kardeen," Charley repeated when he accepted the letter.

"That's right," I said.

"Just tell the guard or whoever you meet first that the king gave you the letter," Lesh said. "The whole family has the rings."

Charley nodded.

"One thing Varay needs is someone who knows how to build bridges," I said, smiling. "Nothing very big or fancy maybe, but bridges."

"Might be nice to get back to practical engineering," Charley said, looking at his wife. "The only thing I've built in the last six years is a barbecue."

"We're ready," Aaron said. The Ingelses and I stood.

"I'll probably be a few weeks yet before I get back, but don't worry about anything. It's a good place."

"Thank you," Mary said. "I'd about given up all hope."

"Hope is very precious," I said.

"Right over here." Aaron guided them over to his crude doorway. "I'll open the passage. You'll notice a sort of green shimmering in it. That's a radiation shield. Going through it should also take care of any radiation you've picked up."

He touched both sides of the makeshift doorway, and Castle Basil appeared on the other side—which was almost too much for the adult Ingelses to bear. Charley backed away, almost knocking his wife over in the process. Aaron moved to the side, holding the passage open one-handed.

"It *is* magic," Charley said, looking first at Aaron and then at me.

"Yes, magic," I said. "When you step through, turn left. That'll take you in the direction of the great hall."

Mary clutched her baby tighter against her. She looked at Aaron and me, then at Lesh and Timon. "I never thought I'd see this," she said. "I never really believed it."

"Believed what?" Aaron asked.

"The Four Horsemen of the Apocalypse."

"No!" Aaron said quickly. "We don't bring famine or death. We're not those dudes." I wasn't even positive what the reference was supposed to mean.

9

Between the Rivers

After we sent the Ingels family through to Varay, we needed another three and a half days to reach the Ohio River west of the Wabash and find an intact bridge. The ride was uneventful, just the way we wanted it. We avoided people along the way, particularly large groups of people. They always seemed to set off my danger sense. And when we camped each night, Aaron wove his spells around us to make us less visible to anyone who might chance on our campsite.

In all those days, we didn't hear the sound of a single automobile engine, of any sort of engine. There was no high-speed traffic moving on any of the roads. There were no airplanes in the sky. There was nothing.

Thinking about the way we had sent the Ingelses off to Varay started me grumbling about our lack of foresight. I realized that we could have saved ourselves a lot of bother with packhorses. Aaron could have opened a doorway at mealtimes. We could have kept someone watching for us in Varay, have our food and whatever else we might need ready to hand through.

"We might have trouble finding materials to make a doorway, or finding the time to put one together two or three times a day," Aaron said, trying to stop my grumbling. "And it's not the easiest magic in the worlds. I'd as soon not have to strain at it several times a day."

It was still something I should have thought of in advance, even if we had discarded the idea as impractical.

The bridge we found across the Ohio River was a railroad span that looked as though it had been there for a century or longer. How it managed to survive, I'll never know, but it had. When we approached the bridge, riding along the tracks, my danger sense started to itch. I saw the old bridge and at first assumed that it was the rickety condition of the span that was causing the alarm, the way the bridge over the Tarn at the edge of Basil Town always worried me.

"We'll have to take a good, long look at this bridge before we cross," I said.

We were riding slowly, not pushing our horses at all. It was late afternoon and I didn't see much difference between camping on one side of the river and camping on the other. Staring at the bridge as we got closer, I didn't really notice the directional shift in my awareness of danger as quickly as I should have. The peril was on both sides of the railroad tracks, *not* out on the bridge.

Two men stepped out of the bushes. Both were armed with shotguns.

We pulled our horses to a stop.

"Well, lookee here," one of the men said. "Robin Hood and his merry men." The men showed the effects of several days in the wild. Both wore jeans and ragged flannel shirts. There didn't seem to be anything wrong with their guns, though.

"Almost," I said softly, becoming aware of more points of danger to either side. More armed men, I guessed. A small band of post-holocaust entrepreneurs had set themselves up in business.

I rested both of my hands on the pommel of my saddle, resisting the urge to grab for one of my elf swords and charge forward. I was very careful, anxious not to make any sudden moves before I absolutely had to. We had walked into some sort of trap. In this world, that meant that there were probably more guns in the underbrush, all aimed at us.

Stupid, I told myself. You're so damned used to the Robin Hood crap that you forgot that guns work here and there are people willing to use them against other people.

And while the Hero magic gives me exceptionally quick reflexes, there was no way I could dodge a volley of gunfire coming from several directions at once. Maybe

Aaron could, but Lesh and Timon wouldn't have a chance. I had to find a better way.

"You folks looking to cross over to Illinois?" the same man asked.

"That's where we're heading," I said, nodding in what I hoped was an agreeable manner. Even the pistol under my shirt wouldn't be much good against a gang of these thugs.

"This here bridge is the only one left crost the Ohio. Ain't nothing else 'tween Louisville and Cairo."

I doubted *that*. If this wreck had survived, I expected that others had as well. Besides, the chances of the only bridge left happening to be just where we needed it to be were too small to bet on, even at long odds.

"Then I guess we were lucky to hit this one right off," I said. I felt a tingling on my skin, and just at the threshold of hearing, I could hear Aaron starting a chant. I didn't know what he was preparing, but I hoped I could stall any violence until he was ready to spring his magic.

"This here being the only bridge left, it's *valuable*," the thug doing all the talking said. He seemed to get an extra syllable or two into "valuable." He was standing ahead of me, to the right. "There's a toll for crossing it."

Surprise. "How much?" I asked.

"That depends on just what you got." This time, it was the other man on the tracks who spoke.

"I'll tell you want," I said, still being careful with my voice. "I'll make you an offer you can't refuse." Maybe they never saw *The Godfather*. Or maybe they just weren't smart enough to pick up the implicit threat. "If you two and all your little friends in the bushes put down your guns and let us cross peaceably, we'll let you live to rob other folks who are unlucky enough to stumble on you."

I guess the easy conversational tone puzzled them. They took a moment to react. And then they just laughed. That was as far as they got.

There was a loud clap of thunder immediately behind the two men who were standing on the tracks blocking our path. Twin bolts of fire—I'd really hate to call it lightning—flashed into the brush on both sides of the tracks. The fire flared with impossible speed, erupting for some thirty feet on either side.

With that sort of distraction, the fight was hardly fair. I spurred my horse forward. Electrum was used to noise and light. He responded perfectly. The instant that the two men on the tracks lost looking to see what the explosive noise behind them was lost them their advantage . . . and their heads. I drew Dragon's Death and took one long swipe that finished off both of them.

The men hiding in the bushes were routed by the fires. Not one of them managed to get off a single shot. Three of the five men were on fire, or their clothing was. Lesh, Timon, and I waded into the fray. We let two men who threw down their guns and ran go. The others fell quickly.

Aaron hadn't moved through the engagement. He didn't need to. He had done his part.

"We should have thought of this kind of thing," Aaron said after the fighting ended.

"*I* should have," I said. "If I hadn't lost touch with this world, I would have."

"Did you hear what that sandy-haired one said when he ran off?"

"No," I said.

"He yelled, 'It's the Four Horsemen.' "

"Again?" I asked.

"It looks like it," Aaron agreed.

"Just what are these four horsemen supposed to be?" I asked.

"Agents of death, famine, and pestilence. One of the signs of the End of Everything." *The End of Everything.* Aaron's use of the phrase was like a kick in the face.

"My folks were big on the Bible," he explained. "Used to read it to me every night. Made me start memorizing passages when I was only five. And my grandma was even worse." He made a face. "I always hated that memorizing and reciting but I was afraid to refuse 'cause I might get sent to hell." He looked around. "Looks like we might be getting close to there now."

"Do we cross the river or camp here tonight, sire?" Lesh asked. He's never been one for abstract discussions.

"We'll cross," I said. "With the fires, we may draw more people. Or the two who ran off may find friends and come back. Let's collect the guns they dropped and pitch them in the river."

"There may be others like these at the far end of the bridge," Lesh said.

"It's possible, but we won't be caught napping again if there are," I said. "I'll lead the way. Let's keep some distance between us. This bridge still doesn't look all that sturdy."

I've never been a real big fan of bridges. One of my vague memories of when I was very little concerns bridges. When the family was traveling anywhere by car, I did a lot of sleeping in the backseat. But all we had to do was find a bridge and I woke instantly, especially those bridges with the metal mesh pavement. Our tires wouldn't have time to complete two revolutions before I was awake.

This railroad bridge was worse. We had to dismount and walk across, leading our horses, trying to keep them calm when they could see through the bridge down to the river, fifty or sixty feet below us. There was a sort of deck along the sides of the tracks, but between the rails there was just the regular spacing of ties, and all that openness between.

Although there didn't seem to be any real chance of a train running the line so soon after the nuclear exchange, I kept listening, straining for any hint of a locomotive pulling toward us. We would have been in a sticky situation, unless we happened to be close to one of the two wide spots on the bridge, where the platform stuck out farther, and even there, I wasn't sure that four people and six horses would fit, or that our horses would be able to stay calm with a train rushing past just inches away. And jumping would hardly be a solution.

Several times, one or another of our horses put a hoof through the old wooden planking that ran alongside the tracks. None of the animals seemed to be seriously injured by their missteps, though.

When we got close to the Illinois side of the bridge, I drew my Smith & Wesson 9mm automatic and held it close to my side, where it would be handy but not obvious. There wasn't much cover close to the tracks on the Illinois side. I couldn't see anyone lurking, and my danger sense had nothing to say.

"We'd better ride on for a while before we make camp," I said when the last of the horses was back on solid ground. "We may have just hit the shift change, or suppertime."

"Speaking of supper . . ." Lesh said. I looked his way, and he shrugged. "Just a reminder that we haven't eaten lately," he said.

"We'll ride on for about an hour, southwest," I said. "We'll make camp and eat then. I want to get a little farther from the edge of this forest. We'll ride due west tomorrow. Shawnee National Forest. It pretty much runs all the way across this end of Illinois. We shouldn't be out in the open very much at all."

Most people think of Illinois as just flat, open prairie, even people who live there. While I was living in Chicago I used to hear variations on the same basic joke, that you could putt a golf ball southwest along the Stevenson Expressway, Interstate 55, and it wouldn't stop rolling until it reached Missouri. Sometimes it was a marble or a bowling ball. Same joke. But there are a few long ridges running through the state, some river valleys, and down in the southern end, some real hilly country and a lot of forest. That area looks more like Kentucky or Tennessee than it does the central and northern parts of Illinois.

"If we ride straight across, it should only take two or three days to reach the Mississippi," I told the others. "We can follow the river north until we find a place to cross."

"There might be a lot of people staying close to the Mississippi," Aaron said.

"You're probably right," I said as we mounted and

started to ride again. "I'll give it some thought tonight."
Going on to St. Louis, we were going to run into people
no matter what way we went, maybe a lot of them, and
we had to look for a way to cross the Mississippi, somewhere south of St. Louis. I doubted that there would be
any intact bridges near the metropolitan area, and if we
went north to cross, we'd have to find a way across the
Missouri River as well coming back south.

"How far do you suppose we are from St. Louis right
now?" Aaron asked. "Straight line, not the way we
might have to go."

"I'm not sure. Probably no more than a hundred miles,
maybe less."

"We get settled in for the night, I'll start trying to find
your wife's family."

"Just how do you work that?" I asked. "Parthet always said he had to be able to see things for most of his
magic."

"Most," Aaron agreed. "But I've seen photographs.
Joy showed them to me. Snapshots. And I've got a good
read on her. I think I can make the link to her family.
But I'm still not sure how close I have to be."

Aaron didn't come up with anything that night. The
next morning, we did head due west. I decided that the
immediate advantages of having all that forest around us
were more important than the disadvantages of too many
people later.

Riding through the National Forest, we didn't see any
obvious signs of nuclear war. Of course, the roads we
crossed were empty of traffic, except for a few pedestri-
ans, and there were occasional encampments of refugees,
but most of the time we might almost have had the world
to ourselves. That was a touchy thought.

Dad and I had talked of camping in the Shawnee National Forest a couple of times. We had even sent away
for brochures and maps. But with so many place to go
outdoors, we just never made it to this area. It's not all
wilderness and trees. There are small towns, villages,
scattered through the area, but we stayed away from

them, the way we had been staying away from any concentrations of people.

"It's not really like Precarra," Lesh said, early on our first full day in Illinois.

"No, not nearly as wild," I said. "There are deer, raccoons, skunks, some other small animals." But they probably wouldn't last for long if masses of hungry people started foraging for survival. Hunting laws wouldn't mean a thing now.

There were even birds in the trees.

We were riding through a thin patch of the forest when we heard the helicopter coming. There was only time to pull in close to a couple of trees and halt, hoping that we wouldn't be spotted. A helicopter would most likely be military, and soldiers would ask too many questions if they found a group like us.

"You know that magic Parthet uses to hide people from dragons?" I whispered.

"Already working," Aaron said.

"At least it means that there's some sort of government functioning here," I said after the Army chopper flew over—not nearly high enough for comfort. But there seemed to be no hesitation, no change in its course. Apparently they hadn't spotted us.

"Maybe they're checking air samples," I said after we started riding again. "I saw something like that in some movie about World War Three, and they did a lot of that kind of sampling after the *Coral Lady.*"

After hiding from the helicopter, I started picking our path with more of an eye to cover, but even with that, we almost rode out of the forest about the middle of the afternoon. We stopped, then turned and headed farther south to keep trees around us and, as much as possible, *over* us. Riding alongside an oiled-gravel secondary road, we stumbled on a little village that had been burned. The fire was recent. Although the ashes and remains were cool, the fine soot and ash was still loose, swirling along the ground.

"Nobody dropped a bomb on this place," Aaron said.

"No." I stopped my horse and dismounted. The others followed my lead. We walked along the road, the only real street the village had boasted, leading our horses. There was nothing left but charred remains—a couple of cars, the foundations of several houses, the axles and metal underframes of a couple of mobile homes, odds and ends like the twisted and blackened frame of a child's tricycle.

"Bodies." Lesh pointed off to the side. Back behind the foundation of a house we found two dozen bodies, all huddled together. Some were burned beyond recognition. The stench was overpowering.

"Someone herded them all together and killed them," Lesh said.

"Raiders, thugs like those people at the bridge," I guessed. Lesh grunted.

"I suppose there are a lot of people like that," Aaron said.

"And if the Army or National Guard spots us, they're sure to think that we fit the description," I said. Reasonable pessimism.

"We'll just have to make sure they don't spot us," Aaron said. After a slight hesitation, he added, "Or if they *do* see us, we'll have to make them think we're something they really don't believe."

"You have an idea, I take it?"

"We might as well be those Four Horsemen. Folks want to think we are anyway."

"Disguises?" I asked.

"Just my kind of disguise," Aaron said. "If I can remember—let's see, a white horse, a red horse, a black horse, and a pale horse."

"That still leaves two horses," I reminded him.

"The packhorses. They won't count. You got the sword—one of the riders is mentioned with a sword, maybe more. And we've got to look like something that can't be, real movie-monster stuff. Let's find us a place away from these bodies and I'll take care of it."

"Hang on a second. How many different magics can you hold on to at one time?" I asked.

"I don't know. How many names do you remember?"

"It can't be the same."

"No. Wait, you said you studied computers?" I nodded. "Do you remember any of the programs you wrote?"

"Nothing longer than a half-dozen lines," I said.

"Oh." Aaron shook his head. "I guess that comparison won't work then. It doesn't matter. Most of the magics don't need my constant attention. I start them up and they run, they keep running. Sometimes I have to goose 'em a little later on. Only a few are more demanding. The big ones, mostly."

I still didn't understand, but he was the expert.

We followed the road out of the little village, still on foot, leading our horses. When the road bent a little and took the ruins out of sight, Aaron turned off the road, into the trees. About fifty yards in, we stopped, near a creek.

"The horses should be cool enough to drink their fill right off," Lesh said. "We been walking 'em long enough."

"Okay, you and Timon take care of it. But stick close." I wanted to watch Aaron do his stuff. Magic still fascinated me.

"I've got to see you all to do this," Aaron said.

He sat under a tree and rested his back against it. He stared at me when he started chanting. After a moment, he turned his attention to Lesh and then to Timon. Finally, he stared at each of the horses we were riding, in turn. He chanted the entire time, and the tingling of active magic was so strong that I had to fight the urge to scratch. Before Aaron stopped, he moved over to the creek and knelt next to it. He leaned over so he could see his own face reflected in the water.

When he got up, he cleared his throat and looked my way.

"I think that'll do it," he said.

"Do what?" I asked. "I don't see any disguises."

"We're not trying to hide from us," Aaron said. "We're inside the magic, not looking in."

"Then how can you be sure it's working?"

"It's my *job* to know," Aaron said, with an unusual firmness to his voice.

I nodded. "Let's get a few more hours of riding in," I said. "I don't want to camp anywhere near that village."

We went back to the road and followed it, staying off to the side so the horses wouldn't have to contend with all that oiled gravel. The road went southwest, deeper into the forest, just what I was looking for. I wanted to make sure that we had plenty of cover. But we would have to head west again before long.

"There's a car up ahead," Lesh called out after we had gone about three miles farther.

"I see it," I said. "Let's be careful about this. The people who burned that village may have run out of gas."

"You *feel* anything, sire?" Timon asked.

I hesitated long enough to take stock of my danger sense. "Nothing special," I said.

But we slowed down anyway. The car was intact, a rarity along this ride. As we got closer, Aaron said, "You want to see our disguises? Look in the rear window of this car when we get right up to it."

The four of us bunched up. I guess the others wanted to see what the magic had done too.

Until we saw it.

I looked down into the rear window and saw the reflections of four skeletons draped in ragged, bloody robes.

10

The Camps

I didn't sleep well that night. I was haunted by the reflections I had seen in that car window. It was worse than the Congregation of Heroes dream, or vision, whatever *that* was. Lesh and Timon had both been hit hard by the reflection too, perhaps even harder than I was. They were more thoroughly Varayan, a land where myth and superstition lies much closer to reality than in the land I was raised in. We rode on in almost total silence after looking in that car window. The silence continued when we finally camped. There was only the most essential conversation. Aaron erected his nightly shield. We lit a fire and cooked our supper. And we kept a close watch on the sky.

Rain was threatening again, so we pitched tents, lightweight nylon jobs that had come from the sporting goods department at Marshall Field's in Chicago. As usual, I took the first watch of the night. When the rain came, I pulled down the bill of my Cubs cap and stood next to a large tree, leaning back against the trunk, trying to escape as much of the falling water as I could. It was a steady, heavy downpour that fell almost silently and blotted out any normal night sounds. There was no wind to drive the rain, no thunder and lightning to divert attention from the soaking.

It was a thoroughly miserable night. I missed Joy. I worried about the way she had carried on, forcing this expedition. I worried about the extra moons that I couldn't see because of all the clouds and rain, the Doomsday they were supposed to presage. Several times,

I fancied that I saw the four skeletal faces staring at me out of the rain.

When the downpour seemed to slacken off, just a little, I woke Lesh. He replaced me next to the tree trunk and I crawled into my tent, trying to leave as much of the water outside as I could. That didn't work very well, but I went through the motions. I crouched at the end of the tent and stripped off my weapons, boots, and wet outer clothes before I got into my blanket. I had dry clothing in a saddlebag, but I didn't want to get into it until I had to—preferably after the rain stopped. If an alarm came in the night and I didn't have time to get dressed, I would just have to meet it in my underwear.

Even though I was exhausted—every day of riding and moping left me feeling more drained than the day before—sleep took its own time and some of mine before it arrived. Rain hit the tent. When I closed my eyes, I saw the four specters staring at me, mocking me, laughing at me.

But, eventually, I did sleep.

And sometime later, I saw the face of the Elflord of Xayber hovering over me.

His face was as clear, as sharply defined, as it was when we talked in Castle Basil, but only his head and shoulders appeared this time. He was speaking, but I couldn't hear a word he said. I had a long, suspended bout with panic, fearing that I would miss the most vital message in history. Only gradually did I realize that this was only a dream, not the message I was waiting for.

Only a dream. If only the whole mess would turn out to be no more than that! But even after my logical self decided that this visitation from the elflord was only a dream, my heart continued to flutter. I needed more convincing. The dream woke me. I lay awake for ages, nervous, keyed up, heart pounding, caught in the real adrenaline rush of my dream fear.

The rain had stopped, for a while at least. We had ridden through a lot of rain the last few days, off and on—dirty rain, heavy rain, as the atmosphere started to reject much of the dirt and debris forced on it by the nuclear explosions. The sky had even cleared now, for the most part, and we hadn't seen much of clear skies since we left Varay. I looked out through the tent flap. Aaron was on guard. . . .

And there were four moons in the sky, lined up one after the other, barely separated by their own diameters.

I was more tired than I could remember ever being when I finally crawled out of my tent a few minutes after dawn—a red dawn, with the sky still hazy but mostly clear, the brightest dawn we had seen since stepping through to Louisville.

"I'm starting to pick something up," Aaron told me.

"Joy's family?" I asked.

"I think so. Off in that direction." He pointed roughly northwest, maybe closer to north-northwest.

"Unless I'm way off the way I remember the map, St. Louis should be about there," I said. "This magic would only find them if they're alive?"

Aaron nodded. "At least one of them must still be alive. I can't be more specific than that."

"Maybe we should give up on my idea of staying down here in the forest and just follow your magic magnet. I'd get worried if you lost the trace." Well, I was already worried, about a lot of things, but it got my meaning across.

"You saw the moons," Aaron said. There was no hint of an interrogatory in his voice, so he must have seen me looking out of my tent in the night.

"Four of them," I said. "And when the count reaches seven, that's the end, according to Xayber."

"We knew that time was going to be critical."

"Sometime today, we should hit Interstate 57," I said. "If we start heading northwest now, we should hit 57 north of the fork. It splits just south of Marion; 57 goes south to Cairo and Memphis, 24 goes to Paducah."

"Interstate means maybe a lot of people," Aaron said.

I nodded. "Refugees from anywhere to anywhere. My guess is that any relief efforts would have to start along the major highways, where they're still usable."

"I sure wish we knew just how bad things are. Other than what we've seen for ourselves," Aaron said.

"You're not the only one."

There were so many unknowns yet. After the *Coral Lady*, people would have been nervous. The genie had been let out of the bottle. But had there been enough warning before the big war to start people migrating away from the cities? Had there been a chance to start any evacuations, make any preparations? I could remember Dad talking about how seriously people took Civil Defense in the fifties and early sixties—bomb shelters, air raid drills, Conelrad—and then nothing, because of indifference and budget restrictions. World War Three was the bogeyman who would never come. People were so indifferent to the danger that even the dramatic changes in the Communist world in the late eighties and early nineties couldn't decrease the level any further. If the United States came out of this much worse than the Russians or the people of western Europe, it would be because of that longtime ho-hum attitude. Forget Nostradamus. Aesop had us pegged in his fable about the ant and the grasshopper. And we were the grasshoppers.

"Maybe the elflord was right," I muttered.

"Right about what?" Aaron asked.

"That it's all for the best if this world passes away."

"Why the sudden funk?"

I told him.

"Then it's still going to be up to you to see that something better comes after, right?" He said it very seriously, which didn't help my mood.

Right, I thought. *Fat chance.*

"We'd better get cracking or we'll waste the whole morning," I said. That was easier than arguing. I could continue my funk while we rode.

"That what we saw yesterday, that really how folks will see us?" Lesh asked not long after we got into our saddles again.

"That's how they'll see us," Aaron said.

"What happens if they get so scared that they start

shooting right off?'' Lesh had a practical mind. He saw that possibility before I did.

"There was always the chance that people would shoot at us," Aaron said. "Those men at the railroad bridge were ready to start shooting and they saw us the way we are."

"I got me an itch at the back of my neck," Lesh said.

"You'd better be careful," I said softly. "I may give you the Hero job."

Lesh sputtered a little and didn't recover until I started laughing. "It's okay, Lesh," I said. "We're all nervous about this. Anyway, people who shoot at ghosts are usually too scared to hit them."

"And fear can be cultivated," Aaron said. Then he clucked at his horse a couple of times and moved out ahead of us to avoid answering any follow-up questions.

"Come on, Lesh. We'll worry about shooters when the time comes," I said.

Aaron led the way all day. Guessing from the position of the sun, we were heading just a little west of northwest, not quite the direction he had indicated that morning. A couple of times, we stopped and Aaron did a minute or two of chanting. Both times, we changed course—just a little.

"It gets a little stronger every mile we ride," Aaron said.

And later, "Your wife's parents turned Varay down once. You sure they'll want to go back? Even with all this war stuff, they may want to stay in a world they know."

"I can't see anyone choosing to stay here if they had a chance to go to a place that hadn't been touched by the war." Deep breath time. "Much as I hate to even think about this, we're going to have to take them to Varay whether they want to go or not, even if Lesh and I have to tie them up and carry them through."

Aaron didn't comment.

"The problem we *may* have is keeping other people from trying to crowd through the doorway," I said after a couple of minutes. "If folks are panicked enough, they'll even risk your Four Horsemen to escape."

"And?"

"If we can do it without a riot, we can take some people through. Varay can always use people, a few thousand anyway." As long as they didn't all get in and expect to find a quaint but familiar version of back-home-before-the-war. And maybe some of them would go through to Varay and then want to leave after they saw what it was like.

"We take people back, maybe we ought to look around for a head shrinker to take along to take care of them," I said. It lightened *my* mood a little anyway.

Several times that morning and into the early afternoon we heard helicopters. None passed directly overhead, and we were in a thicker stretch of forest, so we didn't stop, didn't worry quite as much about being spotted. The route the helicopters were taking seemed to pass a little north of us.

Then, about three o'clock, we came out of the woodlands, right by the interstate highway—*and* a large refugee camp.

Aaron and I halted our horses without comment. Lesh and Timon moved closer to us before they stopped.

"Must be several thousand people," Aaron said, looking out at the huddled rows of tents along the side of the highway.

"That's where the helicopters have been going." I pointed. One helicopter, a large military cargo carrier, was on the ground. People were unloading it. "There's Army here." And it was too late to turn around and melt back into the forest. Maybe they couldn't make out any details yet, but sentries had seen us.

The back of *my* neck was itching now. My danger sense got very active.

" 'Into the valley of death,' " I mumbled, and I started my horse forward. "I guess we're going to find out how good these disguises are now," I said.

We kept the horses at a slow walk. Ahead, someone had given an alarm of some kind. A squad of soldiers came forward at the double, their rifles held at the ready. Farther back, I saw activity behind two machine guns.

"Don't anybody reach for a weapon unless I do," I said in a stage whisper. "These guys are going to be trigger-happy."

The squad of soldiers came to a ragged halt about sixty yards in front of us . . . not on command. I guess that's when they were close enough to get a good look at the public faces Aaron had conjured up for us.

"Aaron, if things look iffy, you think you can make their weapons too hot for them to hold or something like that?"

"Yes, but that much heat might set off a few shots itself."

"Well, save it until that looks like a better alternative than whatever else looks ready to happen."

"Gotcha."

We kept riding forward, closing the gap to forty yards, then we stopped. I sat very still, the way I had when we were faced with the toll trolls at the Ohio River. I didn't want the same kind of conclusion to this face-off. *These* men wore U.S. Army uniforms, and from the look of things, they wore the uniforms legitimately.

"My name is Gil Tyner. We've ridden from Louisville, going on toward St. Louis," I announced. Then I started Electrum moving forward again, still very slowly.

"That's close enough," one of the soldiers said when we were no more than twenty yards apart. "All of you, just stay where you are. Don't make a move."

He took a couple of steps forward. I noted the single bar on his collar—a lieutenant. "What the hell are you?" he asked.

Behind him, one of his men whispered, "The Four Horsemen."

"We're no threat to anyone here," I said. "Our business is beyond. Lieutenant, I hope that your men are disciplined enough not to start shooting without orders. I would hate to see this turn unpleasant."

"You're free to pass," the lieutenant said, "but not

until you've turned in your weapons. Only the military is permitted to carry weapons now.''

"Don't try to force the issue, Lieutenant," I said. "You can't kill death." I stood in my stirrups, stretching to my full height. I looked down at the arc of twelve men backing up the lieutenant. A few of them cringed back a little.

Come on, big-shot Hero, I told myself. It's time for a little theater.

"Who dares challenge me?" I shouted. I guess Aaron played games with my voice, because not only did the men in the lieutenant's squad jump, but people turned to look off in the camp, quite a distance off.

I sat back in my saddle again.

"I don't want to make a big deal over this, Lieutenant. I'm tired and I just want to get on with what I have to do. We would appreciate any news. All we've heard was that there was an exchange of nuclear weapons, and we hardly needed the radio to tell us that. We're looking for a few people, family, and we have reason to believe that they got out of St. Louis before the war. I'm assuming St. Louis was hit.''

The lieutenant nodded.

"Aaron, which way do we need to go?" I glanced his way and he pointed, straight through the middle of the camp. We could have detoured around it easily enough, but I decided to carry on with the show—no matter how much my smarter self, and the danger sense of the Hero, complained about the idiocy of the gesture.

"Shall we go, Lieutenant?" I scarcely gave him time to respond but started riding forward again, still slowly. The lieutenant took a few steps to the side to give us room to pass. His men split apart in the center. They stared at us as if they were afraid to look away. I glanced around the arc. Most of the men looked to be older than me, many in their thirties and forties, reservists or guardsmen, I guessed. Only the lieutenant looked really young.

I reined in Electrum and turned to look at the lieutenant.

"You and your men had better all stay even with us," I said. "That way, we can keep our eyes on each other." I grinned and I thought that the lieutenant was going to pass out. His eyes got wide, his face paled, and it looked as if his knees were trying to buckle.

I didn't try to rush the soldiers. Electrum was a little boisterous about being held to such a slow walk, but I wanted to make sure that the men on foot had absolutely no trouble keeping pace with us. Soldiers on the flanks, us on the inside, almost as though they held us in custody—except that we were mounted and they were on foot, and we still had our weapons. Lesh and Timon moved up until they were only half a length behind Aaron and me.

"Lieutenant, just how badly did the war go?" I asked once we were all moving along together smoothly. He was about six feet to my right.

"Bad enough, I guess," he said, glancing nervously at me with every step he took. "They don't tell us a lot, but I think all our cities were hit. But I guess we hit the Russians just as bad. Not that it makes any difference now," he added.

"It *was* the Russians, not the Chinese or somebody else?"

"Far as I know," he said.

"We saw Louisville and Fort Knox," I said. "There's nothing at all left there. Where are you from?"

"Carbondale. I was home on leave when it happened. I was stationed at Fort Gordon, Georgia. I had a telegram to report back immediately, before, but I didn't even have time to start for St. Louis to catch a flight before it all happened."

"And now you're part of the relief effort?"

"Little enough anyone can do. We bring in food, try to keep people from killing each other. We watch while people die of radiation sickness. There aren't enough doctors or hospitals to treat one percent of the casualties."

"You have a lot of those here?" Aaron asked.

"Maybe two hundred left," the lieutenant said.

"We've had more than that die already. It's almost impossible to dig graves fast enough. We don't have any heavy equipment."

"Ah, Lieutenant, we may be able to help some of the sick—if they're not too far gone already," Aaron said. He looked to me, and I nodded.

"You're a doctor?" The lieutenant's voice couldn't have expressed his skepticism any more clearly.

Aaron grinned and laughed. "No, I'm not a doctor. I'm a wizard." I felt a light tingling, and guessed that he had just removed our disguises. The way the lieutenant stopped and let his mouth fall open was a pretty good clue as well. One of his soldiers finally broke and started running away from us at a pretty fair clip.

"We do have a way to help, but we'll need a little assistance," I said.

"I'm not in command here," the lieutenant said. "Major Abrams is the CO."

"Then let's go see Major Abrams," I said. "Where is the command post?"

The lieutenant pointed. We had been headed more or less toward it anyway. "By the way, Lieutenant, what's your name?"

"Kurt McAndrews. How am I ever going to explain you people to Major Abrams?"

"Let us worry about it. Now, what we'll need most is a little perimeter security. We don't want to be mobbed while we're trying to help the sick. And we'll need some sort of doorway. Just a frame will do, two sides and a top, even if it's just three pieces of wood nailed together."

"Whatever the major says."

"He may need a little convincing. Aaron, you have a decent demonstration in mind? Ah, maybe something a little less stark than the Four Horsemen?"

"I'll take care of it," Aaron said.

We were given a clear path through the camp as we rode to the command post. People backed away quickly, but they did stare. Four men, weapons, six horses. The

two claymore swords across my back would have drawn
stares anywhere, if not always for the same reason.

Major Abrams met us in front of his tent. Abrams had
light hair going gray. He was tanned and looked fit. At
a guess, I figured he had to be Regular Army, one of the
survivors.

"Lieutenant, what's the meaning of this?" Abrams demanded.

"They say they can help some of our casualties,"
Lieutenant McAndrews said. "The black says he's a wizard." McAndrews choked over that, and the look Major
Abrams gave him would have been worth thirty seconds
of canned laughter on any sitcom.

"Aaron," I whispered. I heard a quick, soft chant from
Aaron and Lieutenant McAndrews started to lift off the
ground, straight up.

"Don't panic," I told the lieutenant, just as he started
to do precisely that. Aaron parked him ten feet up, then
picked up the major the same way and lifted him to the
same level.

"He says he's a wizard," McAndrews said, with more
poise than I would have believed possible. "I think he
may be telling the truth."

"Do you need any more proof, Major?" I asked. He
didn't answer. He may not have been capable of speech
at the moment.

"Set them down gently, Aaron," I said, and both officers floated back to the ground, landing with scarcely
a bump.

"Major, I told Lieutenant McAndrews that we may be
able to help some of the radiation casualties. I also told
him what help we need to do it. May we proceed?"

The major looked at me, then at the lieutenant. Abrams nodded, very curtly.

"The dispensary is right over here," McAndrews said,
gesturing to the right. We followed him over.

There were three large tents with screened-in sides, like
the mess tent on *M*A*S*H*. Two of them were packed
with people on cots and on blankets on the ground. Half
of the third tent was filled like that too, with the rest

given over to the people who were trying to help the casualties.

"The tent doors look like they might serve," Aaron said. "Wood all the way around."

"You want to try three different times, or just bring everyone through one door?" I asked.

He thought about it for a second. "Could get confusing directing traffic if we just do it once. People inside that tent heading out. People from the other tents have to go in before they can come out. Or the other way around."

"Lieutenant, do any of the sick people have family members here that aren't sick?" I asked. I didn't want to separate families if we could help it.

"A few, maybe," McAndrews said. "But in most cases, if one had radiation exposure, they all did."

"Well, let's make sure we've got everybody. I want to keep any families together."

McAndrew nodded. "Just what are you going to do?"

"Well, the ones whose condition isn't too bad, we'll"—I hesitated a second, uncertain how to phrase it—"we'll send them through to a place where they can get the help they need. That's why I want to make sure that any kin they have here don't get left behind."

"You're just going to take them somewhere? Where?"

"*That* is a little harder to explain. Let's just say that it's something like the Never-Never Land in *Peter-Pan*."

"I am crazy," McAndrews said.

"That's the usual reaction," I assured him. "That's even what I felt the first time *I* went there. Look, a few months ago, you remember hearing about Tessie, the dragon that was killed over south of Fort Knox?"

"I heard about it. I'm not sure I believed it."

"Believe it. They had the body there. I'm the one who killed it. My third dragon."

"Hey, do me a favor, please? Don't feed me any more of this. True or not, I don't think I can handle much more."

"Okay. Just get the families together for us."

He seemed glad of the excuse to get away from me.

We were drawing a crowd, and from some of the conversation I overheard, news of our original appearance
had spread. There were soldiers keeping the civilians
back, but we were in the center of a solid ring of people.

"Aaron, give my voice a boost. I want to talk to everybody." He nodded.

"If any of you have relatives here who are being treated
for radiation sickness, please come forward. We have a
way to help them, and we want to keep families together
while we do it." That was a lot safer than saying we
were going to evacuate just the sick and their families.
The thought of evacuation might start the mob scene I
was afraid of.

I nodded to Aaron to let him know that I didn't need
the public address system any more, then said, "I think
we'd better set this up so the people are coming out of
the tents going into Varay. We do it the other way around
and everyone will see that they're going to someplace
really different."

"Okay. Makes no difference to me, magic-wise."

"Let's talk to some of the people inside. Make sure
they want to go."

We walked through the three tents, talking to small
groups of people, most of whom showed the effects of
exposure to modern warfare. Some had burns. More were
emaciated, dehydrated. The smells of vomit and diarrhea
competed with the smells of disinfectant, sweat, and fear.
I told the people that we had a treatment that would help
many of them, but that it would mean going to a strange
place. Despite that and my strange collection of weapons, not one of the casualties who could still talk turned
down our offer.

Lieutenant McAndrews returned long before Aaron and
I finished our tour. The lieutenant had the relatives waiting, not more than two dozen. Aaron asked him to match
the wounded with their kin and we would get started.
Then we went back to the center tent, the one with the
fewest people in it. Lesh stayed outside with our horses,
holding them so they mostly hid the door we were going

to use from outside observation. I brought Timon inside with Aaron and me.

"Timon, as soon as Aaron opens the passage, you run through and find Baron Kardeen. Tell him what we're doing and have him get people to help take care of the casualties we send through. Then get back as fast as you can. We may need your help on this side."

Aaron opened the first doorway. A green shimmering appeared over a view of the hallway that ran from Baron Kardeen's office to the rear of the great hall. The view was enough to brings gasps and a variety of oaths from the people inside the tent. When Timon stepped through the green veil, turned right, and disappeared, the reactions were even louder, more fearful. I heard one "I'm not going through there!" that was quickly followed by "We have to. It's our only chance."

"Quickly, please," Aaron called out. He moved to the side of the doorway and held the passage open with one hand. "When you step through, this green field will neutralize the radiation you've received, but you'll have to remain on that side to get built up again and for it to keep working." That was more than half a lie, but it might stop a traffic jam of people stepping through and then trying to come right back.

The parade started slowly. I stood near the doorway, across from Aaron. The two of us encouraged the people going through, verbally, and occasionally with a hand to help propel them through the green shield. We told them to move off to the right and to make room for the others who were following them. When Timon reappeared in the corridor, he had several people along to help move the refugees off. Baron Kardeen was only seconds behind Timon. The chamberlain stood at the side of the flow in Castle Basil, and we talked through the doorway.

"Sorry to dump this on you without warning," I said.

"We'll manage. Timon explained. It's a good idea. That other family, the Ingelses, are doing well. They're still a little nervous, but they're adapting."

I nodded. "Tell Joy that Aaron is picking up some trace—of at least part of her family. We may have several days' riding left to reach them. Things are as bad here as I feared.''

Some of the refugees could barely walk. They were helped by others, some of whom weren't in much better condition. It reminded me a little of the shots of the Israelites crossing the Red Sea in *The Ten Commandments*. Only the scale was smaller. Once the people got through the green (which was rapidly turning orange with all the radiation it was absorbing from the people), there were plenty of hands to help, castle staff, soldiers, anyone who could be found—and more were arriving every minute.

''We're about ready to move on to the next batch,'' I told Kardeen. Timon slipped back across before the last of the people from the center tent crossed into Varay. ''We have two more groups here, both larger than this one, in other tents. A few minutes to start the next.''

I noticed a growing commotion outside the tent. After Aaron broke the first connection to Varay and we stepped outside to move on to the next tent, we could see the crowd pushing closer, agitated. They knew that something major, and strange, was up. The troops, heavily outnumbered in any case, were having trouble holding the civilians back. Our horses may have obscured the view for some people, but enough had seen all of the sick people disappear from the center tent.

''We'd better not hit any snags before we finish,'' I whispered to Aaron as we hurried to the next tent. ''The natives are restless.''

''Another display?'' Aaron suggested.

''Not if we can avoid it. The way those folks are carrying on, it might backfire.''

There were less than two hours of daylight left by the time we finished guiding through the last of the radiation victims. The crowd around the tents had gone from angry noise to stunned silence. There were occasional shouts, but not as concerted as before.

''That should ease the burden here, Lieutenant,'' I told McAndrews before Aaron broke the last connection to

Castle Basil. "You want to go through? I can always use good officers."

"You?" he asked.

"Ah, yes. The place through the gate is a castle in the kingdom of Varay. I'm the king."

I feel absolutely *stupid* saying things like that, but I guess McAndrews had seen too much to doubt me. He looked through the portal, then shook his head.

"I've still got family here, and my duty."

I nodded. "Duty" was a word I could understand. Aaron took his hand away from the doorframe, and Castle Basil disappeared.

"We'd better get on our way," I said. There was no way I would chance sticking around that camp after more than two hundred people had "vanished" because of Aaron's magic. We wouldn't have lasted the night. "We may need some help getting through the crowd."

"I'll see to it," McAndrew said. He still sounded a little shaky, but he had stuck right with us through it all. Major Abrams had been conspicuously absent the whole time.

When we were mounted and Lieutenant McAndrews had his squad ready to escort us out of the camp, I asked Aaron, "Which way?"

He pointed. I looked around in the direction he pointed, then back to where we had entered the camp.

"That's not the direction we were heading before," I said, and the change was a lot more than the minor corrections we had made before. "You're aiming a lot more to the north now."

Aaron looked around the way I had, closed his eyes, and after a couple of seconds, he pointed again, in the same direction he had a moment before. He opened his eyes and shrugged.

"They've moved then, or I'm just getting a stronger signal now," Aaron said.

"Lieutenant, is there a map of Illinois around?" I asked.

"There must be one at the CP. I'll send someone for it."

When the map arrived, Aaron pointed in his direction again. McAndrews produced a compass. The line Aaron said we had to take now would pass fifty miles **east** of St. Louis.

"Are there more camps like this one, Lieutenant?" I asked when I handed the map back to him.

"There must be dozens of them this side of St. Louis," he replied.

I looked at Aaron and shook my head. There was no way we could keep stopping and shipping crowds through to Varay at every camp. Time would run out on us. *Time itself* would run out on us. And I *had* to try to find Joy's family.

11

The Falling Wall

The last of the field corn had been caught in the field by the war and by the rains that followed. Drying cornstalks stood in ponds while the fodder for livestock rotted. There weren't the people or machines around to harvest the grain. But then, there weren't as many animals to eat it either. It did give our horses a change from their diet of grass, though. I didn't have any hesitation about collecting enough corn each day for the animals. It would just have gone to waste.

The rains came almost daily, and they lasted for hours at a time, dirty, stinking rain that brought more filth than cleansing. One front would pass. For a few minutes or hours we would see clear sky—a reddened sun at day, the moons and stars by night . . . with the dimmer stars obscured by the dust in the atmosphere and the competition of four moons. Then the next bank of war-enhanced clouds would cover us like a shroud. At night, the temperatures started to approach the freezing mark, not so unusual for the latter part of October in Illinois, I guess. Three nights after we left the first refugee camp, the rain turned to snow. Little of it stuck, and the thin veneer of ice that formed on standing water thawed soon after the dawn brought a lighter shade of gray to the sky.

We had passed several other refugee camps since the first. Each time, Aaron had shielded us as soon as we saw people and we detoured around them. We passed by more hundreds, maybe thousands of people we could have helped. I felt guilty, but forced myself to ride on.

Quixotic, I thought. You help once, then pass by other sufferers, leaving them to their painful deaths. "I gave at the office.'' Condemn all those hundreds on the chance of saving maybe six people who happened to be related to Joy.

No wonder I had nightmares every night. The word ''Hero'' was beginning to leave a dirty taste in my mind.

''We don't have any choice,'' Aaron told me. I hadn't spelled out why I was in such a rotten mood—and getting worse all the time—but maybe it wasn't that hard to see. ''Even if we weren't so rushed for time, we couldn't save the whole world, couldn't ship everybody to Varay. We've done as much as we could, maybe more than we *should* have. And if you don't manage to get to the Great Earth Mother in time, none of it matters anyway.''

I didn't answer. I didn't say much at all during those days.

My grumpiness did have one benefit. We made better time, nearly thirty miles a day, although that wasn't straight-line distance toward the signal we were following because of the long detours we had to take to get around the refugee camps. When we made camp three nights after handing through the one batch of radiation casualties, we were east and maybe a little north of St. Louis, approaching I-70, maybe twenty or twenty-five miles west of Vandalia, Illinois. We had stayed on the same bearing, as much as we could, since leaving that first camp. If Joy's family had moved while we were rescuing sick people, they had stayed put since.

''The signal's getting a lot stronger,'' Aaron said while we were pitching our tents. ''But then, I don't know what the maximum will feel like. They might be fifty miles away yet or just down the other side of the next highway.''

''Even if it's that close, we'll have to wait for morning,'' I said. ''We can't ride after dark, not this close to another interstate. I'd hate to stumble on another camp in the dark.''

I hardly slept at all that night. Whatever the primary cause—guilt, fear of nightmares, or anticipation—I was simply too keyed up to sleep. We had several showers during the night, which kept me in my tent more than I really wanted to be. I stood an extra-long turn on sentry, then stayed up a while longer after Lesh came out to relieve me. When the rain started again, I went into my tent, but I only stayed in until the rain let up again, shortly after Aaron got up to stand guard.

"If nerves mean anything, we'll find them today," I said.

"I think it's likely," Aaron said. "I feel them close. But remember, they're probably in a camp by now. We're going to have another scene like we did before."

I shrugged. "We get Joy's family through. Then we can get as many others as we can. If we can." Maybe it had been necessary to ignore all the people we could have helped along the way, but once I accomplished my primary mission, I wasn't going to just step through and ignore any people who were close enough to go with us.

"Do we go in like the Four Horsemen again?" Aaron asked.

"Unless you can come up with a better disguise, something to get us close without getting shot."

"They may have heard about us from the other camp," Aaron said. "The Army must have radio communications. And we know they have helicopters. The news has to be spreading. I'm surprised they haven't been out looking for us."

"You think anybody who wasn't there to see us will believe it?" I gave him a sour laugh. "If Major Abrams tried to report exactly what happened, they'll have him locked up, either for being crazy or for massacring all those missing casualties."

"Hey, I know what's eating you, but don't you think it's about time to lighten up? You didn't get so down when it looked like the whole world was falling right on our heads at that shrine. You think a Hero should do more. All those dead Heroes in the crypt thought the same thing. That's how they got dead. And you got work to do yet." He paused, but I didn't say anything. "Besides, you're spoiling my ninth birthday."

"Your what?"

"I'm nine years old today. Didn't you know?"

I looked at him in the flickering light of our campfire. Aaron was three inches taller than me and a few pounds heavier, and had a respectable beard on his face. None of us had shaved since leaving Varay.

"Nine years old?" And then I started laughing, almost hysterically—enough to wake both Lesh and Timon. Lesh came rolling out of his tent with a sword in one hand and his battle-axe in the other.

"Sire?" Lesh said. He got to his feet and looked around, ready for battle and looking for foes.

"Today is Aaron's ninth birthday," I said, squeezing the words out through continuing laughter. It was a painful catharsis. It didn't release all of the agony I felt, but it did make it easier to get through the next hours . . . and I could hardly think farther ahead than that.

Dawn saw rain falling again, heavy rain, dripping off the bill of my Cubs cap, soaking my head behind it. We broke camp in the wet and got up in the saddle. The rain had been too heavy to get a fire going, so we had to start the day without coffee or a hot breakfast.

"There is one way we could maybe find out how close they are," I told Aaron as we started riding north again. "We could ride either east or west for five or ten miles and see how much the direction changes. Triangulation."

"What, and lose an hour or two of riding?" Aaron asked. He smiled. "Anyway, I didn't get that far in math. We were just doing simple fractions in the third grade."

So we rode straight north. We were an hour short of I-70. Climbing the rise to cross the highway, we popped into sight of another refugee camp, sitting right at the north side of the road.

"We're the four riders," Aaron said quickly. I felt the tingling of active magic and nodded.

Sentries at the perimeter of the camp had spotted us, but we still angled off to the right, toward the nearer side of the camp. We had gone only about a hundred yards before Aaron pulled to a stop.

"They must be in this camp," he said. "The pull

changed, off that way.'' He pointed. ''That what you meant before?''

''That's what I meant.''

We gathered a lot of intent attention from the camp as we approached, but nobody came out to intercept us. The sentries, and a crowd of civilian onlookers, moved apart to let us ride in without challenge. I saw people crossing themselves or waving the horns toward us to ward off evil. I glanced around, looking for familiar faces.

''Ditch the disguise, Aaron,'' I said as soon as we were inside the perimeter of the camp. ''I don't want to spook my in-laws any more than they already are.''

This camp was a lot larger than the first one we had seen. There had to be more than five thousand people here. Rows of wall tents paralleled the highway. A United States flag flew over a tent in the center. That had to be the command post. There was an open space at the west end of the camp that had to be set aside as a heliport, but there were no choppers on the ground at the moment.

The officer who came out to meet us was a captain, and he didn't approach until we were halfway from the perimeter to the center of the camp.

''You're the ones we heard about?'' he asked when we reined in our horses.

''Since I don't know what you've heard, I can't say if we're the ones you heard about,'' I replied, softly, trying to sound very friendly and nonthreatening. ''I'm looking for my in-laws, Captain. I have strong reason to believe that they're in this camp.''

''You're the one who took off all the cases of radiation sickness?''

''Yes.''

''We have about four hundred and fifty of them here.''

''And you want us to help them?''

''We certainly can't do much for them here. By the way, my name is William Travis Thompson.''

''Gil Tyner. This is Aaron Carpenter. Lesh. Timon.''

''The Four Horsemen,'' Captain Thompson said.

''Some have called us that,'' I admitted. ''As I said,

I'm looking for my in-laws, my wife's family, and I think that at least some of them are here in your camp.''

"We have a roster at the command post," the captain said. "Can you help our injured?''

"You seem awfully anxious to trust someone you know nothing about, Captain. Are you *that* desperate?''

"Yes," he said, *very* softly, but without the slightest hesitation. "We just can't handle so many. We don't have the facilities, the medical personnel, the drugs. All we can do is watch as people get worse and die, some that could be saved—according to the book—if we had the means to treat them.''

"We'll do what we can, Captain, as soon as we find the people we're looking for.'' There was no way I would even think of turning him down. "Are you in command here?''

"Ah, technically, no. But the colonel has four camps to look after, so I'm the ranking officer here at the moment.''

When we reached the command post, Captain Thompson asked me for the names of the people we were looking for, and I told him: Joy's parents, Dan and Rosemary Bennett; her brother, Danny, his wife, Julia, and their children, Dawn and David.

The roster was alphabetical. Thompson had my answers almost immediately.

"Danny and Julia Bennett and two children, tent D-4. That's toward the northwest from here. Rosemary Bennett, dispensary. Just down the line here. Dan Bennett died the day they arrived. Radiation.''

Now Joy's lost *her* father too, I thought. It was getting to be an epidemic.

"Can you tell me how bad Rosemary's condition is?'' I asked.

"I don't have the daily status reports here," Thompson said. "The doctors keep those.''

I nodded. "We'll go to the hospital tents first.''

Rosemary Bennett was in critical condition, bedbound. She hardly seemed aware of who I was. But Danny was with her when we arrived. After I said hello to his mother, Danny took me off toward the door, away from her.

"What the hell did you do to Mom and Dad?" he demanded. I had only met Danny a couple of times while I was going with Joy. Danny had his own family, and Joy and I were in Chicago most of the time before Joy moved to Varay.

"Joy and I tried to give them, and you and your family, a chance to escape all of this," I said. "Joy was worried when we saw this coming. Your parents didn't want any part of it."

"Part of what? All this fairy-tale hocus-pocus?"

"It's real, Danny, whether you want to believe it or not."

"Then what are you doing here?"

"Looking for all of you. Joy's going crazy with worry. I'm here to take the whole bunch of you through to Varay."

"You think I'm crazy? I'm not a gullible fool."

"Neither is Joy. Neither are the two-hundred-odd people we helped through from a camp by Marion, Illinois. Ask Captain Thompson here about that. We can help your mother. Going through to Varay will reverse most if not all of the damage from radiation. Varay is the only hope she has. And it's probably the only chance your kids have for a decent future too."

"Oh? Do you have Mother Goose there to tell her own stories?"

"Get your wife and kids and bring them back here. We can't waste all day. We make people nervous."

"Yeah, I heard that story about four skeletons riding across the country. All the hellfire preachers are making a big noise about it. Judgment Day is almost here."

"They may be right," I said. "Now, get your family. If it's a fraud, you'll have your laugh soon enough. But it isn't, and you'll see that quick enough too. Look at it this way. You've got nothing to lose but a few minutes, and you've got everything to gain."

For a moment, I thought that Danny was going to just tell me to go to hell and refuse. But he didn't. I sent Lesh along to help him bring his family back to the hospital tent—and to make sure he didn't change his mind and take off in the other direction.

"Timon, as soon as Aaron gets the first doorway open, take the horses through and then find Baron Kardeen again. We'll all be coming through this time. If Joy's there at Basil, find her and tell her that we're bringing through her family. Got it?"

"Yes, sire."

That brought looks from the people around us. Aaron and I started giving the same kind of pep talks we had given to the casualties at Marion. There were five tents filled with radiation cases here, though, larger tents than at the other camp, and more of these people were in really bad condition. Closer to St. Louis, and several days farther along, I guess that was inevitable. We finished talking to the people in the one tent, then went outside to wait for Lesh to get back with the other Bennetts.

"Look, if you don't mind," Aaron said, "after you get your wife's people and all the casualties through, I'll hang on at the door to let as many of the others through as want to come. Can we handle that?"

"It might strain things for a few days, but go ahead." I might have suggested that if Aaron hadn't. "Just one caution. Stand on the Varayan side of the door. If things get out of control then, all you have to do is pull your hand away."

"That'll mean no second chance. I'm not sure I could open the way back to one of these tent doors."

"I know, but it's the only way, Aaron. I can't take any chance of you getting trapped on this side. Crowd gets out of hand, you might get trampled before you could whip anything up."

"You may be right," Aaron said. "Parthet didn't give any guarantees about old-age pensions in this job."

I turned to Captain Thompson. "Once we open the passage here, you'll need to make arrangements for the people in the other hospital tents. Bring the people in through the door on the other end of this tent. We'll funnel them through this way." I had decided on a change in tactics. Shifting from tent to tent had done little but give the onlookers more time to get worked up at the other camp. "Tell the people that we have a treatment for radiation sickness. And try to get the families of the sick people here matched up with one another so we can send them through together. That cuts down on the anxieties. Then—and keep this quiet until we get all the casualties through—we'll hold the door open as long as we can. Anyone who wants to go through to a place where there hasn't been a nuclear war is welcome. As long as it's orderly and there are still people who want to go, we'll keep the way open. But if things get out of hand, we'll break the connection from the other side. If that happens, that's the end, no way we can open it up again."

Thompson nodded, then repeated the gist of what I had said. "I'll get my people busy rounding up the families now."

Julia Bennett, Danny's wife, looked like a complete wreck—understandably. I would never have recognized her. I remembered a pretty, thin blonde who had laughed a lot. World War Three had aged her at least ten years. The kids were quiet. Their faces looked too old too. Julia didn't say much more than hello. She went to Rosemary and talked to her.

Lesh and Timon brought our horses inside the hospital tent despite the screamed protests of two doctors. Then Aaron opened the way to Basil right away, and that shut off any complaints about animals in the hospital. Timon led the horses straight through. Lesh stayed on the Illinois side of the doorway, across from Aaron.

"Okay, Danny," I said. "You and I will have to help your mother through. Julia, you can manage the children?" She just nodded. She didn't even ask where we were going or what kind of insane magic—or simple insanity—was up.

Rosemary Bennett had lost a lot of weight. That seemed to be one of the major problems of most of the radiation cases.

"I thought this was supposed to cure her," Danny said after we passed through the green veil.

"It gets rid of all the radiation in her system," I said. "She'll still need some care to recover from the side effects. Food and liquids, a lot of them, and a little time. But this buys her the time." I hoped it would buy her the time. She looked awfully close to the end.

Danny stared at me for a minute longer before he looked around. We were in the keep of Castle Basil, on the ground floor, and just off to the side of the passage from the refugee camp. Timon had the horses outside already. *Someone* had taken them, anyway. Timon came running toward us with Baron Kardeen and Joy almost immediately.

The relief of the reunion blunted the immediate pain Joy had to feel when she learned that her father was dead. She questioned me about her mother's condition. All I could do was repeat what I had told Danny. It was something Aaron and I had considered. We *thought* that recovery would be fairly quick.

The first minutes of the reunion were too chaotic for anyone to chronicle them. We moved Joy's mother through to the room above Parthet's workroom. It had already been converted for use as an intensive care ward, and a couple of people were still there from the Marion camp. Once everyone was satisfied that the senior Mrs. Bennett was well settled, Joy and I took her brother and his family down to the great hall for a meal.

"One thing you'll like here," Joy told Danny. "You can eat all day and night and not get fat."

Danny still didn't have a lot to say. He looked around a lot, frowned even more. The kids—Dawn was six and David four—perked up a little when Joy told them that it was the biggest castle in the kingdom. They ate and asked a host of questions. Julia perked up a little too. The improvement in the children's dispositions helped hers. But Danny was a lot slower to open up, and I didn't have time to waste at the moment.

"I've got to get back to Aaron," I told Joy. "I'm afraid he'll get bogged down trying to get everyone through."

Baron Kardeen had stayed right at the portal to organize our end of the rescue. After the earlier practice, he had the methods down pat. I even recognized a couple of people from Marion helping direct the new arrivals through.

"You did it, sire," Kardeen said when I stopped next to him.

I nodded. "What little I could. How's it going here?"

"We're still bringing through the injured," Kardeen said. Aaron and Lesh were still on the Illinois side of the door.

"This is going to be a much larger group," I told Kardeen. "More than twice as many injured, and maybe several thousand who aren't. How much trouble is that going to be?"

"I've had people out stocking extra food since the first refugees came through. We're even making arrangements to buy supplies from Belorz. Parthet and your mother went to Castle Curry to see to that. And the fleet at Arrowroot is putting in extra hours fishing. We figured that you would be bringing through a lot of people. We'll manage. And there is something else you need to see right away. If Parthet were here, he'd have dragged you up to the battlements already."

"What is it?"

"You really need to see for yourself, sire. Now?"

I nodded. If Kardeen thought it was that urgent, it probably was.

"Lesh, Aaron! You two get on this side of the door when you get the last of the sick people through. Don't take any chances after that."

"Aye, sire," Lesh said. Aaron nodded a reluctant agreement of his own.

Kardeen and I climbed to the top of the keep.

"Parthet thinks this may be just as dire as the extra moons in the sky," Kardeen said just before we reached the top. We went out and he pointed south. I didn't have any trouble at all figuring out what he was talking about. The peaks of the Titan Mountains were barely visible at the horizon.

"They seem to sink measurably day by day," Kardeen said. "Parthet says the barrier between the seven kingdoms and the lesser world is fading away."

"Did I do that, letting so many people through?" I asked.

"I think not, sire. It has been going on almost since you left."

What happens when the mountains are no longer a barrier? I wondered.

12

Autumn Leaves

There are times when taking any action at all is wrong, when the only proper thing to do is sit back, close your eyes, and let everything sort itself out. The trick to effective management is knowing when to leave the chaos to others and to time, and when to wade in and take an active hand. After we returned from fetching Joy's family, it was a time for me to sit back and wait—mostly. I had confidence in Baron Kardeen and the people he had trained at Castle Basil. All I could do by butting in was get in the way and slow him up.

It was well after dark in Illinois, and near sunset in Varay, before the last of the refugees made it through the portal to Castle Basil. The captain and half of the Army detachment had chosen to come through as well, and they brought some of the supplies from the camp—not nearly everything, because the captain would not have shorted the refugees who remained behind, but enough to ease the start of life in Varay for the more than four thousand people who came through from the camp. Bedding was a big item.

Lesh had to help support Aaron on their way to the great hall. I got them both seated at the head table close by me, and gestured for someone to bring more food and beer. I knew that Lesh at least would have about a two-gallon thirst.

"How many came through?" I asked, after both men had their beer.

"About forty-two hundred, Baron Kardeen said," Lesh said. "Call it sixty companies. If they were all fighting men, we'd have an army to match any in the buffer zone now.''

"Some people didn't come through?" I asked.

"About a thousand, according to that captain," Lesh said. Aaron was still concentrating on food and drink exclusively. Magic was a drain. Parthet had often told me that. And Aaron had been holding a particularly active magic for a lot of hours. "He said two hundred soldiers were staying and the rest were civilians who didn't want to chance our doorway."

"Well, dig in. There's plenty of good food coming out of the kitchen, some of it stuff that I've never had in Varay before."

"I heard, sire," Lesh said, helping himself to another tankard of beer. "Talk is, some of the folks we sent through t'other day are working in the kitchens. Two of 'em was cooks before. They wanted to earn their way right off the mark here."

That sounded like good news. We were going to have to find ways for a lot of our new citizens to make their way in the buffer zone—if anyone had a long-term future. We could support refugees for a time, but not indefinitely.

Baron Kardeen was in and out of the great hall a dozen times that afternoon and evening. Then, as soon as the last of the refugees came through, I made him sit and take a long break so he could do some eating and unwind a little. I mentioned the new cooks and he nodded.

"Two cooks, and a couple of the men are already training with the castle guards. A few others have asked about work. Most will still need a few days of rest and eating before they're really up to anything."

"We need to do some kind of survey, find out what kind of talents our new citizens have," I said. "Charley Ingels is an engineer, a bridge builder among other things, so we can find work for him and a crew or two. We'll probably have quite a few farmers among the two batches." I hoped we would, anyway. Farming is *the* major occupation in the buffer zone. "At least people who have done enough gardening to learn the rest. But we'll probably have a lot of people who don't have any skills that will translate directly. If they have military service in their past, we can fill out the Army a little, and some of the people are soldiers already." I chuckled. "But they'll have to learn the weapons we use here. And there might be a few artisans and craftsmen. Well, you know the kind of information we need. Once we get everyone settled who won't need complete retraining, we can give more attention to the ones who only know TV repair or something like that."

"I've already been asking about carpenters and other building trades," Kardeen said, nodding vigorously. "Those are the skills we need first."

Very softly, I said, "Seeing as how we don't know yet if any of us has a lengthy future."

This time, Kardeen's nod was almost imperceptible. "But we will need places to house everyone. The nights will be getting quite chilly soon." Varay had an extremely short, and usually mild, winter, but late autumn could see some downright cool days and nights.

"Any problem with building materials?" I asked.

"A shortage of seasoned wood," Kardeen said. "Parthet or Aaron should be able to help with that. And rock will have to be quarried. But we will have a lot of laborers, even if they're mostly untrained."

Several times, before and after that break, Kardeen came to get me to open up passageways to the other castles. There were simply too many extra people around to house them all in Basil, castle and town, even for a day or two. We sent contingents of refugees through to all of the castles in Varay, spreading out the work. That is, we sent them to all of the castles but Arrowroot. Baron Resler already had the crew of that Russian frigate to deal with . . . and I didn't want to get our American refugees and the Russians in the same place. That would have been asking for trouble.

I even did a little work myself that evening—of an appropriately "regal" nature. Okay, it sounds rather hokey to say it like that. It felt just as bad thinking of it in those terms at the time. Once I had sated my hunger and thirst, my responsibilities started to weigh on me, my duty as king—*and* as the person responsible for the sudden population explosion. I felt guilty just sitting around, even though I knew I was more likely to get in the way than be a real help if I tried to get actively involved in the problems of getting all of our new citizens settled in for the night.

I walked around the courtyard where most of the people were milling about waiting to be told what to do and where to go, and I toured the areas inside the castle where refugees were being put up for the night—approximately every square foot of the castle, except for the private apartments.

I talked to people.

"Where is this place?" was one question that I heard over and over.

"It's a land between our world and the realm of Fairy," I'd say, or, perhaps more often, "It's something like Never-Never Land in *Peter Pan,* except people do grow up here." Or variations on those themes.

More people wanted some kind of reassurance that they hadn't gone completely crazy, that this wasn't all hallucination, some unexpected side effect of their radiation sickness. I did what I could to put their minds at ease, knowing that only time and full recovery would be really convincing. And, at that . . . well, there were still times when *I* found it all a little hard to swallow.

There was one other thing I had to do in the hours after getting back from Illinois—check in frequently on Joy and her family. And *that* wasn't simply a result of my sense of duty, or guilt.

The room above Parthet's workshop was crowded and still cluttered with Parthet's stacks of books and odds and ends. Rosemary Bennett was on the single bed left in the room. When I returned after supper, she was awake and propped up against several pillows.

"There you are," she said when I entered. I smiled, relieved that she was conscious and alert finally. When we carried her out of Illinois, she was comatose and seemed near death.

"Here I am," I agreed. "You're looking better."

"I'm still alive," she said, and then she closed her eyes.

"She's kept down soup and a little solid food," Joy said. She was sitting on the edge of the bed next to her mother. Joy looked as though the weight was off of her. Danny and Julia looked more relaxed too. Danny looked and sounded as if he was still nursing a grudge, but not one as bitter as before. He didn't say much more to me than a simple hello. Julia had come out of her daze. Food, a little wine, and the general improvement in conditions helped a lot, I think.

I helped a little more by taking the kids, my niece and nephew, on a tour of the castle. Dawn and David both managed to work up a refreshing enthusiasm for the novelty of being in a castle. A couple of candy bars from my private hoard helped.

When I took the kids back to their parents after our tour, Joy had the family housing sorted out.

"Dan and Julia and the kids will have your old room here," she announced. "Part of it has already been partitioned off to make a second small bedroom." It was certainly big enough. The *bed* in that room was almost the size of my entire bedroom back in Louisville.

"Uh, fine," I said, "but I thought the Ingels family had that room. The first family Aaron and I sent through from the other world," I added for the benefit of Joy's family.

"Northeast tower now," Joy said. "They're in the apartments traditionally assigned to the royal builder or some such title. Charley Ingels did say that you wanted him to build a bridge?"

"I guess I did. Maybe he knows something about building houses too."

"Baron Kardeen already has him working on that," Joy said. Of course. Kardeen usually managed to anticipate. That's why everything flowed so smoothly at Basil.

"And all our stuff has been moved here from Cayenne," Joy added.

"The royal apartment?" I asked. I had avoided visiting Grandfather's part of the keep since my return. Joy nodded.

"I'll see you up there when you get everyone tucked in," I said.

Joy's mother was sleeping. Dawn and David had settled down on a bench as soon as we got back. They both looked ready to nod off with the least encouragement. I felt about that ready for sleep myself. I was exhausted.

"I won't be too long," Joy said. She got up to give me a quick kiss.

When I left the room, her brother, Danny, came after me.

"Hey," he said as soon as the door closed behind us, "I know I've been a bit surly. Sorry. Joy told us what you had to go through to get to us. Thank you."

I shrugged. "It's not easy for anyone to accept the reality of this place at first. It wasn't easy for Joy, or even for me. Four years ago, I had never heard of it. Back in our world, the idea *has* to sound crazy."

"Maybe, but that's no excuse for me acting like an asshole. And even if this *is* crazy, it's a better insanity than that shit back there."

I couldn't argue with that.

I wandered through the bedroom and study that had been my great-grandfather's for a century. The bedroom had been changed around a little, and the decorations showed a new hand. The study was still about the same as before—undoubtedly waiting my decision on what to do with it. I wasn't up to thinking about that yet. Finally, I crossed to the private dining room. That was less *personal* than the rest of the suite. A new keg of beer was on the sideboard, the wood still damp from the ice that Parthet kept supplied down in the beer cellar. I helped myself to a stein of beer and sat at the table. The hall door was open. I would hear Joy when she approached . . . unless I fell asleep.

Time and quiet—precious commodities, usually.

Keeping busy, riding across the war-raped middle of America and then watching the confusion swirl around me back at Basil, I had been able to keep from worrying myself totally crazy about the one quest I still had to face—the need to find and seduce the Great Earth Mother before she could put the chop to me—and the uncertainties that even a best-case scenario left. I was acting as if there were sane purpose to rescuing people from the other world, planning to build new bridges, houses, *a future,* when there might not be a very long future for anyone.

Crazy? The situation went so far beyond crazy that language can't do it justice. The Mad Hatter has his tea party on the deck of the *Titanic. Dr. Strangelove* has *Breakfast at Tiffany's.*

"Crazy" is a totally inadequate word.

It must have been close to midnight when Baron Kardeen came up the back stairs into the dining room.

"We have everyone fed and settled in for the night," he reported. "Unless we come up with another plague of dragons in the eggs, we're stocked for breakfast."

"Good. Grab a mug of beer and take a load off your feet."

For once, he didn't hesitate. I know that I upset his sense of propriety quite often. Sometimes I could almost hear him reminding himself that I hadn't grown up in Varay, that allowances had to be made for foreign ideas of manners. I had only once seen him sit in Pregel's presence, for instance, and that was at the formal breakfast after we buried my father. But Kardeen was tired, which must have happened often, and *showing* it, which was rare. He filled a mug, half-emptied it, then topped it off and sat at the side of the table.

"It's been a hectic day," I said. "I really dumped a load on you this time. And, as usual, you managed to handle it."

"It has been a hectic day," Kardeen agreed.

"How are our Russians doing?" I asked. It seemed strange to me even at the time, but I couldn't work up a good hate for them even after seeing the results of the fighting back in my world—maybe *because* I had seen the results. I recognized potential problems, but I didn't have the slightest inclination to take the war out on the crew of that frigate.

"They're not completely satisfied," Kardeen said. "The reality of Varay is beginning to sink in, though. I doubt that they know what happened in your world after they left."

I smiled. "It's okay," I told him. In his own delicate way, Kardeen was trying to make sure that I wasn't about to do anything rash about our Russians. "I don't have any yen for vengeance." Kardeen smiled back at me and nodded.

"We'll try to put anything more off until tomorrow," I said. "I can't think straight right now, and I imagine that everyone must be just as strung out as I am."

"There is one more thing I need to mention," Kardeen said with obvious reluctance.

"Go on," I said when he hesitated.

"I had a report from Baron Hambert at Coriander this evening, passed through when we were sending him his share of our new people. One of his patrols came across scouts for a moderately large force of Dorthinis in Battle Forest. The wizard you blinded has apparently found sight again. He may have as many as five hundred soldiers with him, not enough to stage a major invasion, but certainly enough for a large raid—likely for food."

A blind wizard is of no use to anyone. That's what Parthet had told me after the Battle of Thyme. The Etevar's wizard was blinded during the fight, when the dragon he was controlling was blinded. I hadn't seen any purpose in doing anything more drastic to the wizard afterward.

Now he was back, and Kardeen said he had eyes again.

"Doesn't he have any idea how critical this time is to all of us?" I asked.

"I don't doubt that he does. He may see it as his best chance to get himself a real base. Dieth has kept the pressure on the warlords of Dorthin. If this wizard gets himself a base right on the border, he can strike in either direction."

"How much time do we have to meet him?" I asked.

"Hambert said he has a few tricks prepared but that the Dorthinis could still reach Coriander before sunset tomorrow. Coriander is in no immediate danger. They're warned and there aren't enough troops coming to take it by assault."

"That still doesn't leave much time. They may not bother with the castle if they're looking to steal part of our harvest. And *that* is something we can't afford to lose, not with all of our new citizens."

Kardeen nodded.

"Still, it has to wait for morning. I'm too tired to think straight now. At breakfast, here. You, me, Aaron, Parthet if he's back from Curry. I believe that Joy will probably want to eat with her family. That reunion will be going on for days."

"As you wish."

I stared at Kardeen for a moment. He had a working knowledge of the other world, but entirely secondhand. "Can you even begin to comprehend the destruction back in my old world?" I whispered.

"The queen, your mother, and I have spent many hours discussing the possibilities," Kardeen said. "The descriptions they give . . . It all sounds unbelievable, unreal, impossible."

"About the way that most people from there view *this* world."

"I have noticed that," Kardeen said. "Some of the people you sent through have become almost hysterical for a time."

"Strike the *almost*. That's why Joy's parents were back in that world when the shit hit the fan. They were here once, briefly, and they couldn't handle the idea. As a result, Joy's father is dead."

"Because he could only imagine one reality?" Kardeen asked.

Exhaustion helped overcome my uneasiness over sleeping in the bed that my great-grandfather had died in. Sleep. That's all Joy and I did that night, even after my latest absence. Her pregnancy was just starting to show, but she hadn't lost her enthusiasm for what got her that way. We were simply both too tired to get from A to B that night. And there wasn't time in the morning. We were wakened before dawn. I told Joy about the planning conference at breakfast and suggested that she do the honors in the great hall with her brother's family, that I would join them as soon as I could—but probably not until after the morning meal was finished.

"It was bad, wasn't it?" she asked as we dressed.

"As bad as anyone could imagine," I said. "Louisville, Fort Knox, they simply ceased to exist. I imagine that all the cities were like that, and all the military bases. I'm sorry about your father."

Joy came into my arms. I held her for a moment. "We did everything we could," I told her.

"I know."

"But it still hurts. I know how it feels, Joy. We were too late to save *my* father too."

Then I had to go to my meeting.

The others were all there already, waiting for me. Protocol: the king makes his entrance after everyone else is present. Kardeen had already told the others what was happening. We started on our talk while we started on breakfast. Aaron and I would need several days of concentrated pigging out to recover from our trip to the other world. Parthet always ate as if he hadn't seen food in a week. Kardeen was a little more "normal" in appetite, but he was eating this morning, not standing next to the throne being the court functionary. Maybe I was finally succeeding in my efforts to get him to loosen up a bit.

"We could funnel through enough soldiers to meet this renegade wizard and his soldiers," I said after we had talked through everything two or three times already. "But soldiers alone won't do it, not if that wizard got his eyesight back." I stopped for a moment and shook my head.

"Dammit anyway, this really isn't the time for us to be out playing this kind of game. If only we could hang out a detour sign and send him somewhere else."

"They *are* in Battle Forest," Parthet said, very point-edly.

I looked at him. "What's that supposed to mean?"

"Aaron?" Parthet said. The younger wizard looked at his mentor and shrugged.

"I don't know the country up there," Aaron said.

Parthet looked from him to me. "I'm not absolutely certain this will work. If I were the only wizard available here, I'd say that it wouldn't, not against the Dorthini. But with both Aaron and me—and maybe an assist from what's left of Vara—we just might be able to hang out that detour sign for you."

"Shift the Dorthinis north into Xayber?" Kardeen asked—a beat faster on the uptake than I was.

"This is one I can't guarantee," Parthet said. "But something I saw in the old scrolls I had Aaron study makes me think that it may be possible, with all three of us involved."

"There's something I want to hear more about before I agree," I said. "Just how do you plan to make use of 'what's left of Vara'?"

"Nothing uncomfortable," Parthet said quickly. "You'll simply be one point of our base."

"How close do we have to be?" Aaron asked.

Parthet tapped a knuckle against the edge of the table several times before he answered. "If we can do it at all, we should be able to do it from the battlements here." He looked at Kardeen. "We'll need one of the large maps, one that shows all of Battle Forest and the nearer reaches of Xayber."

Kardeen nodded. "I'll get it now. I assume we'll do this immediately?"

"We'd better," I said, looking to Parthet for confirmation.

He nodded. "Give Aaron and me a few minutes to lay out our program. Once we get started, we won't be able to stop for conferences in the middle."

"Okay," I said. "The map." Kardeen was already heading for the back stairs. "You two with the hocus-pocus, and me with my two cents' worth. I'll start up to the roof now. Just one question. What will the Elflord of Xayber think about us dumping our trash over his fence?''

Parthet started to answer, then stopped while he thought back through my question. ''We can always let him know what we're doing. It might even amuse him, especially if that Dorthini wizard *is* a renegade out of Fairy.''

I guess that I had some intuitive understanding of the basic idea. The force that the Dorthini wizard had assembled was inside Battle Forest and we were going to get them lost. No matter which way they headed, they were going to move north onto the Isthmus of Xayber—if it worked. The Dorthini wizard had been a powerful magic force before he went blind. He had been much better than Parthet. I *thought* that Aaron might prove to be his superior, but I couldn't be certain. Neither could Aaron, not until the confrontation came.

By the time we all gathered on top of the keep, the idea seemed even more familiar. It was something the bad guys usually used against the good guys. Come on down to the riverside and get eaten by a tree. That sort of thing. But . . . I really didn't want to waste the time and men to take a force up to Battle Forest to chase the outlaws back to Dorthin for Dieth to take care of. Force of arms is no more certain than the force of magic.

I stood looking out toward the north, toward Fairy and the Mist, though I couldn't see anywhere near that far, while I waited for the others. The morning was overcast, gloomy, promising rain, the same kind of day I had seen too much of back in the other world. It was a perfect day for sorcery and moping. We were getting ready to take care of the sorcery. I figured I could manage the moping all by myself afterward. It was that kind of morning. All that was missing was the kind of thick, mysterious fog that had come in over Castle Arrowroot to cover the retreat of the elflord's army several years before.

''It gets like this a lot in autumn, sire,'' Kardeen said, just coming up off of the stairs. He had a huge scroll tucked under one arm. "Sometimes we go for a week or more without seeing clear sky."

"And this autumn is far from ordinary," I said. That was the least negative remark I could come up with. The arrival of our wizards spared Kardeen the necessity of a reply.

"Lay out the map aligned with the compass points," Parthet said. "North to north." Aaron helped the chamberlain get the scroll uncoiled and situated. "We may get the parchment a bit soiled. At least one of us will have to stand on it."

That turned out to be me.

"You're the apex of our triangle," Parthet told me, adjusting my position down to the inch. "Don't move your feet or turn your body."

Parthet and Aaron were the bases, facing me. A line bisecting the Parthet-Gil-Aaron angle would touch the corner of land where the eastern shore of Xayber broke north from the mainland, just north of Coriander, where Xayber, Varay, and Dorthin all touched.

"Now, remember, don't budge," Aaron said. "And watch the map. If this works, you'll see the results."

The map was one of Baron Kardeen's large, classy hand-drawn jobs, in four colors, with a lot of detail drawn in. It was "illuminated," in the style of those ancient monastic books, a real work of art. And I had my combat boots planted firmly on it, over the Eastern Sea, just beyond the corner of land where the three countries meet.

Parthet and Aaron started chanting together—point and counterpoint, not in unison. They carried on for several minutes before I started to feel a strong tingle that was highly localized . . . in what was left of Vara. It was almost like a jolt of static electricity that didn't go away. It wasn't comfortable, but I remembered Parthet's injunction and didn't move an inch.

Slowly, the map got hazy. Then, something happened. The closest I can come is to say that the map appeared to turn into a large television screen showing the territory covered by the map as it was, not as it had been drawn. It started out like a high-altitude shot, like some of the

pictures taken from a space shuttle, first of the entire
area, and then zooming down on the area in Battle Forest
north and east of Castle Coriander.

It was like being there, hovering overhead, real enough
that it made me dizzy. And then, we saw the soldiers
riding west. I held my breath for a moment, as if I was
afraid that they would hear me. I didn't even dare rub
my eyes, afraid that I would move too much and spoil
the magic.

Then the map itself moved, or the forest it showed did.
Paths, creeks, everything shifted around. Aaron and Parthet kept chanting. I kept watching. After maybe five
minutes, the column of soldiers stopped. There was a
flash of light near the head of the column, a bright orange
glow, almost like a flame. The light faded and the column started to move again, northwest, closer to north,
bending more and more toward Xayber.

I can't say how long I watched that remote picture.
There were two more pauses by the soldiers, both marked
by the orange glow near the head of the troop. I eventually figured out that the orange flashes were the Dorthini
wizard's efforts to identify and nullify the magic being
used against him.

"Okay, lads, that should do it," Parthet said. I looked
up. Parthet had backed off from his corner of the triangle. Aaron blinked rapidly several times and rubbed at
his eyes. I stepped off of the map. It was once more just
a drawn representation.

"Don't you have to keep it up until they get out of our
territory?" I asked.

Parthet shook his head. "Unless the Dorthini wizard
somehow manages to break the spell, it will hold of itself
. . . long enough. And we'll know if the spell breaks."
He chuckled suddenly. "And *you'll* probably be the first
to know. If the Dorthini wizard manages to penetrate the
spell, the backlash of energy will likely raise your lance
ready for the joust." He pointed toward what remained
of Vara. I got his point.

"Okay, so we'll know if it breaks. Now, when do we
notify the elflord that he's got visitors coming?"

"Might as well do it now while the air is hot." Parthet said. He had to be referring to different air from what I felt. The morning was decidedly chilly.

"I'll make the link," Aaron said. "I built in a short-cut the last time we talked to him." Parthet just nodded, and Aaron let off a short chant.

The elflord appeared on the battlements with us almost instantly.

"I was just about to call you," he said, taking one step in my direction.

13

On the Roof

"You know where I can find the Great Earth Mother?"
I asked.

"Yes." Xayber looked down at the map and then
around at my companions. "I gather that there is something else in the wind this morning, though."

"That's why we made the contact," I said. "That Dorthini wizard is about to intrude on your domain, with
about five hundred soldiers."

The elflord raised an eyebrow.

I smiled. Xayber didn't make me nearly as nervous as
he used to. "The Dorthini wizard thinks he is invading
Varay, probably to steal as much of our harvest as he can
grab for his outlaw band. But we're a little pressed at the
moment, so we diverted him. I thought you might enjoy
a little amusement." I shrugged. "This wizard sees only
a chance for his own aggrandizement and vengeance in
the current chaos, maybe a chance to take over much of
the buffer zone."

"Yet you managed to 'divert' him?" Xayber said. He
seemed to find a little amusement in the idea.

"The three of us in concert," Parthet said.

Xayber nodded as though he understood completely,
which was more than I could say for myself.

"I suppose we can arrange a proper reception for the
fellow. Give me a moment. I shall return." The elflord
vanished without fanfare.

Kardeen rolled up his map and left. He had plenty of
work waiting for him below. Our new arrivals would
likely keep him busy for ages . . . perhaps for as long as
the world would last.

"So far, so good," Aaron said softly. Parthet nodded. And then the elflord was back.

"My compliments on that bit of work," Xayber said. "Quite nicely turned—for outsiders."

I walked a few steps to the side and leaned back against one of the crenels. "What about the Great Earth Mother?"

"She *can* be found," Xayber said. He moved to sit down, and there was a chair under him when his butt got that far. "It is even possible that you are the one who can find her and do what must be done." He didn't sound as if he had any great confidence in that, though. Well, fair is fair. I didn't have much confidence myself.

"You can tell me how to reach her?"

"I can tell you where she is, where you'll have to go. The question is whether or not you can even manage to get there. She bears you a deep hate."

"I know."

"And there is the question of time." Xayber looked up at the cloudy sky. "There are five moons now."

"Where do I find her?" I asked.

"Her central temple," Xayber said. His voice got vague-sounding. "It is located beyond Fairy, in a place where nothing is constant, nothing reliable. I can't even call it a 'land' of a certainty. It is—a place that is strange beyond belief."

"By *your* standards?" Parthet asked. When the elflord nodded, Parthet seemed to blanch noticeably.

"How do I find this place?" I asked. The elflord seemed reluctant to get down to practical matters.

"Yes," he said. "I will give you what directions and advice I can, but there is something I would like from you first." He raised a hand quickly. "I do not speak of the return of my son at the moment. I merely wish to speak with the girl Annick, the hellhound. Merely talk."

I didn't see *why* he might want to talk to her, but I had no objections.

"Uncle Parthet, is she still at Curry?"

"She was last night. Sir Compil has proved to be a most capable guardian. Shall I fetch the lass?" I nodded.

"I'll go," Aaron said quickly. "If there's any difficulty, I can handle her easier."

"It'll take a few minutes," I told Xayber while Aaron hurried down the stairs. Xayber nodded.

"If you are to have any hope of reaching the Great Earth Mother in time, you'll have to start your ride from my estate here," Xayber said. "I can transport you through, along with my son." *Now* a reminder.

There wasn't much choice. Right into the parlor. I nodded.

"I did promise I would return your son," I said.

"Even leaving from here, there is no guarantee that you will have time enough, but you—we all—will have some chance."

"*We* all?" I asked.

Xayber smiled. "Some hope of a new world, a posterity of any sort, is the only hope any of us has in these latter days."

I felt the frown jump across my face and tried to remove it. Something didn't ring true about what he said. I couldn't pin it down at the moment. We were still dealing with the most nebulous of legends that *seemed* to be supported by the dire realities around us.

"And I gather that I need to start as soon as possible," I said.

"Immediately would not be too soon," Xayber said. The expression on his face was more one of extreme distaste than a frown. "And I am not one normally given to consider hours or days."

"Well, no matter, I'll need a couple of hours to get ready," I said. *At least!* I thought. "I have to assemble my supplies and make a few arrangements for while I'm gone."

Xayber shrugged. There was little more he could say. We both knew what we were up against, the price of my all-too-likely failure.

"Why is it so important for you to talk to Annick?" I asked when the silence became uncomfortable.

"There is a thing I must tell her." Xayber frowned clearly this time. Deep lines appeared on his forehead.

"A thing she should hear directly from me." He stood, his chair vanished, and he started pacing. I glanced at Parthet, but neither of us said anything.

At least we didn't have much longer to wait. We all heard footsteps hurrying up the stone stairs and looked that way. Aaron emerged from the stairwell holding Annick by the wrist. She pulled loose when she saw Xayber.

"You wanted to talk to me?" Annick asked, as defiant as ever. She moved slowly toward the elflord.

"I did," he replied. "Stand there a moment, if you would?" I think it was more the polite tone than the words that stopped her. Annick looked at the elflord, then around at the rest of us.

"Yes, it is so," Xayber said after a moment.

"*What* is so?" Annick asked.

"After our previous meeting here, I decided that I should learn the identity of your father. My suspicions have been confirmed." Xayber's face was a study in shifting emotions, everything from deep sorrow to strong pride. I couldn't tell which were prevailing.

"And?" Annick prompted. Her fists were clenched at her sides. The only emotion on her face was hate.

"Your father is dead," Xayber said, and I thought, Another lost father! That Annick had long been looking to arrange that fate for him didn't enter into my thoughts at the moment.

"Then who was he?" Annick demanded.

Sadness deepened on the elflord's face, an emotion that made him look almost human. "He was my son, slain in combat by the Hero of Varay."

Oops.

"That makes you my granddaughter," Xayber continued. "That means something to me."

It obviously meant something very different to Annick. She screamed—a painfully high screech like the death call of some mythical bird. Her entire body seemed to tighten up and enter into the scream. Blood vessels stood out on her forehead and temples and along the sides of her neck. She went up on tiptoe and sort of stretched toward the sky, almost as if she had been caught in some monstrous muscle spasm. But she kept her arms down, her fists pounding against her thighs in short, rapid movements, like a nervous tic gone mad.

The contortions she went through were fearful to watch. I was afraid that the convulsion might lead to a stroke, that she might drop dead on the spot.

After a moment, she screamed again. This time it was a tortured but recognizable *"No!"*

Xayber whispered, "Yes."

And then Annick collapsed. Her muscles all went limp and she pitched forward, crumpling as she fell. Aaron had been standing at least eight feet away, but he managed to catch her before her head could smash into the stone. He lifted her easily. The stark white of her half-elven skin contrasted strongly with Aaron's deep black . . . and almost perfectly matched the narrow streak of white left from the face of Wellivazey.

Her dead father.

"She's just fainted," Aaron said. "She's breathing easily. I'll take her downstairs."

I nodded, even though Aaron wasn't paying attention to anyone but Annick. He was staring at her face. Xayber took a couple of steps toward them. I was surprised to see real concern on his face. He started to speak but didn't. Aaron carried Annick toward the stairs.

"I'd better get downstairs and start getting things ready for your quest," Parthet said.

Always the quest, I thought. It was becoming a four-letter word to me.

"Parthet," I said. He stopped and looked at me, his face troubled. "This time, I *will* be going alone."

"There is no other way," Xayber said, but without any force. He was still staring at the stairs and the disappearing forms of Aaron and Annick.

"Alone?" Parthet asked.

"Alone," I repeated, as firmly as I could without raising my voice. Parthet nodded and left. I turned to the elflord again.

"Annick is your granddaughter?" I asked after the

sound of footsteps on the stairs faded. "And that changes how you think of her?"

His nod covered both questions. "She is my blood," he said.

And knowing that might screw up Annick's mind worse than it already was. This time, when I wondered about psychiatrists among our refugees, I wasn't making a joke.

Xayber and I didn't have much more to say at the moment. He continued to be distracted, obviously troubled by Annick's reaction to his announcement. I wondered at that, and at the importance the elford placed on family ties—even a tie that resulted from a rape his son had committed.

"I'll get ready for the trip as quickly as I can," I told him. "I'll have Aaron give you a shout when I'm packed and ready."

He nodded. Rather disjointedly, he told me that he would transport me, my horse, and his son to his estate at the northern end of the isthmus, give me such detailed directions and advice as he could, and see me "safely" out of his territory.

"And there," he added, "all safety ends."

Then I had to go downstairs to tell Joy that I would be leaving in a matter of hours, less than a day after getting back from my last jaunt.

She was with her mother, in the room above Parthet's workshop.

"You're looking much better this morning, Mrs. Bennett," I said when I went in. Rosemary was sitting up on the side of the bed. She still looked frail, but a lot more alive than she had the night before.

"I feel better," she said with a listless shrug. She closed her eyes for a second. "Joy and I have been talking." She stopped again for a moment. "If we had listened to her before . . ."

"I understand," I said. "I know it's hard, but try not to dwell on it. You're here now. Danny and his family are here. Joy and I are here. That's something to hold to. I know that Varay is strange, but you'll get used to it. I promise."

"She says that the radiation sickness is gone," Rosemary said.

"Completely gone," I agreed. "Once we get you fed up, you'll be good as new. That's part of the magic of the place."

"Magic." Rosemary reacted to that word the way I was beginning to react to "quest." "I never believed in magic," she said.

"I didn't either, until I got dumped in the middle of it," I told her. I turned to Joy then. "We have to talk for a few minutes."

Joy nodded, but her eyes told me that she had a fair idea what we had to talk about.

"Danny and Julia will be right back, Mom," Joy said. "This may take more than a few minutes."

"Go on, children. I'll be all right." She did manage a sort of smile for us. "I've got a lot to keep my mind busy."

"You're leaving again already, aren't you?" Joy said as soon as we left the room.

"Just as fast as I can get packed and ready," I said. "Maybe two hours or so. I don't dare wait much longer than that."

Joy wrapped her arms around me. "This is the big one, right? The one that determines whether there are any tomorrows left?"

"The final quest," I said. If I failed, there wouldn't be anything for anyone to quest after. If I somehow managed to succeed . . . I planned to retire from the Hero racket. King Gil. That's senior management, time to find somebody else to do the harebrained, dangerous stuff.

We started to walk down toward the great hall together. I had to make sure that the preparations were well in hand before I did anything else. It *is* wonderful to have reliable staff. Kardeen came up and started listing the things that were being packed for me to take along. I would ride Electrum and lead a packhorse. Since there was no way to know how long I might be gone, and considerable question as to whether I would be able to find any victuals in a region that was weird by even the loose standards of Fairy, I had to figure on toting along a lot of provender.

"Are you sure you must go alone this time?" Kardeen asked—an obligatory question, I suppose, one that Parthet probably put him up to.

"Absolutely certain," I told him.

A few minutes later, Lesh asked the same question in the great hall and I gave him the same answer. "I have something more important for you to do this time, Lesh," I added. "While I'm gone, I've got just one duty for you. Take care of my family for me—all of them."

"Aye, sire," Lesh said.

"Joy will make sure that all her relatives know you're looking out for them. And Baron Kardeen will make sure you get any help you need. We'll leave Harkane to continue caring for Cayenne, though you might check in on him from time to time to make sure everything is okay there."

"We'll manage, won't we, Lesh?" Joy said.

He grinned at her. "Aye, my lady, we will at that, I suppose."

"We're going up to our apartment now," Joy said. That was news to me, but no real surprise. "We're not to be disturbed for anything."

"I'll make sure of it," Lesh said.

And then, as quickly as we could reach it, Joy and I were alone in the huge bedroom we had inherited from my predecessor and great-grandfather. And the huge bed. There was so much to say that we didn't speak at all for quite a time. We got undressed, slowly, wasting minutes. Soft caresses, tender kisses, and an occasional stray tear that was blinked away quickly. I was getting ready to leave Joy on a mission to find and have sex with another female—who might not, technically speaking, be even remotely human. That was something that Joy and I couldn't even begin to discuss. At the moment, it really didn't matter. It was part of some very iffy possible future, something too unreal to come between us.

We more or less rolled to the center of the huge bed,

pressed together, both conscious of every second we were spending in what might be our final time together—a slightly out-of-focus long shot with petroleum jelly smeared on the camera lens to give it the proper dreamy appearance; soft music in the background, becoming slightly louder as we caught fire and hurried on to the climax. In the movies, it would be fade to black—or cut directly to a different scene with a different pacing.

We weren't on film, though.

Stolen breath. A moment of panting while we recovered—still holding each other, still clasping, clinging. Sweat and flushed faces. A few more tears, hidden from each other because we had our cheeks together.

"Come back to me," Joy whispered after a too-short eternity.

"I will." The promise hurt because I didn't know if it would be possible, and this time, I was almost certain that it wouldn't be. Even if I succeeded in reaching the Great Earth Mother and putting to work what remained of Vara, I didn't know what there would be afterward. And I *did* know how lonely any new world would be without Joy.

"I will," I repeated. "I love you, Joy, more than anything else, ever."

I was glad that she couldn't see my tears. I rolled us a little more to the side so my tears wouldn't drip on her neck and face and betray me.

"They'll all be waiting for you downstairs," Joy said finally. "They *must* know what we're doing up here." A sudden touch of embarrassment warmed her face.

I laughed softly. "If they do, then they'll be damn sure not to interrupt us before we're ready." But time was passing. We disengaged, with more slow kissing and whispered tendernesses that almost delayed us further. There was only time for me to hurry through a quick, and cold, bath. I didn't have a tank installed to provide hot water at Basil yet.

Joy pulled on her clothes quickly, then helped me to dress in all the crud that questing requires—weapons, armor, heavy boots and trousers, all the way up to my swords and lucky Cubs cap. Going into Fairy and beyond, I wasn't even going to bother carrying a gun. There wasn't a chance in a million that one would work in the farther reaches.

We walked down to the great hall with our arms around each other—but carefully, because of all the hardware hanging off of me.

"Everything's ready for you, sire," Lesh said. "The horses are in the courtyard, and the cooks have put together a hot meal for you before you start."

"Thanks, Lesh," I said. No matter what, find time to squeeze in a banquet. It's not show in the buffer zone. It's the calories that power the whole setup.

After the more than three and a half years since my arrival in the buffer zone, I was used to cramming in food at an alarming rate. And washing it down with quarts of beer and wine and coffee. Nobody passes up a chance for a meal.

But, all too soon, it was time to go out to the horses. The head and body of Wellivazey were on a stretcher. Electrum was saddled. My packhorse was loaded.

"Whenever you're ready," Aaron said. I nodded, and he did the quick chant to contact the elflord.

This time, we saw him as a large face in the sky, like an image projected against the clouds, the way Parthet and I had seen him following the Battle of Thyme. Aaron, Joy, and the rest of *my* people backed away, leaving a large clear space around me.

"Anytime," I said, conversationally. And Castle Basil disappeared from around me.

14

The Three Mirrors

It would look like a simple optical effect on the screen, a jump cut from me sitting on my horse in the courtyard of Castle Basil to a similar shot of me sitting on my horse in the courtyard of the elflord's manor, with the packhorse on my left and the stretcher with the remains of Wellivazey on my right. There is no change in that foreground tableau, just the change in setting, in background.

I had no sensation of movement. This transition was even simpler than stepping through one of the magic doorways, and I was so accustomed to those that I rarely thought of them as magic any longer. But the motionless jump from Basil to northern Xayber left me dizzy and disoriented for a moment.

It had been late morning at Basil, ten, maybe closer to eleven o'clock, and the sky had been thickly overcast. I reached the elflord's estate at the northern end of the Isthmus of Xayber on a crystal-clear night. The stars were sharp specks in the sky, the five crescent moons a chilly reminder of the way that time was running out.

Even that shouldn't have shaken me up the way it did. There was a time difference of about three hours between Varay and Louisville or Chicago. The change involved in that move had never really disrupted me, not even the first time. There were enough other weirdnesses to distract me that first time through one of the magic doorways.

But this shift *did* bother me, in ways that I could hardly explain. There was a tingling of my Hero's danger sense, but not the all-out alarm that signals imminent deadly peril. I sat still on Electrum, my knees squeezed tightly against my horse's flanks, while I waited for the dizziness to pass. The night air was quite cold. I could see my breath, and the breath of both horses. The cold actually helped, I think. It jogged my mind with familiar sensations, let me concentrate on those until the discomfort passed.

When my head quit spinning and I was able to think of things beyond the boundary of my skin, I noted that I was just in front of a wide staircase leading up to what had to be the main entrance to a huge manor house—or palace, if you like fancier terms. I was on a circular drive about the size of the racetrack at Arlington Park. The house looked to be at least five stories high, well over two hundred feet long, with wings projected toward the front at both ends.

I dismounted just as the front door of the house opened and a flood of light jumped out to repel the darkness.

The elflord led the way. He had a crowd of retainers with him. Only a few showed any weapons, and none of the blades I saw were being brandished. My training, and the paranoia that the elflord induced, led me to notice things like that. The servants—or slaves, whichever they were—were mainly human, though I did spot a couple of the vaguely porcine faces of troll-kind. But Xayber was definitely the only elf in evidence. Most of the servants carried lights, torches that burned as bright as halogen headlights, but without smoke. Those servants who came out of the house empty-handed went to the stretcher that held Wellivazey, the son of the elflord . . . and the father of Annick.

"You might as well come inside and be comfortable for a while, while you may," the elflord said in neutral tones. "Dawn is yet a time away, and we have much to do before it comes."

I nodded. I didn't want to speak for fear that my teeth would chatter from the unexpected nip in the unexpected night.

Xayber turned from me to look down at his son. He touched a pale cheek, then grasped his son's shoulder.

The elflord stood motionless for a long moment before he gestured toward his waiting servants.

"Take him inside and have him prepared for the vigil."

Those servants led the way toward the door, flanked by others with the torches. Xayber turned to me and gestured after them, while a final two servants took the reins of my horses.

"You bested him in single combat when he had every conceivable advantage, a costly miscalculation on our part," Xayber said. It wasn't an apology, but I hoped I was right in reading the statement as a "let bygones be bygones" sort of truce.

"In some ways, your son and I were not so different," I said, choosing my words with exceptional care and making all sorts of mental reservations. "Both of us doing what we saw as our duty. This may sound banal, but there have been times when I wished that we had known each other before he died as well as we did after."

We stopped at the top of the stairs, on a porch or patio that was long enough to hold a half-dozen shuffleboard courts end to end.

Quite seriously, Xayber said, "I thank you for that."

The ultrapolite, almost warm, welcome from the elflord made me more nervous than open hostility could possibly have.

I'm not sure what I expected from the elflord's mansion—something exotic, no doubt, with sparkling lights, invisible servants, rooms perhaps marked by indefinite and shifting boundaries and optical illusions, something ostentatiously magical. The reality was considerable more mundane—lavish, luxurious, but endlessly mundane—with no more obvious feeling of magic about it than the great hall of Castle Basil. I had no real chance to fully gauge the size of the place, inside or out, but it *had* to compare with some of the largest "stately" homes of England. The first room inside the front door was almost large enough to hold my parents' Louisville house, garage, chimney, and all.

The elflord's son had already been taken beyond that room. I didn't know where. The elflord and I went off to the left, to a relatively small room, one that was only about forty feet square. The chandeliers and candelabra made the room as bright as day. The walls held paintings and plaques. There were statues standing in the corners.

"Please sit," Xayber said, pointing me at a very comfortable-looking chair by a large fireplace—everything about the place was large, including the chair. It was built for someone a couple of feet taller than me. But I managed. I slipped off the rigs for my elf swords and sat, holding the weapons across my legs. My feet barely reached the floor.

Xayber took a similar chair a few feet away and angled toward mine. The only weapon he showed was a long dagger with a jeweled hilt, more or less the equivalent of the monogrammed breast-pocket handkerchief in parts beyond the world I was born in.

The heat from the fireplace was welcome.

"There's really no point in setting out before dawn, unless you've learned to see like an elf," Xayber said after a silence that must have lasted all of five minutes.

I shook my head. "That magic is not mine."

"Some wine?" Xayber gestured, and a servant entered the room immediately, carrying a gold tray with wine in a fancy crystal carafe and two matching goblets.

There was no question of me refusing wine, or anything else. If Xayber intended harm, he had no need of subterfuge.

"Where do I head from here?" I asked after I had sampled the wine—sweet, but not too bad. Actually, it was probably a top vintage for its type; I'm just not crazy about sweet wines. I'd prefer a decent beer any time.

"Due north, from anywhere," Xayber said.

"You mean it's at the north pole?"

"Not precisely, but if you were following a compass, you would need to follow it north, even from the north pole."

Right, that doesn't make sense, but it was no more impossible than a lot of other things that I had encountered in Fairy and the buffer zone. I accepted Xayber's statement as the literal truth.

"What am I likely to meet along the way?"

"Anything you could possibly imagine, and much that you couldn't." He gave me a self-conscious smile. "I'm sorry. I really can't be more specific than that. It is simply not possible. You know some of the dangers of Fairy." That was, I assumed, an oblique reference to my earlier foray along the Isthmus of Xayber. "The deeper into our territory you go, the more common are the hazards, especially to outsiders. The hazards are stronger and stranger. In the lands beyond Fairy, even that is no sure guide. You will likely face hazards that no one has ever seen before, that may not have existed before your arrival. That is the nature of the region, if it can be said to have a nature . . . if it can even rightly be called a region." He paused and lifted his wineglass in my direction.

"And you have the added handicap of the recent and intense hatred of the Great Earth Mother."

"You don't think I can even reach her, let alone do what I have to do then," I said. I didn't bother to make it a question.

"No, but you are the only chance." He stared at me for a moment, then closed his eyes and stared some more. I had no doubt that he was still looking at me, still seeing *something*.

"But then," he said after another long silence, "I imagine that it had to be like this when the time came. Your people have some legend about a Golden Age returning. A Golden Age *you* were supposed to initiate simply by being both King and Hero of Varay." I nodded when he hesitated. "Perhaps some garbling of the truth is necessary over so many generations of mortals."

"You mean that instead of just bringing back the Golden Age of Vara, reuniting the titles had to bring back the chaos that he ended?" I asked.

"That is certainly how it has worked out, anyway," Xayber said.

It was as I had guessed, but having my fear confirmed didn't make me feel any better. Talk about your monumental screwups. Like that party game where the host or hostess whispers a story to one guest and the tale has to pass through everyone at the party and the final result is compared with the original story. At a party, the evolution of a simple story into something that bears little if any resemblance to the original is a gas. Translated to reality on this kind of scale, it loomed as the ultimate tragedy.

"Then, along with everything else, the only way to get to this new Golden Age is for me to manage what Vara did, despite the difficulties."

"My memory may be failing me, but I do seem to see some resemblance to Vara in you. Perhaps, despite everything my mind tells me, you do have some chance."

"You remember Vara?"

"The memories fade in time, or they would not be bearable," Xayber said, closing his eyes again. "Vara, or the one before him." He shrugged and opened his eyes to stare at me again. "This is not the first universe that has ended."

"And you have survived the chaos before?"

"What do the legends of Varay say of the time before time?"

"That the Great Earth Mother roamed the void until she found a mate she considered suitable. There is nothing about what she was roaming on or where the mate came from if there was nothing around before."

"You see the gaps then," Xayber said, and I nodded.

"But if nothing comes after the dissolution this time, no one will survive, not even the Great Earth Mother, in the long run."

It was Xayber's turn to nod.

"Yet you think she'll kill the only chance for a continuation?"

"Why should she worry about continuation?" Xayber asked. "An end is only an end, not the bleakest of prospects for one whose memories go back too far."

I understood less about the elflord with every sentence he uttered. This was the man (or whatever he was in essence) who had tried so diligently to kill me? Who had sent his son to kill me after he failed to do it directly?

Who had made a career of trying to conquer Varay? He was starting to sound a little like Uncle Parthet.

"You should eat before you leave," the elflord said, an invitation that didn't particularly surprise me. "My servants will have a meal prepared and waiting for us now."

We both stood. I carried my sword rigs in my left hand. Xayber led the way to a dining room that could have fed the entire population of a large university dormitory. The table was a good thirty *yards* long, without exaggeration. The sides were lined with chairs, but only two places had been set, together, at one end of the table. As we entered through one doorway, a stream of servants entered from another over to our left.

This meal was even more of a feast than a meal at Castle Basil. Since we were deep in Fairy, a land even more bound up in magic than the buffer zone, the caloric demands made on residents were even greater. There was a wide variety of food, and to be honest, most of it tasted better than the best fare served in Varay. The plates were something even finer than the finest china I had come across in my world, delicate, almost translucent. The silverware was real silver, the goblets crystal and gold with decorations of rubies, emeralds, and diamonds. I doubted that any of it was fake.

Xayber kept me company, talking enough to prevent any long silences, yet he still managed to eat more than I packed away. I did myself proud, though, cramming in the equivalent of three or four Thanksgiving dinners, even though I had eaten a full meal just before leaving Castle Basil, and an equally full breakfast just a few hours before that. Back in the real world, that kind of gluttony could have proved quickly fatal. In Fairy, it scarcely gave me a bloated feeling.

"It is nearly dawn," Xayber said as the meal wound down. I was still eating, but just forcing the food in now, a small cache against days of light rations to come. I nodded. There were no windows in the dining room, and the elflord certainly hadn't consulted a watch or clock, but I didn't doubt what he said.

"I should leave as quickly as possible," I said.

He nodded. "I have been thinking. Before you leave, there is one thing that may give us both some idea of your chances for success."

"That sounds like it might be a dangerous thing to know," I said.

He watched my face for a moment before he said, "If you would rather not know?"

I paused before I answered this time also. "There's a saying back in my old world, 'Where ignorance is bliss, 'tis folly to be wise.' But I don't think that I could possibly have lower expectations than I do now. I have no objections, if it's something *you* want to know."

"You turn my question back on me," Xayber said, sounding surprised, as if no one had ever done that to him before. "Very well. I can see now why my son chose to help you." I took that as a compliment. I'm not certain why. "We shall put it to the test then."

"What kind of test?" I asked, suddenly feeling a stab of caution.

"Merely to gaze upon yourself in a mirror."

Despite my nervousness, I had to fight back the impulse to crack a joke about that being hazardous enough without magic.

"Where is this mirror?" I asked. Maybe I was looking for an out. Even without knowing exactly what Xayber expected me to see, I was working up a real fear about it.

"Here in the house. Not too long a walk."

I stood up and moved away from the table to hook up my sword rigs. That was easier than continuing to carry two six-foot swords around. "Then we might as well get it done so I can make my start."

"Yes. There is a need for some haste now that light approaches."

The elflord's idea of a short walk turned out to be a little different from my own. This one turned out to be something like playing three holes of golf. He kept his strides short enough to avoid making me run to keep up with him, but we didn't dally. We left the dining hall and went along a corridor, then up a grand staircase past the second floor to the third, headed down another corridor that was even longer than the one below, turned, then went up another staircase—a tight circular staircase that seemed designed to snag my swords every other step—into a small room with windows on two adjacent walls.

"The mirror," Xayber said with a gesture toward the corner of the two walls without windows.

Mirrors. Plural. It looked like a deluxe version of one of those three-panel mirrors that they have in clothing stores, front view flanked by two angled mirrors to let you see more of the garment you're trying on.

I stepped in front of the mirrors, and the elflord started doing a little chanting of the conjuring sort. It was a fairly long chant, but I could tell that something was happening almost from the start of the spell. The mirrors fogged over, or *under,* since the fog seemed to be within the mirror, not on the glass.

The panel on the right cleared first. I focused on that panel and saw myself. There was nothing at all unusual about the image. It was just me, the way I would expect to see myself in any mirror—all decked out in my questing garb.

When the panel on the *left* cleared, I almost jumped. It wasn't me in the mirror, though the image duplicated my moves perfectly—like the Marx Brothers' mirror sequence in *Duck Soup.* The face *looked* familiar, somewhat, enough to start me glancing back and forth between that image and my own face in the panel on the right.

"Who?" I asked, though I already suspected the answer.

The elflord didn't confirm my guess directly. He continued to chant, and then the center panel started to clear, and *it* showed a double exposure, me and this other person.

"Almost a perfect match," the elflord said softly. "He was considerably taller and heavier, but still . . . it appears that you *are* Vara's true heir."

"This other guy here. That's Vara?"

"It is," the elflord said. "Vara as I remember him."

Not *quite* the figure I had seen in my dreams of the Congregation of Heroes, but not totally different either.

"The Great Earth Mother thought that I was him for a moment, after I got the second ball," I told Xayber, thinking about the confrontation with her apparition in the shrine out in the Mist.

"Perhaps you do have a chance," Xayber said, but still without any real confidence in his voice. All three images faded from the mirrors, leaving panels that showed the room behind me but didn't show me.

"There is only one more piece of advice I can give you for this quest," Xayber said. "When you get beyond Fairy into the nebulous regions beyond, if a time comes when reality seems to flee completely and you can find no other anchor to hang on to, reach down with both hands, grab what you have of Vara's, and hold on with all your might. Your rings on the jewels may help you win through the moment."

Yeah, what a fine public pose *that* would be for a Hero.

15

North

The sun was resting on the horizon when I caught a glimpse of the dirty red ball out a window while the elflord was leading me from the room with the mirrors down to the front courtyard. Most of the courtyard was still in shadow. The eastern wing of the manor hid the sun. The morning felt even chillier than the night had been. I didn't see any frost or ice on the ground, but it wouldn't have surprised me.

"You will need two solid days of riding to clear my demesne," Xayber said after I mounted Electrum. "You should be relatively safe until then. All of my subjects know that you travel with my countenance, and there are no outsiders within my borders." He shrugged. "In these times, *that* is subject to change. Your danger sense will have to guide you."

"And after I leave your lands?" I asked.

"There *is* no safety beyond." He said that so flatly that I shivered. I tried to blame that on the cold but knew better.

"Any idea how long this trek will take me?"

"Till the end of time," Xayber said. He sure had a way with words. Much more of that kind of talk and I would have headed south.

"Then I had better get started," I said.

Xayber nodded and pointed north. I started riding. Before I could go north, though, I had to go around the house, and a series of linked outbuildings.

Riding alone over long distances can do strange things to the mind. I learned that on the ride north from the elflord's. It's a special kind of solitude. You talk to yourself. You talk to your horse. You retreat inside yourself, viewing the world around you as out of a bubble, like the Starchild at the end of *2001: A Space Odyssey.* You register your surroundings, after a fashion, but seldom recall details—only of the most extraordinary moments, especially when danger seems particularly close. There is more the constant feeling of the saddle against your butt, jarring and chafing; the cramps in your fingers from holding the reins, even loosely; the smell of sweat, the horse's and your own, even in cool air.

I had been riding Electrum for more than two years, if not exclusively. I knew how strong he was, had some idea of his endurance, though I had never ridden him as hard as I would have to on this trek. At six years of age, Electrum was in his prime. He gave what I asked, and took what I offered. He knew his job. And he knew when it was time to stop for a break.

Altogether, we managed about fifteen hours of riding that first day, from shortly after dawn until long past dusk. Five moons, even in the first quarter, provide considerable light on a clear night, enough to cast strong shadows, enough to let a rider pick out a path with considerable confidence.

When we finally stopped to camp for the night, I unsaddled Electrum and lightened the load on Geezer, my packhorse. I rubbed both animals down with a worn scrap of blanket, found them grass to graze on, and made sure they had water while a small fire heated my supper and a pot of water. I had hot chocolate instead of coffee for the evening.

The campsite was a small clearing bounded on three sides by brambles that would keep the horses from wandering. I strung two lengths of rope across the open side and tied the horses to a picket line, double insurance to keep them from wandering off during the night.

We had ridden through mostly civilized countryside all day, past small villages, through fields that had been harvested many weeks before. No one had challenged us.

The few peasants we saw had seemed anxious to avoid close contact.

We, us. One day on the road and I was already thinking of me and my horses as *we.* Maybe it was just because I was so used to having other people around. Back in Varay, even in the other world, I usually had to make a special effort to get time alone, do things like go down into the burial crypt at Basil to get completely away from people.

"We did good today," I told the horses when I checked on them before I bedded myself down for the night.

I crawled into my small domed tent, rolled two thermal blankets around me, and slept—no dreams, no alarms. There was simply a blank between closing my eyes and opening them again in the morning, the way sleep should be but so rarely is for me.

When I woke, just before sunrise, there was a thick layer of frost on the ground outside my tent. I used a can of Sterno to get a fire going to heat my breakfast and more water—this time for instant coffee. I needed a caffeine fix to start me off. I was stiff and sore. Hurrying through the morning routine to get into the saddle as quickly as possible seemed the best remedy.

The second day and night passed about the same as the first. We crossed out of Xayber's lands about an hour before sunset. I knew exactly when we passed his border. My danger sense shifted to a fast idle. His people had been instructed to let me pass. He had no control over anyone beyond this boundary. I reined in Electrum and toyed with the idea of camping again on Xayber's land, putting off the threat of other elflords until the morning of a full day, but I decided to press on that evening as long as we could.

Time. I couldn't afford the luxury of wasting riding time for one last night of comparative safety. By the time I finally stopped to camp, we had traveled about ten miles beyond Xayber's lands.

I didn't sleep as soundly that night, but it passed without incident and we got an early start the following morning.

The heart of Fairy was a lot different from the portions of the Isthmus of Xayber that I had seen during my first foray into the land of the alleged immortals. The isthmus was wild territory, populated mostly by various beasties and wild trolls, patrolled by the armies of the Elflord of Xayber. There had been the swamps and mangled forest, tangled and dripping with danger. But that was all marcher territory, Fairy's buffer against the buffer zone, like the minefields on the East Berlin side of the Berlin Wall . . . before the Wall came tumbling down. Deeper inside the territory of the elflords—Xayber and whoever owned the land that I entered after I left Xayber's demesne—the land looked tamer, little different from land in the seven kingdoms. There were regular roads, fields that had been harvested for food and fodder, vast park-like tracts, and stands of wood that looked as if they were regularly tended and manicured. The place was just dripping in folksy scenes that wouldn't have been out of place in a Currier and Ives print.

Wagons loaded with produce moved from village to village, or on to some manor house or castle that I never got close enough to see. The people running the wagons gave me nervous looks—which I imagine I returned fully—but no one challenged me or set my danger sense into convulsions. The two elf swords slung over my shoulders would have stopped any of the common folk from setting at me. Even small bands of soldiers, had I chanced on any, might have been daunted by such evidence of martial prowess . . . unless they were led by an elf warrior.

Despite Xayber's warnings of constant danger once I left his lands, I didn't have any trouble at all during the first week after I crossed that border. I rode with the sun over my right shoulder in the morning, directly behind me at noon, and over my left shoulder in the afternoon. Past sunset each night, I rode by the light of five silvery moons until I was too tired to go on any longer. The nights got colder, the days started to remain quite chilly. But the skies remained perfectly clear. There was no rain or snow.

Even the cold got boring.

My one-sided conversations started to repeat themselves. Memories came and went, and came again, until it seemed that I had reviewed my entire life in more detail than I really wanted. I sang old songs just to break the silence. At times I felt like standing in my stirrups and screaming for *somebody* to do *something,* just to break the monotony.

I wasted a lot of time wondering how much time had passed back in Varay. Nine days in the heart of Fairy might translate to more than three weeks back at Castle Basil, perhaps considerably more. Aaron and Parthet would be examining every bit of news and rumor for new hints of the speed of the general dissolution. Kardeen would have surveyors marking how much the Titans had shrunk since the last measurement. Cooks would continue to crack open eggs with trepidation, wondering if the next one—or the one after that—would hold a tiny dragon. Joy would be worrying. By now, she probably had her fingernails chewed halfway to her knuckles.

And all I could do was keep riding north, pushing Electrum and Geezer as hard as I could without driving them into the ground, not having the slightest idea just how long a ride we might have. At least Geezer's load decreased a little with each passing day.

There were no maps of the farther reaches of Fairy back in Varay. I didn't even know whose land I was trespassing on after I left Xayber's demesne. But none of the other elflords seemed disposed to block my progress. There were no questing presences seeking to identify the interloper.

It was just a matter of time before the Great Earth Mother took note of me, though. I knew that with a surety that didn't require the occasional tweet of my danger sense.

Ten days out from Xayber's land, I reached the end of the civilized regions of Fairy—for all practical purposes, perhaps the end of Fairy itself. I couldn't be sure exactly what the border meant—Xayber's explanation hadn't been

as clear as it might have been—but the demarcation line
itself was as clear as a brick wall. A slightly rolling
meadow came to an abrupt end at a thin creek. Beyond
the trickle of water there was a tight tangle of gnarled
and thorny trees, something like crabapple gone berserk.
The road I had been following extended right to the edge
of the creek. Beyond, there was only a very narrow trail
that immediately started bending back and forth, making
it impossible to see more than a few horse lengths ahead.

I reined to a halt on the Fairy side of the creek.

"This is it, kids," I said, not the first time I had ad-
dressed my horses that way. It had been a *long* ride already. "We might as well stop for a good lunch and a
short rest before we cross."

Electrum whinnied as if he understood what I was saying.

Caution suggested that we get back a safe distance from
that tangle of trees first, though. Even though the leaves
had fallen, an archer in good camouflage gear could get
almost down to the creek to launch an arrow without
showing himself, if he was careful. I dismounted and led
Electrum and Geezer back two hundred yards from the
water. No archer I had ever come across could get an
arrow that far over level ground, certainly not with
enough force to do any damage.

While I ate, I stared at the wild forest across the water.
My danger sense kicked up anytime I looked *away* from
it, as if warning me not to turn my back on the hazard.
I got the message. There are different levels of danger,
levels of unknowns. Once we crossed that creek, we
would be in territory that even the Elflord of Xayber
found fearful, a land that he said got stranger and stranger
the farther you penetrated into it.

The challenges would start once we got inside the forest. I tried to imagine possibilities, but the elflord had
warned me that my imagination wasn't equal to that task.
That didn't stop the musing, of course. I ate. The horses
grazed. When we got back to the creek, I let them drink
for a few minutes before I mounted Electrum and led
Geezer across the boundary.

The trees got taller, thicker, more coarsely tangled. It didn't matter that the leaves had fallen off most of them. There were enough trunks and branches to obscure the view.

The elflord was right about my imagination. I couldn't have foreseen the first challenge if I had spent a lifetime pondering the possibilities. And it came not an hour after we crossed the creek.

The trail started out narrow, and it didn't get any wider. The thorny trees pressed so close on either side that I had to give Geezer extra rein so he could follow directly behind Electrum. The path wasn't wide enough for the horses to walk side by side. At times the trail seemed too narrow for even *one* horse. My knees and thighs got stuck a number of times. The thorns reached right out to prick me whenever they could—or so it seemed.

It was damn slow riding. I had to keep looking back to make sure that the line to Geezer didn't get tangled in the trees when the path jigged right or left—every couple of minutes. And I had to keep looking ahead because my danger sense wouldn't let up. I could trust Electrum to pick his way along the path, but there might be other threats. Holding a compass heading was impossible. I hoped that the briar patch wouldn't go on forever.

Still, the thorns were only a nuisance, even though some of them were more than four inches long. The danger came when we reached the first clearing.

Twelve (count 'em folks, *twelve*) naked women were standing in a short arc near the far side of the clearing. Call it a sampler of feminine pulchritude: complexions ranging from the pure white of elvish skin to a deep swarthiness (but no blacks); hair colors from white-blond through red to chestnut and a deep black that was almost the blue of Superman's hair in the comics; figures stretching from the barely nubile budding of adolescence to one woman with the most exaggerated dimensions I could imagine. And no matter the size, all of the breasts were firm and jutting, like the best that plastic surgery and the photographer's airbrush could manage in tandem. The smiles of the ladies seemed right out of the finals of

any major beauty pageant. Their skin was uniformly perfect, their hair fit for Madison Avenue. Twelve beauties—
any one of them was enough to raise an erection on a
dead man. And I wasn't dead.

I reined in Electrum while my danger sense went into
extra innings, banging my head back and forth like the
clapper on a church bell on Easter morning.

Maybe I was a card-carrying Hero, but I wasn't stupid.
Even if it hadn't been for the location and the forty-degree
temperature, I would have guessed that there was something rotten about this presentation. I also knew that the
safe course was to turn around and head back to the creek
and find another route before I found myself up that creek
without the proverbial paddle.

But I couldn't waste that much time, not when I could
expect *any* route north to be defended against me. I
clucked softly and Electrum moved a few steps forward.
Then he stopped again. He's a smart horse.

"Ladies," I said. It came out a little cracked, so I
cleared my throat. " 'Had we but world enough and time,
This coyness' . . ." I stopped. The ladies had started
walking slowly toward me, strutting, parading their, ah,
virtues. They didn't seem interested in my weak attempt
at humor. That's always my luck.

"Welcome, stranger," one in the middle—a fair ringer
for a young Ann-Margret—said. She spread her arms in
a welcoming gesture that invited me to leap right off my
horse and onto her. "We're looking for a Hero to keep
us warm and satisfied."

Sure, every day.

"Too cold," I said. "It'd freeze right off." I was sitting balanced for combat, ready to reach for both swords,
through I kept my movements casual. I tied the lead for
Geezer to the pommel of my saddle and looped Electrum's reins loosely over them. Those twelve naked
women scared the crap out of me, even though I could
damn well see that they weren't concealing any weapons.

"We won't let you freeze," the big mama with the
most exaggerated figure said at the end of the line. Call

the measurements 48D, 28, 42, all firm and jutting. Unreal.

"I took a vow," I said. The only exit from the clearing, other than the one behind me, was over on the other side. I would have to ride straight through the middle of the line of chippies. The defensive line of the Chicago Bears couldn't have looked so intimidating.

"We took a vow too," the one in the middle who had spoken before said. "If you don't do each of us, we'll do you—for supper."

"Eat 'im up, eat 'im up," a number of the others chanted. Their smiles turned to grins. Their toothpaste-ad teeth turned to fangs of the carnivorous sort. They weren't talking about oral sex.

I dug my heels into Electrum and reached for my elf swords at the same time. In just a second, the harmonizing battle tunes of my swords drowned out the dinner chant of the women. The swords didn't seem to intimidate them. The line charged at me. The closest ones leaped for me, arms spread, fangs showing. I probably imagined the sounds of stomachs rumbling in hunger.

My swords were hungrier, and faster. They took off two lovely heads quickly, then bit into more beautiful flesh before Electrum beat a hole through the center of the line. It's a good thing there were no newspapers or electronic media around, even better that the Great Earth Mother didn't have one of the many students of Dr. Goebbels on the payroll. I could see the headlines on the tabloids: MAD SLASHER GOES ON RAMPAGE DURING GIRLS' SCHOOL OUTING. The reality was jarring enough.

The fight took only a few seconds, but I didn't get away scot-free. By the time the last of the women fell wounded or dropped behind, I had dozens of deep scratches. Some of the women had claws that would do a Bengal tiger proud. One even slashed through the thick leather that cushioned my chain mail.

The thorns that encroached on the path didn't seem nearly so bad as I raced to escape the horny and hungry vixens. I kept looking back to see if any of the women had managed to hitch a ride on Geezer or if they were following me. My vision got blurred, and it took me a moment to realize that it was because I was crying. And it took even longer for me to discover that all those naked women had done more than just arouse me. They had pulled the trigger as well.

I still hadn't fully recovered my breath or my poise from that incident—I was still pounding along, and so was my heart—when Wrigley Field dropped out of the sky, the lights flashing on and off, flags showing a wind blowing out toward right field. Wrigley Field, home of the Cubs. Wouldn't you know it: they finally put in lights for night baseball and just about the time people are beginning to forget that they weren't always there, World War Three erupts. In a way, that figured. The same thing might have happened if they had won a World Series.

But it was only the stadium that dropped, not the playing field itself. That would have put an early end to my quest. I was crossing where second base should have been, heading in the direction of the visitors' bullpen. The force of the crash when the stadium hit the forest split the stands and I was able to ride straight through, though not with the aplomb that a Hero might be expected to show. Geezer needed some calming, but Electrum was rock-solid. He had faced dragons and didn't know anything about baseball.

Once we cleared the cracked stadium, we continued to follow the path through the thorny trees. Wrigley Field really gave me something to think about. First off, there was the matter of how it got out of Chicago intact through a nuclear war. Secondly, how did anyone know to drop *that* particular stadium on my head? I adjusted my Cubs cap and looked back. Evidently the Great Earth Mother was very big on "Know your enemy." That didn't, as they say, bode well for my mission.

There were no more challenges through that day, but after the Amazons and Wrigley Field, I was so nervous that I feared new disasters at every turn. I was so hyper by sunset that a simple "Boo!" behind me would have launched me at least as far as geostationary orbit.

We stopped so I could cook my supper. I got a fire going that was much larger than I needed, too large for the prudent outdoorsman in a tinder-dry forest. I chopped down several small trees and hacked the thorny branches into small lengths with Dragon's Death, using up some of the adrenaline that had been pumping through my veins all day. I cooked up four of my ready-to-barf dinner packets and ate them. Then we rode on, away from the ashes of the campfire. Warmth would be nice during the night, but after that day's adventures, I had no intention of camping next to a beacon. There might still be a few of those hungry houris on my trail.

Two hours later, I finally made camp. But I didn't sleep much. Between reliving my confrontation with the voracious lovelies (and only the most exaggerated of them hadn't done much for my innate lust) and wondering what was coming next, sleep didn't seem to be the best idea in the world, not in that crazy forest where a threat could drop on me before I could even see it. I wasn't ready to put full faith in the danger sense that a Hero of Varay has instilled along with his initiation. It had never stopped me from posting a guard at night when there were several of us along on a mission.

The night was freezing. I sat in my tent with my blankets wrapped around me. I was still cold, especially my nose—which ran continuously except when it felt as if it were about to fall off. I thought a lot of cold thoughts in the night. I had to keep heading north, no matter how far—like Dr. Frankenstein pursuing his monster across the icefields. I was equipped for quite a bit of cold, but not for a polar winter. Thermal underwear and a fleece-lined parka will take you only so far. I wondered how cold it would get before I reached the central temple of the Great Earth Mother—where it would likely get much too hot for comfort. I worried about frostbite—even though it wasn't really *that* cold yet—and I remembered a Jack London story about a man freezing to death and getting so deliciously warm just before the end. And I managed to think about how ironic it would be if I reached the Great Earth Mother, got her in the proper mood for what had to be done, then found that the important bits had been frostbitten and wouldn't work. The Hero, unable to rise to his final challenge. I didn't laugh.

Five moons passed overhead, or rather, somewhat to the south, one after the other, getting closer to the full.

By morning, I was shaking with the cold, miserable, and just about soured on the whole business. The only problem was that there was no alternative to pressing on to the bitter end—and I couldn't have been more convinced that the end would be bitter, from the cold, if nothing else.

A little before noon, my fourteenth day out from the estate of the Elflord of Xayber, the scraggly little thorn jungle came to an end the same way it had started, bounded by a puny trickle of water. I was anxious to get away from the arthritic thorn trees, but I still reined in Electrum to sit and look out at the new vista before we crossed the creek.

Solid trees south of the water; not a tree in sight north of it . . . very little of *anything,* actually. The plain was barren to the horizon around half of the compass. Only a little thin grass grew in the sandy, or gravelly, soil. It looked as though it would crunch underfoot. "Miles and miles of miles and miles," came to mind. I had no idea where I first came across that phrase. I still don't.

"Well, Geezer, I hope you feel up to carrying an extra load for a while. I think we're going to have to carry enough wood for our next few campfires with us."

Geezer didn't answer, which was just as well. A talking horse wouldn't have helped my nerves a bit. Geezer's load had been getting gradually lighter as we traveled. Each meal I ate lightened his burden a bit. I got busy and chopped down a bunch of little thorn trees. I had been wearing lined gloves and my parka against the cold, but chopping wood warmed me enough to do without them for quite a while. I built a fire and heated a couple of meal packs for lunch, then got busy baling wood to take along. I had no way to know how far the next suitable fuel might be, so I kept going until Geezer was carrying as much as he could handle.

The horses grazed and drank while I worked and ate. They were both ready to move on by the time I was.

Riding across a flat, barren plain did offer one nice bonus that made up for a lot of shortcomings. I would see any approaching threat with plenty of time to plan a response . . . unless it materialized right on top of me, of course. The reverse was also true. Any threat would see me with a lot of warning, but I didn't consider that to be much of a flaw. The only threats I anticipated would come from the Great Earth Mother, and I was already certain that she knew just where to find me.

The only outside threat, unconnected with my present mission, that is, might be a dragon, and no dragons had been spotted (at least not over Varay) since the herd of them rained out of the sky when I scarfed down the balls of the Great Earth Mother. Dragons. I wished that there were dragons around that people could ride, something straight out of Pern. That would have taken much of the drudgery out of the Hero work.

I took a compass bearing when we crossed the creek. Without reference points, I expected to consult the compass quite often, but at least I wouldn't have to worry about the vagaries of a twisting forest path out on the empty plain. I could aim north, hold the heading without any trouble, and be able to make much better time.

That's what I *thought,* anyway.

About a half hour after we started on the plain (and yes, the rough soil did crunch underfoot), I looked back to get some perspective on our progress. That damn forest looked like it was no more than a couple of football fields away, and that was ridiculous. We had been riding at a brisk walk the whole time.

"Optical illusion," I muttered, and I started us north again, maybe at a trot for a few minutes now and then.

The next time I looked back, we might have been a quarter mile from the forest, still nowhere near as far off as we should have been.

"I think something's wrong," I said, having sudden

flashbacks to my first nightmare visit to the Congregation of Heroes. In that, I had climbed the stairs from the crypt up to the living levels of Castle Basil without making anywhere near the progress I should have.

And in the Titan Mountains, the maze guarding the first shrine had refused to get any closer as we walked toward it, until I closed my eyes and damn near walked into a wall.

I got down off of Electrum and looked around, then knelt to grab a handful of the gravel and sand. It felt normal. I've been on beaches with that kind of mixture, up above the high-water line. I held out my arms, aimed back at the forest, and sighted past my thumb, the way you see artists doing it—at least on TV and in the movies. I held my thumb so it covered one tree. After a couple of minutes, the edges of the tree started to appear from behind my thumb.

That really wasn't what I expected.

"The ground's sliding back toward the forest," I announced. Well, *sometimes* Electrum almost seemed to know what I was saying.

We had made some progress away from the forest while we were moving, but every minute we stayed in one place, we lost ground because the ground was moving south. A slow treadmill. We had to move north faster than it moved south to get anywhere.

I mounted Electrum again and pushed it—canter, trot, walk, canter. I kept the horses going as fast as I dared, using the walk sparingly, as a rest, trying to keep Electrum and Geezer speeding along as much as possible. We did make noticeable progress, but there was no sign of any relief to the north, no promise of any end to the treadmill. The motion of the ground wasn't pronounced enough to feel, but in a ten-minute break, we might lose close to a hundred yards. We didn't take many breaks. And I refused to even think of stopping for longer than ten minutes until we got clear of the mess. A good supper and a night's sleep might put us all the way back at the forest, and I couldn't bear to think of wasting an entire day and facing the same challenge the next morning.

The day seemed longer than it had any right to be, especially so far north at that time of year. November. So far north? Latitude isn't really the same in Fairy and the buffer zone as it is back in the other world. It's not like saying you cross from Canada into the buffer zone and then Fairy in the far north, nothing like that. The climate in Varay is beautiful. Winters are short and mild, the summers don't get extremely hot. It's really too ideal for anywhere in the "real" world, though there are certainly enough tourist boards and chambers of commerce that claim that sort of climate. There is *some* relationship between distance north and weather in the buffer zone and beyond, just not as much as back home. I hoped that the general rule continued to hold in the lands north of Fairy. Each increasingly cold night cooled my optimism, though.

We rode. Every so often, I looked at my compass and made sure that we were still heading due north. If the ground could slide south under us, it might also be able to get us turned around. More often, I looked back over my shoulder. At a very rough estimate, we were sliding two steps back for every three we took forward. The entire day passed like that. I didn't stop for meals, didn't stop for anything but the most essential of personal needs and to rest the horses for a few minutes when I feared that they couldn't go on without a stop.

I watched five moons come up, one by one, getting near the full. We kept riding. Our pace fell off, but I figured that we were still managing a *little* forward progress. But even if we had been doing nothing but staying in place, we had to keep moving, keep trying, to keep from losing ground.

It was a long night after a long day. At times I got down and walked to give Electrum a little relief. I thought about discarding some of Geezer's burdens, dumping some of the wood I had packed up, but that seemed too desperate a measure to take yet. There might be weeks left to travel, and the items I might dump now could be the ones that would make the vital difference later, whether I abandoned wood or anything else.

The moons crossed the sky and started to set. I was so exhausted that I could hardly keep my eyes open even when I was on the ground walking in front of my horses. A few more hours of this treadmill and all the determination in the world wouldn't be enough to keep us going even fast enough to stay in place. It would be so much easier to camp, to promise myself that it would only be for an hour, just long enough to get a little real sleep and to rest the horses. But that kind of promise is too easy to break. One hour becomes two. Two becomes four, and four hours might easily cost us every inch we had gained in a long day and night of effort.

We kept trudging north, into the brief interlude of dark following the setting of the fifth moon and the start of dawn.

I stumbled and fell flat on my face. I felt *movement* under my chest. I slid my hands around. *The edge!* The gritting sand seemed to be coming out from under something. The ground beyond was stationary, as far as I could tell. The spot where I fell was like the start of an escalator, where the steps come out from under a platform.

I nearly cried with relief.

Maybe the "nearly" could be struck from that.

Right along the boundary, the ground was the same on both sides, the coarse mixture of sand and gravel. But it started to change quickly once we were free of the treadmill, less grit and more real dirt mixed in, and more grass growing out. My horses and I were too spent to travel far beyond the boundary, but edges make me nervous. They're too easy to fall off of.

We lost more than half a day there, not fifty yards from the boundary. I didn't even bother to fix myself a meal before I pitched my tent and crawled in to sleep. I got the horses taken care of, hooked together on a long picket line staked to the ground where they could graze to their hearts' content without straying back into the moving zone of ground. There was water just within their reach as well, another trickling little creek, this one wandering crookedly from northeast to southwest—not a straight boundary creek like those that had bracketed the forest.

Judging from the sky, it was nearly noon before I woke and took a good look at the land around and ahead. I built a fire, then got water and several meal packs on to heat, then trudged to the top of a low ridge just north of us to have a good look at the next stretch.

We had stopped in a good place. Beyond that ridge, things started to get crazy again.

The ground sloped away quickly into a wide valley north of the ridge. The valley seemed to be filled with a tropical jungle. And the few creatures I could see in the air above the jungle looked suspiciously like pterodactyls. These weren't dragons, but even more primitive flying reptiles.

I couldn't see any way around the jungle either. It extended as far as I could see, east to west.

"Okay, I guess it's time to do the Professor Challenger bit," I mumbled. At least it looked warm in the jungle, wherever the heat to power it came from. I packed my coat and gloves. It was still chilly out in the open where I was, so I didn't bother to shed the thermal long johns.

"If I was sure we could get all the way through that in one day, we'd just stay here and rest up the rest of today," I said. I was doing a lot of my talking out loud, even when I wasn't talking directly at the horses. "But there's no way to know that, so I guess we should get started today. You boys have seen dragons, so I doubt that there'll be much in there to really give you a fright."

You have to understand. After dealing with dragons the size of the *Love Boat,* nothing out of the Age of Dinosaurs is going to give a regulation Hero or his steed much of a fright. *Tyrannosaurus rex?* The species only got to be about fifteen feet tall—a mere bagatelle, child's play. And the really huge beasts of that age were all vegetarians, slow-moving, with peanut-sized brains. The only thing to fear from one of them would be if it tripped over its own feet and fell on you. If the advertising was correct.

It did occur to me that those prehistoric jungles might

have contained threats that didn't leave such impressive remains—venomous bugs or slugs maybe, creatures that didn't leave huge piles of bones around. For that matter, a toxic fungus might prove to be more dangerous than all the carnivorous dinosaurs that ever lived.

"We can at least get down to the edge of the jungle," I said when I finally hoisted my saddle back on Electrum. "We're still a few hours short on sleep from last night."

The slope down to the jungle was longer than I thought, which meant that the jungle itself was also more massive than it had appeared from the ridge. We spent nearly three hours going down the slope, angling back and forth to keep from edging into a headlong rush, because the slope was also steeper than I had thought at first. There was a breeze coming out of the jungle, soft, light, but full of wet, earthy smells, bringing with it a strong hint of warmth that had no business existing just north of a plain where the temperatures had been flopping back and forth across the freezing mark at night. I saw huge ferns in the moderate distance, and a lot of lush trees that looked like they would be uncomfortable with nightly lows even thirty degrees above freezing.

There was a lot of movement inside the jungle, but at first I couldn't tell if any of it was caused by the local fauna or if it was just the movement of the wind through the branches. I saw those flying reptiles from the ridge, but it wasn't until we were well below the level of the jungle canopy that I saw anything else.

The first animals I saw on the ground weren't any of the giant dinosaurs that make such lovely movie monsters. The first dinosaurs I saw were about three feet tall, skinny and long-legged—maybe the Cretaceous version of the road runner. Beep, beep. They *were* running, and they looked as if they might be catching flying insects and eating them on the run. I stopped and watched them for a few minutes—from about a hundred yards away and up on the slope. Maybe they were full-grown, and maybe they were young, with Mama hanging by just out of sight. They ran around like kittens at play. But their long, narrow, tooth-filled snouts looked like they could take a decent hunk out of meat a lot bigger than a dragonfly.

"I hope they sleep soundly," I said when I started Electrum down the slope again. I toyed with the idea of setting up camp for the night outside the jungle, waiting until morning until I actually entered. If it hadn't been for the cruising pterodactyls (or whatever they were), I probably would have done just that, parked right at the base of the slope. But the flying reptiles seemed to be doing their hunting out on the verge of the jungle, where they could get some speed into their dives . . . and see anything out in the open.

Since I didn't know which was the frying pan and which was the fire, I decided to get under cover of the jungle, where I could at least escape long-distance observation.

It wasn't just *warm* when we reached the bottom of the valley and moved under the cover of the jungle, it was downright *hot*, maybe fifty degrees warmer at dusk inside the forest then it had been at noon on the ridge just south of the valley.

Dusk seemed to flick past in a matter of seconds inside the jungle. Sunset meant *real* darkness under a thick canopy. It was an exotic jungle, and only looked somewhat like a modern tropical rain forest. The soil seemed ridiculously poor and thin to be supporting so much, but I guess that's the way those rain forests in Africa and South America are too, everything actively tied up in the ecosystem, depending on very tight recycling to keep it all going. There was a lot of rock in this forest, some of it barely covered by a few inches of soil, some of it sticking up in large knobs and low ridges. To support themselves, the trees had to depend on extensive systems of roots, many of them almost entirely aboveground, and various kind of natural buttresses. Thick vines coiled around trunks and led from one tree to the next, locking vast sections of the jungle together in a massive web. There was relatively little ground cover or underbrush. The trees and vines hoarded most of the available resources.

About twenty minutes after we entered the jungle, I

spotted a nook protected on three side by a hefty elbow-shaped rock and decided that it would make a dandy campsite, even if there was only one way out. That meant there was only one way in too, and I was more worried about large animals than I was about trolls or any other thinking enemies. I set aside part of the thornwood Geezer had been carrying to build a night-long fire, and used the rest to put up a half-assed barricade across the open side of the nook. Those thorns wouldn't even inconvenience many of the saurians I had read about, but maybe it would slow up the little ones that I had actually seen. And maybe the fire would keep all of them back . . . if it didn't attract them by its novelty. Dinosaurs weren't covered in any of the survival manuals or camping guides Dad had made me study while I was growing up. Maybe dinosaurs wouldn't know that animals are supposed to be frightened of fire.

Somehow, I just *knew* that I was going to have to do battle with at least one of the monsters of the Dinosaur Age before I got through the jungle. I was a certified Hero, on a Mission. There had to be a battle to justify the set.

I did sleep that night. I was still so exhausted from the treadmill plain that nothing could have kept me from getting some sleep. But my danger sense kept waking me. I heard crashing noises in the night, clear enough to assure me that there were some of the big dinosaurs around even though I hadn't seen any before sunset. I slept sitting up, with my back against the rock outcropping, both of my elf swords on my lap, my hands on the hilts. During one drowsy period, halfway between sleep and waking, I found myself wondering which variety of dinosaur I would have to face. The two likely candidates that came to mind (there weren't all that many that I knew by name) were *Triceratops* and *Tyrannosaurus rex,* both late Cretaceous types. *T. rex* would make for a more exciting spectator sport with its quick movements and huge mouth. *Triceratops* would be more difficult to dispatch, from the Hero's point of view. Those three big horns on its head and the big armored flap stretching back to cover the neck would be a bitch to get past. I knew that there were many other kinds of dangerous or dangerous-looking dinosaurs, but if the dangers were as personalized as the falling Wrigley Field seemed to indicate, I felt relatively sure that it would be one of the two I could call by name. I *thought* that *Triceratops* was supposed to be a vegetarian, but it was sure equipped to fight. Hell, rhinoceroses are vegetarians, but they're sure not house pets. If I lost to any of these dinosaurs, it wouldn't matter much to me if I was on the supper menu or not.

My horses didn't like the smells or the noises in the jungle. They were restless all night, sometimes waking me even when my danger sense wasn't active.

I got up as soon as there was any hint of light in the jungle and fixed breakfast. The horses settled down a little then. I don't know if they were lulled by the resumption of familiar routine or if they just knew that breakfast meant that we would soon be moving away from this place where they were so nervous.

There's no real drama to riding through a forest like that—if all you have is the forest. With no underbrush and with all the tall trees reaching to get to the sunlight before they start to put out branches, you don't even have to worry much about bumping your head on anything. It's as safe and comfortable as riding down the center aisle of a cathedral. Sure, it's spooky with the light dimmed and tinted green, with the thick smells, but the jungle itself is just a collection of trees. It's the animals that provide the danger, and the sound effects. Dawn brought a lot of noise, especially from the canopy, from animals or birds I couldn't see or hope to identify by call . . . and by the occasional splattering of waste being dropped from high branches.

Compass out, I started us off toward the north again. There were individual trees that had to be detoured around, but it was nothing like the forest of thorn trees where I had no choice but to follow a narrow, twisting path. Here, there was more path than forest.

About midmorning, I saw my first large dinosaur, one of the really huge ones, in the shallow water at the edge of an even larger pond. The water wasn't in my way, and the dinosaur, a brontosaur or something similar to my nonexpert eyes, showed no inclination to climb out of the water to investigate me. In size, even the brontosaur was nothing compared to the dragons I had faced close-up and personal.

The main event in the jungle didn't start until after noon.

In this corner, Gil Tyner, Hero and King. In the other corner, a whole damn *family* of *Triceratops*. The two little ones were each the size of Electrum. Mama was about three times as big and must have gotten up on the wrong side of the bed that morning. Or maybe *Triceratops* dinosaurs were habitually in a bad mood, like rhino.

"Hey, lady, let's make a deal," I called out. "You don't bother me and I won't bother you."

She lowered her head so those three giant spikes were aimed directly at me and charged about three steps. Electrum and Geezer went into reverse just as quickly. When Mama T stopped, so did my horses. The big *Triceratops* pawed the ground. The two small ones did the same. I started looking for the emergency exit. At the moment, those dinosaurs looked a lot less vulnerable than any of the full-grown dragons I had seen, though some of them could have eaten Mama T in one gulp.

I tugged on Electrum's reins to shift him toward the right. We started moving slowly, all of our eyes on the armored nasties. And they were watching us just as closely. One of the small ones did a mock charge, coming a little closer to us than Mama had. Then the other small one had to show its bravery.

Well, there comes a time for bravery, when you have to swallow all the fear and insanity and "do what a man has to do." But as far as I was concerned, that wasn't it. As soon as we had a little room, I put my heels to Electrum and we exercised the better part of valor. We ran like hell.

Maybe I was finally learning how to be a smart Hero.

* * *

It was getting dark inside the jungle when we reached the edge. Beyond, the ground started upward, gently at first, then more steeply to another ridge, perhaps twice as high as the one we had descended on the southern side of the jungle. I spotted a cozy-looking ledge about a third of the way up and decided that we would spent the night there. Twilight was almost wasted before we got up to the ledge and started to settle in for the night. I still had a little wood left after reclaiming most of what I had used for the picket fence in the jungle, and the air was still fairly comfortable up on the ledge, thanks to a warm upflow of air from the valley. I fixed supper and got ready for a good night's sleep. There didn't seem to be any need for the tent, so I just wrapped up in my blankets and stared into the sky. I felt pretty good after escaping another of the traps in my path. Put the white feathers on me and teach me to crow. I didn't give a damn. I knew there would be sufficient Hero work ahead. There was no need to take chances that didn't have to be taken.

I counted moons again as they appeared one after the other. The good feeling ended quickly when I saw that a sixth moon had joined the parade.

Time had taken another bite out of its own vitals.

16

Her Central Temple

The horses needed time to sleep, to rest, and so did I—an eternity or more. But it looked like I might get it sooner than I wanted. There were six moons in the sky at the same time, each showing the familiar patterns of the one moon that should have been there. Together, six full moons reflected a lot of light, soft but bright, enough to read by—if I had had anything to read.

Six moons also meant that there was no chance that I would sleep that night. One more moon and it was all over, even without Milliways, and I didn't know how much time I had left, how much time *everyone* had left, before the celestial parade was complete. Moon number seven might not appear for two or three weeks, or it might show up tomorrow night. As far as I had been able to determine, there were no regular intervals between new arrivals in the sky. The central temple of the Great Earth Mother was still somewhere farther to the north, and I couldn't be sure how much farther, how many days—and nights—of riding it would take for me to reach it. I just had to keep plodding along as quickly as I could, hoping to get there in time. Averting total catastrophe when, or if, I got there was another problem, still too far off to take the primary position in my catalog of worries.

Sleep? Not only did I have to face *that* night without sleep, there was a chance that I would never sleep again, not until the entire universe came to an end.

But I had to rest, and I had to give Electrum and Geezer some time. Even if I was a veteran, certified Hero, I couldn't go on forever without stopping, and the horses were just horses. They would give what they had, but there were limits.

Six full moons in the sky. There would be plenty of light to ride all night once we started again. I figured that we had to rest for at least three hours before we resumed the almost hopeless quest. Three hours of fidgeting, staring at those moons.

"You'll just drop off sooner or later," I mumbled. "You can't go that long without sleep. It just isn't possible."

I shrugged. "Well, maybe I'll be able to doze in the saddle when I get that far gone." But the horses would probably be stumbling from exhaustion by then.

I once read—in some book of criticism I had been assigned to read in some literature class, I think—that the typical hero was always portrayed as a guy who was all balls and no brains . . . or words to that effect. The irony of that had to grate with me carrying around a spare set of the former, and maybe not using all of the latter.

"We've got to keep trying," I mumbled, pulling my blankets tighter around me. It was warm on that ledge above the jungle, but I couldn't get warm enough, even though I was sweating.

After a few minutes, I closed my eyes and pulled the bill of my Cubs cap down to shut out some of the glare of all those moons. Even though I couldn't blank my mind enough for sleep, I tried to steer my thoughts to pleasant memories—to times I had shared with Joy, not nearly enough of those; to epic drinking bouts with Lesh and Uncle Parthet; to long conversations with Parthet and Pregel; to all of the fun my father and I had while I was growing up, before I learned of the deception. But I had trouble holding on to happy memories. It wasn't a good time for nostalgia. It wasn't a good time for much of anything. All that was lacking for an atmosphere of total gloom and resignation was a soundtrack from Wagner. Maybe the Valkyries would ride to carry me to Valhalla or some such place when the end came. If even a place like Valhalla could survive the total destruction that threatened.

I had my bouts with wishful thinking in the night too. Perhaps the temple was just beyond the next ridge. Perhaps the Great Earth Mother would let bygones be bygones the way the Elflord of Xayber had—you know, shoulders to the wheel, let's all work together in this crisis, and all of the other clichés that come up when the shit is ready to hit the fan—so we could get right to the important work.

Work? Being a Hero was starting to sound a lot like being a prostitute.

Maybe, better yet, maybe I would wake up and find that it was all a dream, like that year of *Dallas*. Maybe I had snapped under the pressures of my senior year at Northwestern and all of my memories of the last forty-four months or so were merely delusions.

Yeah, and maybe I was just starting to crack up now, and all of creation would go down the drain because the only Hero with the balls to do the job didn't have the balls to do the job—to mix the literal and the figurative.

Somewhere in the night, I remembered what the Elflord of Xayber said that I should do if I felt reality starting to slip away from me. I reached down under my blankets with both hands and held on, trying to save whatever link to sanity I might still have. *Four balls all in a bag, hold 'em and roll 'em and . . .*

The elflord's advice didn't seem nearly as ludicrous as it had when he said it.

Exhaustion and worry, the feeling that I was on a hopeless and hopelessly quixotic quest, and loneliness— maybe I *was* flirting with the edge of insanity that night. Time swirled around and through me; ''Where it stops, no one knows.''

I had a moment of extreme lucidity and realized that I had been sitting there rocking back and forth the way some people do who have been locked up in mental institutions too long. I opened my eyes. No such luck. I wasn't safe in a nut house. I was crouched on a ledge, partway up the side of a hill, somewhere in the uncharted regions beyond Fairy.

The sixth moon was directly overhead, so I got up and got ready to ride. Both horses whinnied their disapproval of the decision, but they didn't mutiny, so we continued up the slope, away from the anomalous Cretaceous jungle toward who could say what next terror.

There was no temple visible when we reached the crest. I didn't realize how fervently I had hoped for that until I felt the flood of disappointment when I looked north from the crest. North of us, there was another plain, not more than twenty feet below the ridge. There appeared to be a similar ridgeline several miles away. I couldn't be completely sure of the distance, not even with all of the moonlight.

"I hope this isn't another treadmill," I said as we moved down toward the plain. That would have defeated us without any doubt.

It wasn't a treadmill, but before we had gone fifty yards across the flat ground, I knew that there was something equally strange about it, something that slowed the horses almost as much as the treadmill had, something that annoyed and frightened them no end. We stopped and I dismounted. My feet sank in the ground to my ankles, but no farther. When I lifted my feet, they came up clean, but there was a sucking sort of pressure. I squatted. Electrum's legs were sunk in the stuff above his hoofs. I felt the ground. It was like a very soft, semiliquid rubber. It molded itself to hand or foot but didn't cling. Like gooey mud without the goo.

"Just a nuisance," I said softly. I got up to try to reassure the horses. I stroked their heads and talked easily to them. "I know, it's a drain on energy, and you don't have all that much pep left. We'll just have to put up with it for now. This plain doesn't look all that wide. Maybe we can be out of this stuff by dawn."

I drew Wellivazey's swords and probed the rubbery ground with it. I could sink the blade in almost to the hilt with very little effort. It came out just as easily as my feet did, without a hint of clinging dirt. I got down on one knee and sank a hand into the ground. It felt like rubbery jelly. If I really pressed, put all of my strength into it, I could get my hand, even my arm, down into it, about halfway to the elbow. The stuff below had the same kind of texture, it was just thicker, firmer.

I shook my head as I climbed back into the saddle. The obstacles on this trek seemed designed more to test my sanity and my threshold of boredom than my strength or bravery.

"I think I'm missing something here, kids," I said. "I just can't figure out what it is." If there actually was something more subtle going on, maybe I really was the hero who was all balls and no brains, too dense to puzzle it out. If the Great Earth Mother was really the Big Bad Mama she was cracked up to be, she ought to be able to show a little more power.

Of course, even with the piddling tests that had been thrown in front of me, I was almost out of it. If I hadn't been so thoroughly exhausted by then, I might have felt some humiliation.

The rubbery plain slowed us more than I had guessed, whether because the horses were so tired, the gumbo was so thick, or the plain was wider than I first thought, I'm not sure. It may have been a combination of any or all of those. But we moved on steadily through the night. Several times my danger sense hiccupped and I saw low shadows moving—or thought I did. But the shadows didn't come close and I couldn't make out what they might be.

By dawn, I was so tired that I had trouble keeping my eyes open. The rubber plain was a slate gray and there looked to be a little more than a mile left of it. At the slow walk that seemed to be the most efficient pace for the horses in it, we would need another twelve or fifteen minutes to get to the ridge ahead of us . . . with no real guarantee that the ridge marked the end of this slop.

Then I saw another of those shadows on the plain. With sunlight playing on the ground, the shadow was low, triangular, and black, moving almost directly toward us, cutting through the rubber surface without any difficulty at all. It looked exactly like a shark fin cutting through the surface of the ocean. The way my danger sense started ringing my head as the shadow came closer, I was ready to concede that it *was* a shark—some weird variety that could swim through semiliquid rubber almost as quickly as its marine cousins could swim through water.

There was no *Jaws* theme in the background, getting louder as the shark approached. The fin came on, changing direction to come straight at me. Off to the side, a couple of hundred yards away, I saw three more fins, idling, I guess, moving in lazy circles. I pulled Dragon's Death and urged the horses on toward the ridge . . . and what I hoped was the end of the rubbery "ocean." I watched the first shark as it came on, and I turned Electrum at the last second, leaned over, and slashed at the front of the fin. My sword slowed drastically when it hit the rubber, fighting through the surface, losing much of the force of my blow.

But there was still enough juice behind it to wound the shark, to make it break surface.

It opened gaping jaws to shows rows and rows of flat needlelike teeth. My second blow shortened the snout by a foot, and blood flowed onto and into the gray rubber surface. Off in the distance, the other sharks quickly caught the scent of blood and homed in on it. I gave Electrum my heels and he *tried* to gallop. The result was an awkward, bouncing run like a carousel horse gone out of control, but we were moving faster than the remaining sharks, and that was all that mattered. Two of them continued toward the blood and the thrashing of the shark I had wounded. The last shark changed course to try to intercept us.

The race was close, but we got out of the goop onto firm, sandy soil with maybe two seconds to spare.

Okay, stick another white feather in my cap. I had run from danger again. I was getting to like it. But I also felt that I had to make a gesture, more than the shark I had given the nose job to. That was unavoidable, not heroics. I dismounted and walked back to the edge of the goop. The shark that had tried to intercept us was circling right

close to the shore (I guess I have to call it that). I drew
Dragon's Death again and waited for him. When he was
as close as he could get, I stabbed down with my six-
foot elf sword—stabbed rather than slashed this time—
aiming for that same point just in front of the fin. The
shark struggled for a moment, and I pulled my sword
out. The shark went belly up in a hurry, and drew the
other two, with more fins visible in the distance, coming
on at full speed.

I didn't wait. I had made my gesture, thumbed my
nose at convention.

When we got to the top of the ridge north of the shark
pond, I rudely reined Electrum to a halt and dismounted
in such a hurry that I almost fell, not quite getting my
foot clear of the stirrup. When I got to the ground, I
dropped to my knees. It wasn't an act of faith. It wasn't
prayer. More likely, it was disbelief. I couldn't quite accept what I was seeing.

I could see the shrine, the central temple of the Great
Earth Mother.

This time, I know I cried, and I couldn't do anything
but let the tears come until there were no more left to
shed. Then I looked to the sky, fearing some final cruel
trick by fate, the appearance of the seventh moon, showing up just soon enough to torture me at coming so close.

There were no moons at all in the sky at the moment. The
sixth had set just before dawn.

The temple was still some distance away—at least ten
miles, I figured, perhaps more. It was at the far end of a
very large, very flat valley. The temple was up on a broad
shelf a little above the valley floor. The only thing I had
to base my estimate of distance on was a rough guess
that the central temple had to be at *least* as large as the
two shrines that had held the balls of the Great Earth
Mother. That would make the shelf that the temple sat
on approximately two miles wide and deep. The temple
certainly looked like it had been fashioned from the same
basic design, at least on the outside, a pseudo-Greek temple with rows of columns around it.

And there seemed to be one more series of obstacles in the way—a real doozy.

Call it a million dominoes, just to keep the number very even. I wasn't about to try counting them. I wasn't even going to go to much trouble to make a respectable estimate. There were certainly at least one million, perhaps two or three.

Dominoes. I didn't see any pips or any dragon designs, but I didn't have any doubt about what they were. These dominoes were about twenty feet by ten feet by three feet thick. Even at a distance the colors looked vivid: black and white; bright red, orange, yellow, blue, green, and purple; various shades and tints of those colors. Virtually all of the dominoes were standing on end, and they appeared to be arranged in an elaborate pattern like those you see on the news when college kids go after the constantly escalating record for tumbling the most dominoes in a single, spectacular chain reaction. The entire floor of the valley, as far as I could see to east or west, and completely across from north to south, was covered with those gigantic dominoes. On the far side, maybe a mile east of the temple, there were several stacks—dominoes that hadn't yet been added to the display, or perhaps just extras left after the pattern was complete.

And I thought *I* was bored? I didn't care to meet the person who had placed all those dominoes out there, but I had a sneaking hunch that I had discovered the secret hobby of the Great Earth Mother.

I had another sneaking hunch as well, a premonition I would have wagered heavily on if there had been anyone to take my action. I would have bet that those dominoes were going to get tipped before I got to the temple on the other side of the valley. Being that certain, I spent a lot of time studying the patterns that the dominoes were arranged in, trying to pick out the safest route through the mess.

''I wonder how long it will take all of those dominoes to fall once they start?'' I asked.

Nobody answered, which was just as well.

I could remember an announcer on television talking

about a setup in some college gym in Japan. The dominoes would need more than half an hour to fall, and those were regular-sized dominoes, and a lot less than a million of them. I guessed that it would take several hours for all of these to fall, especially if it was set up so that they would go one at a time, not with parallel lines dropping together.

I didn't *see* anything that looked like it might be a trigger for several rows going simultaneously.

"Let's eat first," I decided. I used the last of the wood Geezer was carrying to build a fire. I wasn't worried about giving away our position. If the Great Earth Mother didn't already know exactly where we were, she wouldn't be much of an adversary. Anyway, those camping meals are just so much cardboard unless you eat them as hot as possible.

I decided to eat big. Like as not it would be my last meal, so I splurged, fixing a full half-dozen of my packaged dinners. It still wasn't a proper Varayan feast, but I did what I could and let the horses graze while I was doing it. The only thing missing was beer. A six-pack of Michelob Dry would have topped everything off perfectly.

When I finished eating, I stood and let out a couple of well-deserved belches before I mounted Electrum and said, "Let's go, boy." I have never, to the best of my recollection, used the phrase "giddy-up" to a horse. I'd be too self-conscious . . . I just *know* any self-respecting horse would turn his head to laugh at me.

Before we could get to the valley floor and all of those humongous dominoes, we had to descend a long, gentle slope, too easy to pose any threat even to tired horses unless they were galloping full out, and mine weren't. I was looking ahead, still concentrating on the patterns of the dominoes, when somebody started playing games with the law of gravity.

All of a sudden, *down* was straight out to my left. Abruptly. We were still on the slope, and the horses kept walking, but my senses started screaming that we were about to fall sideways, parallel to the ground. The horses seemed to be doing a fly act, walking on the wall. Then we flip-flopped just as suddenly and down was straight out to my right. After yet another hiccup of reality, down was straight up. It never changed the actual working of things, just the perception. We didn't fall, but the horses neighed and tried to break and run . . . and I ended up losing most of that big meal I had just eaten.

It did take my mind off the dominoes for a time.

Then we reached the beginning of the domino pattern. There were still no pips visible on any of the blocks, but the proportions were right. They *were* dominoes to all intents and purposes.

At least up and down straightened themselves out before we got to them.

I had spotted a lane between two rows of dominoes that seemed to extend about a third of the way across the valley before giving way to rows running east and west. I couldn't be sure of a safe path beyond that. The angle had been wrong from the ridge. Navigation would have to be by guess and luck once we got that far, if we got that far. And as near as I could judge from the spot where I had done my studying, the pattern appeared to start and end right over under the temple—the way golf courses start and end right by the clubhouse.

The moment I edged Electrum between the first two dominoes, I heard a distant thump, and I knew that the pattern had been tripped. The thumps came regularly— all too close together—and I hurried the horses down the lane I had chosen. If the dominoes were all aligned properly, we would be safe there even if the blocks on both sides of us went down.

The metronomic precision of the heavy stones falling came closer and moved farther away, came back, paralleled us. Distance translated to volume, which gave me a constantly updated clue as to where the action was taking place. I stopped at the end of the safe lane I had picked up from the ridge and looked both ways, trying to decide which way to go next. There was a section that looked terribly confused just ahead, as several rows of dominoes met, crossed, and went off at different angles.

I chose the shortest path to another straight row, and this time I really put my heels to Electrum. The sound of falling blocks was coming straight toward us.

It was our closest call. Half a step slower, and Geezer would have lost his tail, and perhaps more.

Fear drove us on from there. Electrum and Geezer both gave me everything they had, without waiting for my urging. A row of dominoes just to our right chased us for several minutes, then passed us by. The racket of that got the horses moving a bit faster than they should have been capable of.

We had to zig left, then right, past another collapsing row. I had trouble holding the horses on course with dominoes coming toward us from in front—on our left side. But then we had a clear track ahead of us. The dominoes along that lane were already down, clear to the north side of the valley.

We were nearly up to the level of the temple before the horses were willing to check their speed. By that time, we were above the tops of the dominoes. I finally got the animals stopped and looked back across the valley. As near as I could tell, less than ten percent of the blocks had fallen—in more than an hour.

"It's going to take all day for them to finish," I said, somewhat awed by the thought.

I watched for a couple of minutes, fascinated by the display. But the break also gave the horses time to catch their breath—if little more—and when I turned away from the falling dominoes, Electrum and Geezer were ready to climb. Maybe they sensed that the end of our journey was near.

The ledge was even larger than it had appeared from the south ridge. It had to be at least five miles wide and four deep. The temple was situated close to the exact middle of the shelf, and it was perhaps twice the size of the other shrines.

A couple of modest creeks came across the ledge from the hill behind. Electrum and Geezer started walking toward the nearest. They were moving slowly, and they stopped to graze whenever I gave them a slack rein.

"Go ahead, you're entitled," I whispered. I couldn't let them just run for the water in any case. With all the running, they needed time to cool off before they drank. I turned them a little, so they would need longer to work their way to the water, and when we finally got there, I dismounted and dug out the picket line. I hooked the horses to the line so they could get their fill of green grass and cool water. They would be content. Me, I turned and walked toward the temple.

I finished my journey on foot, the way pilgrimages are supposed to be made. I walked the last mile, and I had a feeling that the phrase was appropriate. I had to go around to the south face of the temple again. There were no doors on the west, where I had left the horses.

No soldiers came out to challenge me the way they had at the shrine in the Titan Mountains.

No sea serpents coiled around this temple the way one had around the island temple in the Mist.

No companions walked at my sides.

This temple did have large gold doors, just like the others, only much larger. The gold was beaten into fancy designs. I stood in front of the doors for several minutes and just stared at them. When I took my next step forward, the doors swung open.

I waited until the doors stopped moving, then stepped forward again. I didn't need a formal introduction to know that the woman waiting just inside was the Great Earth Mother.

17

Great Earth Mother

I'm not sure what I expected. Okay, that was a frequent occurrence. But the apparition of the Great Earth Mother I had seen in her shrine on the island in the Mist hadn't been very promising. Part by part, I guess there was nothing wrong, but as for the combination . . . the word "hideous" springs readily to mind. Beyond that apparition, I had never been able to completely shake the thought that—just maybe—the Great Earth Mother was really the myth I had taken her for in my early days in Varay, just another primitive fertility symbol. Sure, I should have known better, but I had twenty-one years of "real world" experience compared to less than four years of the buffer zone and Fairy.

I walked through the doorway into her temple, and she was standing there, hands on hips, legs spread a bit, waiting for me. I saw one immediate problem. Scale. The Great Earth Mother was at least fourteen feet tall, maybe a little more—considerably taller than the eunuch who had guarded her shrine in the Titan Mountains. If I had bumped into her . . . there is no delicate way to express the images that flickered through my mind at the time. I could have put my face right *into* her. A problem of scale.

Fortunately or not, I didn't bump into her. I got inside the door and stopped. And stared. She was put together properly, if you allow for proportion, not all mismatched the way her apparition had been. She had dark hair, and curves that kept my eyes roaming over them. She even looked a little familiar. The resemblance wasn't exact, but she reminded me of Raquel Welch back in *One Mil-*

lion B.C.—but the Great Earth Mother didn't have even the scantiest of clothes on. Fourteen feet tall, stark naked: that's a lot of skin. She didn't have so much as a jewel in her navel. For that matter, she didn't even have a navel. I noticed that after a few minutes of noticing other things like the fact that if I stood close to her, she would provide shade for a good part of the day.

The Great Earth Mother was certainly beautiful enough to make any man horny, but mortal flesh will only stretch so far, no matter how aroused it gets. She needed more than a Hero, she needed at least a hero and a half.

What a way to go, I thought.

"You're here," she said. Her voice was a bit too deep and husky for my tastes, but I suspect that was a function of her size.

"The obstacles you put in my way weren't really very daunting," I said.

"They amused me."

"And the dominoes?"

She chuckled. "Those have been waiting for just this time. When the last one falls, it will catapult the seventh moon into orbit and the last of Vara's get will be gone."

"You're that ready for your own oblivion?" I asked. I was trying to be cautious. She hadn't immediately snapped my head off, but I had no way to judge how far her tolerance might extend. My danger sense had blown a fuse when I walked through the door. It went crazy, and then it went dead.

"I seem to be the last of Vara's get, as you put it, and I also have the souvenirs you clipped from him," I said. "If *we* go, there's no chance for you to find someone else to make a new plaything with. No one who could possibly live up to expectations. The way I understand things."

She shrugged, and her huge breasts jiggled with the motion.

"I've been debating that question ever since you set the destruction in motion."

"And what have you decided?"

"I haven't, not yet."

"Not deciding is a decision in itself." And then I tried to recall just where the hell I had come across *that* line. It sounded hokey as hell, but it did seem appropriate.

"We have a little of your time left. You must be hungry. Come with me."

I followed her butt across a corner of the main central room of the temple. As long as I thought of her as a figure on a movie screen, I could keep from being totally overwhelmed by her size. We went between two interior columns and into a room at the side of the temple. The room was large enough that the Great Earth Mother didn't look out of place in it. There was a table set up—about the size of the table in Xayber's banquet room. The Great Earth Mother settled herself on a pile of fancy pillows on one side of the table and gestured me toward a chair—a normal, human-sized chair—on the other. We were almost eye to eye when we were both down.

"Eat," she said. "If I do decide to play with you, you'll need all of the energy you can possibly find. If I don't—well, then you might as well meet your end with a full stomach."

If I had any shreds of sanity left when I reached the temple, I think they had started running for cover as soon as I saw the Great Earth Mother. When she said, "Eat," my eyes locked onto one of her nipples and my mouth started to water.

"A little wine to start the meal?" she suggested. She pointed at a decanter and it got up and poured dark red wine into a fancy goblet in front of me. I gulped down about a pint of the strong, heady wine and felt the alcohol burning on its way down.

"Eat," the Great Earth Mother said again. She reached out and grabbed what looked like a whole leg of lamb and started gnawing on it. In *her* hand, it looked about the way a chicken leg looks in my hand.

Soft, unobtrusive music started playing in the background. It wasn't elevator music, but something that sounded classical even though it didn't remind me of any composer that I knew anything about.

Since I had already decided that sanity was no longer a factor in anything that was going on, I ate with all of the enthusiasm that a big meal deserved. There were about two dozen different dishes on the table. The hot foods stayed hot and the cold foods stayed cold—without Styrofoam packaging. The serving platters and bowls remained full. The loaf of bread kept growing to replace the chunks that the Great Earth Mother and I ripped off. The decanter kept filling my goblet, varying the wine to go along with whatever I happened to be eating at the moment. Same decanter, same goblet. Different wines: sweet, dry; red, white. When I got to the salted fish, there was even beer in the goblet.

"You do look remarkably like Vara," the Great Earth Mother said after we had been eating for about ninety minutes.

I told her about the three mirrors that the Elflord of Xayber had.

"I killed Vara finally," the Great Earth Mother said— flat, conversational tones.

"So I hear. But not for nearly two hundred years after you had sex with him."

"I don't act rashly."

It was time for the White Rabbit to run through the room looking at an oversized pocket watch and screaming, "I'm late, I'm late." I would have greeted him like a long-lost brother.

"Vara was more my size than yours, wasn't he?" I asked a few minutes later, after I had given up hope of seeing the White Rabbit.

"A little more than you, a lot less than me."

"Wasn't that a little awkward?" I was worried about the logistics of the situation.

"I am *always* capable of ensuring my own pleasure." That sentence had haughtiness dripping from every word.

"And those who give you pleasure?" I asked.

She stared at me for a long time then. Under the pressures of the moment, I met her stare rather then turn my attention to her other attributes again. She got a look of concentration on her face. I wondered why that question took so much time for her to answer.

"Would you get sentimentally attached to a warm fire in winter?" she asked.

I started to flip back a quick answer but decided that a question that took so much time and thought to ask needed at least that much time to answer. I thought about it. I repeated the question silently, watching her eyes while I did, and searching for the trick in the words.

"I might if I had been cold for several thousand years," I said finally.

"When you could build a new fire whenever you wanted it?"

"I might worry that I wouldn't have the materials handy to build that next fire," I said. "There might not be any wood left, or a match to strike a spark."

We did some more staring at each other. The eating seemed to be over. Neither one of us paid much attention to the food.

"You're not Vara," the Great Earth Mother said next.

"No, but I have something Vara didn't have, no matter how good he might have been."

"Oh?" A raised eyebrow, a hint of interest.

"A *couple* of things Vara didn't have. I have his balls, and I have my own."

"The dominoes are falling," she said, a pointless reminder. Even though I couldn't hear them clunking into each other while I was inside the temple, I was very aware of them, especially since she had said that the last one would launch the seventh moon.

"How many dominoes were there?" I asked.

"Who counts? There were as many as were needed. What more matters?"

"How many of these cycles have there been?" I asked next. "Do you really want the one that is ending now to be the last?"

"How many?" She smiled. "Who counts?" she repeated.

"And were they all the same?"

"Enough alike to get monotonous."

"Then you might welcome a diversion that offered the chance for something different. Four balls might introduce some novelty," I suggested. "Who knows, you might even produce twins—two cycles running at once, parallel, maybe even running in different directions. That would ease the monotony."

She considered it for a moment. "It might at that."

More silence. In my mind I could hear those damn dominoes clunking toward oblivion.

"Ah, if we're going to conceive a new world, don't you think we should get about it? This would be a poor time for coitus interruptus."

"How quaint," she said, wrinkling her nose.

"And what's the gestation period for a universe?"

"Have courtship rituals fallen so far?"

"A, it's better than offering you twenty bucks for a trip around the world. B, who know's what's proper here; I've never made love to a goddess before. And C, we just don't have time for chocolates and roses."

She shook her head. "Is it really worth it then?"

My smile was forced. I had gone into the close too soon. I could almost feel every muscle in my face to get the smile in place.

"You'll never know unless you try." I was feeling decidedly perverted by then, like a dirty old man offering a little girl candy to show him what was under her panties. Which was really a ridiculous way to feel with this naked giant sitting across the table from me.

"Very well, little man, show me that it's worth it." The way she said that, I wondered if I would even be able to get it up. I felt little enough compared to her size; I didn't need the sarcasm. I had heard about psychic impotence. I figured this would be a bad time to have my first personal experience of it.

"Here?" I asked, and I tried to make the single word sound sarcastic all by itself, a sort of "how gauche" expression. The Great Earth Mother laughed in my face, a loud, raucous bass rumble. I could feel myself shrinking even more.

"There's not *that* much hurry," she said. "We have more time left than *you'll* be able to manage."

Forget "Fire and Ice." The world was going to come to an end without a replacement because the Great Earth Mother liked to indulge in sexual put-downs.

"We'll go to my bedroom," she said, uncoiling herself from the stack of pillows on the floor. I took one last pull at my wine and got up.

I'm tempted to say that the bed of the Great Earth Mother was the size of a football field, but that would be a gross, and obvious, exaggeration. *But,* if you put one corner of the bed at home plate on a baseball diamond and lined up the adjacent sides along the foul lines, the pitcher's mound would cause the bed to wobble. The bed and bedroom looked like something from a Hollywood art director's idea of a fantasy harem in some *Arabian Nights* picture. The bed was immense but low, only about a foot off the floor. The coverings looked like satin. The wall hangings were of the same material. There were piles of pillows and cushions everywhere, on the bed and on the floor. The colors were pastels with a few dark accents. There were neither torches nor candles in the room, but it was well lit. The lighting was indirect with a vengeance. I couldn't spot where any of the illumination was coming from. There was simply light where it was needed, in just the proper amount.

"This is my playroom," the Great Earth Mother said. She went to the bed and crawled out toward the middle of it, her butt moving provocatively as she moved directly away from me. She got near the center and flopped over on her back, spreading her legs wide.

"Are you just going to stand there with your clothes on?" she asked. "I thought you were worried about the time."

I started the process of undressing, taking off my swords, mail shirt, and so forth. The Great Earth Mother reached down between her legs. What started as a casual scratch turned into something more specifically erotic. Then she held out her hand, thumb sticking up.

"This is what you have to compete with," she said. A *big* thumb. It was going to be close.

I finished undressing.

"Come to Mama," she said.

18

The Big Bang

I looked out at the Great Earth Mother lying in the middle of that huge bed. Her breasts jutted up yet, very little flattened because she was on her back—two volcanoes waiting for my attention. There was still a problem of scale. If I got my head up to her breasts, my feet would be dangling over her genitals. —Okay, that was a bit of an exaggeration, but the working parts still wouldn't have connected. As I started crawling out on the bed toward her, I thought, I'm still sixteen and this is just the wildest wet dream ever. Somewhere inside me, another voice said, *Go with the flow.* If I had been just a little less frightened, I might have considered singing a chorus of "Climb Every Mountain."

But that long crawl did give me time to get aroused. It was a unique point of view, a unique pilgrimage.

Her thighs were as thick as my waist, but on her frame, it looked right. I wondered how much *Playboy* or *Penthouse* might pay for an eight-page centerfold spread on the Great Earth Mother—if either magazine was left after World War Three and the current dive into chaos . . . and if the Great Earth Mother could be bought.

That crawl seemed to take an hour. I passed the level of her feet and moved on toward the other end of that special box canyon. Yeah, a lot of bad puns came to mind. I managed to cram several hours' worth of them into the few odd minutes that actually passed. I crawled to her and up over her. I homed in on her breasts and face, not worrying too much about trying to keep my weight off of her.

Her breasts were firm. The nipples rose to hard peaks

under my hands. I slid between her breasts and moved
farther north until our faces were level.

"This is going to be even more awkward than I imagined," I said. Then, taking my boldest move yet, I lowered my mouth to her, ready to kiss—ready to risk having
her bite off half my face if she got a little carried away.

The Great Earth Mother laughed again, but this time
it was a more friendly sound. "I told you I always make
sure of my own pleasure," she whispered.

Then I felt her skin crawling against mine, her whole
body seemingly involved in some strange migration. My
first thought was that she was changing into some hideous monster to do me, and with her arms wrapped
tightly around me, I didn't have a prayer of escaping. I
needed a few seconds to realize what was really happening. She was shrinking herself down to my size.

I knew that she was making herself smaller and not
making me larger because more of the pattern on the
pillow under her head became visible.

"Is that better?" she asked when the shrinking act
ended. She had matched my size quite closely.

"Much better," I said. "I don't have to worry that
I'm making love to a movie screen now." *Now,* I adjusted my position to take some of my weight off of her.
It was probably still not necessary for her comfort, but
it was for mine.

Patterns, textures, sequences.

I guess that we all fall into habits in lovemaking as in
everything else. The first time with a new lover, two sets
of habits can clash, making the session less than satisfactory, or they can mesh, leading to something that can
be quite extraordinary. Who does what, and when, and
how? Once the Great Earth Mother and I got cooking,
habits took over, saving some of the wear and tear on my
overloaded brain. I had done this before, often enough
that I didn't have to think about what came next.

The Great Earth Mother was every man's dream in
bed, responding, anticipating, encouraging, driving me
to a frenzy that went on and on. The hero with four balls
was making love to a real sex goddess. Time seemed to

rest on the sidelines to watch. Our foreplay was more extended than I had ever managed before as the big mama bared all my nerve endings and kept me just short of ejaculation. I didn't even have a chance to worry about the End of Everything coming before I did.

"Okay, Hero," she said at last, her mouth all over my ear. "Fuck me." Well, that's what heroes are supposed to do best, isn't it? *All in a day's work, ma'am. Just part of the job. Service with a smile.* Service as a verb.

I entered her slowly, cautiously, more for my own comfort than to try to tease her. The Great Earth Mother had strung me out to such a pitch that the gentlest touch against the head of my penis was a ragged shock, threatening to tip me over the edge into premature orgasm and painful release. Maybe all I *needed* to do was make sure that the release was into her, but I had to hold out for a while at least, show *some* staying power, a touch of class, a hint of style. She had a poor enough opinion of Heroes without my giving her additional reasons.

I also had to avoid thinking too much about all of that to keep from triggering what I was trying to hold.

But it started very nicely even with all of the screaming tension of my extended arousal. The Great Earth Mother got me so crazed that I had trouble remembering just who she was and why I was screwing her. There was magic in the air, in the bed, the way it's always supposed to be according to the trash—an air of conquest. *Me Tarzan, you Jane.* She might be Mother Goddess to the world, the creator of everything with the help of *any* appropriate stud, but she writhed around under me like any woman caught up in the moment, apparently as strung out by our match as I was. What a letter it would make to one of the skin mags! It was an Olympic performance, a level I had never reached before and never expect to duplicate. I'm not sure that I could even survive a rematch of that intensity. I'm only human.

The theme from *Rocky* would have been appropriate background to this affair.

Sweat-slicked skin, the aromas of active sex, the sounds of heavy breathing, garbled nothings, grunts, and gasps, it went on and on. I felt the Great Earth Mother scratching my back, felt the sting of flayed skin, and that finally brought some measure of awareness back to me.

She wrapped her arms and legs around me and said, "Let's see what you're made of, Hero."

Then she pulled me tightly against her, her arms and legs overpowering in their strength, crushing the breath from me, forcing my orgasm to match hers: bucking and yawing, a scream that sounded as one even though it was drawn from two throats.

And then I felt her skin crawling against mine again. There was a swelling sound like the "ocean's roar" from a seashell.

And then I fell in.

Alice fell down a rabbit hole into her strange adventures, but Alice was just a little girl, facing a little girl's dream fears. Me, I was a Hero, full-grown, tested in battle and in bed. While the Great Earth Mother grew beneath me, I slid out of her arms. I was still anchored to her at the groin. I slipped between her breasts and across her smooth belly without a belly button. I tried to grab hold of the cascades of pubic hair that were suddenly as thick as tangles of heavy rope, but my hands kept sliding off and I tumbled down into the dark well I had been pumping so vigorously not long before.

I fell into the Great Earth Mother. My shadow fell before me, and seemed to race away from me. I was losing my shadow, the way Peter Pan did, and that provided a focus for my panic.

Light reflected in wet, glittering patches from the walls of the shaft. The walls receded, became barely visible in a growing distance, then disappeared completely.

And I continued to fall.

At first—a *long* first—I was totally caught up in the fear of falling. There was a moment of utter terror that extended beyond eternity. There was no room in my head for anything else, no sense of how impossible, how *Freudian* the entire scene was . . . or how appropriate it might be to go out like this. I'm sure I screamed, maybe a number of times, baring my fear, reducing my throat to a raw pain.

The Hero was stripped of both form and substance, tumbling an inconceivable distance down a channel designed for conception.

> *Jack fell down and broke his crown,*
> *And Jill came tumbling after.*

But the fall went on and on and my mind eventually grasped for some sort of crisis equilibrium. *The fall went on and on?!?* Trying to rank utter impossibilities is even more useless and confusing than trying to rank infinities. As near as I could tell—from everything that my terrified senses told me—I had already been falling for minutes, many of them, perhaps even an hour's worth. I felt wind streaming past me, or rather (as a misplaced moment of logic informed me) I felt the air as I streamed through it, but I didn't seem to be accelerating any longer. I had apparently reached terminal velocity, whatever *that* might be under the circumstances.

I spread my arms and legs like a skydiver in free fall. There was enough air whipping around my naked body to make the tender parts ache again.

Full extension of my extremities seemed to slow my descent, just a little. I knew that everything that I was experiencing was impossible. *(There's that line again.)* There was no way I could really have fallen into a vagina, no way that such a fall—even if it had been possible by any stretch of the imagination or flesh—could have lasted so long. *A bottomless pit? A black hole? Impossible.* It was something to drive a psychiatrist to *his* psychiatrist. Compounded impossibilities finally softened my panic. Some semblance of rational thought struggled to regain control of my mind, even though the surroundings were completely irrational.

The light at the top of the shaft was too far away to be more than the merest pinprick of light, a single distant star in the otherwise absolute void. Around me there was only the deepening darkness and the continued sense of falling.

"In the beginning . . ." thundered through my head, but I ignored the litany and it went away.

I rolled over to look back the way I had come, and I had to fight down a resurgence of panic at falling backward. I looked toward the distant point of light and another voice in my head urged me to wish upon a star to have my dreams come true. That seemed somehow more reasonable than the first proclamation. I had to consider this one for a moment before I let it drift away.

"Twinkle, twinkle . . ."

"Shut up!" I screamed. I twisted back around so that I would meet whatever might be coming head on—as if that made any difference when I couldn't see anything, not even my hand in front of my face—not the slightest silhouette.

Time. Time. Time.

Seconds ticked and hours donged. My head throbbed in some nonphysical pulsing, an inner metronome. I passed in front of my whole life. Hallucinations were projected against the void I was falling through. But it all whizzed by too fast for me to grasp anything of what I saw.

I have no doubt at all that enough time passed for me to have fallen all of the way to the center of the earth and beyond—if any of the laws of nature that I learned in school still held . . . which, apparently, they did not. I would have gone through the center, carried by my momentum, to eventually slow down as gravity caught up with me. There would have been an instant when I would have hung in equilibrium, and then I would have fallen back the other way.

If any of this insanity had been possible in the first place, which it obviously wasn't—even though it was actually happening.

Or I thought it was.

Of all the crazy ideas my father came up with for doing things together while I was growing up, I only flat refused one, when he suggested that we try skydiving. "I don't see any sense in jumping out of a perfectly good airplane,'' I told him, and no matter how many times he brought up the subject, I continued to refuse. Not long after that, I saw a feature on some news show about people tying themselves to bridges with long rubber bands and jumping off, aiming to stop themselves as close to disaster as they could. The reporter called it bungee jumping, or something like that. I knew that if Dad saw that story he would want to try it. For months I worried, but Dad had just gone off on one of his vague ''business trips'' when the story aired, so he never saw it, as far as I know. Of course, I didn't know then that his ''business trips'' took him to Varay, far from any television and all the spiffied-up reporters who went looking for crazy stories to fill airtime with.

I'm fal
     l
        l
           l
              ling.''

Gibraltar and the Rockies did their crumbling and tumbling, along with all the other clay that made up the world. It all broke down. The universe exploded like a balloon filled with too much air.

Fall down, go BOOM!

I became part of the extended void. There was nothing but me, my awareness, and the infinite hole I was falling through. A hole in a void. Even the point of light back at the entrance had disappeared—sometime. There was no light at all now. The only sound was the vague whistle of wind as I streamed through the air.

Minutes, hours, days, months, years, centuries, millennia, eons—who could count? I fell through a time when there was no time, through a distance where there was no distance, no dimensions of any kind.

I fell beyond that void into my memories.

There was a sharp transition at that point, in my mind, in the pit, wherever, a boundary that I will never be able to adequately explain in mere words. There was an alteration of perception, a change in state, a cusp. At one point I was falling through this dimensionless void. At the next, I was walking on air, falling through my mind.

Slower.

Joy, Annick, Lesh, Aaron, Timon, Harkane. Parthet and my mother. Baron Kardeen. Even the Elflord of Xayber. Clear memories—something that seemed to match my notion of what the "Vulcan mind meld" was supposed to do in the original *Star Trek* series. I became them and they became me. And we were all together. Altogether. It felt like something a long way beyond mere memory. It was more a current, an ongoing communion. They were there, inside my mind, realities of this peculiar present, not relics of a now-vanished past. I could reach out and touch. . . .

My memories of my father, my predecessor as Hero of Varay, and my great-grandfather Pregel, my predecessor as king, were dimmer, vaguer, two-dimensional, fleeting. I saw them laid out in the crypt of Castle Basil, about to be slipped into their niches along the wall and capped over with marble.

Castle Basil. Basil Rock. The crypt. The town. Cayenne, Chicago, Louisville.

I fell through layer after layer of memory, through many repetitions of the strongest recollections, the tightest bonds. Each repeat painted the scene in stronger colors, more vivid, more *real,* cementing the past to the present, extruding it toward the future.

If there was a future.

Vaguely, gradually, I became aware of memories beyond the memories, a widening net of poorly understood rumor and secondhand histories coming from the people I recalled most strongly, tying me to people and places I had never seen myself. There was a statue of the Brothers Grimm. I had seen photographs of it, but now I was seeing the real thing, and I knew, for the first time, that it stood in Marketplatz in some town called Hanau, in Germany. I had never been to Germany.

And, weakest of all, I felt synaptic vibrations of yet

more distant connections, a web reaching out even to the stars.

"History is a lie that most people agree on."

"We recreate our past every minute of every day. Some people do it more effectively than others."

"He died because he could only imagine one reality."

And then, finally, I *knew* what I was doing, what I had yet to do, what the entire point of this vaginal odyssey was. As if to match this sudden inner light of revelation, there was outer light. I seemed to be inside a tight sac, a moving point of ivory luminescence, surrounded by a horde of similar vehicles, each of them containing a replica of me, wrapped closely in a helical structure I remembered from science classes. Many of those other *me*s were looking at the *me* I was looking out of. Repeatedly, I met my own gaze as those other eyes turned to meet mine.

The seed. The sperm. Life offered.

Ahead, below, I could see myriad larger blobs of light, iridescent bubbles, each containing a potential universe, each spreading across the requisite billions of light-years.

The seed. The eggs. Life accepted.

One of me would have to penetrate one of the countless possible universes waiting there in the infinite womb. Each of them was different, with its own past and future, its own rules. We would unite and become one. The future that resulted would draw its parameters, its reality, from both of us, the Great Earth Mother and me. There were possibilities within possibilities. All of the images of myself that I could see in the flood around me were actually ME, as fully as I was. Split personality? That only touches the edge of the reality. I felt my individuality, but I also felt the union of us all.

It might not be me who created the new universe, but it would still be ME. Did I worry that one of those other selfs would succeed instead of the self I was most aware of? Yes, but in a subtle, detached way. There was just too much going on for me to focus on that particular question.

"God doesn't play dice with the universe."
Oh yeah?

I knew, *realized, decided,* that I needed to force as much of *me* as I could on the resulting cosmological genes. The crapshoot of heredity: I had to try to load the dice if my memories were to prove dominant over chance, over the efforts of the Great Earth Mother to give birth to a universe in *her* image.

The Great Earth Mother and the Hero of Varay are pleased to announce the birth of their . . .

Take one from column A and one from column B.

Cheat if you have to.

I concentrated on Joy and our shared memories. She was my anchor. I could see her, touch her, get inside her head the way I had gotten inside the Great Earth Mother's womb. *Womb?* Do people still use that word? It did pop into my mind. Joy. I saw her there with me, beautiful, pregnant, warm, wonderful. In a very real way, she was the center of *my* universe—and I was delighted and relieved to have her there.

I saw Aaron and Parthet chanting their magics, moving in a tight circle around Joy and me, part of the helical structure that held me. Aaron and Parthet, a strange pair. Uncle Parthet, Uncle Parker: he was a half-baked wizard if ever there was one, but he came through when he could. Maybe if he could see better, remember better. And Aaron now: there was a constant strength emanating from him, and not just as a result of his magics. He was an enigma with less past than he needed. The streak of elvish white down the side of his face seemed appropriate, *necessary.* Maybe he would disagree. I wasn't sure.

Baron Kardeen and Lesh were two more anchors in my hurricane, orbiting not far beyond Parthet and Aaron. Kardeen and Lesh were solid men who did their duty and still had room for friendship.

My mother was there in the group as well, but I couldn't put much thought to her yet. There were still the barriers of memory, of resentment for the years of deception.

Annick was there too, farther out in the electron web

around me, half elf herself, granddaughter of the Elflord of Xayber, burning with hatred for all that came from Fairy. That was a waste, draining her of so much that she could be.

Beyond the inner circle, a growing sea of faces and names, people I knew in Varay and beyond, on the other side of nothingness, back in the world that was. Names and faces, little bits of poorly remembered data clouded around me. Strangers stood and swam around and around, outward and outward in concentric spheres around the core.

Castle Basil, the center of Varay. Basil Rock, supposedly the hub of the universe.

The Congregation of Heroes and the genealogical tree of kings.

And dragons. "If we have to have dragons, at least give us *useful* dragons, like on Pern."

Fact and fancy. Science and magic. Myth and history. Tomorrow and yesterday. Now and then.

Oh say can you see. . . ?

A new world, a new universe.

How about a minor correction to physics? Let's make nuclear explosions impossible, without subtracting any other use of the equations. Suns are possible. Bombs are out. It violates natural law? Hell, we're writing a new law, adding an exception, a footnote that invalidates nuclear weaponry without deleting any of the necessary uses of nuclear energy. $E = mc^2$, except in bombs.

Little green men and bug-eyed monsters in the merry month of May. Flying saucers and starships that travel instantly between the stars. People, people everywhere . . . and assorted other beings. Hell, let's even make room for Alf.

Make Room, Make Room.

"It's My Party."

This Immortal rides to Amber and finds Lazarus Long lecturing my heroes. Bogey and the Duke chain-smoke and argue into the night while quarts of booze go by the wayside. Errol Flynn checks out his new Robin Hood duds in a mirror, preening and stroking his mustache. In the imperial observatory, Hari Seldon ties together *The City and the Stars*. Detour signs are put up at the on-ramp to *The Glory Road*. No hobbits served, please, "Never on Sunday."

Honest car salesmen. Commercials and politicians that tell the truth. We'll make *that* a natural law.

There's no room for broccoli or cauliflower in my world. Asparagus is a prescription hallucinogenic, strictly for medicinal purposes. *"Ninety-nine bottles of beer on the wall . . ."* Nothing you eat or drink can hurt you. doesn't it say something like that in the Bible?

What the world needs now is . . . *laughter*—all of the laughter it can get. Laughter is immortal. Those who give it to us should be too. Jack Benny for President. *He* can balance the federal budget if anyone can.

If wishes were horses, then beggars would ride.

While we're wishing, how about elves who are cute little creatures who clean kitchens and help shoemakers and sing cheery little songs around campfires in the wild? Magic for convenience—good, useful sorts of magic, not the evil spells of witches and warlocks.

If I Ruled the World.

If I'm not as loony as I think I am, maybe I've gone one better than that.

Gravity getting you down? We'll have to do something about that, provide a way for people to nullify gravity when they need to.

Frog went a courtin' . . .

As long as he didn't catch a disease in the process. All sex should be safe sex. And while we're at it, let's do away with all these limits on how often a guy can perform in a night.

"Those Were the Days." My friends.

Joy. Always Joy, my love, my partner—always. Forever is a long, long time.

A burning fever. What have I forgotten? There's so much that has to go in that I have to have forgotten a lot, maybe some of it important. If I had my druthers . . .

I guess I'll have to try a simple et cetera. Let's include

everything I would have thought of if I had the time to think of it and sort it all out.

My World. We'll make it a beautiful place. I deserve it. *Everybody* deserves it.

The bubble universes-in-waiting are closer now. The ultimate moment of truth, the moment of ultimate truth, will come soon, perhaps *too* soon. Some of the bubbles have popped, their potential wasted, spilled into the void. Others are off behind, above me now, out of reach, no longer possible. How will I know which of the remaining choices is the right one?

The options decrease with every thought.

Time. I can feel it now, a living, breathing entity. I can sense the way it is fluttering.

That one! Straight ahead, below. It calls to me, beckons, *pulls*, demands me. I straighten out my body, extend my arms like a diver ready to enter the water . . . and I hold my breath as I plunge toward it.

There is a quick instant of resistance. Then I penetrate the outer membrane. The resistance ends but it rips apart the sheath that protects me. I am caught up in the explosions of creation. The helical strands around me are ripped apart and cast into the maelstrom.

Goodbye.

19

After the Ball

I hear the screams of the multitudes, tortured souls praying for release. I know the torments of the damned, the weighing of the scales of justice. There is a thumb on the scale. It lifts itself off—there is no hand attached to it—and waggles a couple of times. *This is what you have to compete with.*

A uniform gray, boundless in every direction. *The Earth was without form, and void.* No time. No space. No energy. No matter.

No matter.

Duration where there is no time, in a place where there are no dimensions. *I think that I think, therefore, I think that I am.*

But I am not.

Sound in a vacuum, plodding, regular, assaults ears that do not exist and echoes in a mind that has neither substance nor form.

I am tired to the death, but there can be no death where there is no life. I have no conscious thoughts because there is no such thing as consciousness in this eternal gray limbo.

But I am aware.

I am aware that there is no awareness, nothing to be aware of.

The screams of the multitudes. The memories of the dead. Sound in silence. There is nothing. There has never been anything. There has never been nothing.

No past, no present: it will always be the same.

* * *

Tell St. Peter at the Golden Gate . . .
Peter, Peter, pumpkin eater . . .
Cinderella. Glass slippers. Midnight.
While the mice are away, the cat will starve.
No, it can always eat the bats in the belfry.
They all left to drink the blood in Transylvania. The
Count is throwing a dinner. The main course is bat bat-
ter.
Batter up!
"Once a king, always a king, but once a knight is
enough."
A Hero Ain't Nothing But a Sandwich.
The Earl of Sandwich and the Marquis of Queensberry
request the honor of your presence at high tea, to be
served in Madison Square Garden, precisely at the count
of eight, nine, ten, you're out.
Out: *There is no in.*
There is no room in the inn.
Ninety-eight bottles of beer on the wall . . .
"Hello, Walls."
"Hello, Goodbye."

Goodbye? I said that, didn't I?
There is only the light gray in every direction, the gray
of a winter sky when snow is threatening. I look around.
I look up and down. There is no texture to the gray, no
hint of its dimensions. Like me, the gray simply *is*, without definition.
I am is a major step forward. That simple awareness is
the result of eons of chance, and of chance associations
and movements. It takes even longer for me to realize that
I am is not an end result but merely a signpost along the
way. I cannot see the end result. I cannot imagine it yet.
I'm not sure what it will look like, how I will recognize
it, what it will be . . . what it will be . . . what it will be.
I am!

> *Snowballs have a chance in Hell,*
> *But only if they ring the bell.*
> *"Ding dong bell,*

> *"Pussy's in the well."*
> *Well, well, well.*
> *Who was Pussy banging?*
> *And is that his tail*
> *By which I see him hanging?*

Pale Gray for Guilt. Once upon a Mattress. Two for the Road. Three Balls in the Fountain.
"Ball four. Take your base."
"Take Me out to the Ballpark."
Barefoot in the Park.
"Park it here."
"Oh, Johnny."
"Heeeeere's Johnny."
"When Johnny Comes Marching Home Again."
"Where's the john? I've got to go."
Go directly to Jail. Do not pass GO. Do not collect . . .
Butterflies?
Butterflies Are Free.
Born Free.
Born to Boogie, Bogey.
"Born to Be Wild."
I am. I am!
Says who?
Says me.
How do you know?
"The Shadow Knows."
Know thyself.

I've heard that.

I look directly down my front and notice several things that I hadn't seen before, whenever "before" was. I appear to be fully dressed: mail shirt, jeans, boots, straps across my chest to hold the swords I can feel on my back, part of a saddle under me, a horse under the saddle—Electrum. I reach down and forward to pat his neck. "Good boy," I tell him. He snorts an answer. His hoofs plod on through the gray, clopping softly on an indistinguishable surface.

I look around me. Geezer plods behind Electrum and

me, a leather line running from his bridle to the pommel of my saddle. Geezer blinks at me, a gesture of recognition. He looks put-upon, which isn't unusual, but the load on his back is less than it was before.

The thought *I'm alive* surprises me so much that my feet almost slip out of the stirrups, but I don't know why that thought should be such a shock. There are vast blank areas in my mind, as gray as the vista around me. The one seems to be a reflection of the other and I can't guess which is the primary and which is the reflection. My horses, their loads, and I provide the only form in this dimensionless universe, and even *we* lack color yet. We are merely darker shades of gray than the nothingness across which we are riding, a classic movie that Ted Turner never reached with his Crayolas.

"Are we going the right way?" I ask, but not only is there no answer, the question appears to be meaningless, *without form.*

> *"Jack and Jill went up the hill,"*
> There are no hills here, or valleys.
> *"To fetch a pail of water."*
> I wonder how much water we have left.
> *"Jack fell down and broke his crown."*
> Varay has no crown.

Varay. The word triggered first a strong flood of emotion—longing, distaste, fear, affection—all mixed together; then a series of memories, thoughts that I had to speak into the void.

"I am Gil Tyner, Hero King of Varay. My wife is named Joy; my wife, my queen. My mother is Avedell Tyner, granddaughter of Pregel, my predecessor as king, widow of Carl Tyner, my predecessor as Hero."

Each memory triggered another series of associations, the memories rippling outward, increasing, multiplying, filling many of the blank spaces in my mind. I pulled on the reins. Electrum halted. Behind us, Geezer stopped when we did.

"I remember Varay," I said, and even the odors of

castle and countryside seemed to return in a sudden del-
uge of sensation. But there was still only the gray void
around me.

No, there *was* a difference, a change. Color had returned to me, to my horses, their gear, and the things
they carried. We had become a bright smear at the center
of the infinite gray. We *had* to be the center; there was
no other color anywhere in sight.

"I'm alive," I said, though I knew that I couldn't prove
it, except possibly to my horses.

I'm alive.

I looked back the way we had come: featureless gray.
That way lay madness.

I looked forward at a similar featureless gray. I had no
idea what lay there, if anything.

I looked down, at still more of the same gray, around
and beneath the hoofs of Electrum. I wondered what
would happen to me if I dismounted. Just because the
gray supported my horses, there was no reason to believe
that it would support me. Since I was going to have to
find out sooner or later, I opted for sooner.

The gray supported me. There was a firm surface beneath my feet, though I couldn't distinguish it. It was
firm, with no give, even when I stamped and jumped up
and down. It held me, but I couldn't really touch it.

"There doesn't seem to be any grass around," I said,
holding Electrum's bridle and stroking the blaze on his
face. "I think there are some fresh veggies back on Geezer. At least they were fresh when we left Basil. We'll
all have to make do for now." There was no way to heat
water to cook my survival rations, and they're virtually
inedible cold . . . though I would have to eat them anyway. "And I'll see how much water is left too," I added.

I walked back to Geezer, spent a moment talking to
him, and then I started sorting through the packs he carried. It was a time-consuming process, so some sort of
time was running in this place that wasn't a place. I found
that I didn't remember where the various items had been
stowed. Mostly, I wasn't even sure what was in the packs.
And I was distracted while I searched. Memories were

still trying to force themselves to the front of my mind, trying to claim my attention, but I just let them flow through and pass into the web of my mind. There was no point in dwelling on recollections. They could only bring pain at the moment. My only immediate curiosity was directed toward learning what Electrum, Geezer, and I had to eat and drink. That occupied me fully.

There was one warm, if puzzling moment. I found four cans of beer tucked into one of the packs. That would help the water last a little longer, but I would have sworn that I hadn't packed any beer on this trip. If I had, I would have packed a full six-pack, and I was as positive as I could be that I hadn't had any beer along the trail.

Not all of the food was the instant heat-and-eat sort. There was beef jerky, there were a few packets of military field rations, and there were the vegetables I recalled, some carrots and onions mostly, and there were a dozen apples—those I also didn't recall.

We all ate, if sparingly. I didn't know how long we had to stretch our supplies. I had one beer and I let the horses drink just enough water to wash down their food and wet their throats.

"I'm tired, and I bet you guys are too," I said after we finished. I didn't know why I was tired. The concept itself needed a moment's thought, as if it was something completely novel. A long rest seemed appropriate.

"Don't start wandering, huh?" I said as I lay down. There was no place to anchor the picket line—I couldn't pound the stake into the gray void no matter how hard I tried—so I just wrapped one end of the rope loosely around my wrist. My swords hung from the pommel of Electrum's saddle.

There was enough support for me in the gray void. It seemed to mold itself to me.

I slept.

When I woke, I was thinking about when I came home from college for my twenty-first birthday. That was the day I found the note on Mother's lilac-colored stationery that sent me through a magic doorway into Varay. I recalled questing after my parents, with Lesh, Parthet, and Timon as my companions. We found Mother standing sentry over my father's body in a small cottage in an orchard in the easternmost part of Varay, not far from Castle Thyme.

The wages of heroism.

I sat up. I couldn't ignore these memories, couldn't push them aside to find their places in my mind. This was my past, my history. The Etevar of Dorthin. The Elflord of Xayber. Annick—white fire.

My memories were finally coherent. They were also compelling. I relived the last four years of my life, seemingly in real time, which was no more impossible than a thousand other impossibilities I had experienced during those years. The sequence finally brought me to the Great Earth Mother and the final insanity I entered between her legs. My memories ended with a universe-ending explosion and resumed after an indeterminate gap in this gray limbo.

I looked up at my horses.

"It looks like we failed," I said, but that explanation wasn't really at all satisfactory. It didn't explain how *I* had survived, or my horses. The animals had been tethered outside the temple. My clothes and swords had been dropped at the foot of the Great Earth Mother's bed. I had left the world the way I entered it—naked and through a woman's birth canal.

I stood, strapped on my swords, and mounted Electrum.

"We'd better ration our supplies, boys," I said, and then we rode off across more of the gray void.

Time still had no real significance. Perhaps that is what allowed the food and water to last. The gray of the void got a little darker as we rode. There was also some contrast to it, finally, as a lighter gray mist formed and swirled, always at an indeterminate but considerable distance.

"Maybe we're making some progress at that," I said.

There was nothing to do but continue to ride, no matter how pointless it might seem—not knowing where we were going or why, having no known goal, it did seem pointless. I couldn't guess where we might be headed, or if there would be anything there when we arrived. I had no real plan. The best I could think of was to continue riding in a straight line, if there was such a thing as "a straight line" in this dimensional limbo, holding to the course we were on when I first became aware of movement . . . when I first became aware of awareness.

I had no feelings of danger or even anxiety, and at the time I didn't even consider that lack unusual. Reality was a nebulous concept then, as vague as the limbo. We rode on, going as far as we could, and then stopping to eat and sleep. I slept without dreams, without difficulty.

The gray went on, and so did we. The mist advanced and retreated, increased and decreased, cavorted in subtle patterns of almost-nothingness. I welcomed the variety, limited though it was.

Days passed, surely, maybe even weeks or months. I had a sense of duration, of time passing, but it was impossibly vague, uncalibrated. Time had meaning again, but not much.

And then, eventually/finally/already, there was *something* on the horizon—something that defined a horizon for the first time simply by being there. It was a dark speck, nothing more, but it was the first dark speck to intrude on the endless gray. I couldn't guess what the speck was or how far away it might be, but since there was nothing else around—and hadn't been in the eternity of my ride—it had to be where we were supposed to go.

"Something survived, so I guess maybe there is some hope yet," I said.

Hope was a new concept.

We rode until exhaustion returned. The dark speck might have grown just a smidgen, but it was still much too distant to show any clear form . . . if it *had* clear form. I only knew that we had to try to reach it.

My sleep this time was shallow, disturbed. There was *hope*. That meant there was also room for despair again. Electrum and Geezer seemed to pick up my feelings, or perhaps they had also seen the distant speck on the horizon and realized that it had to be our goal. Whatever, they didn't rest easy either. They tugged on the picket line I had wrapped around my wrist several times for the "night."

Another long ride brought the beginning of form to the distant object, and I started to harbor some hope of eventual recognition. We rode to exhaustion, but this time we took only a short rest before we started out again. The horses and I were all too keyed up to stay put very long.

In an hour or thereabouts, by my vague awareness of time in this place, I reined in Electrum.

"That's Basil Rock," I said.

Electrum whinnied. Geezer snorted.

We rode on, a little faster now.

At times, the mist completely obscured the still-distant rock, churning anxiety into me until the rock came back into view. The mist came and went. When it cleared, even momentarily, the rock was always there, always larger, always closer, looking more naked than I had ever seen it, without the trees below hiding its lowest reaches, without any hint of the town that nestled at the foot of its southern and western flanks.

But the distance decreased with maddening slowness, and I wondered if the rock was only a mirage put there to torment me and to drag me back down into the void of insanity.

After another sleep that was forced by exhaustion and hunger, my rested eyes were able to discern the outline of the ramparts of Castle Basil atop its rock. My heart started thumping with more hope than I had known since World War Three sent me racing off to find Joy's family . . . and then, the Great Earth Mother.

"They called Basil Rock the hub of the universe," I informed my horses, as if they might care. Now, for the first time, I had to admit to myself that *that* legend might be accurate, unless we were chasing a mirage.

We ate the last of the food. The horses drank the last

of the water. I drank the final beer. If the rock ahead of us *was* a mirage, the end would not be too far off.

"This is it, kids," I said when I climbed aboard Electrum again. "We ride until we get home or until we drop."

It was a close thing.

Time took charge of my mind again and dragged its heels over every pulse of blood and thought. It wasn't just slowness, it was . . . it was . . . it was something I can't describe, vaguely similar to the last few notes coming from a spring-wound music box, just as the spring is winding down fully. That is as close as I can come.

We rode. Occasionally, the horses managed a soft canter for a few minutes. They rode with their ears angled forward, almost as if they could hear the sounds of home, or expected to hear those sounds. But Basil grew with incredible slowness. Hunger returned, and exhaustion. The horses fell into a walk that seemed about the speed at which a baby might crawl.

Basil Rock. Castle Basil.

Joy might be there. I could hardly control myself when that thought assailed me. I could hardly think beyond the possibility that Joy might also have survived. It might be a fool's dream, but I had nothing but fools' dreams to hold me anyway. In all of the destruction, how could anything or anyone have survived?

I survived. My horses survived.

Perhaps all logic died with the universe of Vara and the Great Earth Mother. My apparent survival might mean nothing. It might only be the hell to which I had been condemned.

We rode a little farther. The horses were beginning to stumble over their own feet. There was certainly nothing else for them to stumble over.

I could see some detail in the Rock, in the castle walls, but no matter how tightly I squinted, I couldn't make out any movement at the crenels, any sign that there were people—living, breathing people—within the castle.

Basil Town was definitely missing. Basil Rock rose straight out of the gray limbo. No town, no River Tarn, no Forest of Precarra. I had to ride halfway around the rock to the south face. I tried calling. I shouted, but the grayness seemed to swallow my words.

We climbed the path up toward the top of the Rock and the castle gate. It was a slow climb, but it still almost proved to be too much for my horses. I dismounted and walked ahead of the horses up the incline, tugging on the reins to give what little help I could, as if I might be able to hoist them behind me. Halfway up, I stopped and un-loaded Geezer, dumped the tent and blankets, the coffee-pot and a few remaining cans of Sterno, everything but Geezer's bridle and the leather lead strap. I lightened Electrum's load as much as I could too, unsaddling him. He hadn't carried much besides me. I set everything on the path. Maybe it would still be there when there was a chance to retrieve it. If there proved to be any point to retrieval.

"Just a little farther now," I whispered. "If we're lucky, there'll be all the hay and oats and water you could possibly want."

The path up the Rock had never seemed so steep be-fore. And the time was still a little crazy. We needed a lifetime to reach the gate at the top of the path.

The gate swung open.

20

The Rock

No hands had touched the gate. It opened of its own accord. I led my horses through the gateway and stopped in the courtyard. The gate closed behind us, by itself. The bar that normally needed two strong men to slide it home slipped across without a single hand helping—real *Twilight Zone* stuff.

I didn't see anyone in the courtyard or up on the walls. The hoofs of my horses clopped loudly on the stone of Basil Rock as I led them toward the stables, across the courtyard from the keep, around the corner. What I *wanted* to do was leave the animals to find their own way while I ran for the keep to try to find Joy, or anyone else, *some* assurance that I wasn't totally alone in the universe. But I forced myself to look after Electrum and Geezer first. They needed my attention, deserved it.

There were other horses in the mews. That was encouraging, enough to increase the pounding of my heart. The castle had survived, and there were horses. I got Electrum and Geezer out of their bridles as quickly as I could, set up a solid meal of hay and oats for them, made sure they had water available but didn't get into it too soon. Even the slow walk they had been making the last part of our journey had been taxing for them. They were hot, sweating. They needed a few minutes to cool down.

Precious minutes that I had to wait with them.

"I'll be back later to give you a good rubdown if I can't find any of the stable boys," I promised when I finally let them at the water. The stable boys would do a better job of taking care of the horses after a long journey than I could. "If there's a later," I added. That was still a major uncertainty.

The other horses looked as if they had been tended regularly—if not to the usual standards of the royal stable.

"*Somebody* must still be around," I said, more to reassure myself than the horses. I wanted to believe, I thought there was *reason* to believe . . . but I was *afraid* to let myself believe in anything until I actually saw it, touched it.

I went back out into the courtyard and looked up at the tops of the walls again. Normally, there would be at least two or three sentries visible, more in times of trouble. But there were none now, not a one. Then I looked at the keep. No guards stood at the entrance.

After standing and looking around for what had to be several minutes, I took a deep breath and walked to the huge doors. They were bolted on the inside. I raised a fist to pound, but heard the bar sliding across its brackets on the inside. But the door didn't swing open by itself the way the gate had. I had to push.

There was no one in the entryway. Across the corridor, the door to the great hall was closed. I went to it, then hesitated for a long moment before I pushed it open.

There were people in the great hall.

Relief washed over me so frantically that I nearly fainted from the overload. Blood drained from my head. Dizziness bubbled through. My heart actually seemed to stop pumping for an instant.

People!

Eyes turned to look at me. There were at least a hundred people in the great hall, some at the table, some sitting on benches near the hearths or along the walls. They were nervous people with nervous eyes, looking at me as a drowning man might look at a lifeguard who was *just* too far away to help.

I looked around at familiar faces. For a moment—a long, suspended moment—the tableau was frozen in silence. The great hall was crowded with soldiers, servants, clerks and cooks, refugees from the camps in Illinois, adults and children.

Despite the crowd, Lesh was the only person sitting at the head table, down near the end of it. Even he needed time to react to my sudden entrance.

Then the room erupted in sound. Lesh stood and had to grab the edge of the table as his knees threatened a mutiny, started to buckle under him—enough that I could see it from the doorway. Then he straightened up and started toward me, stepping down from the dais, walking quickly—then stopping uncertainly.

"Sire?" he called. We moved toward each other.

"Joy?" I asked.

Lesh stopped walking, and his answer was delayed just long enough to let fear throw the hangman's noose back around my heart.

"She's upstairs, lord, with the others."

I felt another surge of relief. I stumbled, almost went down, and Lesh was at my side in an instant, supporting my weight while I recovered enough to hold myself up again.

"We nearly gave up hope for you, lord," Lesh said.

People started to crowd around us. It was impossible to make out much of what they said with dozens of people talking at once. All I could get was some of the flavor. Part of it was relief at my return and the promise that it held. More of it was fear, even panic, over the unprecedented isolation of Castle Basil and the endless gray outside.

"There is hope, real hope now," I said, loud enough to cut through some of the clamor. That silenced the rest momentarily.

"Where is Joy?" I asked Lesh.

"In your private dining room, sire, with the chamberlain and the others."

"Take me there, Lesh. I don't think I have the strength to make it alone."

Lesh took me at my word. He damn near carried me. It might have been faster if he had. I kept stumbling in my rush, and without Lesh at my side supporting much of my weight, I would have fallen.

"Has it been bad here?" I asked when Lesh and I were on the stairs, away from any other ears.

Lesh hesitated. I knew him well enough to figure that he was trying to find the most precise way he could to tell me what it had been like.

"The terror," he said finally. "The whole world and the sky both disappeared in an instant, like, and we was all alone. Them as was even down in Basil Town just vanished. Folks here are mostly too terrified to set foot out of the keep, fearing like they'd be gone too. It's hard to get anything done at all."

It was a tremendously long speech for Lesh. It took all of the way to the top of the stairs. I stopped there.

"You'd better go ahead and warn them, Lesh. Tell them I'm back." The shock might still be considerable in two stages, but I thought it would work better that way than if I just barged in without warning.

"Aye, lord." Lesh let go of my arm and waited to make sure that I wasn't going to fall down before he hurried down the corridor to the small dining room. I followed more slowly, not entirely by choice.

I had taken only three or four steps before I heard Lesh announce, "He's back," right in the doorway to the dining room. Then I heard chairs scrape against the floor, and voices that climbed all over each other.

Joy met me at the door and flung her arms around me, almost knocking us both over. As soon as we got our balance, we went through the obligatory mad-reunion scene, replete with kisses, tears, and totally incoherent words. It was so intense that I wasn't sure I could make it through the next minutes. Emotion? That's too tame a word. I had long feared that I would never get to see Joy again, but there we were.

There was right in the doorway, so the others in the dining room couldn't get out to surround us. When Joy and I finally separated to catch our breath, we moved into the room. I finally had a chance to notice the others, a chance to get a better look at Joy.

I gave her an up-and-down look. "How long have I been gone here?" She looked about ready to bust, she was so big around the middle.

"Five months or more," Joy said. "It's been hard to tell how much time is passing." I knew what she meant by that.

"It should be late March now, spring," Baron Kardeen said, but with less certainty than usual.

"I told everyone that I refused to have the baby until you got back," Joy said.

Slowly, with much confusion and delay, I got everyone seated at the table. I collapsed into my chair at the head of the table.

"Is there any food?" I asked. "I've been on tight rations for an eternity." Kardeen sent two pages scurrying down to the kitchen. Lesh poured me a mug of beer from a keg right there in the room. As soon as I took my first drink, he filled a second mug and set it on the table in front of me. I mentioned the horses. Timon ducked down the back steps for a moment, then came running back and told me that the animals would be tended immediately.

I drained off the first beer and started the second while Lesh refilled the first and brought it back. I looked around the table. Except for Joy, everyone looked thinner than I recalled, especially Parthet. He seemed to be scarcely more than a wraith.

"Have you been sick, Uncle Parker?" I asked.

"Not sick," he said, very softly, "but *my* world has passed. I finished the memoir you wanted, what I could recall."

Not that *I* wanted, that *he* said he should write: I remembered that. I stared at Parthet. The others were silent, an indication that they knew more about his condition then he was telling me.

"We can speak of all that later," he said. "What of *your* travels?"

My travels. I did need to speak of them, and once I started talking, it became a catharsis I could barely control. The food came—a full meal's worth for everyone. I ate, I drank. So did the others. But mostly I talked and studied the faces and reactions of the others. The two beer mugs were refilled as often as I drained them, to keep my throat lubricated for talking and eating. But the focus was always on what I saying.

Joy sat right at my side, where she belonged, where I wanted her. Her face was pale, chalky, almost as white as Annick's or the elford's. Joy held on to me and did a lot of silent crying. I could feel her trembling through the hand she kept on my shoulder. I interrupted my recital early to ask about her family. They were alive, safe— her mother was fully recovered from the side effects of her radiation sickness—but the Bennetts were all as terrified as everyone else in Castle Basil, perhaps more terrified than some.

Baron Kardeen appeared to have aged twenty years. His hair was grayer, his eyes showed the memory of his own fear. But there was still an air of competence in his every word and move . . . even if his hands did tremble just a little now and then.

Lesh, as sturdy as ever, tried to hide his feelings, but his face was ashen, like that of someone who has just had a serious heart attack. It was a fit color to match the infinite gray outside the castle. But although Lesh tried to hide his feelings, he gave himself away clearly, acting the page, moving to refill my mug every time I emptied one, pushing platters of food my way.

Timon was at the far end of the table, listening with transparent awe, sometimes forgetting to stuff anything into his mouth for minutes at a time. Awe and fear. They do belong together.

Mother. She was showing signs of stress too, more than I had ever seen from her before. Even when we found her waiting with father's body she had been collected, fully in control of herself. She wasn't like that now. There were plain lines on her face and indications that she had been biting her lips a lot.

"This was all inevitable from the moment I became both king and Hero," I said, staring at her. Perhaps that wasn't the right time for that kind of "I told you so." I might have avoided any mention of it just then or glossed over it. But I couldn't hold it back. I couldn't be silent or consoling about it.

"The legend you and Dad were so eager to claim somehow got mixed up over the years. It wasn't a Golden Age that had to come when the same man was both king and Hero, it was Doomsday, the end of the universe that Vara sired." I had been bitter about the way that my parents had secretly groomed me for the twin roles, denying me any real choice in my own life. What I had gone through and seen certainly didn't dull the anger I felt. Mother didn't reply.

Parthet looked as frail as Pregel had in the days just before his death, and I knew that I was going to have to force that long talk with Uncle Parthet *very* soon if we were ever going to have it.

"Where's Aaron?" I asked, interrupting myself—whatever I had been saying just then.

"Either in his workroom or somewhere with Annick," Parthet said.

"Safe?"

"Safe," Parthet assured me.

"But Harkane's gone, sire," Lesh said. "He was at Cayenne."

"None of the magic doorways works now," Parthet said. "Even Aaron can't work a passage to any of the other doors, not even the ones here in Varay."

I talked, and then I listened while Kardeen and the others told me what they had experienced.

There had been neither day nor night at Castle Basil since the arrival of the gray limbo outside. There was still food and drink, enough to last a minimum of another three months even with the added mouths of about one hundred and fifty refugees who hadn't been permanently relocated before the end came. Castle Basil was always stocked against the faint possibility of siege, even though it had never been invested by an enemy and the doorways had always provided a means of resupplying it.

The End (everyone referred to it that way) had been

eerie at Castle Basil. A thick snowstorm had obscured
most of the sights the morning the End came. The snow
was remarkable in itself, heavier than anyone could remember any snowfall at Basil, where the winters are gen-
erally mild and short and two inches of snow in a month
is rare. This snow had been blizzard-thick, but without
the wind, obscuring vision but drawing people outside to
watch it and frolic. But the snow came to an abrupt halt.
Beyond the castle wall, even the flakes in the sky on their
way down vanished. Inside the castle, the snow already
coming down landed. Then there was nothing but the
solid gray above the castle and beyond its walls. The
Rock was visible, and the path leading down, but nothing
beyond.

"It was a terrible day," Parthet said. "When the world
disappeared so suddenly, we knew that it was the End.
The conclusion was inescapable. The End of Everything
had come. You had failed. I've never known a time of
such thorough despair in my considerable life." He
looked down at the table, his hands clasped together in
front of him.

"The despair was so complete that it seemed ages before I saw the flaw in it." He looked up at me then, but
his voice remained somber.

"*We* hadn't disappeared with the world around us."
He shrugged.

"Of course, when that did penetrate my skull, there
seemed to be several possible answers. The isolation
might be our hell—damnation to an eternity like this. Or
we might simply be the last place to fade. That seemed
to be the most likely explanation at the moment—that
Basil Rock actually *was* the hub of the universe and would
simply be the last to fade. And, finally, there was a
chance that you had achieved at least partial success.

"When the castle persisted, the second explanation
became less and less likely. When the gray outside *also*
persisted, the first became *more* likely. Until you returned."

Baron Kardeen had attempted to send scouts down the
trail to Basil Town, that first day and on many after, but

the gate refused to open. It even proved impossible to lower men from the wall to the path outside. The gray prevented any exit from the castle.

Before long, no one would even attempt to leave, not even men who had families down in the town. People huddled together inside the castle, stewing in their fear. There had been a few suicides—a previously unheard-of occurrence in Varay. A few other people had gone raving mad. Aaron and Parthet had been able to help them, but their magic was weak, more draining than usual. There were severe limits to what they could accomplish.

Seven weeks had passed since the universe disappeared from around Castle Basil. Seven weeks . . . as close as anyone inside could tell.

I already knew about the crazy way time seemed to sneak around its own backside, messing up internal rhythms and providing no external clues. Even simple references to time were apt to get screwed up by the reality. The telling of tales in the small dining room may have taken two hours or ten. We all ate and drank, if not as intently as at a "regular" meal, then at least without breaking off the "meal" completely. There was always food on the table. Anyone could grab a helping or two of anything, and everyone did, whenever.

Aaron made an appearance, but he didn't stay long. "He spends most of his time with Annick these days," Parthet told me. I sensed that there was something more to the statement, but—like everything else that day— Parthet didn't seem anxious to talk about it, at least in front of others.

Even in limbo, Castle Basil needed some management. Baron Kardeen excused himself a number of times to see to one thing or another. Lesh went out a couple of times too. Now that I was back, he figured that it would be possible to reestablish regular watches on the walls. "It may all come back as quick as it went, and we won't want to miss it by a second, right, sire?" he said. I grinned and nodded, and Lesh hurried off to see to it. Whether or not anything ever came back, Lesh seemed to have found the perfect line for us to take under the circumstances.

"If you are a true heir of Vara, you may be able to see that some portion of this world is recreated in the next." There had been no promises in what Xayber said. Maybe this was all I had been able to save. And there might be no next world to graft it on.

I didn't know what to think.

Later, an indefinite later, after the urgent histories had been exchanged, I decided that it was time for me to make an appearance downstairs. "And then, I think it must be time to sleep," I told the others. I was feeling considerably stronger after consuming a couple of days' worth of food and beer—even by Basil standards—but ten or twelve hours of sleep would really help a lot.

"I'll wait for you in our room," said Joy. "I really don't like to take all those stairs more often than I absolutely have to." She put her hands on her belly to make sure that I knew what she was talking about.

"I won't be long," I promised, and then I gave her a kiss that almost became more urgent than the appearance in the great hall.

The rest of us went down to the main floor together, but Mother and Parthet both turned off to go to their own rooms. Mother had sat through the entire discussion upstairs, wearing her guilt quietly. She had never tried to argue the point I had made, never tried to shift the blame. I didn't press the matter. I mentioned the facts. She took it from there. Parthet had also sat through the recitation, doing his share of the eating and drinking, and perhaps dozing for a few minutes a couple of times. He hadn't seemed to miss anything important. When we started down the stairs, he had to take them more slowly than usual. He seemed to be having difficulty, but he managed on his own after refusing offers of help from both me and Lesh.

There were more people in the great hall than when I had made my first appearance there earlier. Everyone seemed to be waiting for me, as I had sensed they would.

They had questions. I was the only one who might have answers.

I went to my seat at the head table. People stood, and sat when I gestured them down. Kardeen sat next to me. Lesh and Timon stood behind us. Pages brought beer and bowls of pretzels.

"I know you've all been frightened," I said. "I have been too, for ages and ages. Nothing like this has happened in thousands of years." I paused. "But it *has* happened before, more than once, perhaps many times, and people have survived." A brand-new thought hit me then, and I had to wait for it to run a couple of laps around my mind before I said anything about it.

"In fact, the last time this happened, the new world was a lot better, in the mortal realm for certain, and almost certainly here as well." A lot of the people in the great hall were from the other world. "It marks the sudden leap from the late Stone Age to the early civilizations of Egypt and Mesopotamia." It was a beautiful theory that made so much sense to me that I didn't doubt it in the least: the sudden appearance of written language, widespread settled cultures, pharaonic Egypt.

"We can't be sure yet what will result this time, but I'm as confident as I can be that the gray outside won't be eternal. *Something* will return. We have to wait for it, as patiently as we can. After all, we're not going to run out of food or anything else anytime soon."

There wasn't much more I could say, so I didn't try. Someone else could pass along the details of my journey north . . . and beyond. I hoped that folks would exercise a certain amount of discretion in that.

"Will there really be a new world?" Joy asked when I got back to her.

"I believe so," I said. "Apparently, this kind of situation has happened a number of times in the past. Xayber said that he had gone through several of these cycles, and the Great Earth Mother confirmed that there had been many." I was reluctant to go into any real detail about my time in the temple of the Great Earth Mother with

Joy, even about the talk that had preceded our session in bed. Under the circumstances, I had no reason to feel guilty about that. With the entire universe *in extremis*, what I had done could hardly be considered infidelity. Still, I couldn't entirely suppress an uneasiness. I would have been extremely uncomfortable giving Joy a blow-by-blow account. I would have if she had demanded it, but she didn't.

We got undressed and into bed. Joy had me feel the baby's kicking, a startling sensation the first several times. We lay together, holding on, for a long time, but there was no question of sex, not when I was afraid that Joy might pick about any second to shoot our first child into the world—or whatever it was out there beyond the castle walls.

Joy had less trouble getting to sleep than I did. Her soft breathing lulled me to the edge of sleep, but I needed forever to tip across that edge. I remember thinking, *I hope* this *part isn't just a dream,* and then there was that inner void finally ready to claim me.

When I woke feeling that it must be time for morning, I decided that I had better find Parthet as soon as possible. Joy slept on. I dressed and went around to ask somebody where the old wizard had been sleeping lately. The room above his workroom had been turned over to Aaron, and so had the workroom. According to Lesh, Parthet had announced, loudly and often during my absence, that he was retired, that Aaron was now the wizard of Varay. I learned that Parthet had claimed a small tower room that gave him fairly direct access to the kitchen and great hall. He was in the kitchen when I started through there for the tower stairs.

"I don't sleep much anymore," Parthet said, greeting me with an answer to a question I hadn't even thought of asking.

"I think we need to have a talk," I said.

He smiled over a mug of coffee. "I expect we do," he said. "I know what I look like."

"Like Grandfather did, except you're trying to tell me that you haven't been sick."

"I haven't been sick, and I'm not sick now. But . . ." He looked around. "This isn't the place for our talk. I think they're about ready to start toting your breakfast upstairs. We could talk up in your dining room. As homey as this kitchen is, perhaps this particular conversation deserves a different setting, and fewer ears to listen."

Once we got out in the corridors, away from other eyes, Parthet only made a *pro forma* protest against the support I offered him. I brushed aside the protest and held his arm while we walked, supporting as much of his remaining weight as I could.

"You talk as though you've made all your preparations for death," I said when we stopped to let him rest for a moment halfway up the stairs.

"Most of them," he conceded easily. "There's not much left to do." He started walking again, and I couldn't get anything else from him until we were seated at the table in the private dining room upstairs.

"I'm part of Vara's world, Vara's universe," Parthet said when he was settled in a chair. "It seems that I am—or was, to be more accurate—an integral part of it. Perhaps you'll understand that better if you get a chance to read the book of memories you forced me to write."

"It was your idea, not mine," I reminded him. "But I'll read it, never fear." And then, for the first time in ages, I thought of my grandmother's *Tower Chapbook*. Mother had left that for me with the note that brought me to Varay. Over the years, I had glanced at it a few times, read a few short sections, but I hadn't really sat down and thoroughly *read* it yet. "I'll read it," I told Parthet again, but I was talking about both books.

"When you forced the memories back, you forced the memoir," Parthet said. He snorted. "Vara's world. And now, that world is passing, almost dead. Your world is a-borning. When the transition is complete, I will be gone."

"That sounds rather melodramatic, Uncle," I said.

"Perhaps, but true. It's not an old man's fancy. You

can see yourself what has become of me. There is no chance for me to see the world you've made. I *would* like to see it, at least enough of it to judge how well you did.'' A wan smile. ''A ripping good show, I'm sure.''

''Can't Aaron do something to help you?''

''Not a thing, no more than he could help Pregel. The lad will do you proud, Gil. He's a better wizard than I ever was—tenfold, maybe a hundredfold. He'll serve you and your children and their children for ages to come.''

''I'd as soon have you around longer, bad eyes, dirty jokes, and all.''

''I thank you for that, but there simply is no way. Call it a natural law, one I've only recently discovered.''

He was as serious as he could be. I could tell that from the sound of his voice and the look on his face. And I never even considered that it might just be a case of an old man talking himself into a delusion. Not Uncle Parthet. And he didn't simply *think* that he was going to die soon, he was positive, he *knew* it.

''There's no precedent for a wizard dying here, no tradition,'' I said. There was another smile to go with his shrug. ''It leaves a big question. We have places for kings and we have places for Heroes in the crypt. Where do you fit?'' That lack was one of the clues that had led me to guess how far back Parthet's past went.

''I'm afraid you leaped to the right conclusion through the wrong hoop, lad,'' Parthet said, smiling again. He let me stew in that for a moment before he continued.

''I'm afraid that there won't be any remains for you to visit, so you don't have to worry about their disposition. Look at me! If there was a bright sun behind me, you could see straight through me now.'' He said that almost harshly, then softened his tone. ''If you'd been around as long as I have, there wouldn't be much left of you either, lad. I'll simply fade away, leaving only memories in the minds of others. And in time, even those will fade. In a few generations, people here will never remember that Varay ever had a wizard besides Aaron, and in a lot more generations, if he lasts as well as I think he will, even he may come to believe it.''

"Aaron. What's going on between him and Annick?"

"They share a bed, if that's what you mean."

"Only partly. The jailer and his prisoner?"

"No, no," Parthet said. "This all began almost immediately after you left, after Xayber acknowledged Annick as his granddaughter. She already had her hatred for all things of Fairy, and then to learn that her father was the son of the Elflord of Xayber, the primary focus of her hatred . . ." Parthet shook his head. "The snow-white skin of Fairy. And there stood Aaron, the antithesis, his skin as black as an elf's is white."

"That sounds suspiciously like a racist remark, Uncle, if you know what I mean by that."

"Racial perhaps, but not necessarily racist. There *is* a difference. Isn't 'opposites attract' a properly senile adage in the world of your birth? But relationships grow sometimes. You'll simply have to watch and decide for yourself."

I felt that there was something missing in the distinction that Parthet was trying to draw, but he didn't give me a chance to think it through.

"There's something more important that you should be thinking about," he said.

"Such as?"

"Such as your relationship to the world that's about to be born."

"What do you mean?"

"Now, it wouldn't be the same if I gave you the answer, would it? Think about it, lad. That's the action that's important."

Even without Parthet's cryptic advice, I would probably have found my way down to the catacombs under Castle Basil that day. I had a habit of going down there when anything was bothering me, and after my return from the Great Earth Mother, a catalog of the things that were bothering me would have been approximately the size of the combined Chicago telephone books. And I just had to see for myself that the crypt far down in the center of Basil Rock was still there.

It was.

The room was the same as before. There were no changes along the burial wall. There had been no Lazaruses in Castle Basil.

I paced back and forth the entire width of the burial wall, from Pregel to my father, stopping occasionally in the center, in front of Vara. I kept my curses silent, but they came, regularly. I related my adventures again, all the way though, just talking, listening to the echoes. This time I went into more detail than I had to my living audience upstairs. Motor mouth. Maybe I was still trying to convince myself that it had all really happened the way I remembered it . . . or maybe I was trying to convince myself that none of it had happened at all.

When I ran out of things to say about my adventures from Fairy to the inner temple of the Great Earth Mother, I found myself thinking about what Parthet had said I should be thinking about—my relationship to the new world. *He* had no doubt that a new world was coming, and I was glad to have all the reassurance I could find. But *relationship?*

I thought about the crazy time while I was supposedly falling into and through the Great Earth Mother. That had to have been insanity, a hallucination, or a metaphor. So I performed a ritual of some sort that might permit a new world to follow the old. Maybe there was something like LSD in the food or wine that I had before we headed to that bedroom. The idea that my session with the Great Earth Mother would make the new universe my literal descendant, in the same sense that the baby Joy was about to have would be, was ludicrous. All of the mental raving, the images of DNA molecules, egg universes, and such had to be part of that coital craziness.

It had to be.

My world? No way. That would make me . . .

Aaron and Annick found me in the crypt, just as I was getting ready to start the long climb back to the living levels of the castle.

"I figured you'd be here," Aaron said.

I nodded, looking first at him and then at Annick. She was the major surprise. For the first time since I met her, years back in Battle Forest, there was no tension in her face. She hadn't turned into a bubbling airhead or anything like that, but she wasn't instantly marked with the stigma of her hate.

"You look almost happy," I told her. She actually smiled, but there was also a sudden edge to the grin, a cutting edge that told me that the hatred was still there, only held at bay for the moment.

"There's nothing left of Fairy now, is there?" she asked. Challenged.

"I think not," I said.

"Once you asked me what I would do when all those I hated were gone. I told you I would find something. I did."

I looked at Aaron.

"It's not just this," he said, holding his black hand next to her white face. It wasn't the first time that Aaron had almost seemed to know what I was thinking. "Not even mainly this." The trace of reservation I heard in his voice didn't seem to be about what he said, but—I think— about how I might react. Aaron had changed while I was gone. Perhaps it was just maturation. Or perhaps he expected disapproval, or even jealousy, from me.

"Are you sure?" I included them both in the question, tried to make it sound friendly, hopeful. Some languages have devices for those situations, constructions that say that you expect or hope for a positive answer.

"It's not even this," Annick said, tracing the white blaze on the left side of Aaron's face—the only remains of Annick's father.

Annick took Aaron's hand then, and I reached out to clasp their hands in mine. "As long as you're both certain," I said.

"This is going to sound silly as hell coming from me," Aaron said with an embarrassed grin, "but it's magic."

After my ride through the gray limbo and the way that limbo continued to envelop Castle Basil, I was getting used to the nonchalant mood of time in this new environment. The gray nothingness persisted, leaving time to mark itself slowly, however it wanted to, for perhaps a week after I returned.

When things finally started happening, they all seemed to happen at once as time tried to catch up with itself. I don't mean that things just *seemed* to happen one right after the other, or simply coincidentally close. I mean that everything *did* happen precisely at once, which makes it especially difficult to chronicle coherently.

I was in the great hall, sitting at the head table, putting considerable effort into my drinking but only eating haphazardly. The constant munchies are common in Varay anytime, and they seemed to be even worse during the limbo. Perhaps forty other people were in the great hall, some doing the same things I was, others just sitting around or even sleeping. Personal biorhythms were hit hard by the general weirdness of life and time.

The first indication I had of the maelstrom that was erupting was when somebody disturbed the King's Peace. I heard a loud metallic clanging, something that sounded like a sword being repeatedly smashed against a suit of armor.

"What the hell's that racket?" I asked, an instinctive thing. Somebody quickly got up from the table and went out to the hall to look.

"It's Gorfal attacking a suit of armor," was the report.

I swore under my breath and went to see for myself. Gorfal was one of the guards who had been in service to the crown for years, one of the men I had encountered the first morning I came to Castle Basil with Parthet.

"Gorfal, what the hell do you think you're doing?" I shouted when I got out to the hall and found that he was indeed attacking an empty suit of armor. I was usually a lot gentler with people. That morning, I don't know, I was just in an unusually foul mood.

"The enemy, sire," Gorfal screamed, hysterical but puffing for breath.

"It's all right, Gorfal," I said, softer, but still nearly shouting to make sure he could hear me over the clanging.

I didn't want to hurt him, but my danger sense was acting up. I took a couple of cautious steps toward Gorfal. The sword he was swinging was just a normal broadsword, nothing to compare with my two elvish blades. I didn't draw a weapon, though. I wouldn't, unless it became clearly unavoidable.

"They's tricky, sire," Gorfal said, panting harder, continuing his assault on the empty metal. "They pretends to be dead, then they comes at you from behind."

His blows were slowing down a little. He was tiring rapidly. But I was going to have to wait a while longer before it would be safe to dash in and pin his arms. I was still the Hero, after all. It was up to me to take the foolish risks.

Before I could take any action, Mother came hurrying out of the great hall, almost at a run.

"Joy has gone into labor," Mother said. "She's calling for you."

Almost as the full stop on that, Lesh came barging in from the courtyard. He glanced toward Gorfal, but ignored him for the moment to report.

"Sire, there's something happening outside the castle walls. A change in the gray."

"Stay here, Lesh," I said. "As soon as he slows down a bit, grab him and put some sort of restraint on him until Aaron can work on his head."

That seemed to be the next cue. Aaron came running around the corner at the far end of the corridor, behind me.

"Come quickly," he shouted. "Parthet is starting to fade. He says he's going to vanish into his past."

As I said, everything happened at once. I hadn't mastered the art of being in two places at once, still haven't, and I had never even thought of needing to be in four places at once. I put Gorfal out of my mind right away. I knew I could trust Lesh to look after him. But the other three crises all demanded my immediate attention.

"How long will it be before Joy really needs me there?" I asked Mother. She was almost a doctor at that.

She would be of more use to Joy now than I would anyway.

"There is a little time, but I wouldn't dally long."

"Lesh, can you describe what it is that's going on outside?"

"The gray seems to be closing in on us, getting thicker. We can't see the lowest stretch of the path leading down now."

"Where's Parthet?" I asked, turning to Aaron.

"In the workshop. He was adding something to the end of the book he wrote for you. Suddenly he said, 'I can see through my hand,' and then he sent me for you. He said to come at once."

"Okay, I'll go to Parthet, then up to Joy, and from there to the battlements," I decided. That gave me an efficient route from one place to the next—a back stair from the workshop to my apartments, then a connection from the keep to the curtain wall of the castle.

"Mother, get back to Joy and tell her that I'm on my way. Tell her about Uncle Parker." Even four years after learning that his real name was Parthet and not Parker, there were still times when the pseudonym he had used in the other world came out instead. "I'll be with her as quickly as I can." Mother nodded and left.

"Lesh, as soon as you get Gorfal quiet, get back to the wall, then catch up with me if there's been any change. You heard where I'll be?"

"Aye, lord."

"Try not to hurt him, Lesh. He's just sick." Lesh nodded, and I turned to Aaron.

"Let's go."

I didn't run flat out, but I didn't waste any time as I hurried along the corridor, back the way Aaron had come. Aaron came a lot closer to running. He waited at the corner for me, then went on ahead again, getting to the workshop a good twenty paces ahead of me. Annick was in there with Parthet.

And Parthet was staring at, and *through*, his hands. He held them out toward me. I could see his face through his hands, but very faintly, both because there was still a little substance to his hands and because his face, his head, was also beginning to get less opaque.

"It will happen very soon," Parthet said. "Your world must be nearly ready to appear."

"Lesh says that there's a change in the gray outside," I said. "How much longer do you think you have?"

Parthet chuckled. "I don't know of any possible way to judge that, lad. There are no precedents that I am aware of. At a guess, maybe an hour or two." He shrugged. "Perhaps much less."

"Joy is upstairs getting ready to give birth," I said.

"Then that is where you should be, lad. You need to see both of your children being born, your son and your world. I'll walk along with you. I suddenly find movement particularly easy. There is so little of me to move around now."

Annick handed him a pair of glasses.

"Yes," Parthet said, fitting them to his face and holding his hands as if to catch them if they happened to fall off or through his nose and ears. They stayed in place. "I should like to see as much of my final moments as I can."

I didn't know how Joy would respond to having a crowd around just then, but we had once discussed the way that royal births used to require witnesses of the proper rank and position. At the time, it had been something of a joke between us.

Mother was there as midwife and obstetrician. Doc McGreary had made it to Varay before World War Three broke out, but he had been out of the castle when the gray came, so he wasn't around to do the honors. Either Parthet or Aaron could help if help was needed, except that Parthet was having his own rite of passage at the moment.

Joy was on the huge bed, near the edge, sweating, gritting her teeth and puffing. She looked as if she was suffering.

"Uncle Parthet?" she said when the contraction ended. He went to her side.

"You're going to have a healthy son, lass," Parthet

said. "I'm not sure if I mentioned that before or not. And though you might not think it just now, I do see a relatively easy delivery for you."

Joy seemed to focus on Parthet then. "You're fading?" she said, lifting her head from the pillow.

"My time to leave, your son's time to arrive. It balances out, really. I'm about to see if there's anything beyond, if any of the religious fairy tales are real. I've often wondered."

The windows along one wall of the bedroom looked outside the castle, where the keep met the curtain wall. Those windows had been shuttered continuously since the limbo came. I opened one and looked out after going to Joy and giving her a kiss and a few words of encouragement—which sounded phony to me and probably to her as well, because we both knew that I couldn't really know what she was going through.

The gray. It *was* different, but I needed a moment to put my finger on the difference. There was a hint of *form* to the gray, shape, an appearance of substance rather than just a void . . . and it did seem to have moved closer to the castle. It was darker than before as well, and after I had watched for a moment, I started to see what appeared to be a swirling within the gray, almost cloudlike patterns.

And there was a breeze for the first time since the gray had formed.

I stared out the window. After a few more minutes, I felt that I could see something beyond the gray, something down toward where the River Tarn and some of the local farms should have been, had been before. Joy had another contraction. I started to go back to her side, to hold her hand and offer what encouragement I could, but Mother shooed me out of the way.

Aaron was off to the side chanting up a spell. I assumed that it was something to help Joy. Her face got relaxed, almost dreamy, as though she had been given an anesthetic. Her breathing got freer.

Annick watched for a moment, worrying at her lip, then she went over to stand by the window, where I had been before. Uncle Parthet stood in the center of the room, looking vaguer all the time, like a television or movie ghost.

"Uncle Parker?" I said when I noticed that I could see the open window right through his once-substantial body.

"The time is almost here." His voice sounded the same as ever, though, full of life, hearty. "Did you do what I told you to do?"

"You mean that bit about my relationship to the new world?" I asked. He nodded.

"Some," I said. "Down in the crypt and since. It just doesn't make sense."

"It doesn't matter whether or not it *sounds* true, but that it *is* true, and it is." Parthet shook his head. "I thought I would have a *little* more time."

"I can see the river!" Annick shouted. "The gray is fading."

So was Uncle Parthet, quite rapidly now.

"Remember this," he said. "You are Father to this world, its Creator. You have responsibilities, duties. I have great confidence in you, lad. I couldn't be more pleased in you if you were my own son."

I never had a chance to respond to him. Once again, everything happened at once. A baby cried its first breath.

Annick shouted, "The sun is out."

And Parthet vanished.

I glanced toward the window, then back at the spot where Parthet had been, and in just that second, he was gone. I turned toward the bed.

Joy's eyes were closed, but she was breathing freely and there was a smile on her face. Aaron was still chanting. Mother held the baby, her first grandchild. She wrapped a blanket around the tiny form and turned to me.

"You have a healthy son," she said.

I looked at the tiny face framed by the blanket, then at Joy. Joy had opened her eyes. She mouthed the words, "A son." I smiled at her, then at the boy.

"His name has to be Parker," I said. Not Parthet, but

Parker, the name I had known the original by for most of my life.

"Of course," Joy whispered, and Mother seemed delighted by the choice.

Lesh came rushing into the room without knocking— an unprecedented breach of etiquette for him.

"Basil Town is back!" he shouted. "It's *all* back!"

21

My World

An end and a beginning. Mother chased Aaron, Lesh, and me out of the bedroom. She kept Annick to help with Joy and the baby—my son, Parker.

"We should try the magic doorways," Aaron said as soon as we got out of the bedroom.

"One step at a time," I told him. "The world may not extend very far yet. If this rock is the hub of the universe, we may have to wait awhile yet before there's anyplace very far from here to go to."

"How far away's the sun?" Aaron asked.

"I don't have the foggiest idea. In the old universe, it was something like ninety-three million miles from earth. In this one? We'll let the astronomers answer that, if there are any astronomers."

"Sire, are you saying that we can't count on *anything* until we see it?" Lesh asked.

"I guess I am." I hadn't really thought of it, but that was indeed what I was saying. "If what happened to me at the temple of the Great Earth Mother really happened, then the new world, the universe, should be a mixture of my memories and hers."

"You still don't believe it," Aaron observed.

"Not until I see it. Maybe not even then." We were heading down toward the great hall. The commotion there was audible while we were still on the stairs, some distance away.

"Let's start by seeing if the front gate will open," I said. "I left a lot of stuff on the path coming up because I didn't think the horses would make it carrying anything more than their own weight."

The people in the great hall were more animated than I had seen anyone since my return. Something more important had returned. *Hope.* I saw some folks already heading out into the courtyard, toward the stairs up to the ramparts of the curtain wall. They wanted to see for themselves as quickly as possible. Most of the people who were still in the great hall were toasting the event before going out to confirm it, giving other people a chance to take the first risks.

"I need some hands to open the gate," I said from the doorway of the great hall. There was only a very brief pause before men started coming, raising their hands to volunteer. As soon as it was clear that there were enough volunteers to do the work, the rest of the people started to crowd together toward the door, willing to come out and watch.

I led the march out to the front gate. Men climbed up to watch from the wall. Others moved to slide the large bar out of its brackets, and more got ready to pull open the two heavily reinforced wooden gates.

Baron Kardeen came hurrying out of the castle. "I just heard," he said, sounding embarrassed that anything had happened in Castle Basil without his knowing it virtually at once.

"There's a lot more than this," I said. I was watching the gate, though, not Kardeen, too intent on that to mention the other happenings yet.

The gate had refused to open at all from the beginning of the limbo . . . except for my return. I had supervised a couple of equally futile attempts to open it since I got back. We had been able to slide the bar out of the way, but no number of people could force the gate open, and no one could climb down the outside wall.

But there was no need for anyone to try scaling the wall now. The gate swung open as soon as we tried.

After all I had been through, I didn't have the slightest hesitation about being the first to walk through the open gate. If nothing else, I had been the last one to come through it.

I walked straight through the middle. Aaron, Lesh,

and Kardeen all moved right with me, only half a step behind. Protocol. We walked across the short drawbridge that I had never seen drawn and stood at the top of the path leading down to the town. I could see people moving around in the streets below.

"I wonder what *they've* experienced," Aaron said.

"I imagine that we'll find out soon enough," I replied. I turned to the crowd of people at the gate.

"I need four volunteers," I said. "When I returned from the temple of the Great Earth Mother, I had to leave much of my gear halfway up the Rock. I would like to see it retrieved as soon as possible."

There was some shuffling around, with a few men ducking back out of the front rank, but it didn't take long to get volunteers. They went down the path slowly and came back fast. I thanked them and promised that their bravery would be remembered. When I glanced to my side, I saw that Kardeen was making sure that he knew who they were. Having Kardeen along is like having floppy-disk backups for all the files on your hard disk.

"There's the Bald Rock Inn," Lesh said, pointing.

"You think their brew has suffered?" I asked.

"Won't hurt to find out."

I laughed. "Soon enough, I imagine. Let's make sure everything's in order first."

"Aye, lord," Lesh replied.

"Okay, Aaron, let's go see if the doorways lead anywhere." I turned to go, but Lesh stopped me.

"Look, sire." He pointed down the side of the Rock. "Looks like the miller's on his way up with a delivery." Kardeen moved closer to the edge and confirmed it.

"I'll leave the miller to you," I told Kardeen. "Find out what you can."

The sea-silver-lined doorways to the other castles in Varay worked normally enough. I tried them all, held them open while I waited for some warning from my danger sense. No warnings came, but I still didn't go through to any of the other castles. Not yet—I didn't want to rush anything. Conferring with the various castellans could wait until I was certain just what was going on around Basil.

But when I opened the way to Cayenne, Timon ducked through to find Harkane. I didn't have time to stop him, so I held the doorway open until Timon and Harkane both came back through to Basil.

"Are you all right?" I asked Harkane.

"Aye, sire, right enough. Though we were beginning to wonder why we hadn't heard from anyone for so long."

'How long?" I asked.

"Why, lord, since . . ." He stopped, surprised—*shock*—locking onto his face. It was almost as if he had gone catatonic. I waited a moment. He didn't even blink.

"What have the last two months been like?" I asked. Harkane blinked then, and he looked more and more confused. He started to speak several times, but he just seemed to sputter a little. It was almost as if he were choking on food.

"Aaron, can you ease the way for him?" I asked.

Aaron did a short chant that seemed to tranquilize Harkane almost from the first phrase.

"Why, sire," Harkane said, "there's a *hole* in my mind, an empty place. What happened to us?"

"That'll take some explaining," I said. I smiled and took hold of both his shoulders to reassure him. "But later. We've got plenty of time now, I think. Go on down to the great hall and get some food and something to drink. Take Timon along. He can fill you in on a lot of what's happened."

"Are you going to try the doors to the other world?" Aaron asked after Timon and Harkane left.

"I have to," I replied, though I had consciously by-passed those doorways on our progress through the castle. The doorways to the other world were the final link. They would tell me how much fantasy and how much fact there was to my memories of my encounter (my "connection," as Parthet would have phrased it) with the Great Earth Mother.

I went to the bedroom that had been mine as Hero. Joy's family were all there. They were still a little reticent about mixing with the locals most of the time. Everybody treated them as part of the royal family, and I think that unnerved all of them . . . the three adults, at least.

"Joy's just had our baby, a boy," I told them. "They're both doing fine." And then I sent them up to visit.

I went to the doorway that had led to my parents' bedroom in Louisville before the war. I stared at the silver tracing for a moment and wiped my sweating palms on my trousers.

"This is it," I said, looking to Aaron. He nodded.

I stretched my hands out to the silver, and hesitated again before I finally completed the circuit. The other bedroom was there, the way I remembered it from before the disaster. There was no trace of fire or any other damage.

"It's there," I said, and my hands were shaking when I pulled them away from the door. "There's something there."

Then I went to the door that had connected to my bedroom in the Chicago condo—a building that must have been totally destroyed by the nuclear missiles that must have hit Chicago.

It was just the way I had left it before the war.

"It's as if that war didn't even happen," I said.

"Probably didn't, not in this new world," Aaron said. "Why don't we go through and check it out?"

"Not yet," I said—without hesitation. This time it wasn't just my reluctance to push things too quickly, or even the fear that had come without any prompting from my danger sense.

"I want to wait until Joy has recovered enough to go along," I said.

Joy's recovery took only four days—with the fourth day probably an unnecessary safety margin—thanks to Joy's own constitution, the easy delivery, and a little help from Aaron's magics. I spent much of my time during the wait learning as much as I could about the hole in time in Varay. I talked to the castellans and to people from Basil

Town. I spent a little time back at Cayenne and in the private apartments in Castle Basil searching through the belongings Joy and I had brought along from the other world, finding the things we would need when we made our visit back to that other world—money, bank and credit cards, suitable clothing. And I spent as much time as I could with Joy and our son, Parker.

In Varay, most of the people simply didn't realize that they had lost a big chunk of time unless they had their faces rubbed in it, one way or another, and even then many of them refused to accept it. People had superficial memories of life-as-normal, some sort of psychological defense mechanism, I suppose. Those memories wouldn't stand up to determined scrutiny, to detailed questions, but they were more comforting than the truth.

But life picked up right where it left off in most ways. Deliveries to the castle resumed. Families that had been separated were reunited; those members who had been in Castle Basil had full memories of the time that wasn't while their relatives who had been outside the castle walls didn't. Life went on.

The Titan Mountains had grown back to their previous heights—though there appeared to be a couple of new gaps. Those would have to be explored in time.

In time.

I had one major task to deal with in those days—among a myriad of other demands on my time and attention. I was more than a little nervous about confronting the captain and crew of that Russian frigate, but I had little choice . . . and the longer I put it off, the harder it was going to get. I did wait until the morning following the return of everything. I took Lesh and Aaron along and we stepped through to Arrowroot. Captain Sekretov had gone far beyond outrage.

"What have you done with my ship?" he demanded when I walked into the great hall of Arrowroot. He came toward me so rapidly that Lesh interposed himself.

"What are you talking about?" I asked, trying to sound calm.

"My ship has disappeared. It was there yesterday morning, but last night it was gone."

"Slow down, Captain," I said. "A lot has happened, but no one here has touched your ship." I had a good guess. The *Kalmikov* was an anomaly in the buffer zone, and when the new universe was born, it either didn't include the frigate or it returned it to the world where it belonged.

But getting that, and everything else, through to Commander Sekretov took up a good-sized chunk of the day. Only my promise to get him and his men back to the other world in a couple of days even started to calm the captain down.

"We need to get a supply of formula for Parker," Joy reminded me when we were finally getting ready to leave for Chicago. "That powder that comes in cans."

She had been nursing the baby the old-fashioned way pending availability of something else. I wasn't sure what kind of powder she was talking about. My experience with babies was pretty much limited to diaper and tire commercials on television. But I nodded anyway, just to be safe.

Lesh, Aaron, Joy, and I were making the trip. Aaron had somehow persuaded Annick to wait for the next time, reminding her that he could open the passages whenever they wanted to visit. Annick could help the two grandmothers care for Parker while we were gone this time.

Despite the apparent return to normalcy, we were a nervous lot as we stepped through from Castle Basil to my apartment on Lake Michigan, but nothing untoward happened. The utilities in the apartment were all connected. None of my stuff (what remained after Joy and I had hauled off everything that we thought we might find a use for in Varay) had been carted away. That meant that the financial system still worked and that I hadn't gone broke. All of my routine bills had been handled automatically by one of the banks I had dealt with before the "recent unpleasantness," and those arrangements had to still be in order. My frequent absences on Hero business had demanded some sort of automatic arrangement.

After the four of us stepped through to Chicago and looked around just enough to make sure that there was a city outside the windows, I opened the passage back to Castle Basil and held the way open for the Russians to come through—all but the dozen who had decided that they wanted to stay in Varay. My apartment wasn't nearly large enough to hold all of the sailors, so Lesh and Aaron took turns escorting batches of them downstairs. I let Commander Sekretov call the Russian consulate—not all that far down Michigan Avenue from my place—and arrangements were made quickly.

It was a little strange. We were no longer in the buffer zone, so I didn't have the translation magic, and I don't speak Russian. But as the conversation went on, I found that I could follow the sense of it without the buffer zone's magic or a working knowledge of Sekretov's language. The longer the captain talked, the closer I could follow.

"Good luck, Captain," I told him, holding out a hand.

He hesitated, looked at my hand, then nodded. We shook. "I will need that luck," he said.

"It may not be quite as hard to convince your superiors as you think," I told him. Sekretov did not appear to find that reassuring.

I went downstairs with Sekretov and the last of his crew, then Lesh, Aaron, and I all went back upstairs.

It had been about nine-thirty in the morning when we arrived in Chicago. We were in no particular rush, so we took time for hot showers before we ventured out. Aaron spent some time listening to WBBM, the all-news radio station, but when I asked him what was going on, he just chuckled and shook his head.

"You'll find out sooner than you want," he said.

"Joy, I don't know what will happen," I said after we had both finished showering, "but why don't you try phoning your folks' number in St. Louis?" She flashed me a puzzled frown but went to the telephone and dialed.

Somebody answered. I could tell that from the look of

total bewilderment on her face even before she said her first word.

"Dad?"

She half collapsed into the chair next to the phone.

"It's Joy." Over the next ten minutes she did a lot of crying and even more confused explaining. Her father had trouble grasping that his wife and Danny's family were safe . . . and in Varay. There had been no World War Three. Papa Bennett wasn't too clear on when or how everyone had left, just that they were gone. He finally agreed to fly to Chicago that afternoon and go back to Varay with us—though he wouldn't promise to stay.

"Aaron, do you know your telephone number?" I asked softly when Joy seemed to be about finished with her call.

"I know it, but it won't do any good," Aaron said. "It was hearing that my parents were dead that sent me to Varay the first time, and hearing about my grandmother sent me back the second time." He gestured toward Joy. "She never accepted that her daddy was gone."

I nodded. I knew pretty much what Aaron meant. I had seen my father and great-grandfather dead and buried. Even in the throes of my "connection" with the Great Earth Mother I had only seen them dead. They hadn't returned. They wouldn't.

Aaron did go to the telephone after Joy hung up, though. He dialed and listened. "That number is not in service," he reported. Then he tried his grandmother's number and got the same recording.

"Wouldn't have done much good anyway," Aaron said. "They'd never believe that I'm me."

We used the magic doorway to take us to the office I kept in the Loop to save time. Then we took an elevator down to street level and went outside. There were crowds on the streets, shoppers, workers, the normal bustle as we walked over to the State Street mall.

"It's like nothing at all happened here," Joy said.

"Something happened, all right," Aaron said, giving me a look—your patent "significant look," I guess.

"Well, I'm going to get the papers and see what I can

find," I decided. We were approaching a corner kiosk. I picked up a *Tribune* and a *Sun Times* and handed the old guy tending the stand a ten-dollar bill. He returned my change and I pocketed it without even looking at it, let alone counting it.

I turned away from the kiosk before I even glanced at the headlines on the papers. They started strange things going on in my throat. The words were in English, but they didn't all register at once.

"What the hell's happened here?" I whispered when I could get anything out.

"You happened," Aaron said, just as softly.

GASA REPORTS ANOTHER ALIEN CONTACT
A spokesman for the Global AeroSpace Administration has announced that a GASA survey team has found another intelligent race of ETs. This makes 34 known sentient . . .

ASIMOV QUITS SPACE
Isaac Asimov, emeritus Barrie Professor at Boston College and pioneer in the development of metaphysical Stardrives, has resigned as director of SPACE, the Special President's Advisory Committee on Exploration . . .

JACKSON: NO SECOND TERM
President Jesse Jackson has announced that he will not run for a second term. Instead, he will embark on a goodwill tour to the home worlds of the members of the Federation of Sentient Races . . .

"Hey, you do that?" Aaron asked. He was reading over my shoulder.

"I guess I did," I said. "I seem to have done a lot."

"You're even better than I thought."

"Let's find someplace where we can sit and read," I said, looking around. We were jamming up pedestrian traffic.

"Someplace with food," Lesh suggested.

* * *

We found a small diner not too far off. There was plenty of room, since we had come after the coffee-break rush and before the lunch rush. We all ordered coffee and rolls and read, passing sections of newspaper around. I skimmed mostly, checking out headlines and sometimes a paragraph or two of a story, just trying to get some feel for the extent of the changes.

The Cubs and White Sox were both—according to these hometown newspapers—even money to repeat as pennant winners, with the exciting possibility of back-to-back subway series.

A *new* John Wayne movie, *One Small Step,* was premiering in town. The Duke was playing Neil Armstrong.

The AMA—the American *Magicians* Association—was holding its annual convention at Over-Galapagos, the American geostationary city.

Applications were being taken for emigrants to fill four colony ships—54,000 people were needed.

Laurel and Hardy were costarring in a stage revival of *The Odd Couple* at the Arie Crown Theater in McCormick Place on the lakefront.

The sections of the papers went around the table. We followed our coffee and rolls with a generous lunch. We were all still hungry, but the diner didn't serve alcohol, so we decided to move on someplace else. When I dropped a five-dollar bill on the table for a tip, Aaron picked it up, looked at both sides, then passed it back to me.

"Look at the back, near the top," he said.

I did. Aaron pointed out the line he wanted me to read and I almost choked.

It said, *"IN GIL WE TRUST."*

My immediate response was to look at the rest of the money I had picked up that morning. It all had the same motto, the money I had carried along from Basil and the change that the vendor at the kiosk had given me. My next reaction was an instinct to head directly for the nearest bar and proceed to get totally soused.

—But I had Joy with me and we had to find formula for the baby.

So we did that. I hailed a taxi and Aaron threw in a magic chant to get it to stop for us, and we all piled in. We cleaned one supermarket out of the brand of formula Joy wanted, and we had trouble getting it all in the cab with us for the ride back to my condo. And then we had to wait for Joy's father to arrive, though Joy took a can of the formula mix through to Castle Basil right away. She came back to wait with us, though.

There was no booze in the condo. That had been one of the "indispensable" items I had carted through to Varay back when I was worrying that I might never get another chance to visit Chicago.

But I waited. I could have gone through to Basil for a beer, or asked Lesh to haul back a keg, but I decided to wait.

Joy's father arrived, and we all stepped through to Castle Basil. By that time, I was ready to chug-a-lug the nearest keg of beer, but Baron Kardeen intercepted me before I got to it.

"You have someone waiting to see you, sire," Kardeen said, his face trying without much success to hide some sort of emotion. That was totally unlike my able chamberlain.

"Who is it?"

"The shop steward for the local Guild of Cobblers' Assistants and Domestic Workers." Kardeen's voice sounded more than half strangled getting that out.

"A union steward? I didn't know that Varay *had* any unions."

"We didn't, before. The steward is in the throne room."

I knew that there was something more that Kardeen wasn't telling me, but if he didn't want to spell it out, I wasn't going to order him to. I trusted him too much.

"You'd better don your regalia," Kardeen said when I turned and started to head to the throne room. I stopped and looked at him.

"You mean the swords?"

"Yes, sire. Protocol, not danger."

"I'll get them," Lesh said, and he hurried off toward the stairs before I could say anything.

I nodded to Kardeen. "Okay, this last time. I'm going to start some changes, though. This is a new world, so the old traditions don't have to stay unless we want them too. Those elf swords have got to go." When Kardeen started to protest, I cut him off.

"I know all about that 'they'll come back to kill anyone who abandons them' line. New world, new rules. And anyway, I'm not going to abandon them. I'm going to put them where they'll be safe. I want a pit dug below the crypt. Say a twenty-foot cube. Then I want enough concrete to fill the hole. We'll put my two elf swords right in the middle, finish filling the hole, then pave it over with stone—with bits of Basil Rock itself. Anytime I need to wear a sword, I'll wear my own, or Vara's."

"As you wish, sire."

We started moving toward the throne room again, stopping only long enough for me to strap on the rigs with the two elf swords when Lesh got back.

The throne room has two entrances, one for me and one for people seeking an audience. Kardeen went in ahead of me to make the announcement of my arrival. There were no blaring horns, just the announcement. I knew just how long to wait before I followed him in and headed for my throne.

Before I got there, I knew what Kardeen had been keeping back. My chamberlain was developing a sense of humor.

The Elflord of Xayber was standing in the middle of the throne room waiting for me. He had plenty of open space around him. No one wanted to get close. I don't know why. Xayber didn't look *nearly* as fierce as he had before. Now, he was only about three feet tall, and he was dressed in a cute little children's-elf/Robin Hood sort of outfit.

But he did look mad as hell.

I knew that I had to keep a straight face, that I didn't dare laugh, but holding it back was the hardest chore I have ever had. It made all my prior Hero-work look like a breeze.

"You are the shop steward for the Guild of Cobblers' Assistants and Domestic Workers?" I asked when I was almost confident that I would be able to control my voice.

Xayber took a quick step forward. "As if you didn't know that, *sire*. I won't forget this, I assure you. I'm not totally devoid of power yet. It's just a matter of time. I will remember this insult."

"It wasn't intentional, I assure you, my Lord Xayber," I said. "I do regret the inconvenience. Did you have a particular complaint to bring on behalf of your members?"

The next fifteen minutes were the longest of my life. I knew that I absolutely *had* to hold back the laughter until I got far enough away that Xayber couldn't possibly hear me. And holding that all in threatened to rupture something important. The fairy tale about the shoemaker and the elves had found its way into my new world.

It was just too hilarious.